AN ACCIDENTAL SERIAL KILLER

BY SALLY FISHER

First published in paperback by
Michael Terence Publishing in 2024.
www.mtp.agency

ISBN 9781800949126

Cover image (AI)
by Michael Terence Publishing

Michael Terence
Publishing

This book is dedicated to Neil, Joe, Robyn, Chloe, Rob and Louis and most especially Barnaby, Archer and Phoebe, for all the love, light and laughter you have brought to my life.

In loving memory of my vbff, Helen Smith (1962–2019)
See – the body is not always in the canal!

– Sally Fisher

PROLOGUE

July 2017

"Amy McDonald?" the stranger standing on her doorstep asked in a broad Scottish accent.

"Yes," confirmed Amy, cautiously.

"This is for you," he said handing her a package wrapped in brown paper.

"Am I being served?" asked Amy, having no idea what else could be happening. She hadn't been expecting a delivery of any kind.

"No, not at all, Madam," the man answered with a little laugh. "Please just sign here to say you've received it," he said, passing a clipboard to her with one hand and offering a pen with the other. Amy tucked the package under her arm to be able to hold the clipboard whilst she read the paper attached to it. Underneath her printed name and address was typed:

'I hereby acknowledge I am in receipt of the package handed to me by a representative of Browns Solicitors, 105 Holt Road, Inverness IV3 9ED.'

There was a dotted line underneath for her signature and a space for the date.

Amy was unsure whether to accept the package or not, having absolutely no idea what it might contain. Sensing her hesitation, the man waiting at the door now produced a white envelope from the inside pocket of his suit jacket and said,

"This will explain everything."

Amy's hands were full, so she placed the package down at her feet to take the envelope from him.

"If you wouldn't mind scribbling your signature, so I can be on my way," he said, brusquely.

Amy would have preferred to read the letter first before she signed but it seemed rude to keep him waiting any longer. Sticking the envelope between her teeth to free up her right hand, she scribbled a barely legible signature and the date before handing the clipboard back. The man looked at her expectantly and for one moment she was confused, then she realised she still had his pen and handed it back to him. Tucking the pen into the front pocket of his jacket, the man nodded, then turned and walked back down to the gate. If he'd been wearing a hat, he'd have raised it to her thought Amy as she stood and watched him get into his BMW and drive away. He certainly wasn't your run-of-the-mill delivery driver. The whole experience was quite odd. She took the parcel into the kitchen and set it down gently on the scrubbed pine table, curious as to what it contained. The man at the door had been a little optimistic if he considered the covering letter to be an explanation, thought Amy, once she had opened it and read the scant contents:

'Our client has instructed us to ensure that in the event of her death, you personally receive the enclosed documents. We regret to inform you that our client died on 30th June 2017, and we offer our most sincere condolences.'

"I don't know anyone in Scotland," thought Amy, undoing the brown paper package. Inside, wrapped in white tissue paper lay a cream-coloured notebook bound with string. Between the string and the front cover sat an embossed cream envelope which she detached, leaving the journal lying on its bed of tissue paper. The envelope had her name written in turquoise ink, in handwriting she instantly recognised, and which sent a chill down her spine. Just as she was about to open the envelope, she had a sudden thought. She crossed the room and delved under the kitchen sink. Moments later, now wearing latex gloves, she broke the seal and removed the written pages from within.

Half an hour later, still sitting at the kitchen table with the letter and the journal laid out in front of her, she took out her phone and carefully photographed each page one by one, checking that she had captured the whole sheet before moving on to the next. Then she made the first of two phone calls. It went straight to voicemail.

"Matt, it's Amy. You'll never believe what I've just received. Call me back as soon as you can."

She dialled the second number.

"Good afternoon, could you put me through to DCI Mason please."

PART ONE

"Ricky, I need you to come around to mine right now."

"Right now, Ricky! It's urgent."

"No, I can't pick you up. Just leave now."

"For fuck's sake Ricky I'm not joking. I need you here now!"

"No, I'm not going to discuss it on the phone. I'll explain when you get here, just come over."

"Yes, that's exactly what it is – a matter of life and death."

"Wait, listen. Don't come to the front door. Use the alley at the back of the house and climb over the fence."

"I really don't give a shit about that, just move your fucking arse."

September 1969

She sat on the edge of her bed hugging herself, rocking backwards and forwards, listening out for his footsteps on the stairs, bracing herself for the battering she was certain she was about to receive, but none came. Total silence.

Quietly she got up and tiptoed to the door. Creeping to the top of the stairs she peered down to the hall. He wasn't there. She walked slowly down the stairs carefully avoiding the steps that would give her presence away. She knew exactly where each noisy step and creaking floorboard was in this house. The ability to move silently around the home was paramount for her own protection. Then she heard the sound, something she had never heard before. She couldn't place it, but it seemed to be coming from his study. Again, moving cautiously, stopping after every few steps and listening for the opening of a door or the tread of his heavy feet, she made her way towards the sound. It was definitely coming from his study. The door was ajar and as she approached, she could see him sitting at his desk, leaning forward with his head in his hands. That's when she realised that the noise she heard that she couldn't identify was the sound of him weeping.

Back in her own room she lay on her bed and rested her hands on her stomach. Although when standing she had a defined bump, her belly still felt flat lying down. She tried to picture the life growing inside of her, but it still didn't seem real. Even after the appointment at the new Women's clinic that had opened in the town (she hadn't dared go to see her own doctor), and her fear had been confirmed, she struggled to accept what had happened. And then today, which had been a momentous day for Betty, as for the first time in her life she had stood up to her father. She had given him her news and had not cowered away or broken down, even though the vitriol he hurled at her knew no bounds. He was the angriest she had ever seen him. His rage was so immense that globs of spittle landed on her face as he struggled to get his words out through his gritted teeth.

He had demanded to know who she had slept with; what devil incarnate had impregnated her. The names he called her were foul and unfamiliar, but she certainly got his meaning, and it infuriated her. How dare he! Her own anger grew inside her starting as a small ball of hate in the pit of her stomach and working its way up her body, growing bigger with each verbal assault he threw at her, until she too was shouting, screaming back at him. Telling him the truth. How could she have ever met anyone without him knowing? He kept his watchful eye on her twenty-four hours a day. How, she had demanded he enlighten her, just how did he think this had happened? There was no mystery man. There was and always had been only one man. The only 'devil incarnate' that had ever been near her was standing right in front of her. The only immoral, ungodly presence in her life was him.

She hadn't used those exact words because they were beyond her comprehension, but she had managed to get across to him exactly how she felt, and she saw the truth of her words sting his very soul. He visibly shrank before her eyes. For the first time in her life, she felt strong and powerful. She knew this would be her one and only chance to ensure she got what she wanted, the only time he would be meek enough to agree to her terms. And so, she laid out her plans before him and he accepted them all, including the condition that he never, ever laid hands on her again.

Friday 20th February 2015 – 8:17 pm

Operator: 999. Which emergency service do you require?

Eliza: Hello, erm I'm not sure. Definitely the police, maybe an ambulance, but he's already dead, do I still need an ambulance?

Operator: Can you tell me what's happened?

Eliza: It's my husband, he's been stabbed, he's definitely dead so I'm not sure whether you need to send an ambulance or not, but the police will need to come.

Operator: Can you give me your address caller?

Eliza: The address is 12, Lime Tree Avenue, Brigholme.

Operator: (Repeats address back): 12, Lime Tree Avenue, Brigholme. Is that correct?

Eliza: Yes.

Operator: And your husband's been stabbed, is that correct?

Eliza: (Impatient sigh) Yes.

Operator: Where is he love? Are you near him?

Eliza: He's in the kitchen. I'm not next to him.

Operator: Can you go to him love; I need you to do some checks on him for me.

Eliza: There's no point doing checks. I'm certain he's dead. He has no pulse, he's not breathing and stop calling me love, my name is Eliza, Eliza Kelly.

Operator: Okay Eliza, what's your husband's name?

Eliza: Keith, his name is or er- was Keith. Will you just send someone, now!

Operator: Someone's on their way to you. Do you know who stabbed Keith, Eliza? Can you tell me exactly what's happened?

Eliza: My son, Zac. My son. He's stabbed my husband and my husband's dead.

Operator: You're saying your son has stabbed your husband and you think your husband is dead? Is that right love?

Eliza: I don't think it, I know it. He's dead. Stop calling me love. He's dead okay. Stone cold dead. Just listen, will you? I need you to send someone around to deal with this.

Operator: Alright Eliza, just calm down and tell me where is your son now? Are you in any danger? Is he armed?

Eliza: He's standing next to me. And no, I'm not in any danger. He's 9 years old. He's not armed.

Operator: Sorry Eliza, can you repeat that? How old is your son?

Eliza: He's 9. Are you listening? He's 9 years old. He won't hurt me. When is someone coming?

Operator: They're on their way love, just stay calm. Are you in danger Eliza?

Eliza: Will you fucking well listen. My son Zac is with me and he's not dangerous. He's stabbed his dad but he's not a threat to anyone. I need someone to come and clean this mess up. Where the hell are they?

Operator: Calm down please, they're on their way. Eliza? Eliza, are you there?

The line had gone dead and when the Operator tried to call back there was no answer.

1

It was an early February evening, and the cold was beginning to seep into the house after what had been a remarkably warm day for the time of year.

"Shall I pop the heating on?" George McArthur asked his wife hopefully, as she walked into the sitting room bearing a tray with mugs of tea and some fancy chocolate biscuits, which were always their Saturday night treat. Annie shook her head. Although they were both in their eighties and certainly felt the cold more now their blood was thinner, she had an irrational fear of high heating bills.

"If you're cold I'll fetch you a cardigan," she replied.

George sighed and wrapped his hands around his mug to warm them up a bit.

Just then the piercing sound of sirens split the peace of the night causing George to jump, spilling some tea onto his lap as he did so. It was extremely unusual to hear sirens along the tree-lined avenue on the outskirts of Brigholme, even on a Saturday night. The affluent area had been the target of opportunistic burglars a few years ago and so the police had run an initiative encouraging the residents to fortify their properties with various security devices. With the help of their son, George and Annie had a rather imposing alarm system fitted, which they both were a little fearful of, neither liking to be the one who set it when they were going out or last thing at night lest they triggered the alarm. As their neighbours had also invested in more protection for their homes, including the installation of several CCTV cameras, the crime rate had decreased to practically nothing.

Annie and George went to their large bay window and stared out into the night. All the houses along the avenue were set quite far back from the road, most having large established front gardens, and it was difficult to tell where the emergency vehicle had gone, but it must have been close because the sirens stopped. George could just make out blue flashing lights at the top of the drive of the house opposite them. Then a motorbike raced up the street and pulled into the same drive, it too had flashing blue lights and was emitting a siren.

"That's a paramedic," said Annie with some confidence; she loved the TV medical dramas. "Must be some sort of medical emergency, like a heart attack."

"Why the police car then?" enquired George, who, now his eyes had adjusted to the darkness, could make out the vehicle that had pulled up right next to the house across from them. "If someone's had a heart attack you don't call the police."

"True," replied Annie.

They stayed glued to the window although they couldn't see anything properly due to the darkness and the distance. When, a short time later, an ambulance and two more police cars arrived, they decided it was worth suffering the cold to join other neighbours who had left their houses to get a better look.

"Alright George, Annie?" Tim, who lived in the house on the left of theirs, acknowledged their arrival. "Any idea what's happening?"

"None whatsoever," replied George.

"Isn't the man who lives there that actor?" asked Tim.

"I think so," said Annie.

"Yes, he was in that daytime soap a few years back," said Gayle, Tim's wife, who being active in both the Neighbourhood Watch and the local church, knew most of the residents in one way or another. "He's not been on TV much lately though. His wife's an odd fish. She's a bit up herself if you ask me. Never wants to help out with anything; she's always sent me away with a flea in my ear whenever I've knocked." She turned to look up at the house. "No one ever likes doing jobs for her, always late paying. And she's a snob you know, very la de da. I've never met him, no idea what he's like. Kid goes to private school."

She stopped talking and looked back questioningly at the group. Having run out of information to pass on, she was waiting for someone else to join in. The others nodded at her, but no one had anything else to add as they had never personally encountered the couple.

More neighbours joined them and were brought up to date with the happenings so far. They continued to stand at the bottom of the drive, staring up towards the front of the house. They were unable to see much due to the darkness, even though the house itself exuded light. There was a fair bit of activity going on and they watched as a couple of figures entered the house, visible because of the white forensic suits they were wearing.

"That doesn't bode well," commented Tim. "Not if they've already got forensics in there; maybe someone's been murdered."

"Unlikely, it's probably nothing but a break-in. They have to wear those suits whatever the circumstances," said the woman next to him who was wearing a fluffy dressing gown and furry slippers. She shivered, pulling the gown tightly around her. "If nothing happens in the next two minutes, I'm off. It's too bloomin' cold standing here."

Moments later the onlookers watched as a woman and child were escorted out of the house by two police officers and loaded into the back of a waiting ambulance.

"Whatever's happened, it must be bad," commented Annie, as the small crowd moved out of the way of the departing vehicle.

"Well, they can't be too seriously hurt," remarked Tim, "otherwise the sirens would be going."

A short while later a young constable made his way down the drive. As he approached, the spectators began firing questions at him. Holding his hands up in front of himself as if to ward them off, he asked them very politely to return to their homes, explaining that they would be visited shortly and asked to give witness statements. He refused to answer any of their questions. Turning away, he pressed a button on the control panel that was set into one of the stone pillars, and the bystanders watched as the large black wrought iron gates slowly came to a close. The policeman then stood in front of them, his arms folded as if daring someone to try to get past him.

There didn't seem any point in staying outside, so the neighbours did as he asked and returned to their own properties. Both George and Annie felt a fizzle of excitement at the thought of being visited by the police, and forgetting how tired and chilly they were, busied themselves by getting the kettle on and adding more chocolate biscuits to the plate.

Brigholme Local Twitter – 20th February 2015 – 8:57 pm

Police have cordoned off Lime Tree Avenue in Brigholme after what they describe as a serious incident. Local traffic is being diverted.

~~~~~~

Brigholme Echo Website – 20th February 2015

BREAKING NEWS: Reports are coming in of a serious incident that has taken place at a house on Lime Tree Avenue. The street has been cordoned off by the police and traffic is being diverted. This is a breaking news story, and we will bring you more information as we receive it.

~~~~~~

BBC Local News

We have reports of a serious incident occurring at a residential property in Brigholme. Police are currently at the property and the road has been cordoned off to traffic. More information to follow.

~~~~~~
~~~~~~

2

On the night of Friday 20th February, Detective Inspector Michael Mason was enjoying a rare night at home in front of the telly. He had planned to meet up with his old boss Trevor Harrison, but Trevor had cried off at the last minute. Mason wasn't bothered, he was more than happy to stay in and enjoy a takeaway from his local Indian.

His empty plate was on the side table being surreptitiously ignored by his golden retriever, Monty, who, as always, was hopeful of being on the receiving end of any leftovers. Mason still derived a certain amount of pleasure from leaving his empty plate in the living room, instead of rushing it to the kitchen and rinsing it under the tap to appease his ex-wife. He considered it a luxury to be able to eat the majority of his meals from a tray, sitting in his armchair, comfortably watching TV or listening to music, instead of having to sit formally at the dining table as his ex-wife had always insisted upon; even though, due to the nature of his job, he was usually home too late to eat with the rest of the family. The fact that the house he now lived in didn't have a dining room didn't diminish the enjoyment he got from knowing how much his habits would offend his ex-wife.

He hadn't realised until Claire had left him for the sunnier skies of Spain, jetting off with her new beau, how her exacting standards had meant that he had never properly relaxed in his own home. After the divorce, he had been encouraged by Trevor to apply for the position of a DI within the Sussex Force, and he was currently based in Brigholme, where Trevor had been the DCI. When Mason was offered the position, he had been unsure whether to accept or not, thinking that although the area that the new appointment covered was larger than his current remit, the crime rate was actually much lower. Also, he hadn't been certain that he would enjoy moving out of the city and into the sticks. However, he now considered it one of the best decisions he had ever made. There was still plenty of work for the task force, but it involved far fewer street brawls and domestics that had gotten out of hand.

Having worked with Trevor previously the transition had been fairly painless as both men already had an understanding of how the other ticked, and although Trevor, (who was now retired), had received a promotion to Superintendent not long after Mason relocated, the new DCI who replaced him showed the same amount of confidence in Mason as Trevor had and basically left him to his own devices.

The move to the coast would never have suited Claire, who would have considered it a step down from the life they had been leading, but for Mason it was perfect. There was enough money after the divorce settlement for him to purchase a small, terraced house in the little seaside town of Swilford. The location was close enough to the main police headquarters for him to get to work easily, and being situated in a quiet, side street, close to the harbour, meant it was off the main tourist track. Despite this and having come from a busy, noisy city, Mason still dreaded the influx of Grockles in the Summer. Why was it, he thought, that people spending their annual two-week holiday in the town appeared to leave all common sense at home? They forgot how to use pavements, choosing instead to walk in the middle of the roads, paying no heed to the traffic. They left their litter behind everywhere they went, including the beach, and completely disrespected the local shops and businesses. The inhabitants of Swilford tended to avoid the town centre and the beach during the summer because of these ignorant, ill-mannered visitors, but they tried hard not to complain because the income generated by tourism was a much-needed boost to the town's economy.

Instead of being lonely without his wife and family (his son was a musician and travelled extensively; never staying in any one place for very long, and his daughter was now married with a family of her own), Mason relished the freedom that was now his. He had rediscovered simple pleasures like being able to choose what to watch on telly or what music to listen to, what to eat and whether or not to accept invitations without having to consult anyone else.

Claire had been a social butterfly, insisting on attending every party and event that came their way, never taking into consideration that Mason might be tired and stressed out by his demanding job and that he would both appreciate and benefit from some time off. Despite claiming to support his choice of career, she had never understood that the long hours he worked were a matter of necessity. She also could not comprehend his refusal to climb the promotion ladder. He loved his job and the idea of ending up behind a desk was anathema to him, but Claire had wanted both the prestige of being married to a high-ranking officer and the salary that went with it. Instead of backing him, she felt his refusal to aim higher and the time spent away from the family was his way of punishing her. She just could not accept that when he had to cancel engagements at the last minute it was for a good reason, like a new lead in a murder enquiry and not just because he was purposely trying to make life difficult for her.

When a particularly complex case he was working on meant he couldn't accompany her on the mini cruise that had been booked to coincide with her 40th birthday, it was the final straw for Claire in a long list of straws. She had really thrown her toys out of the pram and instead of cancelling the holiday, she took herself off alone, leaving him behind to carry on with his investigation. It was during this trip that she met Tony, and it wasn't long after that she moved out. Although devastated at the time, Mason now considered that the divorce had actually improved his life. If Claire had not met Tony, then they would still be living lives they both hated and making each other miserable.

He was just contemplating a small whiskey when his mobile began to ring. Sighing, Mason was already heading towards the kitchen, balancing his plate, as he answered,

"Hi Leah, what's up?"

"Sorry to bother you on your night off Sir, but we've got a live one or should I say a dead one. Things are a little unusual and well I think it would be best if you…"

"Give me the address and I'll come now," Mason interrupted her. Leah was a good copper, and he trusted her judgement; she wouldn't have contacted him if she didn't think he should be there. She had only recently been promoted to DS and although she was young, Mason himself had made the recommendation due to her enthusiasm, commitment and attention to detail. She was a hard worker and deserved to be rewarded. Mason believed that she would climb a lot higher within a short space of time.

Intrigued as to what was awaiting him, Mason shrugged on his coat at the same time as giving Monty a treat and a quick pat on the head.

"Don't wait up lad," he told the dog before making his way to his car.

Pulling up in front of some imposing black wrought iron gates, Mason nodded to the officer who was standing at the entrance. If he'd been put there to control the crowd, then his job wasn't proving too strenuous thought Mason, checking out the small group of what he presumed to be neighbours who were huddled together some distance from the gates. The PC nodded to his counterpart on the other side who reached up and pressed a button, causing one-half of the gates to open, enabling the superior officer to access the drive. Approaching the top of the drive Mason took in his surroundings. The house itself was impressive, of mock Tudor design, standing stately, surrounded by gardens on all sides. Light was flooding from every window, and he could see movement both upstairs and downstairs, the team getting to work gathering evidence. He parked his car next to the numerous other vehicles abandoned outside the front of the property.

Leah Cooper crossed the driveway to meet him and started to give him the details, whilst he donned his white forensic suit, booties and gloves. The victim was, Cooper informed him, a 65-year-old male named Keith Kelly. Mason thought he recognised the name, but he couldn't place it. Cooper then gave him a concise report of the initial findings: that Kelly had died as the result of stab wounds and that a kitchen knife, believed to be the weapon used, had been recovered from the scene. The body had been discovered in the kitchen of the house and there were no obvious signs of a break-in or forced entry. The other occupants of the house, the victim's wife and son were currently inside the property with another police officer. What made this so extraordinary, Cooper explained, as they made their way towards the front door, was that the wife was claiming that the son had stabbed his father. According to Eliza Kelly, she had left the house after an argument with Keith and when she returned home, she had found her husband in the kitchen, very obviously dead. Her son, Zac, was also in the room, cowering in the corner clutching a kitchen knife.

"Nothing too out of the ordinary," commented Mason, "I've known plenty of cases where sons have killed their fathers or vice versa; domestic murders are quite commonplace."

"Not when the child responsible is 9 years old," answered DC Patel, who was hovering inside the doorway as Mason and Cooper entered the house. He obviously enjoyed the effect that his dramatic statement had on his senior officer.

I have to say I'm feeling quite exhilarated. It seems to be going well; certainly doesn't appear as if they've found anything that contradicts what I've told them. But what if Zac starts talking? I'm still not certain how much he understands of what's happened, what he's done.

Think Edith, think.

I'll just tell them the truth about him – about how unstable he is mentally. I mean that boy sure has a temper – takes after his mother! Am I overthinking this? I've only got to get through this morning's interview and then, apart from giving my formal statement, that should be it, job done. Still feels unsafe though. Still be really easy for something to go wrong.

Think Edith, think.

Maybe it's time to disappear again. Leave all this baggage behind. Collect the insurance money, sell the house and move on. What about Zac and Ricky though?

Think Edith, think.

Well, Zac's not going to be going anywhere anytime soon so he'll be easy to leave behind. Face it Edith, you're not exactly mothering material, are you? The boy will be better off looked after by the state or even better, maybe they'll make that bitch of a daughter of his raise the boy. Now that would be justice for all she's put me through. Still leaves the problem of Ricky.

Think Edith, think.

Why am I worrying about all this? Chances are it'll never be a problem. At the end of the day who's going to believe a drug addict with a criminal record as long as his arm, over me an upright, law-abiding citizen (at least on paper)?

I've just had another idea about how to raise more funds. I could sell my story to the highest bidder – start a tabloid war – the paper willing to pay the most gets the interview. Could do some TV too, although I must be careful - don't want people to look too closely at me. Wouldn't do for anyone to pop up out of the woodwork right now. Still should bring in another few grand. Then it will be time to fly off to somewhere exotic – new place, new name, new me.

That DI that's supposedly coming to see me this morning is taking his own sweet time. I really want to get out of here and start the ball rolling. Places to go, people to be!

June 1981

Panting, he scrambled to the top of what they called "The Hill", but which was, in reality, a mound of grass-covered earth. It was the highest point of the Common that was situated at the back of his best friend's house and from the perspective of the children, it was considerably high. The Common was where they both spent as much time as they could, sneaking out to meet up whenever the opportunity arose. It was their favourite place. Tucked away in the middle of a thicket of gorse and brambles, they had carved themselves a hiding place, a little den that could not be seen by passers-by. A place where they felt safe, whatever time of day or night, secure in the knowledge that no one would be able to find them.

Sometimes he would throw a stone up at her window in the middle of the night or in the early hours just as dawn was breaking. She would creep out of the house to join him with some smuggled snack for the two of them, and together they would head off to the den for an hour or so, making sure that they were back home before they were missed. Well, before she was missed anyway, it had been very unlikely that anyone would notice that he wasn't there. Of course, all that had changed now for him. Now his escapes had to be carefully planned and were few and far between.

He sat down hugging his knees, watching in awe as orange flames shot up into the dark night sky accompanied by plumes of smoke, white, grey and black, billowing in the wind, swirling around before heading upwards and crossing over the roofs of the houses. There was an acrid smell in the air. Every now and then a sharp crack split the night followed by a mass of bright sparks, hissing and spitting, like fireworks. It was mesmerising, a thing of great beauty; all colour and noise and it gave him the impression that it was alive, and it was talking to him, its creator. Never before had he experienced such a sense of achievement and for a while it consumed him, it was all he could see and hear. He hadn't been around to witness anything like this before. He had only returned to his childhood home after the fire had been extinguished and all that remained were the charred ruins of a property that had once held his entire family.

Gradually he became aware of a change in the atmosphere. The night around him got noisier, busier. Sirens gave way to shouts and cries. Although he couldn't see the house, in his mind's eye he could picture the scene. The firemen rushing towards the blazing building with hoses and ladders, the ambulance crew waiting, anticipating the worst, the policemen holding back crowds of onlookers, neighbours rudely awoken by all the commotion, expressing their disbelief, questioning who might still be inside. Just like the fire that had happened a few streets away only a couple of weeks before.

He sensed the noise dying down and imagined the body now being lifted from the stretcher into the ambulance, its blackened face covered with a sheet. Because he was in no doubt that the sole occupant of the house that night could not have survived the fire; that they would have succumbed to the smoke long before help was able to reach them. He had made sure of that. She had spent a long time in the planning of these incidents, and she had explained to him in great detail about house fires, and how and why so many people died in them.

"There you go." He spoke as if she was standing next to him. "It's done. We're even now."

3

Amy was awoken by a thumping which she assumed was inside her head. '*Surely not the start of a hangover already?*' she thought. It took her a moment to work out that the pounding was not in her head but someone knocking on the front door. She fumbled about on the top of her bedside cabinet trying to find her phone so she could see the time. Squinting, she managed to make out the numbers on the home screen – 1:35 am. Who on earth could be knocking at this time in the morning? They hadn't been in bed all that long and having drunk two bottles of wine between them, Amy was definitely feeling the effects. She nudged Marcus who was snoring loudly beside her. He stirred, muttering, but didn't wake. She was about to shake him when there was a louder knock, almost a hammering, and Marcus sprang upright.

"Who's at the door?" he asked.

"I've no idea," said Amy as she got out of bed and went to the window. Marcus checked the time on his alarm clock and groaned.

"It's the police." Amy had no idea why she was whispering but somehow it seemed appropriate. As she turned away from the window, Marcus was already in his dressing gown and heading for the door.

Following a few steps behind Marcus, Amy's first thought was that something must have happened to one of the children. Rory was 13, nearly 14, and staying overnight at his best friend Kyle's house and 11-year-old Olivia was at a birthday sleepover with some of her school friends. Hence the two bottles of wine she and Marcus had consumed between them. It wasn't very often they got the house to themselves. Amy knew that Marcus would be having similar thoughts, whatever this was about, it wouldn't be good news. The police didn't visit at this time in the morning unless something terrible had happened.

Amy reached the bottom of the stairs just as Marcus flung open the front door and greeted the two uniformed officers standing there with,

"Is this about one of the children?"

The older of the two shook his head and asked if they could come inside.

"Is it one of my parents?" asked Marcus.

"Let's just get inside Sir," replied the younger female officer.

Amy felt an enormous sense of relief flood through her and realised she had been holding her breath, this wasn't about the children, thank God. She had no idea that what she was about to be told would be so appalling and that it would change her life forever.

Amy couldn't recall the exact words the female officer used to break the dreadful news to her, but she did remember that the woman was kind, gesturing for her to sit on the sofa and then sitting next to her and looking her directly in the eyes as she spoke. Thinking back, all Amy could remember with any clarity was wishing that she had cleared away the empty wine bottles and glasses that stood on the coffee table, worrying about what the police officers would think. Such a ridiculous concern under the circumstances. She had got the gist of the conversation – her father had been stabbed and he was dead. She was vaguely aware of the police taking their leave.

After showing them to the door Marcus had taken her into his arms and gently gone through the painful details with her, making sure she understood exactly what scant information they had been given. Her father was dead, he'd been stabbed, it happened in his home, Eliza and Zac were in hospital, but it was just a precaution, neither of them had been injured.

What puzzled both her and Marcus was that the officer had stated that they weren't looking for anyone in connection with her father's death. How could that be? Surely this should be a murder inquiry. The police apologised for the lack of detail but for the time being, this was all that they could disclose, and they were unable to answer any questions. They assured the couple that there would be another visit later the same day and a fuller explanation of what had taken place would be given.

4

Mason pulled into a parking space that was the closest he could get to the entrance of the hospital. There weren't many perks to his job but being able to park where he liked was one of them. He checked himself in the rear-view mirror before he climbed out of the car noting that he looked as tired as he felt. He had been up all night visiting the crime scene, liaising with SOCO, the pathologist and the coroner, putting an investigating team together, updating his superior and carrying out the numerous other tasks that are involved at the very first stages of a murder inquiry, although this case was more likely to be labelled as an accidental death. He still had a lot to do before there was any chance of getting some rest. He'd just have to rely on several cups of strong coffee to keep him going.

DS Cooper spotted him as he walked through the hospital doors, and she approached carrying two take-out coffees as if she'd read his mind.

"How's she doing?" asked Mason. He had instructed Cooper to accompany Eliza Kelly and her son in the ambulance that had taken them away from the scene of the incident last night. He'd told Cooper to stay at the hospital until he could get there himself.

"She's very hard to read," replied the Detective Sergeant. "She's extremely rude and slightly aggressive which I would put down to shock, but she doesn't appear in the slightest bit shocked or upset, definitely not distraught in the way I would have imagined her to be after what's happened. She's treating the whole thing like it's an inconvenience and as if it's not got anything to do with her. The only time she's shown any strong emotion is when she was told she can't leave here yet. She got quite angry. She's accusing us of holding her against her will."

"What about the boy?" asked Mason struggling to remember the child's name.

"Zac," said Cooper. "He's still not talking; the legal guardian is sitting with him. I've got one of the lads in the room under strict instructions to contact one of us as soon as he starts to say anything and to make a note of anything we miss."

Mason nodded his approval. "I think I'll go and visit Mrs Kelly on my own," he said. "You go home and try and get some kip, you look knackered."

"So do you," said Cooper grinning at him. "What if Zac starts to talk?"

"I'll get Danny Boy to come over. I'll be visiting Mr Kelly's daughter later on and he can keep me company. Go on home lass, you've done enough."

"Thanks, boss," Cooper replied, grateful at least to be able to go and shower off the horrible hospital smell that she felt was clinging to her clothes and her hair.

As he waited for the lift to reach the ground floor, which was taking so long it must be coming down from the roof, Mason turned his thoughts to the victim of last night's stabbing. The name Keith Kelly had been familiar to him when he'd first been informed of the victim's identity, but he hadn't made the connection with the actor Keith Kelly until DC Patel had acquainted him with the fact at the crime scene. Mason got the distinct impression that Jay Patel was rather excited about a case involving a celebrity, something to boast about in the staff canteen. For Mason, the body he had viewed on the kitchen floor of the upscale family home he visited last night bore little resemblance to the image in his head of the cocky, East Ender that Keith Kelly had portrayed on a popular soap opera in his heyday. Still, thought Mason, that was a few years ago now.

After eventually reaching the floor he wanted, via the lift, and being pointed in the right direction by a harassed-looking nurse, Mason found it easy to identify the correct room due to the officer sitting on a chair outside the door. He nodded to the young PC.

"Any problems?" he asked.

The boy, Mason could only think of him as a boy, (he was as bad as his dad had been at his age thinking that policemen were getting younger), stood up and shook his head.

"As you were then," said Mason, adding wryly, "you can get back to your paper."

The lad blushed; he'd hoped that he hadn't been spotted hastily tucking the sporting pages of a national rag under his chair when he saw the DI approach.

Mason peered through the small glass panel in the door of the room and then knocked and entered without waiting for a summons. *'Doesn't matter which hospital you're in',* he thought to himself, *'all the rooms look and smell the same'.* This room had the standard bed and side cabinet with a double window that overlooked the car park. *'And they're always so bloody hot!'* Mason thought whilst he slipped out of his overcoat.

The person occupying the bed was sitting cross-legged in the middle of it, dressed in jeans and a T-shirt, her head bent down as she scrutinised the screen on her phone. She did not immediately turn towards him as he approached. He gave a subtle cough, and she swung around to look at him. The first thing he noticed was her eyes, a piercing blue, the sort you associated with someone of Scandinavian descent and yet her hair was dark brown, almost black, rather than the usual blonde that accompanied such icy blue eyes. It was an unusual combination; she couldn't be classed as beautiful, but she was certainly striking. She also looked a good 10 years younger than Mason knew her to be, more like mid 30s than mid 40s he thought, as her eyes swept him up and down immediately dismissing him. Mason was unsurprised, aware that he wasn't anything special to look at, being on the shorter side and rather stocky. His nose was flat, the result of being broken on more than one occasion, and his once dark hair was now a steely grey.

When he introduced himself, however, her whole attitude changed and she sat up straighter, pocketed her phone and swung her legs over the edge of the bed. She looked him straight in the eye.

"You've taken your time getting here," she said. "I've been told I can't leave until I've spoken with you. So can we get on with it as I very much want to go home, I've a lot to sort out."

Her voice was much deeper, and breathier than he had expected, and he would hazard a guess that it was not her natural speaking voice but something she'd deliberately cultivated. He couldn't place the accent. Posh, but with tones of South London, he thought. She gave an impatient sigh as she waited for him to answer. Instead, he grabbed the chair that was against the side wall and hanging his overcoat over the back of it, he moved it next to the bed.

"We did meet briefly last night but I'm not sure if you remember. First of all, I would like to express my sincere sympathy regarding the death of your husband Mrs Kelly. Last night must have been a horrific experience for you and I appreciate how distressing all of this is, the testing, the waiting around and everything, but I would very much appreciate it if you could just run through what happened for me."

She sighed again, louder this time, folding her arms in front of her chest. Being nearer to her face now Mason could see the bruising around her right eye, the black, greenish hue beginning to deepen. Up close she looked much more like her real age.

"For God's sake, how many times do I have to go through it?" she demanded irritably.

"I understand that this is difficult, Eliza, may I call you Eliza?" he waited for an answer but as none was forthcoming, he continued, "but surely you can see it from our point of view. What took place last night was out of the ordinary, to say the least; your husband was stabbed and died as a result of his injuries. Currently, we only have your word for how it happened. Namely that Zac was responsible. We really have a duty to find out exactly what went on and I don't want to add to your distress, but your account is imperative to our investigation." He then added with more sympathy, "Your cooperation at this stage is vital. The more you tell us now the quicker this can be over with."

"I'm not going to add anything to what I've already said," Eliza told him tartly. She folded her arms even tighter together as if to emphasise the point and glared at him. Mason said nothing, he just held her gaze and waited.

After what felt like minutes but in reality was only seconds, Eliza spoke again, "I just don't see why you can't liaise with your colleagues, the ones I've already spoken to," she snapped at him. "I'm not going to say anything different to you than what I said to that woman officer last night. All I'll be doing is repeating myself, which is a complete waste of both of our time. Like I said I have things to be getting on with."

"Such as?" Mason couldn't help himself. Her tone annoyed him and for the life of him he couldn't imagine what she needed to do that was so important at this particular moment in time. '*Get a grip*', he told himself. '*Think of what she's gone through and how she must be feeling.*'

"Well for starters you might be aware that there is an awful mess in my kitchen that needs to be dealt with, and I would like to start notifying people that Keith is dead. I must speak to his solicitor regarding the will, and I need to make some financial arrangements." Eliza spoke as if it was all a terrible inconvenience.

Mason hoped that the disgust he was feeling towards her didn't show on his face. He was expecting her to mention her son's welfare or to talk about the necessary arrangements regarding a funeral, not a mess in the kitchen and her husband's financial arrangements.

"I wouldn't worry too much about the state your house is in for the time being," he said dryly. "It's a crime scene so you won't be allowed back in for a while and my officers will be adding to the mess I'm afraid, taking fingerprints, and the like. We will of course send in the crime scene cleaners once we're done; we have a specialist team," he tried to take the sting out of his words by smiling at her. "As regards other people, we've already sent someone to notify Keith's eldest daughter, and I believe she will contact her brother, as they are the next of kin after yourself. If I were you, I'd wait a little while before letting anyone else know, nothing official can be done until you have a death certificate and that won't be released until we know exactly how Keith died."

If he was expecting her to be contrite, he was mistaken.

"I'm a qualified solicitor so I know how this works," she said. "But I would like to contact his agent and let her know that she needs to settle any outstanding earnings and that he won't be available for future roles." She gave a little laugh.

Mason had dealt with many bereaved relatives over the years, but he couldn't remember ever coming across someone so cold and unfeeling as Eliza. He was aware that people reacted in different ways to shock and to grief, but this woman's responses were, to him, unnatural. If she hadn't been so confident and composed, he could have almost believed she suffered from a form of autism. Mason wondered if she was starting to lose control. It would be understandable given the circumstances.

"I know what you're thinking," Eliza smirked. "You're surprised that I'm not weeping and wailing, ripping my clothes. You're assuming that the way I'm acting is a coping strategy or that the trauma I've suffered has left me unhinged. Let me assure you, Detective Inspector Mason," sarcastically giving him his full rank. "What's happened, happened and what's done is done. I can't change it, I couldn't have prevented it, so what's the point in being upset about it? I must be practical. I have a future and Keith doesn't, so I need to think about myself. If he hadn't died, I'd have split from him anyway. I'm not the sort of woman who would stay with a violent, self-obsessed, has-been. So, are we clear? I'm not emotionally fragile. Keith is dead and I need to move on."

"And what about Zac?" Mason asked. "What are your feelings regarding him and his future?" He hadn't intended to be so sharp but what she had just said riled him. He had noted that she had used "violent" as a description of her husband but decided not to inquire about their relationship right now, those sorts of questions would be asked in due course.

"As far as I can see, Zac has no future," she said harshly. "How or why, he did what he did doesn't matter. It's done and he'll have to face the consequences."

"He's 9 years old," said Mason, appalled by her callous dismissal of her only child.

"What difference does that make? 9, 19, 29, he's still a murderer in the eyes of the law."

"Well," Mason said, not sure how to respond, "I'll be going to visit Zac myself shortly. Hopefully, he will be able to tell us for himself what went on between him and his dad last night."

Eliza got off the bed, so Mason rose out of the chair. They stood face to face as Eliza confronted him.

"You can't question him. Not without an adult present and I've told you I have no interest in seeing him at this time. He wouldn't talk to you anyway, not without me there."

Mason noticed that when she got angry her posh accent slipped considerably.

"Eliza," he said. "You come across as an intelligent woman and, as you've indicated, you have an understanding of the law, so you must realise that you can't be present when we question Zac. There's the possibility that you may inadvertently influence anything he says; surely you understand that. Only you, Zac and Keith know what happened last night. Keith is obviously unable to help me, and I can't just rely on your word. Questioning Zac is incredibly important."

"You are not allowed to question him, not without me." Eliza was almost snarling now.

"Yes, I am," Mason replied curtly. "I've already applied for a responsible adult, a court-appointed guardian, to be assigned to Zac so *someone* will be looking out for his best interests. He's currently being well looked after I promise."

"He won't talk to you if I'm not there," Eliza responded smugly. "So, you'll be wasting your time."

"We'll just have to wait and see, won't we? At least I can check how he is. Would you like me to come back to see you afterwards, and let you know how he's doing?"

"No thank you," Eliza replied bluntly.

"After Zac's told us what happened, I can arrange for you to see him if you like," said Mason.

"Whatever he tells you you're hardly likely to pat him on the head and let him go home, are you? He's going to be locked up one way or another, isn't he? There's absolutely nothing I can do to help him, he's now your problem, not mine. I'm beginning to think that it's probably better for both of us in the long run if I cut contact with him and sever all ties. Whatever happens to him is only going to cause me problems and I have enough problems to deal with right now without having him to worry about, and like you said," she gave Mason another of her sarcastic smiles, "he's being well looked after. I think that would be what's best."

Mason was stunned. He had no idea what to say. If this woman was in her right mind, then she was a terrible excuse for a mother. No matter what her son had done, surely she couldn't be serious about not wanting to see him. He wasn't certain how to proceed from this point.

"Perhaps you'll change your mind when things have calmed down a bit; it's all so raw at the moment. I don't advise that you make any big decisions like that just now."

Eliza smirked at him. "I very rarely change my mind. Now can we just get this over with so I can leave this God-awful place."

5

Neither Amy nor Marcus had seen any point in returning to bed after the two constables, who had broken the news, had left. They had both sobered up and knew that it would be impossible to sleep. Marcus had made coffee and toast, but Amy couldn't face eating. They had both taken showers and dressed and then sat together on the sofa going over what little they had been told, speculating about what could possibly have happened. Amy shed a few tears thinking about the fact that she would never see her father again, but it didn't feel real. It was like a bad dream from which she would wake at any moment; she just couldn't believe it was actually true. Large chunks of time passed where they didn't speak to each other, both lost in their own thoughts.

After one of these periods of silence, Amy said, "Do you think Dad could have killed himself? It's the only reason I can think of as to why they aren't looking for- How did they say it? Not looking for anyone else in connection with his death. Oh God, I really hope that's not what happened. Poor Dad. But they said he was stabbed. Why would they say that? People don't stab themselves to death, do they? They hang themselves or slit their wrists. Dad wouldn't have committed suicide, would he? I mean, I know he's been depressed lately but to do that! This is just unbelievable."

"I honestly don't know," Marcus replied, "It just doesn't make any sense to me either. I think maybe someone else is involved and perhaps they're in custody already, but they couldn't say; weren't allowed to tell us for some reason. It's just so weird. I'm sorry love but with such little detail I think all we can do is wait until they come back and hopefully, then we'll get some answers."

Amy reluctantly agreed. Marcus got up and made yet another cup of tea that neither of them really wanted.

"I wish Adam would call back," Amy said. "I know I can't tell him much, but it feels wrong that he doesn't know Dad's dead." Adam, Amy's brother was currently living and working in Australia. His phone had gone straight to voicemail, but then it was Saturday afternoon for him, so he was probably out and about somewhere.

"He'll call soon," Marcus reassured her.

"And what are we going to tell the kids?" cried Amy, taking the mug from him.

Marcus sat down and put his arm around her.

"I'm going to ring Kyle and Hayley's parents in a bit and ask if the kids can stay a little longer. I can't ring now, it's far too early. I'll just say that we've had some bad news, but I'll ask them not to mention anything to the kids. Perhaps they can make out that we're a bit worse for wear; the kids would believe that. Hopefully, the police won't be too late calling around and when we know more, we can decide when to bring the kids home and what to tell them."

Again, Amy agreed with him, she was in no hurry to break the news to her children that their beloved granddad had died.

"I really feel like I should let other people know that Dad's dead though. We ought to tell Uncle John and Kath and Terry, but what would we say? We don't know anything ourselves." She continued before Marcus could reply. "And what about Eliza? Shouldn't we ring to find out how she is, if nothing else she'll be able to fill us in on what happened."

"I've tried her phone, but it goes straight to voicemail," said Marcus. "Anyway, I'm not sure the police would let us talk to her right now. Not when she's a witness."

"I can't bear this, it's just so awful," moaned Amy.

"I know love, it's horrendous and it's frustrating but all we can do is wait," said Marcus. "There's no point contacting anyone else yet. They'd only be in the same boat as us, wondering what on earth has happened; speculating. Let's see what the police have to say before we talk to anyone else. They might already have been in touch with Adam, you know in the same way they came to us as next of kin."

"No, I told the Policewoman that I would call him," said Amy. "Anyway, he would have phoned me by now if he'd been told."

"I'm sure the police will come round again soon; they must know how desperate we are for more information," said Marcus.

The police were as good as their word and just after midday, Detective Inspector Mason and Detective Sergeant Hobbs arrived at the house. After introducing themselves at the door, Marcus invited them both in and took them through to the kitchen, where Amy had already put the kettle on. Whilst she made tea, the DI and his Sergeant took seats at the wooden farmhouse table. DS Hobbs busied himself with removing his notepad and pen from his suit jacket, as Mason made the introductions again for Amy's benefit, explaining that he was the senior investigating officer handling the case and that he had wanted to visit them in person. Firstly, to offer his and his team's most sincere condolences on the death of her father, and secondly, to bring them up to speed with the investigation so far.

Mason looked around the kitchen approvingly. He couldn't help comparing this welcoming space with its Aga and Welsh Dresser, dog baskets on the floor and piles of folded washing on the table, a pair of muddy football boots chucked into a corner, with the cold and clinical kitchen, all stark white with chrome fittings, where the dead body of this woman's father had been discovered. You could tell straight away that this room was at the heart of family life he decided, whereas the one he'd visited last night was more of a showroom kitchen, for display purposes only.

Amy, having already enquired about milk and sugar, asked them again. She then realised that she was pouring boiling water into empty mugs. Marcus took over, telling her gently to go and sit down. In the time it took for Marcus to deposit the mugs of tea on the table and hunt around in the cupboard for a new packet of biscuits, having discovered that the ones in the biscuit tin were soft, Amy had a chance to study the two detectives. Hobbs was tall and thin, with sandy-coloured hair and light blue eyes. His suit was well-worn. As he folded his jacket over the back of his chair, she glimpsed the shiny patches at the elbows. She estimated that he was a good 10 years younger than his colleague and he certainly looked friendlier and more approachable than his stockier counterpart. Even if he hadn't introduced himself as such, she would have known that Mason was the boss, the one in charge. His whole demeanour was that of a man who would brook no nonsense, the sort unlikely to suffer fools gladly. He would make a formidable opponent she thought. He certainly looked very stern and serious, but as he caught her watching him, he gave her a smile that changed his face completely, and now she could see compassion and kindness in his deep brown eyes. She knew she had reddened slightly having been caught out staring. She always blushed easily; it was something Marcus took pleasure in teasing her about. Then she worried that it was inappropriate to smile and dropped her eyes down to study her mug.

Mason cleared his throat and said,

"I believe our officers visited you at around half past one this morning. I'm not sure how much they were able to tell you, and I'm pretty certain that you wouldn't have been able to take much in any way after a shock like that. So, I'll run you through everything we have been able to establish so far and then if you have any questions, I'll try to answer them. I have a few questions of my own too, if that's alright with you?"

Amy thought she could detect a slight Scottish burr in his accent and for some reason this made him seem softer, less intimidating. She nodded to him to go ahead feeling Marcus squeezing her arm slightly, letting her know he was there. After confirming her full name and saying that she was the daughter of Keith Kelly, Amy felt as if she didn't breathe again during the few minutes it took DI Mason to talk through the events of the night before.

He began by telling them about the 999 call Eliza had made, in which she had stated that her son had stabbed his father and that she was certain her husband was dead. Eliza confirmed several times during the call that despite her son being only 9 years of age, he was solely responsible for the stabbing but was now unarmed and harmless. Amy gasped. '*This can't be happening*,' she thought to herself. She turned to Marcus, and he just shook his head in disbelief.

DI Mason told the stunned pair that neither the call handler nor the attending officers could be certain the circumstances Eliza was describing were accurate. Therefore, the officers were extremely cautious as they approached the property, but Eliza met them at the front door with Zac by her side. After a quick search, it was confirmed that there was no one else in the house, other than Amy's father, who was discovered on the kitchen floor; just as Eliza had stated. The paramedic had quickly established that her father, Keith, was dead and had been for some time, at least a couple of hours, but forensics would be able to provide a more accurate time of death. DI Mason paused at this point to let Amy compose herself and then he continued to tell them the version of events given to them by Eliza.

Apparently, Eliza and Keith had been arguing, and as the argument escalated, Eliza worried that Keith was going to completely lose his temper. She had gone upstairs to check that the shouting hadn't woken Zac. Finding him still sleeping, she made her way downstairs to the front door with the intention of leaving for a short while to enable Keith to calm down. As she went to open the door, Keith tried to prevent her, grabbing her by the arm and pulling her back into the house. As she struggled to break free, he hit her, letting go of her arm in the process which enabled her to run out of the front door.

At this point Amy interrupted Mason.

"She said my dad hit her?" she asked incredulously. "My dad's never hit anyone in his life. He doesn't lose his temper. He's ridiculously soft."

Mason held up his hands.

"I'm not judging your father," he said. "I'm just repeating what we have been told."

Amy nodded and looked down at the table again. Mason waited for a short while and then when she didn't say anything else he carried on,

"Eliza then drove herself to her friend's house."

This time it was Marcus who interrupted. "Eliza doesn't have friends," he said.

"It must have been Ricky," said Amy. "Who else could it be?"

Mason neither confirmed nor denied this. He continued with his narration,

"Eliza waited for a couple of hours at her friend's house and then returned home hoping that your dad would have calmed down and possibly taken himself to bed."

Mason then went on to tell them that according to Eliza this was a regular occurrence between herself and her husband after a row. She had found if she left him alone for a while, he was likely to cool off quicker than if she stayed in the house. Normally, she said she would return home to find him very contrite and conciliatory. This time, however, when she returned, she found Keith slouched on the kitchen floor and Zac cowering in the corner clutching a knife. It was obvious to her that Keith was dead, and as soon as she had taken the knife from Zac, she had called for help.

Zac had only spoken once whilst the officers were present and all he had said was, "I did it for my Mummy." Since then, he had not uttered a word, and they assumed the boy to be in shock.

DI Mason paused again to see if Amy or Marcus wanted to ask anything, but they just sat in stunned silence trying to take it all in, so he carried on. Eliza, he told them, could only assume that Zac had gone downstairs after she had left the house and that he and Keith had got into an argument, the outcome of which was that Zac had stabbed Keith.

The DI went on to explain that forensic evidence had been collected from both Zac and Eliza at the hospital where they had been sent for an examination. Other than the bruising Eliza alleged was caused by Keith, they were both unhurt. Forensic samples had also been taken from the house. A post-mortem was currently being performed on Keith and they were awaiting toxicology results.

Mason seemed to pre-empt the question Marcus was on the verge of asking, by saying there had already been a full examination of the house and there was no evidence of a break-in or forced entry.

He finished by saying there was very little else he could tell them at this point as there was still a lot of investigative work to be done. The results of the forensic tests would take time to come through, but they could confirm that Keith had died as a result of one or more stab wounds. He also confirmed that, from what they had established so far, they would not be looking for anyone else in connection with the incident. They were certain that no one else had been involved and that Eliza's explanation of the events of the night was supported by the evidence uncovered so far. It was just a question now of establishing exactly what happened on the night and they were hoping that Zac, who had so far remained silent, would soon be up to talking to them. He explained that he had visited both Eliza and Zac at the hospital that morning, where he had gone over the events of the night before with Eliza again.

"I'm so sorry," said Mason "but the way it looks to us is that your brother, whether deliberately or accidentally, fatally stabbed your father."

"He's my half-brother," responded Amy. She didn't know why she needed to correct the Detective on this point, but it was important to her.

"Sorry, yes of course," said Mason. "Your mother is deceased is that correct? And Eliza is your…" He had obviously been about to say stepmother but thought better of it. "Your father's second wife?"

"That's right," said Amy.

Then Marcus said,

"If I understand you correctly, what you're saying is that due to an argument getting out of hand, Zac a 9-year-old child stabbed my father-in-law to death! I'm sorry but that just doesn't make sense. Keith would never have hurt Eliza, and I really can't believe that he and Zac would have got into a fight. Zac's 9 for Christ's sake. He's just 9 years old!"

"I know it's difficult to take in," said Mason calmly, "and I appreciate that the circumstances are certainly unusual, but yes that does appear to be what's happened. We will know a lot more once we receive the results of the many tests that are currently being carried out."

"Eliza told you that she and my father frequently had rows?" queried Amy.

"That's right," confirmed DI Mason. "She told us that he was often violent towards her, and she had experience of the best way of dealing with him when he lost his temper."

"That's just not true," Amy's voice was little more than a whisper. "My dad never hit her; he never lost his temper. He hated confrontation. He never shouted at me or my brother Adam, not ever. He never hit my Mum. I've never once heard him shout at Zac, not even when he should have done. She's lying."

"I know you're upset and it's a lot to digest but until we establish exactly what happened, I can't take anybody's word about any of it. I'm really sorry but you'll just have to let us do our job and then we will be able to give you some answers. What was *your* relationship like with your father?"

"Just recently we've been getting on really well," Amy answered. "We've had a few rough patches since he and Eliza got together but we finally seemed to have got past that, and things were good between us."

"Your relationship with Eliza wasn't so good then?" This was the first time DS Hobbs had asked a question, and he looked up from his notes and smiled to let her know it wasn't an accusation of any kind.

"To be honest no, not good," Amy answered. "I think we both tried at the beginning but for the last couple of years, we've basically stayed out of each other's way. I never visited my dad at their house, but he would come here on a regular basis on his own. It was just easier that way."

Hobbs nodded as if he understood how tricky family relationships could be.

"What about Zac?" asked Mason. "What's your relationship like with him?"

"Truthfully, I don't have a relationship with Zac, never have done. I'm not close to him at all."

"Was your father on any medications that you know of?" asked Hobbs. The complete change of subject threw Amy, and she had to think before she answered.

"He took something due to a heart condition, some sort of blood thinner I think but I don't know the name of it."

Hobbs nodded as if this information wasn't new to him. "Was he on antidepressants?"

Again, Amy thought before she answered,

"Not that I'm aware of. He had been very down lately. The last couple of times I saw him he was quite open about the fact that he was struggling, so I wouldn't be surprised."

Mason took over the questioning again. "Any idea what was getting him down?"

"From what I could gather, he had financial problems

and was also struggling with his relationship with Zac. Zac's behaviour was starting to really get out of hand, and I know Dad and Eliza had disagreed over how best to deal with it, and…" Amy stopped and put a hand up to her mouth. "But that doesn't mean they were having severe arguments," she stressed. "Dad wouldn't have hit her. He never physically punished Zac. He just wanted to set boundaries, show him that bad behaviour had consequences, but Eliza wouldn't even agree to chastise him." Amy paused and took a breath. "I'm sorry," she said. "I know it sounds bad, but seriously, it was just minor disagreements." She wished she'd never started on this topic. She felt like she was being disloyal to her father and tears started to stream down her face.

"I'm certain he had some money worries," Marcus chipped in to give Amy a chance to regain her composure, "and that was getting him down. He was struggling to find work. He's an actor as I'm sure you're aware."

Mason nodded.

"He's found it difficult to get any decent roles recently," Marcus continued. "He was talking of packing it in and trying something new, but he had no idea of what else he could do, and I mean at his age, well… he was a bit old to be starting again. I know he was really keen for Eliza to return to work, but she couldn't seem to settle for anything." He stopped now aware that he was rambling. He looked over at Amy for help.

"How is Eliza?" asked Amy, not because she particularly cared but because she'd started over-thinking everything and felt the detectives might find it odd that they hadn't enquired after either Eliza or Zac.

"She's doing remarkably well, given the circumstances, very calm and collected," answered Mason.

Marcus, detecting something in the DI's tone raised an eyebrow at him.

"People react in very different ways when they experience trauma," explained Mason.

"If you mean she's not showing any signs of being upset," said Marcus, "I think you'll find that that's just Eliza. She doesn't do emotion."

"To be honest," said Mason, "she seems more annoyed at not being allowed back to the house than anything else at the moment."

"Obviously it's out of bounds to anyone right now as it's a crime scene," clarified DS Hobbs.

Amy shuddered. Her dad's home was a crime scene? That felt so wrong.

"Where is Eliza at the moment then?" she asked.

"We'll be putting her up somewhere for the time being," said Mason. "She has a FLO staying with her. An FL…"

"It's okay," said Amy "I know what an FLO is." She included Marcus with a tilt of her head as she continued, "We were thinking earlier that we should contact her, show our support or whatever, but her phone's turned off."

"She's stated that she would prefer not to be in contact with anyone for the time being. I'm sure she'll be in touch with you soon. I think she just needs a bit of time. She has just lost her husband and her son after all," said Mason.

Amy was confused for a second, "Oh, you mean Max?" she said.

"Max? Who's Max?" asked Mason.

"Oh sorry, I just assumed that's what you meant when you said she'd lost a son, but you actually meant Zac didn't you? Sorry, I'm being a bit dumb."

"No, no, you're doing great," Mason reassured her. "You're right, I was referring to Zac as obviously he won't be going home for a while whatever the case may be. But could you tell me about Max?"

"Max was Eliza's son from her first marriage, but he lives with his father. Eliza hasn't had any contact with him, hasn't done for years. He must be in his 20s by now. That's who I thought you were referring to."

Amy was very conscious of DS Hobbs scribbling away in his notebook, so she felt it only right to enquire about Zac and his current whereabouts.

"He's being well looked after," was all that Mason would say.

Up until now, Amy had been coping relatively well but the horrendous facts she'd been given were starting to have an effect. Images of her father lying on the floor bleeding, of Zac standing over him grinning whilst wielding an oversized knife above his head.

"Was it quick?" she asked, and seeing the look of confusion on Mason's face, she continued,

"My dad, was it quick? Did he- Was he in pain? You know did he suffer? Would he have been aware of what Zac had done?"

Mason rose from his chair and moved across to her. Very gently he put a hand on her shoulder. "From what I understand," he said, "it was quick and no, I don't think he suffered."

He turned to DS Hobbs and nodded. Hobbs also stood up and began putting on his jacket.

"Mrs McDonald," Mason began.

"Please call me Amy."

"Amy, you've been extremely brave and thank you for answering our questions. I'm so sorry for what's happened, and I know nothing will ever make this right for you, but I promise you I will uncover exactly what occurred last night, and we will keep you updated on our progress."

"Can I see him?" asked Amy. "Can I go and see my dad?"

"Soon," the DI promised. "We'll be in touch to let you know when."

"Where are your children?" asked DS Hobbs, looking at the many photographs slipped in between bits of crockery on the Welsh Dresser.

"With friends at the moment," said Marcus. "They were away last night so they don't know anything yet."

"Oh God," said Amy, "what are we going to tell them?"

"I would just say that their grandad had an accident for now," advised Mason. "You can give them more details when you've got a better idea yourselves. Children are resilient you know, but it's probably best to keep it simple for the time being."

"Have you spoken to my brother, Adam?" Amy asked.

"Not yet," confirmed Mason. "Would you like us to, or would you prefer to do it yourselves?"

"Oh, we'll do it," said Amy. "It'll be easier to hear it from me rather than the police, what with him being so far away. I've already left him a message to contact me, but he hasn't returned my call yet. This is going to be so awful for him to hear. He and Dad were very close even though he's been in Australia for the last few years."

Mason nodded and Amy realised she didn't have to explain where Adam was, he already knew.

"Is it okay if we tell family, like Dad's brother, and maybe some of his friends?" Amy remembered the discussions she and Marcus had had before these officers arrived.

"I'll leave that to your discretion," said Mason. "But again, it's probably best to keep it simple for now. Wait until we've got further with our enquiries before you go into too much detail. One thing I would mention is that obviously there will be a lot of press interest in this case. Your father is somewhat well known and the fact that this was a domestic and the age of Zac. We've not given them any information yet, and I will try and keep it that way for as long as I can, but they've already been sniffing around." His tone of voice revealed exactly what he thought of the media. "The news will soon get out there and then they will do everything they can to get a story."

Amy hadn't even considered this, but he was right. With her father being a celebrity, albeit a minor one, the interest in his death, especially under such dreadful circumstances, was going to be huge. Thinking about it, she realised that the press would be interested if Zac was responsible, whether her father was famous or not. A 9-year-old boy stabbing his father to death was certainly going to be considered newsworthy. The thought of the press attention worried her. It would be hard enough for herself and Marcus, but it would be hell for the children.

"If you have any problems at all with press intrusion, just get in touch," said Mason, seemingly reading her mind, as he handed her a card. "All my contact numbers are on here and if you can't get hold of me ask to be put through to DS Hobbs or DS Cooper. We will look after you, Amy, I promise. And if you have any questions, or you think of something that we might consider useful to the investigation, then please do call."

"Thank you," said Amy, although she wasn't sure quite what she would be able to do to help them. It seemed as if the investigation was already over, there wasn't anything that she could add.

"We'll be in touch again very soon and someone will let you know when you can go and visit your father," said Mason. "Don't worry, we'll show ourselves out."

And with that, the two of them left the room.

As soon as she heard the door shut, Amy let go and completely broke down. She sobbed and sobbed as Marcus held her, rubbing her back and making soothing sounds, feeling totally useless, nothing prepared you for something as horrific as this.

BBC Local News – Saturday 21st February 2015

MAN DIES IN STABBING INCIDENT

Police were called to an incident in Lime Tree Avenue, Brigholme at around 10 o'clock last night.

A man believed to be in his 70s died at the scene apparently from knife wounds. A woman and young boy were taken to hospital and their condition is as yet unknown.

At present no further details have been released.

~~~~~~

Sunday Telegraph – Sunday 22nd February 2015

NINE-YEAR-OLD BOY DETAINED FOLLOWING DEATH OF HIS FATHER

A police investigation is underway after the body of a man was found in a house in Brigholme on Friday night. Reports suggest that the victim was attacked and killed by his 9-year-old son. The boy is currently being held at a secure facility.

The police have confirmed that they are not looking for anyone else in connection with the incident.

~~~~~~

The Guardian – 23rd February 2015

9-YEAR-OLD GUILTY OF FATHER'S MURDER

A nine-year-old boy, who cannot be named for legal reasons, is believed by police to be responsible for the death of his father. The man in his 70s was found dead at his home.

Police were called to an address in Brigholme at around 9 o'clock on Friday 20th February. Police later confirmed that a body had been found on the property. The 9-year-old, believed to be the victim's son, is being held pending further investigation. Police are not releasing any names or giving any further information at this time, although they have confirmed that they are not seeking anyone else in connection with the incident. The police are currently supporting the victim's family.

~~~~~~

The Sun – Saturday 21st February 2015

9-YEAR-OLD KILLS FATHER IN FRENZIED KNIFE ATTACK

A 9-year-old boy is in police custody after he went berserk and stabbed his father to death. The victim, who has yet to be named, died as a result of the brutal assault by his child, sometime yesterday evening.

~~~~~~

6

Mason took it easy as he drove himself and Danny Hobbs back to the incident room at Brigholme Police Station. They left West Wilby, the small village where Keith's daughter and her husband lived, and passed through a few more almost identical villages, before joining the dual carriageway that would take them back to Brigholme.

These villages were all of such a similar ilk. One main street, with the village church taking pride of place, and a couple of pubs, most of which were advertising reasonably priced Sunday lunches. *'Shame it's only Saturday,'* thought Mason. He could do with a nice roast beef dinner with all the trimmings, and it would have been good to put the meal on expenses. Another small perk of the job.

Some of the villages had new estates added to their borders which spoilt the traditional look but all of them were quiet and peaceful, very quiet considering it was a Saturday afternoon.

"I could retire out here," he announced to Danny, "lovely little cottage, not too far from the sea."

"Not on your pension," laughed Danny, "and anyway you live right by the sea at the moment."

"True," said Mason. "But it gets too busy in the Summer. It must be more peaceful being this far out."

"Too quiet for me," replied Danny. "That wasn't as hard as I was expecting," he added, referring to the visit they had just made. "They were a nice couple, weren't they? Don't think it's sunk in yet though, do you? Such a shocking thing to happen. I'm struggling to get my head around it, got to be so much harder for them."

"It's the most bizarre case I've worked on in a while," Mason admitted. "At least their reactions were normal."

"What do you mean by that?" asked Hobbs.

"Well, you know, they were stunned, shocked, upset, definitely not accepting of it. Mrs Kelly," he said her name with emphasis, "on the other hand was cold, calm, completely dismissive of the whole thing. You wouldn't have thought for one minute that her husband had just died. She wasn't bothered about her son, what he had done, she didn't even want to know how he was."

"Well people have their own way of dealing with tragic situations," said Hobbs mildly. "She's suffering from shock; she could be completely different come tomorrow or whenever it starts to hit her."

"I know that, and it's what I thought too, but she said, and I quote, 'What's done is done, I can't change it. I've got a future and Keith hasn't'." Mason actually felt himself shudder as he recalled the interview that had taken place at the hospital that morning.

"I got the definite impression just now that there was no love lost between Keith's daughter and his second wife," he continued.

"That's quite often the case though, isn't it?" remarked Hobbs. "I can't stand my stepmum, but I get on great with my stepdad. In fact, I get on better with him than I do with my real dad."

Mason was surprised. It wasn't very often that he received any personal information from Danny; usually, if they weren't talking about work, they kept their conversations to light-hearted stuff like football or films. '*Danny's starting to get more comfortable with me*', thought Mason, which pleased him; he hated being treated like the boss all the time. Although he could come down hard on a subordinate, when necessary, he preferred a more relaxed approach.

"Do you remember Keith Kelly?" Mason asked his passenger. "It must have been before your time when he was in that soap."

"My mum never missed an episode, so I do remember the character. Can't say I remember seeing him in anything else though."

"No, me neither. Maybe a couple of bit parts, but certainly nothing big, nothing of note. His son-in-law was probably right when he said that a lack of work was what had been getting him down. I understand his daughter being very defensive when it came to her dad losing his temper, but if you look at it realistically he was getting older and struggling for work, the chances of him landing another major role were very slim, and if he had financial worries on top of that it's enough to make a man lose control. And I know I shouldn't be influenced by personal feelings, it's not professional, but if I was married to that woman, I'm pretty certain I wouldn't be averse to giving her a slap."

"I see those politically correct courses they've been sending us on have done wonders for you!" observed Hobbs.

"I'm not condoning domestic violence in any way, shape or form."

Although Mason knew Hobbs was joking, he felt it was important not to be misunderstood. One slip of the tongue these days and you were up for a disciplinary.

"I'm going to insist that Eliza Kelly comes to the station to give her formal statement and you can sit in on it, then you'll see what I'm talking about."

A song he liked came onto the radio and he turned up the volume resisting the urge to sing along. He didn't want to give Danny another reason to take the piss out of him and his singing voice left a lot to be desired.

When the music finished, he turned the radio down and addressed Danny,

"Don't suppose you've heard anything from Zac's guardian, remind me of his name again."

"James, 'call me Jamie' Adams. I've not received news yet. He's a really nice bloke, very willing to help, and hopefully, Zac will start to trust him soon. The hospital was arranging for a psychiatrist or a psychologist, I'm not sure which and if I'm honest I don't really understand the difference between the two, to visit Zac at some point today, and I've asked them to talk to us. Not sure how the patient confidentiality bit fits in with something like this."

"Well, the coroner is going to need a statement regarding Zac's mental health either way, so I can't see why they couldn't share information with us. I had a quick chat with Martha, but you know what she's like, she won't say much until her findings are complete."

Martha Daniels was the forensic pathologist working on Keith's murder inquiry.

"But so far everything is pointing to Zac being guilty, the evidence fits. When we get back to the station, I'll call everyone together and we can go through where we've got to and what still needs to be done but, my thinking is, that this isn't going to be a long-drawn-out inquiry."

"It's really quite sad," commented Hobbs. "Devastating for the family. And you were right with what you told Keith's daughter; the press is going to have a field day with this one."

"The DCI is meeting with the press office as we speak," said Mason. "They're going to release a statement this afternoon. There's no point trying to keep Keith's identity quiet as it wouldn't take the media long to associate him with that address. They won't name Zac of course, but they will have to say that the culprit is Keith's son. I think they'll put a court order in place that stops his name from ever being printed but that won't really help. The boy will end up more famous than his father."

They continued the rest of the journey discussing various football teams' performances so far that season and listening to the updates on the scores of matches being played that day. Neither of them brought the case up again in conversation, both feeling that they needed a break from thinking about how a 9-year-old boy murdered his father.

7

Mason had called his whole team together for an end-of-day meeting just a few days after Keith Kelly's murder. The noise in the incident room as people drifted in and took their seats was more subdued than normal. Murder inquiries usually had an air of, for want of a more suitable word, excitement about them, a buzz created by the need to get answers and find the killer as soon as humanly possible. This case was very different. It had been upsetting for everyone involved and the fact that it already appeared to be drawing to its conclusion was gratifying for all concerned.

Mason stood waiting, leaning slightly against the large whiteboard on which information relating to the case had been written as it had come in. DS Cooper finished handing out the last copy of the reports being given to everyone, then took her own seat, nodding to Mason that her task was complete, and he could begin.

He started by giving them the results of the post-mortem that had been carried out on Keith Kelly. The post-mortem confirmed that Keith had died from an initial knife wound that had punctured his kidney. The blood thinning medication that Keith was taking for a heart condition had caused him to bleed out quickly. The second knife wound, which had been inflicted between his neck and shoulder blade, had occurred posthumously. The positioning of the initial wound was in keeping with someone of Zac's height thrusting forward with the weapon whilst Keith was in an upright position. The forensic investigation of the area where the incident took place now led them to believe that after being stabbed the first time, Keith had grasped hold of the kitchen counter before sliding down to the floor, dying very shortly afterwards. This would explain why he was found propped up against the cupboard and why most of the blood found at the scene was pooled underneath him.

The second injury occurred whilst he was half upright against the cupboard and again could quite easily have been inflicted by Zac. They had been able to confirm that Keith had died in this position and had not been moved at all after death. The time of death had been established as occurring between the hours of 4:00 pm and 8:00 pm, which fitted with the incident having occurred not long after Eliza had left the house.

The toxicology report confirmed the presence of blood thinners in Keith's system, and antidepressants in a larger quantity than had been prescribed, and that there was no alcohol, or narcotics present in the deceased's system.

There was no evidence of a fight or struggle having taken place at the crime scene and no defence wounds were found on Keith's body. None of the neighbours had reported hearing an argument but the distance between the houses had always made that unlikely. The family had been described by those living near them as a seemingly normal family that had never been the cause of any trouble. But no one locally had been close to them, and although they knew Keith by name, that was down to his celebratory status and not because they had made his acquaintance.

Most of the neighbouring houses had CCTV but unfortunately not the house directly opposite the Kellys'. However, the footage that had been obtained showed Eliza both driving away from her property and returning at the times she stated. They had been unable to recover any CCTV evidence from the actual property itself as there had been a malfunction of the equipment, which the technical experts had confirmed had been a problem for weeks before the incident took place.

Ricky Kerr had been interviewed and his recollection of events and the timings supported what Eliza had told them in her interviews. There was also CCTV footage from the area showing Eliza's car parked not far from his flat. Ricky said in his statement that Eliza had arrived at his house in a distressed state, and it was obvious she had been attacked. She refused to let him call the police and also refused his offer to return to the house with her to make sure she was alright. He had received a text from Eliza after she had returned home that read "All okay", and he knew nothing about Keith's death until the police officers turned up at his flat. This message had been sent not long after Eliza had made the call to the emergency services. When questioned Eliza said she didn't know how to explain to Ricky what had happened, so it was easier just to send that text as she'd promised to contact him when she got home.

There was bruising to Eliza's face and finger mark bruising to her forearm, consistent with being grabbed, which also supported Eliza's version of events. Both Eliza's and Zac's clothing that they had been wearing that night had been tested, and blood belonging to Keith had been found on Zac's nightwear and traces of Keith's blood and DNA had been found under his fingernails and on the palms of his hands. A small amount of Keith's blood had been detected on Eliza's sweater, but this was most likely to have transferred when Eliza leaned over Keith checking for a pulse. Which was also the likely cause for there being small amounts found in her fingernail scrapings.

The knife found on the kitchen countertop, which Eliza confirmed was the knife she had taken from Zac, had proven to be the weapon which had inflicted Keith's injuries and only Zac and Eliza's fingerprints were on it. There was a gap in the knife block in the kitchen that the recovered weapon fitted into, and it matched the other knives stored there.

Zac was still refusing to speak to anyone and being concerned about his mental state, it was felt that pushing him in any way at this early stage could do more harm than good.

"So," said Mason, "as you can see there is no evidence that contradicts Eliza Kelly's version of events. Having spoken with those higher-up than us," he bowed his head towards the DCI and the Commissioner who were standing at the back of the room by the door. People turned round to see who he was talking to; everyone had been so wrapped up in what Mason had been telling them that they hadn't noticed the two senior officers entering the room. "It has been decided that there is enough evidence to prove that Zac Kelly was responsible for the fatal stabbing of his father and as such, a report will be sent to the coroner."

Later, DS Cooper and DS Hobbs joined Mason in his office. "What will happen to Zac now?" asked Leah.

"Well, he's currently in a secure children's home where I assume he will remain for the foreseeable future," said Mason. "He'll receive help and treatment from a whole team of professionals, I should think. I don't know who will make the decisions regarding his care or where it takes place. As far as I know, and it's early days yet, his mother has been as good as her word and not been anywhere near him. Not even made enquiries about him. I don't think she even knows where he is. I'm assuming he'll basically be put in care."

"I hope he'll be made a ward of the court," said Leah. "At least then the media won't be able to report anything about him or where he's being held."

"I'm certain that's being taken care of already," Mason reassured her.

"It's Keith's daughter and son from his first marriage that I feel sorry for," said Danny, "and his friends and the other members of his family. Every single person I've spoken to has told me what a nice man he was. They all dispute what Eliza says about him being violent and none of them has ever evidenced him even losing his temper."

"I know," said Mason, "and as you're aware Eliza Kelly is not my favourite person, but there's no evidence to suggest that she is lying about what happened. Keith was depressed and taking medication that could have affected his personality. You know as well as I do that domestic violence takes place in secret."

"Yeah, and Eliza said she's never needed medical assistance, never reported it to the police or told anyone what was going on," added Leah.

"That's right," said Mason. "She was worried that news of it might leak to the press and be damaging to his career. I have to say I think she *would* worry about that. Damage limitation would have been her priority. She also said that Zac had witnessed previous incidents, and she had played them down. She thought she had convinced him that everything was okay, but it had obviously affected him more than she realised, possibly leading to his reaction that night."

"Well, until he starts talking, we'll never know," said Danny. "Personally, I am just grateful that it's over. I'd prefer a good old-fashioned stabbing over a drug deal gone wrong, than a case like this any day."

The others didn't disagree with him.

BBC News – Monday 23rd February 2015

The victim of a stabbing in Brigholme on Friday evening has been named by police as the 71-year-old actor Keith Kelly. The body of Kelly was discovered in the kitchen of the family home by his wife when she returned to the house at around 8:00 pm. In a bizarre twist, the police have confirmed that a 9-year-old boy, believed to be the son of Mr Kelly, is being held on suspicion of being responsible for his father's death and that they are not looking for anyone else in connection with the incident. Mr Kelly rose to fame in the early '80s, appearing as Jeff Walker in the BBC's popular soap opera, Prospect Road.

Here's our entertainment correspondent Rob Harding with more details.

~~~~~~

Daily Telegraph – 23rd February 2015

ACTOR KEITH KELLY FOUND STABBED TO DEATH IN OWN HOME

A police investigation is underway after the body of actor Keith Kelly was found in a house in Brigholme on Friday night. It is understood that the victim was attacked and killed by his 9-year-old son. The boy is currently being held on suspicion of murder. The police have confirmed that they are not looking for anyone else in connection with the incident but have not released any further information, stating that it is an ongoing inquiry.

Keith Kelly rose to fame…

~~~~~~

The Guardian – 23rd February 2015

9-YEAR-OLD GUILTY OF FATHER'S MURDER

A nine-year-old boy, who cannot be named for legal reasons, is believed by police to be responsible for the death of his father the actor Keith Kelly. Kelly, in his 70s, was found dead at his home on Friday night.

Police were called to an incident in Brigholme at around 9 o'clock on Friday 20th February. Police later confirmed that the body found at the property was that of Mr Kelly and he died as a result of injuries he had received. The 9-year-old, believed to be the victim's son, is being held pending further investigation. Police are not releasing any additional information at this time although they have confirmed that they are not seeking anyone else in connection with the incident. The police are currently supporting the victim's family.

Kelly's most famous role was that of…

~~~~~~

The Sun – 23rd February 2015

9-YEAR-OLD KILLS FAMOUS FATHER IN FRENZIED KNIFE ATTACK

A 9-year-old boy is in police custody after he went berserk and stabbed his father, the renowned actor Keith Kelly to death. Kelly aged 71 died as a result of a brutal assault by his own child on Friday 20th February. The boy, who cannot be named for legal reasons, is believed to have had a history of violent attacks. One source revealed that it was only a matter of time before he seriously harmed someone.

~~~~~~

8

Although it was late morning, Amy was still wearing her PJs and dressing gown. Looking out of the window as she filled the kettle, she was pleased to see the rain had stopped and the sun was breaking through the clouds. She was feeling a lot better this morning; for the first time in a long time, she had slept right through the night and not woken up early. For the first couple of weeks after her father's death, she had to rely on medication prescribed by her doctor for her to get any sleep at all, but she would wake up feeling groggy and lethargic. She soon decided that she would be better off without them, but this meant she suffered disturbed nights where she would lie awake in the early hours going over everything that had happened. Her thoughts were always dark at this time and the 'what ifs' and 'maybes' had driven her mad. Lying awake, listening to Marcus snoring beside her, she would imagine her father's last moments, wondering what had been running through his head as his son stood over him. In her mind, Zac would be leering like some demonic fiend brandishing an oversized silver knife stained and dripping with her father's blood. Sometimes she would drift off only to wake up a couple of hours later in a cold sweat and full of panic having had a vivid nightmare, one in which her father had been calling out to her to save him. The anxiety that she lived with every day, especially when the media interest had been at its highest, left her exhausted and unable to cope with the simplest of tasks.

Now though, as time passed, she was beginning to accept what had happened. That there was nothing she could have done to prevent it and there was nothing she could do now to change it. One of the hardest things to come to terms with was that the man Eliza described as being married to was so very different from the father she had known, loved, and would always love. She couldn't countenance that her father had ever been violent towards Eliza, or anyone else for that matter, but Eliza had the bruises to prove it. Something that hadn't proved so difficult to accept was that Zac had been responsible for her father's death. Although he was incredibly young, from what Amy knew of his character, she could concede that he was capable of it.

Whilst waiting for the kettle to boil, Amy's thoughts turned to all that had happened over the recent weeks. People often refer to their lives as being turned upside down but to Amy, that's exactly what this felt like. One minute she was a perfectly ordinary wife and mother approaching middle age and leading, if she was honest, a perfectly ordinary and mundane life, the next she felt like she was appearing in some sort of bad B movie, or that she was a character in a trashy novel. Her father had been murdered and if that wasn't cruel enough, the murderer was her half-brother, Zac, and to top it all he was only 9 years old! Try explaining that when someone asks you how things are going!

She decided that today she would do something positive. Tackle the kitchen perhaps. At least try and clear the kitchen table, which, as usual, had been used as a dumping ground by all the family when they couldn't be bothered to put things away in the right place. Pieces of schoolwork, loose change, dirty mugs, dirty sports kits and folded clean washing all vied for space. She cleared an area amongst the debris so she could sit with her mug of tea. An assortment of vases of all shapes and sizes spread across the surface, although the flowers they had contained had long since wilted and been thrown on the compost. At the beginning, she recalled they had received so many bouquets that she had run out of vases to put them in, resorting to jugs and bottles and even a Wellington boot!

Amy had been overwhelmed by the kindness of people when they first heard about her father's death. Because Keith Kelly was relatively famous, people who had never met him in real life felt as if they had known him because he appeared on their television screens and took the trouble to send cards or write letters of condolence. Neighbours and parents of the kids' school friends dropped off not only cards and flowers but casseroles, pies and homemade biscuits. These gestures of sympathy, however, soon dried up once the press started to circulate stories that condemned her father as a wife-beater. Having initially demonised Zac, making him out to be some sort of child monster, the media then turned him into a hero rather than a villain. They needed someone to be responsible for what had happened and if they could no longer blame Zac, they decided Keith Kelly had brought about his own demise by being a tyrant of a husband and father.

Thinking back to that time Amy remembered how she and Marcus never left the house unless absolutely necessary, the press attention had been so merciless. Even though the night after the incident, the police issued a statement on behalf of the family asking for them to be given privacy during such a difficult time, the media had gathered in packs outside the house. Their use of long-lens cameras meant that Amy didn't even open the curtains, and they spent days not knowing what the weather was like outside. The news crews would have come to the door too if a police officer had not been placed outside the gates to deter anyone from entering; she would be eternally grateful to DI Mason for his decision to offer them this form of protection. Even so, a quick trip to the dustbin led to harassment, photographers calling their names and trying to get them to look over to the gates so they could grab a facial shot. Journalists shouted inane questions at them like, "How are you feeling?" "Was your father ever violent towards you?" or "Are you on your way to visit Zac? Can you forgive him?" They ended up shipping the children off to her in-laws to protect them from the worst of it.

Amy, and she could only assume her stepmother too had been besieged by phone calls from news agencies all over the world offering obscene amounts of money if they would consider telling their side of the story, give them the inside scoop on Zac and his evilness, and then later if they would be willing to spill the beans about her dad and his abusive nature. The police had also been present outside the grounds of her father's property, technically Eliza's property now, thought Amy grimly, in an attempt to stop the press from climbing over the walls and trying to take photographs through the windows.

As it was, the media had been disappointed; both family and friends of her father had taken the joint decision not to speak to the press or to make any comments when doorstepped by journalists. They were aware that anything they said would be taken out of context and their words misrepresented. It seemed as if Eliza must have felt the same way as she had only uttered "no comment", whilst hiding behind dark glasses whenever a member of the press had managed to get near to her. Why Eliza stayed at the house was beyond Amy. Surely, she could have moved in with a friend? But then thinking about it, Amy wasn't sure that Eliza had any friends, not really, only Ricky and she was certain that Eliza would not want to stay in his squalid little flat.

Someone claiming to be close to the family had, however, been talking to the press. Amy was infuriated by this. She had no idea who this person could be and whoever it was definitely did not know her father at all. This so-called "friend" was the source of the horrendously disgusting stories suggesting her dad was an evil wife-beater. Amy suspected that some journalist had taken it upon themself to invent this source to have a juicer story. Either that or someone with a grudge against her father was deliberately trying to paint him in the worst possible light. The family thought it best to leave them to it, trying to speak in her dad's defence would only have made the situation worse.

At the time the media interest seemed endless but in reality it was only a handful of days before the story died off and the press moved on to more fruitful ground. They returned briefly at the time of her father's funeral. Denied access to the actual event they turned up en masse, waiting outside the gates, hoping to catch a glimpse of the family in their funeral attire. They were also present outside the entrance to the crematorium, but only managed to gain a few grainy pictures, taken through the sleet as the small group of mourners left the service, the weather apparently in sympathy with the grieving family. Thankfully, due to the quality of the pictures, it would be difficult for people to identify Amy, Marcus or Eliza, the only family to attend the funeral as there hadn't been enough time for Adam to make arrangements to fly over.

It had been a dismal affair, cold, clinical and organised with unseemly haste. Nothing like her father would have wanted or expected. Before his relationship with Eliza, Keith had expressed a wish to be buried in the same plot as his first wife Angela, Amy and Adam's mother, but Eliza had declared that it made more sense to have him cremated without any fuss due to the circumstances. At that time Amy had been in no fit state to object. Eliza had no interest in what happened with Keith's ashes and so Kath, one of Keith's best friends, had taken it upon herself to collect them and now Amy was keeping them safe at home. She and Adam intended at some point in the future, when all the fuss had died down and people had lost interest in what happened, to hold a proper memorial service for Keith and give him the send-off he deserved with all his family and friends included.

The very last time that Amy had encountered the press had been at the inquest into her father's death, and at that time they had been far more interested in Eliza than in anyone else. Amy had been dreading that day and had been both relieved and disappointed to find that she would not be called upon to speak. Part of her had wanted the opportunity to speak out in defence of her father's character but that would never have been an option. The inquest was held purely to establish the cause of Keith's death and as Amy had no evidence to give in relation to what happened that night, she was spared the ordeal.

Eliza, of course, had given her version of events, the epitome of the grieving widow, smartly dressed in black and wearing dark glasses, which she removed once she was called to the stand, to reveal red-rimmed eyes. She spoke in a whisper and was asked a number of times by the coroner to speak up. She was so unlike her usual confident, strident self. She constantly dabbed her eyes with a silk handkerchief although Amy could see no evidence of actual tears.

Also giving evidence were the police officers and the paramedic who first attended the scene. DI Mason gave a report of the investigation's findings. The forensic pathologist and her father's doctor had both been called to the stand, as had Zac's psychologist and his legal guardian. Zac himself had not been present as he was a minor.

Amy had the support of both her husband and her brother Adam, who had flown in specially. Adam was unable to stay long but promised to fly home again soon so they could spend some quality time together, they both felt the need to support each other whilst they mourned the loss of their father. Also at the inquest to offer their support were her Uncle John and Aunty Maggie and Kath and Terry Lomas, long-time friends of Keith's.

After 3 days of hearing evidence, the coroner gave his verdict of unlawful killing. It was, he announced, the most fitting verdict he could give under the circumstances. He also recommended that Zac be detained under the care of the state for the foreseeable future.

Whilst showering, Amy's thoughts returned to her stepmother. She realised that she had neither seen nor spoken to her since the inquest. Not that she was particularly bothered. She found it difficult to be around Eliza after what happened to her dad. If the woman had shown the slightest bit of grief or even a smidgen of remorse over his death, it would have made the little time they had been forced to spend together easier. Instead, Eliza's complete lack of emotion unnerved Amy.

Amy never mentioned to anyone, not even Marcus, that personally, she felt Eliza should in some way apologise for the fact that it was Zac who caused her dad's death. Realistically, she knew there was nothing Eliza could have done to prevent what happened, but the fact that Zac was her offspring, her responsibility, should surely produce some feeling of guilt.

Amy, herself, had gone through a range of emotions since her father's death; everything from intense anger to overwhelming despair. Her own sense of guilt was enormous, the feeling that she had let her father down in some way, not considering his problems to be as prodigious as they were. Keith told her that his relationship with Zac was deteriorating and things between him and Eliza were tricky, but she never really probed too deeply, aware that her father was a private person who generally looked on the bright side of life and didn't like to talk about his feelings. Discovering, after he died, that he was taking antidepressants, and he hadn't mentioned it to her, made her feel like a bad daughter. The fact that he revealed anything at all about the trouble taking place in his home life should have raised a red flag; even these small disclosures were a sign that her father was struggling. She should have encouraged him to seek help with Zac's anger issues when he first mentioned his concerns to her.

Then there were the conflicting emotions she felt regarding Zac. She hated him, she was so angry with him, but at the same time, she also felt pity for him. How would he reconcile himself with his actions that night as he grew older and became more aware of the atrocity he had committed? She was also troubled by the fact that Eliza seemed to have abandoned him.

As far as she was aware, Eliza had had no contact with Zac since the night her father died. She had not even attempted to visit him. Amy could only imagine how lonely and scared Zac must be, locked up in an institution and surrounded by strangers. But despite that, she could not bring herself to visit him. Not yet anyway but maybe one day.

Amy stepped out of the shower and gave herself a talking-to whilst she dried and then dressed. It was no good going over what had happened, she needed to look forward, to be grateful to have such a loving and supportive husband and two wonderful children. The children seemed relatively unscathed by the events. Amy felt they secretly enjoyed the notoriety; the sudden interest of classmates, previously dismissive, who now wanted to claim friendship. Also, Amy knew that her father wouldn't have wanted her to be miserable. After her mother died, he made sure that although both she and Adam could talk about their mum whenever they wanted or needed to, they didn't wallow in self-pity. "Life is for living, Amy," he told her. "Your mother would hate to think that you were sad all the time. She would want you to love life, laugh lots and make the most of the time you have. Life is short and you never know what's around the corner. Don't waste precious time thinking about what might have been." It was good advice, and Amy was determined to put it into practice.

Having taken the dogs for a walk, cleaned the kitchen and started tackling the mound of dirty washing, Amy looked forward to a tea break. Unfortunately, she'd already used up the last of the milk, and as Marcus was doing a supermarket shop on his way back from dropping Rory at football, and Olivia at her friend's, it seemed futile to make the trip to the local village store. At least Amy felt able to call into that shop again now. For a number of weeks after her father died, she avoided it like the plague. Although she had grown up in the village, and the majority who lived there knew her and her father really well, the views of the villagers had been mixed once the revelations about Keith began appearing on the news and in the papers. The shop was the centre for all village gossip, and it had only taken one visit during which the conversation at the counter had ceased as soon as she entered and had carried on in whispers whilst Amy navigated her way through the cramped space, for her to make the decision to only shop at the large supermarket a couple of miles away for the time being. At least there she could dash down a different aisle if she spotted a familiar face. To be fair, the majority of the villagers had been extremely sympathetic towards her, not believing that the Keith who had lived amongst them for many years could be the man the papers were now portraying. However, a small minority believed there was no smoke without fire and it was these malicious few who Amy went to great lengths to avoid. Now the inquest was over, however, they, like the press, moved on to new pieces of gossip. Keith and his family had become yesterday's news.

Thinking about that made Amy decide to open her laptop and have a trawl through the major and local news sites. To her relief, she couldn't find a single mention of her father or Zac anywhere on the websites let alone in the headlines. She also searched the sites of the national newspapers as she felt certain it wouldn't be too long before Eliza sold her story. That woman would do anything for money and Amy was convinced that the only reason it hadn't happened already was because Eliza was holding out for a higher sum. Forewarned was forearmed as far as Amy was concerned, but she knew that there was no chance of Eliza contacting her to give her a heads up that she was about to slag her dad off in the Sun Newspaper, so the only way Amy would know about it was when the story was actually printed.

At that moment, Marcus came puffing into the room overloaded with carrier bags. She had to laugh at him. He always felt it was too much trouble to go back and forth to the car, so caused himself a great deal of difficulty trying to carry too much in one go. She got up to help him, catching the bag containing eggs just as it was about to hit the floor.

Marcus spotted the laptop on the table still open on a news website.

"I thought we'd decided not to look any more," he said.

"I know," Amy replied. "I just wanted to check and there's nothing, nothing at all on any of them. It's been weeks since they ran a story. That's got to be good news, hasn't it? Maybe they really have moved on. I was just thinking that we might finally have become yesterday's news."

"Please don't tempt fate," said Marcus ruefully just as Amy's mobile began to ring. She laughed at the look of horror on his face and then turned more serious as she saw the name displayed and answered the call.

"Hello, DI Mason."

Marcus was curious, why was the DI contacting them now? He watched as the colour drained from his wife's face.

"No, sorry, I've had no contact with her since the inquest." Amy paused listening and then continued, "Yes, I understand, no don't worry I'm fine, just shocked… Okay then, yes that's probably best… Alright, see you soon."

She hung up and turned to Marcus. "That was Mason."

"And?" he asked.

"He's on his way over. He said it would be easier to explain everything face to face."

"Explain what?" Marcus was getting anxious.

"It's Eliza," said Amy. "She's gone missing. The house has been emptied and they have no idea where she's gone!"

I can't believe that I lost my temper again. What have I done? How the hell am I going to get out of this?

Think Edith, think.

I never meant for that to happen. I just lost it. It's all his fault, what a stupid, stupid man. Why did I put up with him for so long? I should have realised ages ago that he was past it – too old to be offered anything decent. Although the fact that he managed to completely run out of money without me realising is a huge credit to his acting ability!

What a sheer waste of my time it's all been. I suppose I should accept some responsibility. I could have kept a closer eye on the state of the finances instead of just accepting his reassurances. Maybe then tonight wouldn't have happened. I wouldn't have been caught off guard like that. Would have had better control of my temper when he told me of the shit financial state he'd gotten himself into.

I could feel the heat in me rising when he started talking about the need to downsize and take Zac out of Marston's. I managed to contain the fury right up until the point where he told me our love for each other was so strong that we didn't need money. What the fuck? Did he seriously think I loved him? I never loved him. If I'd had the slightest inclination of what the future held, I would've divorced him years ago. Got out whilst I could get a decent settlement from him. Now even that option's been taken away. I can't fleece him – there's nothing left to fleece. Even the house in Spain has gone. The fucking imbecile!

I looked at him clearly for the first time in a long time. He was so unmanly, standing before me sobbing and the pleading was pitiful. He looked so old, so pathetic. Great globs of snot dripping from his nose. It brought into focus just what a fool I had been. I'd lumbered myself with a has-been, a penniless old, aged pensioner. I couldn't believe I'd fucked up so royally. I was mad with myself as well as with him. Then the red mist descended and well, that was that.

Now what am I going to do? Think Edith, think.

Why do I never learn? Why can I not control my actions when I lose my temper? It always causes such problems. What a time to get so mad. I just saw red. Well, what's done is done and now I have to deal with it.

Think Edith, think.

Okay, so he's dead. That means insurance pay-outs, and mortgage paid off. I can sell the house. I'm the sole beneficiary, I've made sure of that. If he's amended his will so that those kids of his get something, I'll fight it. They've already had more than their fair share. Potentially, I can make a killing – ha-ha – I'm so hilarious. Oh, that's great Edith, you'll inherit all this money just in time to go to prison for murder.

Think Edith, think.

There has to be a solution, a way out of this. I've got away with it before surely, I can do it again. Come on Edith, time's running out. Think, think.

What's that noise? Zac! Wait a minute. Now that could work. Think Edith, think.

"Zac darling, it's okay Daddy's poorly but you can help him, come here sweetheart, come and help Daddy. Just do as Mummy tells you, there's a good boy."

PART TWO

1

The man slumped in the chair across the table from DI Mason and DS Hobbs looked distinctly unwell. The signs showed he was desperate for his next fix. He continuously clasped and unclasped his hands to hide how much they were trembling, and a thin film of sweat was visible on his forehead despite the temperature in the interview room being what could only be classed as chilly. The weather outside was cold and rainy but because it was now officially Spring, the heating at the police station had been turned off; another cost-saving exercise. The man awaiting interview was dangerously skinny. He was dressed in a filthy grey tracksuit that hung off his wiry frame, and his copper-coloured hair was matted, in desperate need of a wash.

As a precaution, Mason had asked the duty doctor to give Ricky Kerr a once-over as soon as he had been brought into the station. The doctor gave the all-clear for the interview to go ahead but just to be on the safe side Mason checked whether Ricky would like to see the doctor again.

"No mate, I'm fine," was the reply, although his discomfort was obvious. They had not told Ricky why he was there and had kept him waiting just long enough for the disheveled, unshaven man to become more nervous and more uncomfortable.

"Why am I here?" he asked. "Is this about Ronnie? Only I don't owe that bloke no money. I don't care what he says. He's a liar. You can ask anyone." The way he spoke with each word merging into the next made it an effort to decipher what he was saying.

"Er. No, this has nothing to with, er, Ronnie," Mason answered. "There's just a couple of things we need to clear up with you regarding the night Keith Kelly died."

"Such as?" asked Ricky. "That's all done and dusted ain't it? What's to clear up?"

Mason ignored the questions and pressed on.

"Am I correct in thinking that you only found out that Keith was dead when DS Hobbs here came to see you to collaborate on what Eliza Kelly had told us about her visiting you that night?"

"She didn't 'visit' me like. She came round to ours to get away from the bloke after he'd belted her."

"Right," said Mason nodding his head as if agreeing with him. "So, you didn't go round to Eliza's at any time that night?"

"Course not, I never went round when Keith were there. For some reason, he didn't take too kindly to me socialising with E. No idea why." Ricky grinned across at them, revealing a couple of gaps between his teeth, the remaining ones were dirty brown in colour. As he spoke, he lifted his arms and swept them over his body as if to say, what's not to like? The smell of stale body odour that emanated from him made both officers subconsciously back away.

"So, just to be clear, you didn't visit Lime Tree Avenue at any time on Friday 20th February?" asked Mason.

"No, like I told matey there," Ricky pointed to DS Hobbs, who was fiddling with the computer screen that sat between himself and Mason. "I was home watching telly when E turned up in a right state. I wanted to phone you lot, send you round there to sort him out like, but she wouldn't let me."

"And you had no idea that Keith had died until DS Hobbs told you?" Mason repeated. "Eliza didn't get in touch with you at all?"

"No, I have to say I was shocked when I did find out. Fancy a boy that age doing that to his dad. Still, he were only trying to protect his mum, weren't he? Not really his fault it went so far like."

Mason chose not to address this statement instead he asked the question that had been bothering him since the beginning of the interview.

"Can I ask you Mr Kerr, what is your relationship with Mrs Kelly? How do you know her?"

"I don't understand," replied Ricky. "What do you mean how do I know her? She's a mate, alright?"

"So, you're not related in any way?" Mason asked.

"No, we're just mates, we go back years, met when we were both at school."

"And you've stayed friends all this time, that's quite impressive."

"I know what you're getting at," Ricky sat upright and stared directly at Mason.

"What am I getting at?" asked Mason.

"People are always the same. They can't get their heads around the fact that someone like E could be friends with someone like me."

"I'm sure I don't know what you mean," said Mason innocently.

"Oh, come off it, mate. Her being all la-de- da and me being a smackhead, doesn't sit right with people like you does it, that we could be mates like? But I'll tell you summat, me and her are soulmates. We look out for each other, always have done, always will."

"Right," said Mason as he nodded to Danny, "well maybe that will help explain this then."

Danny angled the computer screen so that Ricky could get a clear view of it.

Ricky shot Mason a questioning look.

"What's this then? You gonna show me a film or summat? Where's the popcorn?" He gave a nervous little chuckle.

"Like I said," replied Mason. "We just want to clear some things up. It'll be easier if we show you. Just take a look at this."

Hobbs clicked the mouse and Mason watched Ricky's reaction as a short clip of footage played showing a man climbing over a fence and disappearing into a garden.

"Who's that then?" asked Ricky. "Where's this?

What you showing me for?"

"Keep watching," said Mason.

After a pause, the footage played again, this time showing the same man climbing from the garden side and landing rather awkwardly into the alley that ran behind the property.

Ricky started to rock from side to side but he said nothing. The screen changed to show two stills next to each other. The first showed a close-up rear view of the man; the image had been enhanced to show the distinctive skull and cross-bone motif on the back of the jacket he was wearing. The second was a close-up of the man's face as he reached the top of the fence just before he jumped down. The picture wasn't crystal clear as it had been dark when the CCTV had captured the image, but it was discernible.

Ricky was clearly agitated. His rocking motion became manic, and he couldn't keep his feet still, bouncing them up and down on the tiled floor.

"As you can see," Danny pointed to a box on the screen. "This footage was captured at 4:35 pm on Friday 20th February 2015 and this one," he tapped the top of the screen by the second still, "was captured at 8:15 pm on the same date."

"So," said Mason, "what were you doing at the Kelly's property the evening Keith Kelly died, Ricky?"

"That's not me," mumbled Ricky. His mouth was obviously dry, and he licked his lips in an effort to moisten them.

"That *is,* you isn't it, Ricky? We know it is."

Ricky shook his head but said nothing, still staring at the screen.

"For the record, Mr Kerr has shaken his head," said Hobbs. Ricky looked across at him in surprise. "Am I under arrest?" he asked.

"No," said Hobbs. "You're just helping us with our inquiries. I would remind you again that you are entitled to have a legal representative present. I know you said you didn't want one, but you can change your mind."

'*Well done, Danny*', thought Mason. Making it sound to Ricky like he might need a solicitor would put the wind up him and, hopefully, make him more cooperative.

Ricky shook his head again.

"I don't need no solicitor," he said. "I ain't done nothing. That's not me."

"Come on Ricky," said Mason. "This is the Kelly's property on the evening that Keith Kelly was killed. Our tech team is enhancing the quality of the footage as we speak but even as it stands, it's obvious that it's you. Also, as you are aware, we have a warrant to search your property and our officers are there right now looking for the jacket that we see you wearing on the film. You know they'll find it don't you?"

Clearly, although it had been explained to him when they first arrived at his home to bring him in for questioning, Ricky hadn't taken on board the fact that his property was to be searched straight away. Now he paled and the shaking became even more pronounced.

"Do you need to see the doctor, Ricky?" asked Mason.

"Nah, I'm fine mate," said Ricky.

"Can you tell me what you were doing there that night, Ricky?"

"It's not me," mumbled Ricky.

"Can you speak up for the tape please," said Hobbs.

"It's… not… me," Ricky stated clearly, leaning forward towards the recorder and then flopping back in the chair before sitting upright again and bouncing his feet on the floor.

"Why didn't you use the front door, Ricky?" asked Mason. And then before Ricky could say anything he continued. "Why didn't you tell us when you were spoken to before that you were there that night? You were there and you were there for *over three hours* Ricky. So, tell us, what was going on?"

"I've got nothing to say," Ricky replied. His nerves were palpable.

Mason and Hobbs exchanged a look. He hadn't denied it was him this time. Mason decided to push on.

"Let me show you something else, something we find extremely interesting," he said, nodding to Hobbs who clicked on the screen.

As the image of the woman in the baseball cap appeared Ricky became visibly more disturbed.

"Can you tell me who that is?" asked Mason.

"You tell me," Ricky said, stroppily.

"Okay," said Mason. "This clearly shows Eliza Kelly climbing over her own fence into her own back garden."

Mason saw no reason to let Ricky know that they had not yet confirmed that the image was of Eliza Kelly.

"Now why would she do that?"

"You'll have to ask her mate," Ricky tried to look unconcerned as he met Mason's eyes.

"Oh, we are," said Mason. He made it sound as if they were talking to Eliza at that very moment. Once more, Ricky began to rock violently in his chair. Mason decided that this was as good a time as any to stop the questioning and allow Ricky a break. A fifteen-to-thirty-minute breathing space would give Ricky just enough time to think about the trouble he was in, and hopefully lead him to opening up about what exactly had gone on that night. So, Ricky, accompanied by a uniformed officer, was led outside to the smoking area for what Mason suspected was a much-needed nicotine fix, although he was certain that the clearly shaken man would prefer something far stronger.

2

The discovery of the surveillance footage that had just been viewed by Ricky Kerr had come completely out of the blue. It was after the inquest had closed that a junior Detective Constable had taken a call from a retired Detective Chief Inspector, who announced that he had important evidence regarding the death of Mr Keith Kelly and that he would only speak to a senior officer. A little put out by DCI Atkinson, Retired, which was how the gentleman continuously referred to himself, and his insistence on what he had in his possession was of utmost importance, Mason himself had driven over to the retired officer's house to see what he was making such a fuss about. However, once there, he had to admit that what he was shown was definitely of interest.

DCI Atkinson, Retired, lived in a generous villa that sat directly behind the Kelly property, separated by an overgrown alley that ran from one end of the quiet neighbourhood through to a small parade of shops that served the local community. Having accepted the inevitable cup of tea, Mason tried to hide his impatience as Atkinson, dressed casually in jeans and a navy short-sleeved shirt, but looking smart and official nonetheless, talked him through his and his wife Dorothy's, Retired Headteacher, decision to move down South from North Yorkshire for their retirement to benefit from the milder climate and to be closer to the sea. Atkinson then went on to inform Mason that he and Dorothy had recently returned from a 3-month cruise around the Caribbean and that he had been reviewing the footage captured by his extensive security surveillance system during their absence with a view to deleting it. He explained that there had been a spate of burglaries in the area some months before they were due to leave for their trip, so he had upgraded his system and included cameras that would overlook the alley, as he felt it was a vulnerable area and a likely place for someone to attempt to gain access to his property.

Wishing that if the retired DCI had a point he would hurry up and get to it, Mason shifted his position on the rather uncomfortable overstuffed armchair. It was obvious that DCI Atkinson, Retired, was relishing having another officer in his home, and he now began a diatribe on the local crime statistics. Not wanting to appear rude but with so many more important things requiring his attention, Mason had finally interrupted the flow and asked if it would be possible for him to see what had caught Atkinson's eye. Atkinson immediately returned to his professional manner and apologised for going off track. He showed Mason into a small office on the ground floor where a couple of monitors were playing images from the grounds of the property. Atkinson had already lined up the sections that he wanted to show to Mason on his desktop computer and it wasn't long before Mason became as excited as Atkinson had been when he first phoned the station. The retired DCI told Mason that he knew he'd found something important when he saw the date and time stamped on the image of the man climbing over his neighbour's fence. The death of Keith Kelly, although at the time the deceased had not been named, was broadcast on every news bulletin as the Atkinson's had journeyed to the port to embark on their cruise and had caught their attention due to the address's proximity to their own home.

Mason went directly to Henderson on his return to the station, and after briefing him on what he'd discovered, he was given the go-ahead by his DCI to re-open the investigation, because if nothing else, the footage proved that both Eliza and Ricky's statements regarding their activities that evening hadn't been entirely accurate. As Mason put it to DCI Henderson, it had set his spidery senses tingling! Causing Henderson to give one of his rarely seen smiles.

After leaving his superior, Mason summoned Danny and Leah to his office and invited them both to look at the two stills displayed side by side on his computer screen, which he had copied from the footage he had obtained from DCI Atkinson, Retired. He told them that the pictures had been captured on the evening Keith Kelly died and the fence belonged to the Kellys. The first picture showed the back view of a male individual scaling the wooden fence at the rear of a property; he was wearing a hooded jacket with a very distinctive transfer of a skull and cross bones printed on the back. The second showed the same man but this time climbing back into the alley and although a little blurry, his face was still discernible.

"That's interesting," said Cooper. "What's the time difference between them? How long was he on the property for?"

"Just over three hours," answered Mason.

"What!" exclaimed Cooper. "He must have gone inside the house. What reason would he have to spend that long in the garden? There was definitely no sign of a break-in, so whoever he is he must have been known to the family. Surely Eliza must have known he was there. Why was nothing mentioned? This puts a very different light on things, doesn't it?"

"Exactly," said Mason. "So, who do we think that could be?" Cooper shook her head but Hobbs, who had been staring at the face on the screen, answered,

"I believe Sir, that we could be looking at Mr Ricky Kerr. It's certainly the right height and build for him and it fits facially. Although I can't be 100% certain, I'm pretty sure that's the very jacket he was wearing when I called round to see him to confirm that Eliza had gone to him when she left the house that night. I remember the skull and crossbones because it took up the whole of the back of his jacket, just like this one."

"I agree with you, Danny. I've only seen his mugshot but I'm hoping that the Tech guys will be able to enhance the face so we can be more certain," Mason replied. "I've asked them to give it a go. I certainly don't think, whoever he is, this man hung around in the garden for nearly 3 hours, so he almost certainly entered the house, in which case someone let him in, and the fact that he was there on that particular night has to be more than just coincidence."

Moving Danny aside, Mason returned to the computer.

"That, however, is not the most interesting part of what the cameras caught. Now, take a look at this." He clicked the screen and a new still appeared. This showed a smaller figure wearing what appeared to be joggers and a baseball cap. Mason again clicked the mouse, and the footage ran showing what was obviously a female jumping at the fence a couple of times before gaining purchase and disappearing over the top. The two other officers stared at the screen dumbfounded.

"So far this is all we have of her," said Mason, "but I've got people viewing all of the footage that I've collected because I believe that there is a good chance that we will see this woman again coming back over the fence and out into the alley."

"Is that Eliza?" asked Cooper.

"I can't say definitively but I very much believe so," replied Mason.

"I don't understand," said Hobbs. "What's going on? If this is Eliza and Ricky, what are they up to and if it's not, who are they?"

"That, my son, is what we are going to find out."

Mason looked more animated than he had for a long time. "It's my belief that these *are* images of both Ricky and Eliza. It's too much of a coincidence that two people who look so similar to them are going in and out of the grounds of that particular property on the night of Keith Kelly's death. And we don't believe in coincidences, do we? Also, if they are two different people, if it's not Eliza and Ricky, we would have found DNA evidence of these strangers inside the house. I've spoken to DCI Henderson, and he agrees that we need to take this further. He's arranging a search warrant so we can visit Mr Kerr, bring him in for questioning, and search his property for the jacket before he knows we are looking for it and has a chance to dispose of it. I don't really want to speak to Eliza until we've interviewed Ricky. She's clever enough to have a plausible explanation but I don't think he is. He's more likely to tell us something useful.

"Danny, you and I will work on Mr Kerr and Leah, I would like you to get in touch with the unit where Zac Kelly is residing. See if he's said anything at all yet about what happened that night. It might be easier if you speak to his legal guardian first as he's more likely to be able to get them to talk to you. I can't remember his name off the top of my head, but it'll be in the file. I've already given instructions for full background checks on both Kerr and Mrs Kelly, and I've sent some uniforms out to see if they can uncover any other surveillance footage, both from inside the alley and at the entrance to it. I also thought it would be worthwhile to get what we can from the surrounding streets, so I've got them tracking that down too. There's a good chance that even if there are cameras in the area the footage of the night in question has already been destroyed or overwritten, but it's worth a try. We might at least be able to determine which direction Eliza came from. It's a shame we didn't collect footage from the alley at the time of the incident, but with what we got from the front of the house confirming what Eliza told us it didn't seem necessary. Still, we have this now and I'm very interested to find out what it's all about, so let's get started."

3

"Come on Ricky, you're going to have to do better than that." Mason was beginning to get frustrated with only receiving shrugs and mumbled replies to the questions he was asking of the man opposite. Topping up on his nicotine had not made Ricky Kerr any more forthcoming with an explanation for his exploits on the night of the 20th.

Before he could pose the next question there was a knock on the door and Leah Cooper entered the interview room. She hurried over to Mason and whispered something in his ear. Mason nodded to Danny as he got up from his chair and walked to the door. Danny spoke for the benefit of the tape, noting the time as the DS left the room. Ricky appeared alarmed at the sudden departure and began once more to rock violently in his chair. His constant movement was really starting to get on Danny's nerves.

"Are you alright Ricky?" he asked, but Ricky didn't say anything, just carried on rocking.

"What is it, Leah?" asked Mason as soon as they were out in the corridor and the door had closed behind them.

"You've got to see this Sir," she said, holding out her phone.

"What am I looking at?" asked Mason as he studied the image on the phone. He had been expecting her to show him a photograph of the jacket that he was hoping had been found at Ricky's house, but although it was clothing, the picture he was looking at was not a black jacket.

"It's jeans, and a sweatshirt, Sir. They're size small, definitely female clothing. There's blood all over them, Sir. They were in a canvas bag stuffed at the back of a closet. We also found, in the same bag, a T-shirt and a set of women's underwear and with them was a running top, tracksuit bottoms, a baseball cap, a bath towel and a tea towel. Oh, and a mobile phone."

Leah was so excited to tell Mason what had been found she almost forgot the last item. "SOCO's taken it all for testing. I used your name, and I told them we need the results asap; I hope that's okay?" She didn't wait for an answer but continued, "I'm certain the running gear matches what the woman on the CCTV was wearing. I've got proper pictures being printed out now. I just thought you should know what was found so you can question him about it." She jerked a thumb in the direction of the interview room.

"Okay, okay slow down," said Mason, trying to take in everything she had just told him. "So, these items were found at Ricky's property?"

"Yes Sir, they were in a canvas hold-all bag at the back of a closet in his bedroom."

"Well, this is very interesting, very interesting indeed. I take it you've arranged for the phone to go for unlocking once it's been swabbed?"

"Yes, Sir."

"Any luck with the leather jacket?"

"Oh, sorry, Sir, I should have said." Leah returned to her phone and after a couple of swipes, she held it up to show Mason a photograph of a leather jacket with the distinctive skull and crossbones motif.

"Brilliant," exclaimed Mason "and have you managed to get hold of…?"

"Zac's guardian, Sir?" she pre-empted him. Mason nodded. "His name's Jamie and he's currently arranging for me and him to visit the home. I'm waiting to hear back from him."

"Great," said Mason, "but for now I want you to take a couple of officers with you and go and collect Mrs Kelly. I think it's time we put some questions to her. Just tell her we've uncovered some new information but don't tell her anything else. I want to catch her off guard. Oh, and send someone down here with those prints as soon as they're ready."

"Will do," said Leah turning to walk back up the corridor.

Mason returned to the interview room.

"Right Ricky," he announced "we've had some very interesting new evidence come to light. We'll be leaving you here for a little while. An officer will come and sit with you, but I think now might be the time for you to call your solicitor or if you don't have one, we can arrange one for you."

"Are you arresting me?" asked Ricky fearfully.

"Not yet," responded Mason, "but you will be cautioned before we interview you again." Then beckoning Danny to follow he left the room with a very despondent Ricky staring after them.

Well, that's that.

I'm ready for my future. New documents, new me.

It's a shame that I have to leave him behind. He's been the only constant in my life. He's just too far gone now. He'd be nothing but a liability and to be honest there's just not enough money for the two of us. Creating my new identity and getting away has used up what resources I had. I'm going to have to keep my head down and I don't need him getting in the way.

I was going to sell my story to raise some extra funds. I quite fancied the idea of playing the grieving widow, but with him being so flaky I think it's too risky. I don't want to draw any attention to myself right now. And I think I might be running out of time.

He's going to shit a brick when he finds out I've left him behind. I don't think he'll last long on his own. He's struggling with keeping so many secrets as it is, and this last one might push him over the edge. Even if he does crack and decides to talk to the police it won't matter to me. He has no proof to back him up and I'll be long gone by then. Good luck trying to find me. I'll have vanished, I'll be untraceable.

He can tell them everything he knows as far as I'm concerned, all of it. The only person he'll hurt is himself.

4

Leah was secretly pleased that Mason had charged her with the task of bringing Eliza Kelly in for questioning. She relished the idea of bringing that woman down a peg or two and sitting her in the back of a police car to take her to the station should do it. It was such a shame that it would be more than her job was worth to tip off the press. Eliza would be furious if a picture of her being helped into the back of the car by uniformed officers found its way to the front pages. Still, just having the upper hand in the situation would be a refreshing change.

Leah was annoyed with herself for allowing Eliza to intimidate her, but with the woman's supreme self-confidence and her open hostility, it was difficult not to be a little cowed when in her presence. Leah was determined that this encounter today would be different.

On the drive over, however, Leah began to have reservations. What if Eliza wouldn't cooperate? What if she simply refused to comply? The last thing Leah wanted to do was to resort to arresting her. How would it look to Mason if that was the only way she could stay in control? What Mason thought of her was important to Leah. She knew that he had been instrumental in her recent promotion to sergeant, and she was inordinately proud of having attained the rank so much earlier than most, but, at the same time, she was aware that due to her age and her gender, she had a lot to prove. Although the Force was now much better at recognising the abilities of women, there was still an underlying sense that females were not as well suited to the job as their male counterparts, or that's the way Leah felt about it anyway. Perhaps it would have been better if Danny had been given this particular job, she thought. Eliza was much more likely to cooperate with the handsome DS, who she had always mildly flirted with than she ever was for Leah whom she had only treated with contempt.

Leah considered herself good at reading people but when it came to Eliza Kelly, she couldn't fathom the woman at all. Kelly's reactions to the awful events that had taken place that Friday night back in February had confused Leah. She had never encountered anyone so harsh or so cold. To show no emotion whatsoever over the death of her husband was, to Leah, just unnatural. Not once in Leah's encounters with Eliza had she witnessed the woman exhibit any grief; she hadn't shed a single tear. Leah was not at all convinced that Keith had been the abusive partner Eliza made him out to be, but she could have found the widow easier to understand if she had expressed signs of relief, at least that would have been an emotion, but to not show anything at all was just weird, extraordinary. And as for her complete abandonment of her son Zac, as far as Leah was concerned no matter what the boy had done, he was still only a child and Eliza, as his mother, should be offering him her support not ostracising him.

She'd arranged for both DC Johnstone and DC Patel to wait for her in their patrol car outside the property, and as she drove down the road, she was pleased to see that they had parked against the verge out of sight of the house. They got out to greet her as she pulled up behind them.

"Shouldn't have too much trouble getting in," announced Jay Patel. "We did a quick drive-by, and the gates are open."

Leah was a little surprised by the breach in security. Usually, the property could not be accessed unless someone inside the house activated the opening of the wrought iron electronic gates. Maybe now the press had lost interest in her Eliza no longer deemed it necessary to keep the gates shut.

"Well, let's get this over with," said Leah. "I'll go on ahead and you follow but wait in the car until I signal for you."

Eliza's 4 x 4 was parked by the front door and Leah pulled up behind it. There was enough room on the drive for the marked car to pull alongside her.

Even before Leah rang the doorbell, she was certain no one was home, she just had that feeling. Having rung a few times with no result she went over to consult with her colleagues.

"Can you two do a quick search of the gardens in case she's about anywhere and I'll have a peek through the windows and see if I can spot her inside. She might just have popped out on an errand. She won't have gone far as her car's still here and that would explain why the gates are open."

The two uniforms split off in different directions to cover the grounds as Leah headed back to the house. Peering through the large bay window of what she knew to be a sitting room that ran the length of the house, Leah's heart sank. The room was completely devoid of furniture. All that was left in the room was the large fireplace. Even the showy chandeliers that Leah had noted when she had been in the room before, thinking how ostentatious they were, had gone. She made her way around the side of the property to the bi-folding doors that ran nearly the whole width of the rear of the building. Nothing… the rooms were totally empty. Leah took out her phone and reluctantly made a call.

5

Armed with the enlarged photographs of the blood-stained clothing discovered during the search of Ricky Kerr's flat, Mason and Danny returned once more to the interview room. Ricky had now been cautioned and the duty solicitor was present. It was patently obvious that Ricky was suffering from withdrawal and Mason knew that it wouldn't be long before the solicitor called a halt to the interview, to allow him to be seen by the doctor. Mason, determined to get some answers before that happened, placed the photographs face up in front of Ricky as soon as he took the seat opposite, announcing what he was showing to Ricky for the benefit of the tape.

Ricky glanced at the photos and visibly paled.

"Can you tell me how you came to be in possession of these items of clothing?" Mason asked.

"No comment," mumbled Ricky.

"These were discovered in this holdall," said Mason pointing to the relevant photograph, "at the back of a closet in your flat. Did you put them there?"

"No comment."

"We also found these items." Mason placed photographs of the underwear and of the running gear face up on the table and pushed them nearer to Ricky, so that he and his legal representative had a clear view of them.

Danny spoke for the benefit of the tape, naming the exhibits that were now on the table.

"Even if you're into wearing women's clothing Ricky, and to be honest it's of no interest to me one way or the other, these are far too small to fit you, so how come you've been keeping hold of them?"

"No comment."

"Were you aware of what was in the bag when you hid it?"

"No comment."

"Did Eliza ask you to look after the bag for her?"

"No comment."

Mason sighed and looked at the duty solicitor who gave a small shrug of his shoulders acknowledging Mason's frustration, but he had to advise what was best for his client and at this moment it was in Ricky's best interests to say nothing. It was how the game was always played but extremely unhelpful to Mason right now.

"Do these items of clothing belong to Eliza Kelly?"

"No comment."

"I think we can both acknowledge that the blood on these clothes is that of Keith Kelly," stated Mason.

"My client acknowledges no such thing," interjected David Davies, the solicitor unfortunate enough to have been on call that day.

Dave was someone Mason knew well, and out of the station they had been known to enjoy the odd pint together, but inside the interview room, they kept to a strictly professional relationship. Mason was about to press further when a knock on the door interrupted him, and a uniform came in to say there was an urgent phone call that he needed to take.

Irritated at being interrupted, Mason got to his feet and left Danny to announce for the recording that DI Mason was leaving the room. Mason was only gone for a couple of minutes. Returning to his seat, he leant across and whispered in Danny's ear, and then shuffled through the photographs whilst Danny noted aloud the time the interview was recommencing and reminded Ricky that he was being questioned under caution.

Ricky sat with his head down, studying his hands which he was clenching and unclenching in his lap.

"You might want to reconsider and give us an explanation as to how you came to be in possession of these items Ricky. I'll ask you once again, do they belong to Eliza Kelly?"

"No comment," mumbled Ricky.

"Do you know what I think Ricky? What I think happened that evening? The evening of the 20th of February."

Ricky shook his head and shrugged his shoulders.

Mason leant further forward until he was close to Ricky's face. Ricky flinched but didn't shy away.

"I think," said Mason, "that Eliza called you on the phone that was found inside the same bag as these clothes." He pointed to the photographs, pushing them towards Ricky with his index finger. "I think she told you when to come round to the house. You went in the back way so that Keith didn't know you were there. Something happened in the kitchen, Ricky. I'm not sure what yet, but Keith ended up being stabbed and Eliza ended up with blood all over her clothes. Between the two of you, you concocted a plan whereby you could provide each other with an alibi. It seems a very elaborate plan and I don't know why - if Zac was responsible for killing Keith - I don't understand why such a plan was necessary. Were you covering up for Eliza or was she covering for you?"

"No comment," Ricky said with his chin down on his chest.

"Did you witness Zac Kelly stab his father or was Keith already dead when you arrived?"

Ricky didn't respond.

"You must see that all this that we've found in your flat and what we have on CCTV makes you a prime suspect for the murder of Keith Kelly."

Ricky sat upright and stared directly at Mason. "I ain't no murderer," he stated firmly.

"So, explain it to me," said Mason patiently. "Tell me what happened Ricky. Why were you there? Why was the bag at your house? It's only a matter of time before the forensics come back. It won't be long until we uncover the data from the mobile. Talk to me now Ricky. It will be so much better for you in the long run."

Ricky said nothing so Mason tried a different tack. "What's Eliza's role in all this Ricky?"

"You'll have to ask her," Ricky tried to sound cocky, but it wasn't convincing. He was shaken up and it showed.

"I would love to ask Eliza," said Mason. "Only your friend appears to have done a runner."

"What do you mean?" murmured Ricky.

"Eliza has scarpered," Mason told him. "She's gone. Cleared out. The house is empty. Even the furniture's gone."

Ricky was alarmed. "I don't believe you," he said suddenly angry. "She wouldn't do that. She wouldn't just leave. She would've told me."

"I can assure you it's true. She's disappeared and she's definitely not intending to come back. Do you have any idea where she is? Didn't she mention she was emptying out the house?"

Ricky just shook his head, the fight going out of him as quickly as it had appeared.

"This is serious Ricky. There are a lot of questions to be answered and by the look of things Eliza planned it so she wouldn't be here to answer them. I'll ask you again, did you hide the bag in your flat for her?"

Again, Ricky shook his head. "She doesn't know I kept it."

Finally, thought Mason, we're getting somewhere.

Dave Davies gave a discrete cough to remind his client he was not supposed to be answering any questions, but Ricky didn't seem to notice.

"Can you explain how the bag came to be in your possession?" Mason asked again.

Ricky appeared to have lost concentration and didn't reply.

"Come on Ricky," urged Mason. "She's left you in a right mess here. You really are going to have to tell us what happened that night."

"No comment," Ricky said again. He slumped back down in his chair and lowered his head.

"She's left you to carry the can. You do understand that don't you?" said Mason.

Ricky didn't respond and it was then that Mason realised that the man was quietly crying. He saw that Dave Davies had spotted it too and nodding his head Mason announced for the benefit of the tape that the interview was being suspended. There was no point trying to push Ricky any further just now. Perhaps a bit of time to think, a chat with his solicitor, and a visit from his doctor, would encourage him to be more forthcoming. Mason gave Ricky one last look before he left the room. Ricky turned towards him as if he was going to say something, making no effort to stem the tears now streaming down his face, but he changed his mind and dropped his head back down. Mason couldn't help feeling a little sorry for the suspect; the man was completely broken.

Mason wasn't in too much of a hurry to get back to the interview room as they still had a few hours left until they needed to decide whether or not to charge Ricky. He had the feeling that once Ricky had had time to digest the news that Eliza had absconded, he would be more willing to cooperate, which would lead to him being charged. Currently, Mason was unsure exactly what he would charge Ricky with, but one thing was for certain, he would be charging him today.

BBC News – 4th June 2015

West Sussex Police have confirmed that they have named Eliza Kelly, widow of Keith Kelly, as a person of interest after new evidence came to light concerning the circumstances surrounding the actor's death. Police are appealing for anyone with information regarding Mrs Kelly's current whereabouts to contact them. It is understood that Mrs Kelly, aged 45, has not been seen for several days and the house she shared with her husband has been abandoned.

DCI Henderson, who is leading the new investigation, made the following statement:

"We would very much like to question Mrs Kelly as we believe she has information vital to our inquiry. Her current whereabouts are unknown, and we would ask that anyone with any information contact us immediately."

DCI Henderson declined to answer questions regarding the nature of the new evidence, but he did acknowledge that a man in his 40s has been detained and is aiding the police with their investigation. However, he refused to disclose whether charges would be brought against the individual, who is believed to be a friend of the family.

DCI Henderson also refused to comment on whether the new evidence will have any effect on the original inquiry's finding that the couple's 9-year-old son Zac, currently residing in a secure children's unit, was responsible for the unlawful killing of his father.

~~~~~~
~~~~~~

6

Kath was already seated when Amy arrived at the cafe, and she waved brightly to her best friend's daughter from the table she had deliberately chosen at the back because it was out of the way. Amy smiled back at her as she made her way between tables, shopping bags and baby buggies to reach her. Seeing Kath always cheered Amy up. She considered Kath and her husband Terry, who had been her dad's golfing partner and drinking buddy, more like an aunt and uncle than just friends of her parents. The two families had always been very close, holidaying together when the children were younger and taking turns to host one another on Boxing Day and at other times of the year. Amy had many happy memories of barbecues and day trips out to zoos and safari parks. Kath had been a teacher back then before she had climbed the educator's ladder to the dizzying heights of headteacher, and she had made trips to museums and historic buildings fun for even the most contrary of children such as Adam. When Amy's mother died, Kath had taken on the role of surrogate mother but had never tried in any way to replace Angela. In fact, Kath was responsible for keeping Angela's memory alive, often referring to the similarities between Amy and her Mum and making sure she spoke of Angela in front of Amy's children, so they had some idea of what their grandmother was like, even though she had died before they were born. Although, now in her 70s Kath was still a force of nature.

It was Kath that Amy had turned to when a rift developed in her relationship with her dad after he married Eliza, and she had been grateful for the way in which Kath and Terry had mediated and guided both her and Keith back onto an even keel. And it was Kath that she had leaned on after her father's death and all that had happened since. Kath had a natural, warm personality but at the same time she didn't put up with any nonsense. She called a spade a spade and Amy often found her honesty refreshing. She had a wonderful, if macabre sense of humour, and was extremely quick-witted. Even when Amy was feeling at her lowest, Kath had the knack of saying something that would make her smile.

"Soooo," Kath began as she motioned to the waitress that they were ready to order, "Eliza has done a runner."

Amy had a quick glance at the menu before she responded. "According to DI Mason, yes, she's disappeared without a trace. He told me the house was completely empty, save for a few pots and pans. The only thing of value left behind was the car, but it turns out that's about to be repossessed. It's on finance and the payments haven't been made for months, otherwise, they think she would have sold that too."

Amy paused as the waitress came to take their order and didn't continue until the girl had moved out of hearing range.

"He really came to warn me that we'll most likely be besieged by the press again because they've made it public that they've re-opened the investigation into Dad's death, and that they want to question Eliza regarding the new evidence they've found. They're hoping someone will come forward with information regarding her whereabouts."

"And he didn't tell you what this new evidence was?" asked Kath.

"No, he refused to talk about it. He wouldn't even confirm that it's Ricky that they have been questioning either, but he did ask me if I knew Ricky at all, if he and my dad were or had ever been close? I answered no to all of it. Told him that I'd met Ricky once or twice, but I didn't know him well at all and that my dad had very little to do with him. I was certain my dad didn't like him. He then asked if I knew what the relationship was between Eliza and Ricky."

"And what did you say to that?" asked Kath.

"That as far as I knew they were just friends, but I always had the feeling there must be more to it than that. I've always wondered if they were related in some way; maybe he was her cousin or even her half-brother, because otherwise why on earth would she be friends with someone like him? He just wasn't the sort of person she'd normally have anything to do with."

"I know what you mean," said Kath. "Terry and I always thought he must have some sort of hold over her, must know something she wanted kept secret. We used to play a game between ourselves of what it could be. Personally, I thought she was probably an ex-prostitute."

Amy laughed at that.

"She would make a very good Madam or a high-class call girl. I could definitely see her as a dominatrix."

Both of them were giggling now at the image in their heads.

"So, what *did* Mason tell you?"

"To be honest, he didn't answer any of my questions, he just asked a few of his own."

"Such as?" Kath was intrigued.

"Well, what you'd expect really. Had Eliza told us she was leaving? Did I know where she might have gone? Do I know of any relatives? Could I think of anyone she might be staying with? Anyone she was in contact with who lives abroad? I couldn't help him at all. I told him I hadn't got a clue that she was even thinking of leaving. I haven't had any contact with her since the inquest, and even if I had, she was unlikely to share her plans with me."

Amy abruptly stopped talking as the waitress came back to the table with their drinks.

'*It's starting again*,' thought Kath, the need to be careful about what you said in public in case anyone recognised you and repeated what they had overheard to the press. Poor Amy had been paranoid enough the first time around, this time Kath hoped the media interest wouldn't focus on Keith's remaining family quite so much.

"He asked if I knew the name of her ex-husband," continued Amy, "and if I had an address or contact number for him. I could only tell him that I thought his Christian name might be Tom, but that's just what my dad told me, Eliza never talked about him in front of me. Did she ever talk about her previous marriage to you?"

"Not that I can remember," replied Kath. "Your dad didn't seem to know a lot either. When he did mention it, I got the impression that Eliza had had a rough time and didn't like to be reminded of it."

"That's how I felt too. I said as much to Mason. The only thing I could tell him for certain was that when she met Dad, she was Eliza Taylor, and he told me that they had found no record of her under that name. No marriage license and no divorce registered.

"That's odd," said Kath.

"Isn't it? Then I stupidly said maybe she reverted to her maiden name after the divorce because a lot of women do, don't they? But of course, that would have been one of the first things they considered. Without giving too much away, Mason told me they were finding it hard to gather background information about her. They haven't even been able to trace a birth certificate!"

"I should imagine they *are* struggling if they haven't even got the name she was born with!" Kath stated. "You'd have thought that Ricky would be able to tell them that!"

"You would have thought so. It does make her seem dodgy though, doesn't it? Like she's got stuff to hide? Otherwise, why can't they find any background on her?"

"Definitely," agreed Kath. "I have to say I have a bad feeling about all of this, don't you? I'd love to know what this new evidence is and how it changes things. It's all very intriguing."

"Well, I hope whatever it is they've discovered helps to clear Dad's name. Proves that Eliza made all that rubbish up; about him being violent I mean."

Kath thought this was unlikely but decided now wasn't the time to mention it.

"Anyway," sighed Amy, "everything is all up in the air again now and I really don't know what to think. Mason has promised to keep me updated, so all we can do is wait and see. Let's talk about something else. Did you manage to book that weekend away?"

Think Edith, think.

I can't believe that I lost my temper like that. What have I done? How the hell am I going to get out of this?

Think Edith, think.

This really is not <u>my</u> fault. It's their fault. Both of them are to blame.

If he hadn't been so whiny, whingeing all the time: "I want Daddy. I want Daddy."

Well, you snivelling little toe rag he's not your dad, he doesn't want you – at least he doesn't want to pay for you. You were my meal ticket and now you're worth fuck all.

And then the other moron, "Let me tell him the truth E, let me tell him I'm his dad."

I warned him the time wasn't right. He's too young. He won't understand. I told him it was too soon. Did he listen? No, the useless imbecile went ahead and broke the news. To say it didn't go well is an understatement. Complete meltdown. So, what does lamebrain do? What he always does, gets off his face. Leaves me with the ungrateful little shit.

There's only so much I can be expected to put up with. He just wouldn't give over. Wouldn't pack in the crying. No wonder I lost my temper with him. He deserved what happened.

But now what am I going to do? I'm not going down for this. Who's going to understand? They'll blame me but it really wasn't my fault.

Think Edith, think.

Yes, that could really work. Yes, that's the answer. The stupid fucker will believe what I tell him. Now how do I get rid of this mess?

Think Edith, think.

7

Mason and Leah were catching up over a bacon sandwich and a cup of tea at the little cafe near the station. Police officers were responsible for most of the cafe's breakfast and lunchtime trade due to its proximity to their place of work, and the owner had greeted them both warmly, commenting on the weather, as they entered at 8:30 that morning. Danny hadn't joined them as he was busy with the case coordinator, going through the leads that had come through overnight, following the press release declaring Eliza as a person of interest.

"So, what's happening with Zac?" Mason asked Leah as he liberally spread brown sauce onto his sandwich. Leah was watching him in astonishment wondering whether he would still be able to taste the bacon after he had covered it in that much sauce.

"Well, the bad news is that he still hasn't spoken about anything that happened with regards to the night his dad died," said Leah through a mouthful of sandwich.

"And the good news?" asked Mason just before he took his first bite.

Leah swallowed and took a gulp of tea to help it down.

"A Teaching Assistant from his school went to visit him and he chatted away to her as if he'd never had a problem talking. She'd been warned to stay off certain topics, not to mention anything regarding his mum or his dad, that sort of thing. Apparently, she did really well and managed to avoid any danger points. In fact, they were so pleased with how it went, and how much happier he was after the visit, they've asked her to call and see him on a weekly basis."

"And that helps us how?" Mason looked confused.

"The psychologist working with him thinks we could use her to get him to open up about what happened with his dad. He says it would have to be done very carefully, very sensitively and the going might be quite slow because if he got at all upset, she would have to stop and change the subject. They don't want to push him in case it causes him to clam up completely again. He suggested that we make a list of the most important questions we'd like her to ask. We could then meet with her beforehand to make sure she understands what information we are trying to get out of him. Dr Jones, that's the guy's name, says that he will speak to the girl…" Leah consulted her notebook, "Lisa Robinson, to see if she's willing. I should hear back from him today. I thought I'd put a list of questions together and then you could approve them?"

Mason nodded his agreement.

"How come she went to see Zac?" he asked.

Leah pointed to the side of her own mouth to indicate he had a smear of sauce on his. Mason grinned sheepishly at her as he wiped his mouth with a serviette.

"Dr Jones said they were getting quite concerned about the fact that he wouldn't speak. The most they've been able to get out of him are single-word answers to their questions. He never speaks first. Never starts a conversation, except that once or twice he has asked when his mum is coming to see him. They tried phoning Eliza on several occasions, but she never answered the phone or returned their calls, even though they left voicemail messages saying how important it was for Zac's well-being that she got in touch. They tried emailing her too and eventually, she emailed back to say that she had no intention of ever seeing her son again. I could tell Dr Jones was really put out by that," said Leah not hiding her own disgust at Eliza's behaviour.

"I should imagine he was, it's a bit brutal," said Mason. "I'd like to see a copy of the email."

"I've asked them to forward it to us," said Leah, a step ahead of him. "Anyway, with no other family members likely to visit, they approached his old school to see if any of the teaching staff had a good relationship with him. It was the Headteacher who suggested Lisa."

"Well, it's certainly worth a try," said Mason getting up to go and pay the bill. While at the counter, his phone rang, and he motioned to Leah that they needed to leave.

"That was Danny," he said. "Apparently Ricky is ready to talk."

Back at the station, Danny met Mason in the foyer, and they walked together towards the interview room where Ricky Kerr sat waiting for them.

"Anything of interest come in overnight?" asked Mason.

"To be honest there weren't that many calls. A few possible sightings," answered Danny. "I've sent uniform out to follow them up. Hopefully, more calls will come in today once people have had a chance to see the news."

"Maybe we'll strike lucky, and Ricky will tell us everything including where Eliza's gone," said Mason.

"I'm not holding my breath," said Danny as he held open the door for his boss.

8

It had taken time, patience and a fair amount of persuasion but in the end, Ricky had given them a full account of how Keith Kelly died and confessed to his part in covering up the true circumstances.

Mason scheduled a team meeting to commence an hour after the interview with Ricky had finished. He needed the time beforehand to gather his thoughts as well as the necessary information that he would need to impart. The first call he made was to DCI Henderson. Giving his senior officer the most salient points, he requested an extension for the detention of Ricky Kerr and the issue of an arrest warrant for Eliza Kelly. Henderson agreed to both and suggested that they meet in the local pub for a late lunch so Mason could give him the details in full. Mason then went to find Leah to pass on what Ricky had divulged and to get her to ascertain the feasibility of bringing forward the questioning of Zac Kelly.

"I'll ask Jamie to get in touch with the Home," she said when she'd been brought up to speed. "I'm not certain how soon they can bring the TA in though," she remarked.

"Just do the best you can," said Mason. "The sooner we get Zac's version of events the better. I know we have to consider the possibility that he'll never talk about it or that he's suppressed the memory, but it would help immensely if we had his version of what went on that evening, especially if it matches what we've already got out of Ricky. He might even add some new information."

Leah hurried away trying to process all that she had just been told.

Both Mason and Danny were amazed by what they heard. It seemed so far-fetched but at the same time entirely believable, it made sense of all the evidence they had recently gathered.

"Aren't we going to charge him, Sir?" asked Danny when they met up again in the briefing room a few minutes before the meeting was due to begin.

Danny had been on the phone to inform the forensic team that this was now an active murder inquiry, and they needed the results yesterday. He received the usual response that everybody wanted the results yesterday, but they would do the best they could.

"Not yet," Mason answered. "I want to interview him again first. That's why I've asked for an extension on how long we can keep him in custody. We also need to decide exactly what to charge him with. So far accessory to murder and perverting the course of justice would stick, but that's only based on what he's told us. It could all be a pack of lies. He might have done the whole thing himself and be setting Eliza up."

"You don't really think he's capable of that do you, Sir? I mean he's not exactly the sharpest tool in the box," responded Danny.

"Oh, I agree, I don't think he could organise a piss-up in a brewery, but it's not what we think that matters is it? It's what we can prove, and you and I both know that Eliza is not only clever enough to have planned all this, but she's also clever enough to be able to deny everything he's said and put the blame wholly onto him. That's why the physical evidence is going to be vital. You never know, we could get lucky with the phone too. Maybe there's an incriminating text message or voicemail."

Mason turned and added another photograph to the whiteboard, this one being of Ricky taken some years ago when he was arrested for stealing.

"But why did Ricky keep hold of the clothing? That's the bit I don't understand," pondered Mason. "It would have made far more sense to destroy all the evidence."

"He did say that Eliza gave it to him to destroy," said Danny. "Maybe he hadn't got round to it yet. Perhaps, being the stoner he is, he forgot all about it."

"Hmm, not something you'd forget in a hurry no matter how off your face you get," said Mason. "I think he kept it because he didn't know what to do with it. I don't think he's clever enough to keep it in case Eliza dropped him in the shit, that wouldn't even cross his mind; look how stunned he was when we told him she'd done a runner."

"Well, I don't suppose for one minute he'd have coughed up like that if she hadn't run out on him," said Danny. "He did seem genuinely shocked when you told him she'd gone. Maybe he's not quite so dumb as we think."

The team arrived in dribs and drabs and took their places. Danny moved amongst them handing out folders containing all the information they had so far, including the results from the original enquiry, photographs of the items found at Ricky's flat along with stills from the CCTV, and a printed-out version of Ricky's confession.

Mason called for quiet and began to relay the new information garnered from Ricky's interview. When he finished the room was completely silent. Then, almost as if someone flipped a switch, everyone started talking at once. Some turned to the colleague next to them and began to earnestly discuss their views and opinions. Others posed questions directly to Mason.

"Okay, everyone," said Mason. "Just settle down and let's go through this together. There's an awful lot to get through. I know we've already made a start but now, on the basis of what we've learned from Ricky Kerr, we need to bring it all together, and of course, we need to escalate our search for Eliza Kelly. We are going to work on the assumption that Ricky Kerr is telling the truth about what happened that night. As you know we have CCTV footage that confirms his account of how he entered and exited the Kelly household. As yet, we cannot confirm that the woman who appears in the same footage is actually Eliza Kelly, but I don't think there's much doubt that it's her, and I would like the team currently canvassing the area for more CCTV to push forward on that. Anything that gives us a clearer image of the woman in that clothing will be a bonus as it's identical to the clothing found at Ricky's flat.

"On the positive side, we now have the initial forensic results from this clothing confirming the presence of Eliza's DNA, to the extent that we can safely say she has worn these items. The bloodstains on the other female clothing found in the same bag is definitely that of Keith Kelly. We're still waiting for the more detailed results to come through, but forensics are confident about this.

"The phone found at Ricky's flat appears to be a burner phone that Eliza used purely for contacting Ricky. Although we don't have the phone that she was using, we have identified a call to the phone in Ricky's possession at the time Ricky says she called him and told him to go over to the house. There is also a text message telling him that the police are on site so he should expect a visit shortly, which in itself is incriminating. There are a couple more text messages in the days after the murder, but they don't give us any new information, they are just updates on what is happening. Unfortunately, there is no information regarding Eliza's plan to leave or where she might have been heading.

"Turning to Eliza herself, we need to track her movements in the days leading up to her disappearance. We currently have no definite date for her departure and are completely in the dark about where she has gone or how she got there. I will be assigning a number of you the task of tracing the items that were sold from the house; there's a list in the folder of some of the missing items and I'm arranging for Keith's daughter and a friend of Keith's to visit the house to see if we can add more items to it. First, we need to ascertain if she used an online site such as eBay to shift the items or, as seems more likely, she contacted a firm to buy them as a job lot. In which case, we need to find that company so we can establish dates.

"Some of you will be tasked with interviewing people in the local area, neighbours, shopkeepers, etc, to find out when they last saw her, and I'll be assigning others to follow up on all the possible sightings of her that have come in from the public. On that note, we have had one call of particular interest from a hairdresser who claims Eliza called into her salon without an appointment and requested a complete change of hairstyle. Danny will be following that up later today but, on the downside, it means there is a very good chance that Eliza has drastically changed her appearance, so any sightings of her so far are unlikely to give us a positive result. Hopefully, we'll be able to get at least an idea of how she might look now so we can knock up a composite photo and get it out to the public.

"We are under the assumption that she has left the country and if that's correct, then she's done so using a different name. Another line of our enquiry will be to establish what name she is currently using. We need to identify how she got false documentation. We are aware that she's changed her name on at least one previous occasion, and so I ask that Ted and his team continue looking into her history. So far all we have been able to ascertain is that her birth name is Edith O'Reilly, and unfortunately, Ricky Kerr was very unhelpful with any background information other than giving us that name. We will be questioning him again shortly and hopefully, he will be more forthcoming. We need to find people who have had contact with her at one time or another as this could help to establish where she was before she met Keith and where she might be now. You will find details of any relevant information we have uncovered in the folder. I suggest you read it, familiarise yourselves with it and do your best to track down as much information as you can.

"Zac Kelly is to be questioned again by someone who he is familiar with, and we are hoping that he might tell us himself what happened that night. If what he can tell us matches what we've been told by Ricky, then our position regarding Eliza is much stronger. Leah and I will be at the Home whilst the interview takes place which is hopefully going to happen tomorrow?" Mason looked across at Leah for confirmation.

"So far it looks as if it will go ahead," she said.

"Right," continued Mason, "If you're not sure of what you should be doing there's a list here by the board." He indicated the whiteboard behind him that was covered in photographs and all the information they had so far, arrows connecting various pieces of information together. "Find out what you've been assigned to and let's get going. I'm sure I don't need to tell you that time is of the essence. If we don't track Eliza Kelly down soon, I'm not sure we ever will."

Ricky sat on the hard single bed in the cell that he had been returned to. He really didn't feel very well. His heart was racing, and he was dripping with sweat yet shivery at the same time. He would give anything for a fix right now. He lay down and covered his eyes with his arm. He started to cry again. How could she have left without telling him? Surely, she had a plan. She must have put something into place. She wouldn't just abandon him, would she? She couldn't, could she? Of course, she could have, this was E. E who didn't give a shit about anyone but herself. The more he thought about it the more he was certain that this was exactly what she would do. Leave him behind, just like she left Zac. Get them both to carry the can for her. Then another thought came into his head. He got up off the bed and began pacing the floor.

"Well E here's the thing," Ricky shouted, his voice echoing off the cell walls, "you thought I'd got rid of the bag, but I never did and now the police have it. They know it was you, so what do you make of that you bitch?"

He began laughing manically. He still didn't feel good, he was so lightheaded. He sat back down on the bunk.

E had no idea that he hadn't got rid of the bag like she'd instructed him to. Oh, he'd tried. He just hadn't been able to think of a way of doing it safely, a way in which he wouldn't get caught in the act or a place where it wouldn't be found straight away. As he'd walked, well really it was more of a run than a walk, back from E's house that night he'd squashed the bag against his front and zipped his coat up over it. It made it look as if he was 9 months pregnant and that had caused him a fit of giggles. He was feeling a little hysterical after all that had happened that night. Everything had an air of unreality about it. He had searched for somewhere to hide the bag on his route back to the flat, not wanting to be caught with it on his person and not really wanting to take it home with him. But he decided anywhere in the near vicinity would be far too close for comfort and he would look conspicuous trying to hide it so soon and so near to where a stabbing had taken place.

Once inside the safety of his own flat, he had contemplated several different ways of disposing of the evidence. He could go to the seafront, weigh it down and throw it into the sea, but would he be able to get it out far enough that it wouldn't be spotted? Perhaps he could bury it in a garden somewhere. It was a shame that he didn't have his own garden to bury it in. It seemed that as quickly as he came up with an idea, he found a reason to discount it. He had no way of knowing that he was facing the same dilemma as E had some years ago when she too was trying to find a way of disposing of an unwanted item. The irony would have been lost on him anyway. In the end, he decided that the best thing to do would be to hide the bag in the flat until he found a solution. He was sure that given time he could come up with the perfect answer and it would be stupid to rush into disposing of it and risk it being found. Waiting until everything had died down made much more sense. At the time, he had imagined how proud E would have been of him for his forward thinking. Now he realised she would want to kill him for his foolishness.

At the thought of how angry she would be, he felt a tightening in his chest. Suddenly the pain was unbearable. He tried to call out, but he could only whimper. He tried to move; to get to the door so he could summon help, but instead, he fell off the bed and collapsed onto the concrete floor.

9

Mason waited impatiently for Henderson to finish his meal. He himself had not eaten much; he was too churned up inside, desperate to get things moving forward. While he waited, he surveyed the room. There was not much in the way of lunchtime trade, just a couple of old men playing dominoes at one table and a middle-aged man enjoying a pint at the bar, a dog lying patiently at his feet, a possessive paw placed on the now empty crisp packet that was on the floor beside it. It was a place often used by officers when they wanted to discuss a case or have a catch-up in relative peace. The landlord was a retired officer, and he wasn't interested in running a Gastro or themed pub. Just wanted to make enough money to supplement his pension. The establishment served traditional homemade pub grub, provided by the landlord's wife, and if the menu wasn't exactly extensive, the food was tasty and reasonably priced. The décor could do with a facelift, it was starting to look a little tired, but it was clean and comfortable.

"So, what do you think, Sir?" Mason asked when Henderson finally put down his knife and fork and pushed his plate aside. "You're happy to issue the arrest warrant?"

"I'd prefer it if we had the forensic results back," Henderson said truthfully. "Being able to prove beyond doubt that the clothing found is Eliza's. But yes, I think just the CCTV evidence and what Ricky Kerr has confessed to, will be enough. She's certainly going to have to come up with something substantial to put herself in the clear. Have you got any idea of where she is?"

"None whatsoever," replied Mason. "It's really difficult. We don't know on what date she left. Although we're currently trying to work out a timeline based on when she sold items and when she was last seen by neighbours, etc. But on top of that, we have no idea how she travelled. We're looking into whether she hired a car or used public transport, but she's almost certainly changed her name and possibly her appearance too. How do we check train stations, airports, and ports when we have no idea when she left, what she's calling herself or what she looks like? We really are trying to find someone in the dark. I was hoping that we'd get more information coming in from the appeal but that hasn't resulted in anything credible so far. To be honest, it's only a gut feeling that she's gone abroad, for all I know she could be hiding in the street next to the station."

"Any luck tracing her contacts?" asked Henderson.

"Well, she has no living family as far as we can ascertain and no close friends. In fact, it's hard to find anyone other than Ricky who knew her before she married Keith, and he hasn't exactly given us any useful information. All we know from him is that they were at school together. I've got people looking into his background to see if they can come up with anything connected to her. She did receive a caution a few years ago for common assault. There's not much detail on file but it seems to have stemmed from an altercation between her and another woman who was her client."

"Client?" queried Henderson.

"I believe at the time she was working as some sort of life coach or something. Some sort of new-aged, hippy-dippy nonsense," Mason informed him.

"I'm considering sending you on another political correctness awareness course," said Henderson, only half-jokingly.

"I've sent someone to speak to the woman involved to get more details. But I don't think it will add much to our inquiry," Mason continued, without acknowledging Henderson's comment. "At least we have Eliza's birth name now, but it's a long-winded process trying to find any information about her, and of course, we can't trust that any of the details she has been using are accurate. The date of birth she gave us is probably as false as the name she was using when she met Keith. I've spoken to her stepdaughter, but she couldn't give us anything of use. It's obvious Eliza's changed her name before, but we have no idea how many times she may have done that. If she's used more than one name in the past, it makes our job so much harder. We've not been able to track down her previous husband yet. I'm still not sure that he even exists. She's clearly an accomplished liar and maybe she made him up. She told me that she was once a practising solicitor, but we've had no luck tracing anywhere that she actually practised, or in finding previous employers or work colleagues either. With no idea of her actual name, we're more than a little stymied."

"Maybe after the press conference, when we've announced the issue of the arrest warrant, it will attract more attention and people will come forward," said Henderson hopefully. "Someone will recognise her and give us more background details on her. Both the press and the public will be far more interested once they know she's wanted for murder and that she framed her child."

"True," said Mason. "The very fact she put the blame on Zac I think will mean that anyone who does know her will want to throw her under the bus for being such a heartless bitch let alone a murderess. Oh, and there's one more thing we've discovered whilst trying to find people who know her," declared Mason. "She told us that the argument she had with Keith on the night he died was over his belief that she was having an affair with her gym instructor. Well, we finally managed to locate the gym club that she was a member of. Turns out she had an infatuation with the owner of the gym, but he wasn't interested. She made quite a nuisance of herself up until he introduced her to his husband!"

Henderson snorted into his glass.

"That can't have gone down well with her. She must have been incredibly embarrassed."

"I sure she was, she stopped going to the gym," replied Mason. "She hadn't been for a number of weeks before Keith died. Puts a bit of a hole in her story. I mean they could still have been arguing about it, but she told me Keith wanted her to stop going to the gym and it was her refusal that set him off. Yet we can prove she hadn't been there for ages. Although, there's always the possibility she'd found another gym and someone else to have an affair with. Bit unlikely though, don't you think?"

"I think you're right about her being an accomplished liar and that she hasn't told the truth about any of it," said Henderson. "I've arranged to do the press conference first thing tomorrow morning. It was too late to get it organised for today."

"Fair enough," said Mason. "I have a feeling there's a lot more to Eliza Kelly than we're aware of. Maybe it'll turn out she's a black widow and we'll find a trail of dead husbands."

"Don't even joke about it," said Henderson. "I take it you'll be trying to get more information out of Ricky, sounds like he's the only one who knows anything useful."

"Oh definitely, I'm going to have a go at him again tomorrow. I just can't help thinking that we missed something in the original enquiry," mused Mason. "It was all a bit too easy. I've been going over it in my head but there was no evidence to disprove the account that Eliza gave us of what happened." Mason fiddled with a beer mat as he shared his concerns with Henderson. "I really hope there won't be repercussions; that re-opening the case won't cast a negative light on our original investigation."

"I understand what you're saying, Mike," said Henderson. "But at the end of the day, we can only work with what we've got and that's exactly what you did. I'm certain that you carried out a thorough investigation and you're right, everything *did* fit. We still don't know for certain that anything different *did* happen," Henderson tried to reassure him.

"But we both know that what's come to light means something *very* different *did* happen," said Mason despondently.

"Yes, but that's the point isn't it," said Henderson. "What you've discovered now was not available to you at the time. It's no good thinking you got it wrong when you didn't have anything else to go on. As the saying goes, hindsight is a wonderful thing. All you can do now is prove your theory that Eliza's the guilty party. Put your efforts into that. If you're right, then when this goes to trial, you'll be able to rest assured that you've done your job and justice has been served."

Mason was relieved, not only that his boss was not going to hold him to account regarding the initial investigation, but that Henderson himself would once again make the press announcement. The last thing Mason wanted was to be besieged by questions from the media that he could not answer. He was reassured now that he knew Henderson believed, as he did, that Eliza had murdered her husband. On his return to the station, however, he was met with news that sent his mood spiralling downward once more. Ricky Kerr had suffered a cardiac arrest and had died en route to the hospital.

BBC News – Tuesday 8th June 2015 – 9:15 am

BREAKING NEWS: Police in West Sussex have announced the issue of an arrest warrant for Eliza Kelly, wife of actor Keith Kelly, for the murder of her husband.

This is a breaking news story, and we will bring you more information shortly.

~~~~~~

BBC News –Tuesday 8th June 2015 – 3:00 pm

Police have issued an arrest warrant for Eliza Kelly, who they now suspect of murdering her husband Keith Kelly at their home in Brigholme. Initially, police had named Eliza, 45, as a person of interest after she absconded. They have so far been unable to trace her whereabouts. DCI Henderson of West Sussex Police issued the following statement:

"In light of new evidence, we have re-opened our investigation into the death of Keith Kelly and are asking for the public's help in locating the current whereabouts of Mrs Eliza Kelly, whom we now regard as a suspect. We have issued a warrant for her arrest but at this moment in time I am unable to give any more information regarding our investigation."

Mrs Kelly was last seen on…

~~~~~~

The Sun – Tuesday 8th June 2015

MURDERER ON THE RUN

In a sensational twist, police have now issued an arrest warrant for Eliza Kelly, the wife of actor Keith Kelly. Eliza who disappeared from the family home a few days ago, is wanted in connection with the murder of her husband.

The police are appealing for anyone with information regarding the current whereabouts of Mrs Kelly to contact them immediately and at the same time are appealing to Mrs Kelly directly to hand herself in to the nearest police station.

Mr Kelly's family have declined to comment.

~~~~~~
~~~~~~

10

After Mason had contacted her requesting her help in identifying items that were missing from her father's house, Amy got in touch with Kath and asked if she'd mind accompanying her. Marcus was away on a business trip and Amy didn't fancy returning to the house where her father had died without someone she was close to by her side. Besides, Kath had visited the house far more often than Amy had over the last few years. She explained to Kath the police were hoping that by identifying items that Eliza had sold, they could work out a timeline for when she had left the property.

The visit turned out not to be as upsetting as Amy had imagined. She had no strong memories of her dad in that house. The worst part had been going into the kitchen where, despite her best efforts not to, she could not help picturing her father collapsed on the floor bleeding to death. She didn't spend very much time in there.

It was DS Hobbs who had conducted them around, making notes of everything they mentioned. As anticipated, Kath was of far more help, for Amy discovered she had no idea of what was missing other than a few things that had belonged to her grandmother, such as a silver cutlery set. The majority of the furniture, ornaments, pictures, etc, were items that Eliza and Keith had purchased together, and Amy had no real connection with any of it. She was glad when it was finally over, and they stepped outside.

"What will happen to the house now?" Kath asked DS Hobbs.

"How do you mean?" asked Danny.

"Well, with Eliza abandoning it, who does it now belong to?"

"I should imagine it belongs to whichever lender Dad borrowed the money from," said Amy sourly. "Dad's solicitor got in touch with me recently to say it was unlikely that Adam and I would receive any money from the estate as Dad was in so much debt. Not that we were expecting anything anyway. You know how funny Eliza was that Adam and I had already benefited financially from both Mum and Granny.

She told me more than once that Zac would be my dad's priority should anything happen to him."

Danny thought it best not to add to this conversation as he had been advised by Mason not to say anything to the two women about Eliza and her suspected role in Keith's death, or to mention anything about Ricky. The arrangement was that after the inspection of the house, he was to take them back to the station for a meeting with Mason. There the DI would appraise them of all the newly acquired information and how it changed, what they believed had happened to Keith, and where the DI would also break the news to them that Ricky Kerr, their only witness, or the only witness to have talked, had himself died.

As they walked into the reception area of the police station, a man wearing a smart dark grey suit, with a white shirt and plain navy tie made straight for them. Even before the introductions, Kath had identified who he was. Although she had never met him, Amy's description of the 50-something DI Mason was spot on, even down to the irregular set of his nose.

"Thank you for coming in," said Mason. "And for agreeing to go round the house. I'm sure it must have been difficult for you."

Mason instructed Danny to escort the women to one of the interview rooms and organise cups of tea for them. He told them he would join them shortly.

Once Danny had delivered the tea and then left the room, Amy turned to Kath.

"I know it's ridiculous, but I can't help feeling guilty, as if I've done something wrong. I think it's the surroundings," she said, looking around the stark room with its high windows and blank walls.

"I get what you mean," replied Kath. "It doesn't help being surrounded by policemen. Every time that sergeant asks me a question, I feel like I'm under interrogation."

At that moment the door opened, and Mason came into the room carrying a takeout coffee and a large folder. He glanced rather guiltily at the untouched cups of insipid tea sitting on the table and asked whether the women would prefer to have him send someone out for coffee. They both declined, and Mason was conscious that they were anxious for him to begin.

"What I'm about to share with you is going to be distressing for you to hear. Also, I am going to have to ask you both not to share anything that is said in this room with anyone other than your immediate family. It is important that nothing I tell you gets to the press as it could jeopardize the case." Mason looked directly at Amy and then turned to Kath. Each of them nodded their agreement and Mason took a sip of his coffee before continuing.

"In light of new evidence that has come forward and information we have received from Ricky Kerr," he addressed Amy, "we now believe that your father was murdered and that it was Eliza who killed him." He watched Amy closely whilst he spoke, unsure of what her reaction would be.

Amy gave a gasp of shock and Kath immediately put an arm around her. Kath, still holding onto Amy looked back at Mason. "So, what's happened to bring you to that conclusion?" she asked.

Mason cleared his throat and began by telling them about the discovery of the CCTV footage of both Ricky and Eliza showing some relevant photographs to them as he spoke. Explaining that finding the footage had given them just cause to bring Ricky in for questioning, and to also search his flat in the hopes of finding the jacket that was seen in the film. Not only had they found the jacket, but they had discovered other significant items of interest. Mason explained about the holdall found in the cupboard and showed them photographs of the joggers and baseball cap that matched the CCTV footage.

He told them of the discovery of the bloodstained clothing and towel but did not show them the photographs. He then recounted Ricky's version of the events of that night.

"According to Kerr, he received a call from Eliza at around 5:00 pm asking him to come to the house via the alley, which he thought was because she didn't want the neighbours to see him." He then explained about the mobile found in the holdall and that a call had been received on that phone at that time. "When he got there," continued Mason, "she made him take off his shoes and walk around the edge of the kitchen. That's when he saw Keith's body and his description matches the position we found Keith in when we entered the property later on that evening. He told us that he, quite naturally, panicked and asked Eliza what the hell had happened. She told him she'd lost her temper because Keith had come clean on just how grave a state their finances were in. Keith had told her they had no choice but to sell the house and downsize. She hadn't believed he was serious until he revealed that he had already sold most of his assets, including the holiday home, but was still unable to raise enough funds to solve the problem.

"Ricky told us that Eliza was aware that money was becoming an issue, but she had no idea of how bad the situation actually was. She had been completely unaware of the sale of the house in Spain. She was totally unprepared for what he was telling her. She was furious. Feeling cheated and deceived, she utterly lost the plot. She told Ricky that in a mad moment of anger, she had picked up a kitchen knife and before she knew what she was doing, she had stabbed Keith with it. She had no intention of killing him, she just lost her temper."

"Just!" interrupted Kath in disbelief.

"Again," Mason continued, "according to Kerr, she was horrified at what she had done. Keith died very quickly, which we know is true from the post-mortem. Whether it was intentional or not, she had stabbed into his kidney, and he bled out in minutes."

Amy began to cry, and Mason reminded himself to be careful about how he imparted certain information. Kath hugged Amy closer to her and nodded for Mason to carry on, thinking it would be best for Amy to hear everything in one go.

"At this point, Eliza realised the enormity of what she'd done and that she would be charged with manslaughter at the very least, certainly facing a long stretch in prison, so this is where her actions turn really dark," said Mason. "She became aware of Zac standing in the kitchen doorway. She wasn't sure how long he had been there or how much he had actually witnessed. He'd obviously been woken up by her screaming at Keith, and it's at this point, according to Ricky, that she formed her plan. She'd still got the knife in her hand, so she cleaned it with a kitchen towel, which was also found in the holdall we recovered, and then she put it down on the counter. She told Zac that Daddy had an accident, and he wasn't going to get better, but if Zac could do something very important for Mummy now, she would be able to take him to live somewhere special, like America. She promised him they'd live in a big house with a pool, and he could have anything and everything he wanted. She encouraged him to pick up the knife and stab Keith, which amazingly he did, stabbing him between the neck and the shoulder blade. As you know from the original inquiry, this is the injury that was inflicted after Keith was already dead."

Mason paused and looked up to find both women staring at him in horror.

"It gets worse," said Mason. "Everything I'm telling you now is what Ricky says Eliza told to him. He wasn't there and he didn't witness any of it. That means we can't be certain that any of this is what actually happened, that Eliza bribed Zac or that Zac did as she asked. We are actively trying to get Zac to talk to us so we can get a better picture of his role in all this. According to Ricky, Eliza then had Zac put his hands into the blood that was pooled around the body," Mason winced as he said this but decided it was best to just keep going. "Then she got him to wipe his hands over his pyjama bottoms whilst she dipped the hem of his pyjama top in the blood. She made him put the knife on the floor and she picked it up and moved it out of the way. That's the version of events according to Ricky."

Amy felt faint and thought she might be sick. Kath could not believe that a mother would do that to her son.

"So, what does he say happened next?" asked Kath.

"That's the moment she summons him to help," Mason told her. "He also said that after she'd told him what happened, he wanted to ring us straight away, but Eliza persuaded him not to, as she had a plan and that he just needed to stay calm. She explained to him exactly what she was going to do next. Ricky says she believed that because Zac was a child, nothing would happen to him. That after he had been questioned and assessed, life would return to normal. So, if they followed her plan the three of them would be able to move away together as soon as the fuss had died down. All they needed to do was to stay calm, put her plan into action and then contact the police. As long as they had their stories straight, nothing could go wrong. She emphasised to both Ricky and Zac how important it was that Zac never told anyone what had happened, otherwise they wouldn't be able to go to America. According to Ricky, Eliza made it all sound so easy, and he was convinced that her plan would work. He sat with Zac and talked to him about how great it would be to move to America and what a fantastic life they could have, all the time reminding the boy of how important it was that he didn't tell anyone about what had happened.

"Ricky said that while he and Zac stayed in the sitting room, Eliza went back into the kitchen and stripped off her clothes. She then went upstairs where she showered and got into clean clothes. She came back downstairs with the holdall and stuffed the clothes she'd been wearing and the towel she'd used, into it. We believe she did a very thorough job of not only cleaning herself but cleaning the bathroom too. She then got Ricky to action the second part of her plan. She knew that Zac couldn't just stab his dad for no reason, so they had to make it look like Keith attacked her, which is why she got Ricky to thump her in the face and grab her arm hard enough to leave fingermarks." Amy lifted her head from Kath's shoulder.

"So, Dad didn't hit her?"

"No, apparently it was all part of her plan. She needed a reason as to why your dad was stabbed and so made it look like he'd given her a beating."

"I knew he never hit her. I said so, didn't I?" said Amy.

"I know, but we had to take her word for it at the time," said Mason, slightly more defensively than he intended.

"Oh, I'm not blaming you," said Amy. "But how come her car was at Ricky's? I mean you had CCTV of her leaving the house and of her car being at his. How did she manage that?"

"I hate to admit it," replied Mason, "but her plan was actually very clever and if that CCTV footage from the alley hadn't come to light, I really believe she would have got away with it. Can I get you anything? Water, tea, coffee?"

"No thanks," said Amy, "I'd just like to know what you know."

"Well," continued Mason, "when Eliza left the house after Ricky had hit her, she was wearing the jeans and jumper that she had on when we arrived on the scene. When she's on CCTV fleeing from the front door, she's wearing her long winter coat. However, underneath the jeans and jumper, she was wearing her jogging gear; she must have had the baseball cap in the pocket of her coat, hidden from sight. Once she gets to Ricky's, she takes off her outer clothing whilst sitting in her car, she puts her hair in a ponytail and puts on the baseball cap. She looks completely different to how she did when she left her house. Leaving the other clothing in the car, she jogs back to the house and does the same as Ricky did, climbs over the fence and goes in through the back. According to Ricky the three of them sat for a couple of hours and watched films and kept on telling Zac how wonderful their new life was going to be, all the amazing things they would do. Then Eliza goes out the back way, hops over the fence and jogs back to the car that's parked down the street from Ricky's flat. There she changes out of the jogging gear and back into her other clothes. The CCTV that captures her arriving back at the house, having supposedly spent a couple of hours with Ricky in his flat, shows her carrying her coat over her arm and we believe that was so she could cover up the jogging gear. When she's back in the house, she stashes the joggers into the bag with the bloodstained clothes and hands it to Ricky, who goes out back, jumps the fence and goes home. Then Eliza rings the emergency services and… well you know what happened after that," Mason concluded.

The room was silent, save for the quiet ticking of a wall clock. Kath withdrew her arms from around Amy and put the palms of her hands against the younger woman's cheeks, turning Amy's face so she could look her straight in the eyes.

"Are you alright?" she asked.

"I don't know what I am," replied Amy. "I'm just in shock. It's just unbelievable. Poor Dad and also poor Zac. How could she do that, to either of them?"

"I know that it's hard to take it all in," said Mason. "It seems incredible that she managed to think all that through in such a short space of time and to carry it out in such a way that we didn't detect any of it. She's an extremely dangerous, evil woman and please believe me when I say that we are doing everything we can to find her."

"And how's that going?" asked Kath. All she wanted right now was justice for Keith.

"I have to be honest and tell you that at the moment we've got nothing," said Mason gloomily. "Everything seems to be stacked against us. We were really hoping that we would be able to get more information from Ricky regarding Eliza, who she was and what she was doing before she met your dad which might give us a clue as to where she has gone now. All he has given us is the name Edith O'Reilly, from which we have traced her early years of schooling but no birth certificate, so we don't believe her birth was registered in that name. We really are struggling to discover much about her before she married your dad," he said looking at Amy.

"I suppose he's refusing to cooperate now," said Kath scathingly. "Too scared of incriminating himself further."

"It's worse than that," said Mason. "It's not that he won't cooperate, it's the fact that he can't. He suffered a massive heart attack two days ago and died in the ambulance on the way to hospital. Apparently, his drug abuse finally caught up with him and we think the shock of learning that Eliza had abandoned him was literally a death blow."

"Oh my God!" exclaimed Amy. "How awful."

"It's devastating from our point of view," said Mason. "We're just left with a second-hand account of what happened to your father, and we have lost the only person who had any real knowledge of Eliza at all. As you can imagine, it's really hard to track someone when you don't know when or how they left and you're not sure what name they are using. It also seems very likely that when Eliza took off, she had a new look. She visited a hair salon some miles away a few days ago, long before we were looking for her, and had a complete makeover. The woman who owns the salon got in touch after our request for information. She worked on Eliza herself and thought she recognised her, but when she asked, Eliza told her she was mistaken. Luckily for us, the hairdresser took a sneaky photo to show to her friends that she had a 'celebrity' attend the salon. From that photograph, we have been able to positively identify that her client was Eliza. Usefully, this woman was able to give us a detailed description of how she looks now with her new hairstyle. We're just about to release a photofit picture to the press. Hopefully, someone will remember seeing her. We are also fairly optimistic that with all the press attention someone may come forward with knowledge of her background."

They sat in silence for a moment while Amy and Kath digested everything they had learned.

"And what about Zac?" asked Amy, breaking the silence before it became too awkward. "What's going to happen to him?"

"Well, like I say, we are very hopeful that he'll talk, but as to whether he can help us find his mother, I'm really not sure. I think it's unlikely. I should imagine he still believes that his mother is going to take him to America," answered Mason.

"No," said Amy. "I was meaning regarding his future. How does he stand now you know he wasn't responsible for killing Dad?"

"To be honest, I couldn't tell you. That will be up to the professionals to make an assessment. I'm sure you'd agree that whatever was behind what happened the night your dad died, Zac's behaviour was far from normal."

BBC News Update – 10th June 2015

Police trying to trace the whereabouts of Eliza Kelly have today released a photofit which they say is how they believe Mrs Kelly, the woman suspected of murdering her husband, the actor Keith Kelly, may now look. The image was put together with the help of hair salon owner Ms Bethany Shears, who created the new look for Mrs Kelly some weeks before she was known to have disappeared.

Ms Shears told reporters…

~~~~~~
~~~~~~

11

Leah was walking through the incident room when a civilian operator waved an arm to attract her attention.

"Could you take this call please, Sergeant? It's connected to the Kelly case."

Without bothering to ask what it was about, Leah smiled and took the phone from her. "DS Cooper," she said. "How can I help?"

"Hi, my name is Tom Bryant."

He said his name as if it should mean something to Leah, but it didn't. When she didn't respond, he continued, "This may sound rather strange, but I've just worked out that Eliza Kelly was my first wife."

Leah was incredulous. "You've only just worked that out?"

The caller gave a nervous laugh, "I know that sounds weird, obviously, but let me try to explain. I was married to a woman back in the early 1990s who looks or looked identical to the photofit, or whatever it's called, you've just released."

Leah was about to interrupt but he hurried on anticipating what she was going to ask.

"I've obviously seen the news, but I never made the connection with Eliza Kelly before because she looked so different. When I saw that photofit, I recognised her straight away. I thought, Oh My God that's Eleanor. I know her as Eleanor. She was Eleanor Cashmore when I met her."

Now he had Leah's full attention. Was this gentleman the first husband of Eliza whose existence they had so far been unable to prove? And if so, would he be able to assist them in tracing Eliza's current whereabouts?

Again, as if he had read her mind, Bryant continued, "Then I thought if Eliza Kelly and Eleanor were the same person, you would have contacted me by now. As you haven't, I thought I'd better get in touch with you, but to be honest I don't think there'll be much I can help you with. I haven't had contact with Eleanor, or with Max for a number of years. I mean Max will be 23 now and he was only 6 when I saw him last."

"Max?" queried Leah.

"Yes," now it was Mr Bryant's turn to sound confused. "Eleanor's son, Max. He used to be my son too but…"

"Used to be?" Leah interrupted. What an odd thing to say!

"Oh gosh, you really don't know anything do you? I, um, er. I'm really not sure how to explain this," Mr Bryant replied.

"Just try," said Leah rather unhelpfully. She was distracted searching on the computer for the scant information they held regarding Eliza's first husband.

"I'm sorry but I think this is going to be really hard to explain over the phone," answered Bryant. "Would it be possible for me to call in and see you? I'm based in Hornby, but I have a couple of free days next week when I could drive over. Is that of any help to you? Oh, and it would be brilliant if you could give me a way of contacting Max. I'd be extremely grateful. I've been trying to find him for years. This must be such a difficult time for him with everything that's happened, so I thought now would be a good time to reach out. I have no idea what his situation is but I'm sure he must remember me, and with Eleanor having no family I felt I should be there for him if he wants me to be. I mean no disrespect to Mr Kelly's family, but it might be easier for Max to talk to someone who's not closely involved. Maybe you could pass on my details to him. That way it would be his choice to see me or not. If that's not allowed, could you just let me know that he's, okay?" Mr Bryant stopped talking, suddenly aware that his nerves were making him ramble.

Leah wasn't too sure how to handle this. According to the file she had just opened, the only information they had been given regarding Max had come from Amy Macdonald, Keith Kelly's daughter. And she had received that information second-hand from her father. Amy believed that Eliza had a son, who was apparently called Max, by her first marriage but she had handed custody of the boy over to her husband when they divorced and hadn't had any further contact with him. The team had tried to trace this first husband and son but without a surname, they hadn't got very far. If Mr Bryant was indeed that husband, then according to the information Leah had, he should know exactly where Max was. It seemed wrong to confess to Mr Bryant over the phone that up until his call today, no one had been certain that Max actually existed. Rather than complicate the matter further, Leah asked for Mr Bryant's contact details telling him she would call him back shortly.

Bryant was a bit taken aback. Then it dawned on him that Leah hadn't acknowledged anything about Max.

"Has something happened to Max? Is he okay?" he asked.

"If you could bear with me, Mr Bryant, I need to speak to my boss," said Leah. "But I really think it's better if, as you suggested, we discuss things in person, so I'll call you back shortly to arrange a meeting."

"Oh God, something has happened to him, hasn't it?" stammered Bryant.

Trying to put him at ease Leah replied, "I really can't give out any personal information over the phone Mr Bryant, surely you understand that? How can I be certain you are who you say you are? Please just be patient, give me your contact details and I will call you back shortly to arrange a convenient time to meet with you."

She hung up as soon as he gave her his number, to avoid him asking any more questions and then scurried off to find Mason.

PART THREE

1990

The slam of the door roused her from her reverie. It took her a moment to work out where she was. She'd been having one of her favourite daydreams; the one where on arriving home after work, she opened the door to be greeted by the aroma of roast chicken and walking into the kitchen, found her daughter slaving away over pots and pans. She rubbed her arms still feeling the warmth of her daughter's hug even though she hadn't actually received one. Sitting up, she just had time to wipe a bit of dribble away from her chin, before her daughter came storming into the room.

"Darling, what a lovely surprise. I wasn't expecting you."

"Well, that's obvious," the younger woman looked her mother up and down and grimaced. "Hopefully if you'd have known I was coming, you'd have made more of an effort."

The older woman sighed and sank back down into the chair. Unlike her daydream, this was the reality, her daughter always criticising her, always making her feel small. But what her daughter said next took her completely by surprise.

"Sorry Mum, I don't want to be mean. It's just you look a bit scruffy sitting there with your clothes all creased and your hair all mussed up. I've come because I thought I could go through your wardrobe with you to pick out an outfit for you to wear to my graduation. If we can't find anything suitable, then I thought perhaps we could go shopping, my treat. I suppose in my head I pictured you looking like the glamour puss we're going to turn you into, so it was quite a surprise to see you looking so dowdy."

The mother didn't know what shocked her more, the fact that her daughter apologised, her daughter never apologised for anything, ever! The fact that she was going to help her pick out an outfit, another of her fantasies was a mother and daughter bonding session over clothes, although admittedly in her daydream, it was a wedding dress and her own mother of the bride outfit that they were choosing, or that her daughter was offering to treat her, something she had never offered to do before. While all these thoughts were running around in her head, all she could do was stare up stupidly at her daughter who was leaning over her. She was struck dumb. She couldn't think of a single thing to say.

"Are you okay Mum?" her daughter sounded concerned which was even more unsettling. What was going on? Where was the nasty, sarcastic daughter she was used to? What was happening?

"Seriously Mum, say something. You're scaring me. Are you ill? Let me go and put the kettle on and I'll make you a nice cup of tea."

At this, the mother gave a little moan. Surely, she was still dreaming. The younger woman had never spoken so kindly to her in her whole life. Maybe, she thought, I really am ill!

"Shall we just check your blood sugars, Mum? Could be they're a little low and that's why you look so pale. Stay sitting down and I'll go and get your testing kit. I'm sure we'll have you feeling better in no time."

Sometime later, she came to. She was aware of her daughter talking to her. '*I must have drifted off,*' she thought. She tried to concentrate on what her daughter was saying but it was a struggle to focus.

"You must have known that I'd work out the truth about my father." The younger woman was pacing whilst she spoke. "Not a single photograph, no family members on his side, no memorabilia. Nothing."

The mother tried to speak but it was too much effort. Her daughter came closer and knelt in front of her.

"No don't try to deny it. Like I said, I worked it out long ago and that's why I did what I did."

Her mother had no idea what her daughter was referring to. Her last thoughts were of how wonderful it was that her only child was finally being so loving, so tender, putting an arm around her and picking up her hand to stroke it.

"Not long now Mum."

She could only assume that meant until help arrived because she really was feeling kind of strange. She'd always believed that eventually, her daughter would show her how much she cared for her and now that was really happening, her heart sang. Fortunately, she was never to know that in actual fact her daughter was awaiting confirmation that her mother's heart had stopped beating before she left the house.

1

Lisa couldn't make up her mind what to wear.

'*This is ridiculous,*' she thought to herself as she surveyed the various skirts, blouses, trousers and jackets strewn across her bed. She'd practically emptied her wardrobe. All she needed to do was pick an outfit that was suitable for the day ahead; why was she finding it so hard? Mainly because on the one hand, she wanted to look smart and professional for the psychologists and the police but on the other, casual and friendly for Zac. When she had visited Zac before, she had worn jeans but that didn't seem to be the right option this time. Trying to find a suitable blend of the two was proving impossible. In the end, she decided on a plain, knee-length skirt with a white blouse and short-sleeved jacket. Slightly smarter than Zac was used to seeing her in, she tended to dress down for school as most of the lessons she was involved in included some form of messy play, but not too severe for him not to recognise her. She'd originally put her hair into a bun to make herself look a little older and more experienced but decided against it and brushed it into the loose ponytail she normally wore. By the time she unlocked her car, she was a bag of nerves.

She arrived early for the appointment and was asked to wait in the reception area. To calm her nerves, she took herself off to the ladies to re-do her ponytail and check her eye makeup hadn't smudged. Two other people were sitting in reception when she returned. A man she judged to be in his 50s and a woman who Lisa thought was only a couple of years older than herself. They stood as she entered the room.

"Are you Lisa?" asked the female and when Lisa confirmed that she was, the woman introduced herself as DS Leah Cooper and then turned to the man saying, "This is DI Mason, he's leading the investigation into Keith Kelly's murder."

This was the first time that Lisa had considered that she was helping in a murder inquiry, and she was surprised by the ripple of excitement that coursed through her. She had a vision of being questioned by her colleagues in the staff room and having to say, 'I'm sorry that's classified'. Her thoughts were interrupted by the female officer whose name she had already forgotten. She mentally chastised herself and tried hard to pay more attention as the woman asked,

"Would it be okay to spend a few minutes going through the questions we'd like you to put to Zac?"

Half an hour later, Lisa was shown into the room where she had visited Zac on previous occasions. Now her nerves were even worse. DI Mason had made it very clear to her how important it was that she extracted information from Zac, without putting words into his mouth. She needed to get him to talk about what happened the night his father died, but she wasn't allowed to ask him direct questions. Quite how she was supposed to achieve this she had no idea, and the fact that both the police officers, Zac's guardian and his psychologist were all going to be watching through the two-way mirror, did not help ease her anxiety. In the end, however, it all turned out to be far simpler than she anticipated.

She walked into the room where Zac was sitting at a table drawing on a sheet of A3 paper. Once again, she was taken aback at how different he looked now, compared to when she first met him in the classroom. It was a shock every time she saw him.

"Hi Zac, how are you?" she said as brightly as she could, trying to use her normal voice but even so she was aware that she sounded nervous.

Zac made no reply but carried on drawing.

"I've brought you some chocolate," she told him. "They said you could have it after your dinner."

Still no reply from Zac. She walked up to the table and looked down at what he was drawing. She gave a little gasp as she realised, he'd drawn the body of a person and was now covering it in red crayon. The significance of this was obvious. Taking a deep breath, she sat down beside him.

"Is that your dad?" she asked softly.

Zac nodded and carried on aggressively rubbing the red crayon over the paper.

"Can you tell me what happened to him?" she asked gently. It was like floodgates opening. Zac looked up at her with huge, wide eyes.

"My mum stabbed him with a massive knife," he said. "There was lots of blood. Then she let me have the knife and she told me to stick it in him. I had to step in the blood. The blood felt funny, it was sticky. He's dead now, my dad is. All his blood fell out."

There was no emotion in Zac's voice, he was just stating facts. He went on to talk about how his mum had called Ricky and how Ricky had sat with him while his mum went out. Then his mum came back, and they ate popcorn and drank coke while they watched a film. He told Lisa how he was going to live in America with his mum and Ricky. They were going to buy a massive house with a cinema and a pool. He went quiet for a while concentrating on his picture, his tongue sticking out the side of his mouth as he worked. Lisa asked what he was drawing now, and he told her that he was drawing the police car. He got very excited as he described how the police had come to the house, how he'd ridden in an ambulance with his mum and gone to hospital and how he'd been given hot chocolate to drink and crisps to eat.

"Mum told me not to say anything about Dad," he told Lisa. "But it must be alright to say it now because Dad's dead and if Dad isn't coming back then he can't tell me off and Mum can't get into trouble, can she?"

Lisa wasn't sure how to answer that, so she just murmured a "uh huh".

Then very matter-of-factly he said how he was glad his dad wasn't here anymore. His dad didn't let him play the big boy video games, but his mum did. Just like his mum let him watch the big boy films but his dad didn't.

"Dad was always telling me off," continued Zac. "He can't tell me off anymore, can he? I'm waiting for Mum to come and get me. Do you know when she's coming? Only it's been like forever."

"I'm really not sure," said Lisa.

"I did everything like she told me to so I'm sure she'll come and get me soon," said Zac.

At this point, the door opened, and Jamie, Zac's legal guardian, came into the room.

"Hi Zac," he said. "It's time for Lisa to go, so say goodbye to her and then we can carry on with that spaceship we're building."

"Bye Lisa," said Zac not even looking at her as he dived into the box of Lego that Jamie had brought with him.

"Well done, Lisa," DI Mason said to her as he met her outside the room. "You did brilliantly."

"I didn't do anything," answered Lisa truthfully. "He must have just decided that today was the day he was going to talk."

"You did great," repeated Mason. "I don't think he would have opened up to anyone else like that. The people here have been trying to get him to talk about that night ever since he first arrived. Thanks very much. I know it must have been hard to hear."

"I just can't believe he's so unaffected by it all," said Lisa.

"Oh, I'm sure he has been severely affected," said Mason. "It will all come out eventually. I'll walk you to your car."

As they walked, Mason asked Leah what Zac had been like at school. She told him that although he was physically big for his age, emotionally she felt he was immature.

"I met his mother on a number of occasions as she was always stopping by to complain about something," Lisa told him. "She definitely babied him and refused to believe he ever behaved badly but, in all honesty, he was an out-and-out bully. He didn't really have friends, most of the other children were a bit scared of him."

Driving home, Lisa thought about Zac and how he didn't seem fazed by any of the recent events; seemingly treating all that had happened as if it was perfectly normal. She considered what Mason had said about it catching up with him eventually and thought he was probably right. Maybe Zac was just too young to process it at the moment; he might feel differently once older and more able to understand exactly what had taken place.

She no longer felt as if she was important. The whole experience left her feeling terribly sad and she knew she would not be discussing the events of the day with her colleagues.

2

Mason's mood matched the cold, grey January day. Taking his frustration out on that new recruit had not helped, in fact, it had left him feeling even more miserable. He was aware that he was growing a reputation as a grumpy bastard and wondered whether he should care more. At this particular moment, he couldn't care less.

His frustration had been mounting over the months since the investigation into Keith Kelly's death had been reopened and it boiled over this morning after his meeting with the powers that be upstairs – hence the growling at the nervous PC, who made the mistake of catching him on his way back to his office before he had a chance to vent his spleen on someone or something more deserving.

Although Mason was unwilling to admit it to his superiors, he knew that they were right. The operation in the search for Eliza Kelly, now wanted for the murder of Keith Kelly, was making very little progress; in truth, it was making none at all. It had completely stalled. Despite numerous public appeals, hardly any relevant information was forthcoming. The scant reported sightings, although meticulously followed up, all resulted in dead ends. Eliza remained elusive.

The team thought they'd finally caught a break when a hairdresser by the unlikely name of Bethany Shears from Charleston Hampton, a village about 12 miles from the Kellys' home address, contacted them to say she had carried out a complete makeover for a client whom she was adamant was Eliza. Bethany claimed that she had immediately recognised Eliza from the media photos that circulated at the time of Keith's death, and she had been elated to have someone "famous" in her small village salon.

Her client, however, had vehemently denied being Mrs Kelly, telling Bethany that she was often mistaken for her and that was part of the reason for having a transformation. This didn't deter Ms Shears from taking a sneaky photo so she could show her friends and her other clients her famous customer. Mason and his team had seen this photograph and were positive that Bethany was right, and that her client had indeed been Eliza. Ms Shears had then been very obliging and provided them with details of Eliza's "new look" once her treatments had been completed. A subsequent photofit had been released to the press but the only person to contact them with anything of interest had been a gentleman by the name of Tom Bryant and that call had only added complications to the case.

On seeing the photofit picture, Mr Bryant made the connection between Eliza Kelly and his first wife Eleanor, believing them to be one and the same person. From the beginning, although they could not be certain of his existence, the operation had been keen to interview Eliza's first husband in the hope that he would be able to provide them with information that could lead them to Eliza's current whereabouts. As they had no idea of the gentleman's name their efforts to trace him had been unsuccessful. Mason had initially been optimistic when the call had come in out of the blue, although there was a little confusion when the man had asked after Eliza's son, Max, as it had been assumed, from the information provided to people by Eliza, that Max was actually living with his father.

Mason had visited Mr Bryant personally and, on hearing his story and seeing photographs of the woman in question, he too was convinced that Eliza Kelly had previously been married to Tom Bryant; although, Mr Bryant had known her as Eleanor. There was no record of their marriage because the circumstances they found themselves in were not ideal and it had been easier for them to slip off abroad and marry in secret. They had never gotten around to registering the marriage in the UK.

Tom had been extremely embarrassed to admit to Mason that whilst engaged to another girl, he had a drunken one-night stand with Eleanor. To his horror, this resulted in her getting pregnant. Eleanor told him about the pregnancy just before his fiancée died in a tragic accident and, as he explained in detail to Mason, the grief and the guilt he felt about cheating on his girlfriend and abandoning Eleanor drove him to do what he considered the honourable thing and he proposed to Eleanor, who readily accepted. He confessed to Mason that marrying Eleanor was one of the worst mistakes of his life. They made each other miserable, and the marriage only lasted a couple of years.

After divorcing they shared joint custody of Max and things were fairly okay between them up until Tom and his new wife, whilst trying to start a family of their own, were informed that Tom was infertile. This discovery led to a DNA test which was when Tom found out that Max was not his son, which in turn, ultimately, led to Tom no longer having anything to do with Eleanor or Max. In fact, he demanded that his name be taken off the birth certificate, which was why, when the document was recovered by Mason's team, the father's name was blank.

Tom had not seen Max since he was 6 years old. He left the country not long after he got the DNA results, to work in Saudi Arabia for just over a year. While he was away, he came to the realisation that he missed Max and still wanted the boy in his life and his wife supported this decision. He had tried to contact Eleanor on several occasions to no avail, and on his return to the UK, he discovered that both she and Max had disappeared without a trace. No one could tell him where they had gone, and he had not heard from either of them since. Mason felt awkward asking Tom if he had any idea who Max's real father might be, but he had no choice. It would be really useful if they could speak to Max but the only information they had about him was that he lived with his father, and if that was not Mr Bryant, it would be helpful to find out who it actually was. Unfortunately, Tom couldn't assist. He told Mason that as Eleanor was at university at the time, and circulated in a large group, there were any number of possibilities, but he had not been aware of her having a relationship with anyone else, other than himself.

Mason's team soon ascertained that everything Tom told them was true. Further investigation uncovered that the last confirmed sighting of Max Bryant, as he was being referred to although there was no way of knowing what name he was currently going by, had been on Friday 13th June 1997 when his mother collected him from Hardington Grange Prep School for the last time. Eliza, who at that time was still using the name, Eleanor Cashmore, having reverted to what Tom Bryant believed to be her maiden name after their divorce, had taken Max out of school mid-term, stating that he would be going to live with his father who was moving abroad. If by his father, Eliza meant Tom Bryant, then that was definitely not the case. No further information could be found about the boy under that name after this date. There was still the possibility that he had actually gone to live with his biological father, but there was no way of identifying that individual.

Keith's daughter, Amy, had been unable to shed any further light on the matter, although she believed that her father referred to Eliza's ex as Tom. According to Keith, Eliza had made a huge sacrifice by giving up all claims to the child to enable her ex-husband and his new partner to raise him as their own. She selflessly agreed for the good of the boy, and the whole episode was too painful for her to talk about, so the matter was never raised again. There was a discrepancy in the fact that Keith had told Amy that Eliza last saw Max when he was 18 months old. Mason knew this couldn't be right because Tom and "Eleanor" had divorced when Max was 3 and then shared custody. It wasn't until Max was 6 years old that Tom discovered the boy wasn't his. This inconsistency could have arisen as the information was being given third-hand, but it didn't help with the team's inquiry. The most logical person to ask with regards to Max's whereabouts would have been Ricky Kerr who was the person closest to Eliza. Unfortunately, that was no longer possible as he was dead!

Honestly, thought Mason, you couldn't make this stuff up. Not only did they have a missing murder suspect, but they now also had a missing child. Well not really. Max would now be in his early twenties so hardly a child and there was no reason to suspect that he hadn't grown up in the care of his biological father. But they couldn't prove it. Despite their best efforts and numerous appeals, neither Max nor his father had come forward. No one had contacted them with any information and that made Mason uneasy.

Then this morning Mason received the instructions from above that he had been expecting. Both investigations were to be scaled down. In truth, with no new information forthcoming, the team had nothing to work with and therefore could no longer justify the number of resources that had been allocated, not when there were far too many other demanding and deserving cases. Although the directive he received from his superiors was inevitable, Mason was still reluctant to make the two phone calls that were the purpose of his visit to his office. He now had to inform Amy McDonald that, although the case against Eliza very much remained live, they would no longer be actively pursuing her. Obviously, they would follow up immediately on any new leads received, and the case would be revisited on a regular basis to ensure all current information had been actioned. He also had to break the news to Tom Bryant that they had no way of tracing Max. There was nothing more the police could do unless some new information came to light. Tom was desperate to reconnect with Max and Mason would have liked to have been able to reunite them, but that wasn't to be. The frustration Mason was feeling, he knew, was down to his inability to bring justice for Amy and of course her father, and answers for Tom, both of whom he had come to know well during the course of these investigations.

Mason sighed and picked up the phone, then changed his mind and instead of calling Amy McDonald, he called his friend Trevor Harrison.

"Fancy meeting for a pint and a chat?" he asked.

He'd decided there was no particular urgency for him to contact either Amy or Tom. Nothing was going to change, and it was probably best to wait until he was in a better mood. A pint and a whinge with his ex-boss would do him far more good.

3

Mason went down to reception to collect Matt, rather than have someone else show the journalist up to his office. It was unlikely anyone at the station would recognise his visitor, but just the same he would rather not have to explain what he was up to. Not that there was anything wrong with what he was doing, he could just do without any hassle.

Trevor had filled him in about Matt's idea of writing a book on Eliza Kelly, or Edith Staples as she had been born, when the two of them met for lunch just after Mason received the news from his bosses that searching for Eliza could no longer be a priority. Mason readily agreed to cooperate with the journalist and give him all the information he possibly could, because he felt that any publicity that kept the case alive was worthwhile. Mason hated the fact that he had so far failed to bring Eliza to justice, and so to him anything that might help them to track down the elusive woman was worth trying. At the same time, the journalist might uncover something of value whilst investigating her background or produce fresh insights that might help identify where she could currently be residing.

Having grabbed them some tea from the vending machine in the corridor, Mason apologised for both its colour and its taste, whilst gesturing for Matt to take a seat. When Mason first started at the station, he had been given a choice of two offices and had purposely chosen the less showy one. Despite it being small, it suited his needs. Matt, for his part, wasn't particularly bothered by the lack of grandeur, he was just relieved that Mason was acting so affably; not how policeman normally behaved in his company.

"Do you mind if I record our conversation as well as take notes?" Matt asked the Detective Inspector.

"I don't give a monkey's what you do as long as you promise this isn't a stitch-up," said Mason.

"In what way a stitch-up?" queried Matt.

"I realise that we might come across as a tad incompetent in our handling of this case," stated Mason. "We accused and basically convicted a 9-year-old boy with the murder of his father, and in the meantime, we allowed the real culprit, his mother, to abscond. During the investigation, our chief witness, Ricky Kerr, died whilst in our care, and we discovered that another child of the accused disappeared without a trace and has been missing for over 20 years. Not our finest work," he said, giving Matt a wry smile.

"Well, when you put it like that, I have to admit it doesn't look too good," agreed Matt. "But I don't intend to lay any blame at your door. I'm sure you'll be able to give me all the evidence that led you to the conclusions you made."

"Exactly," said Mason. "So, as long as you don't make me out in the book to be a complete plonker, everything will be fine."

Matt laughed.

"I'm serious," said Mason. "Don't make me look like a fool or you'll regret it."

"Point taken," said Matt, slightly intimidated by the quick change of character.

"Right, good," said Mason, returning to his affable stance. "Well in here," he said, handing Matt a folder, "you'll find copies of reports like the post-mortem and stuff like that, you know, the usual. There are copies of interviews we carried out; some bits have been redacted but not much, not really necessary. If there's something you think I've missed, just let me know.

"Now, for a quick run-down of what we know about Eliza. She was born Edith Staples, at least that's what it says on her birth certificate. Ricky knew her as Edith O'Reilly and that's the name she was registered under for the doctor, schools, etc. O'Reilly was Betty's, her mother's, maternal grandmother's name. In fact, Betty's grandmother was another Edith O'Reilly. We believe that Betty chose this surname for herself and her daughter to avoid the stigma of being an unmarried mother. Betty brought the baby up in the home of her father, John Staples, who was a Methodist minister. Her mother, Ruth, died a number of years before Edith was born. The birth certificate for Edith states the father as unknown. There's a copy included in the folder for you."

Matt nodded his appreciation and Mason continued,

"So, Edith grew up in Croyston. She moved with her mother to Leambridge at the age of 11, after a fire destroyed their house and killed her grandfather. She must have been an intelligent child because she won a scholarship to Foxford Girls School; it's a private school attended by the daughters of the wealthy. At the age of 16, she transferred to Leambridge County Grammar to sit her A levels and also changed her name by deed poll to Eleanor Cashmore."

"Any idea why?" asked Matt.

"Nope," said Mason. "Nothing we've uncovered throws any light on why she would want to change her name. She appears to have been an excellent student throughout her schooling. She obtained outstanding grades and there are no recorded incidences of any bad behaviour. In fact, at Leambridge Grammar she received a commendation for bravery for attempting the rescue of a fellow pupil, who unfortunately drowned during an end-of-term dance. There's a report of the incident in the file," said Mason foreseeing Matt's question.

"After her A' Levels she attended Oxford University without taking a gap year. She studied law. During her time at Oxford, her mother died. Just after graduation she married Tom Bryant and had a child by him, a son named Max. I recommend that you speak to Tom if you can, so he can explain the circumstances to you of how he and Eleanor, as he knew her, came to be together. I tell you what," Mason scribbled a reminder on the pad in front of him, "I'll give him a ring and make an introduction for you. If he thinks talking to you might help track his son down, he'll be more than willing. Anyway, they divorced after about three years of marriage and then a couple of years after that, Eliza took the boy and moved to Dolford. That sounds wrong. She didn't take the boy as in abduct him, he lived with her after the divorce, but she shared custody with Tom. Tom still saw the boy regularly."

"It's all very confusing with this Edith, Eleanor, Eliza malarkey," said Matt.

"Tell me about it," said Mason. "Do you know something's just occurred to me? I don't know why I didn't see it before."

"What's that?" asked Matt.

"Whenever Ricky referred to Edith/Eliza whatever, he called her E. That was it. Just simply E. I think that's because she changed her name so often, he didn't want to get confused. Maybe it's not a coincidence that all her aliases start with an E. There are bound to be more names she's used that we've not discovered yet. I'm hoping you have more luck there than we've had.

"Right, where was I? So, she moved to Dolford to start a new job. Then Tom discovered he wasn't actually the boy's father – details in the folder," he put up a hand to prevent Matt's inevitable questioning, "and long story short, he lost contact with both Eliza and the boy and hasn't heard from either of them since."

"Is it true that this Tom didn't come forward until quite some time after you announced you were looking for Eliza, in connection with a murder? Why was that?" asked Matt.

"Well, he never realised that his first wife and Eliza Kelly were the same person," answered Mason. "I know," he continued, having registered the disbelieving look on Matt's face, "but honestly, she looked so different. He showed me photos and I agree with him that you wouldn't know they were one and the same. He didn't recognise her until we released the photofit." Mason prodded the file in front of Matt to indicate there was a copy inside. "And the photofit does look far more like the woman he married than Eliza Kelly ever did." Mason stopped to answer the phone on his desk and after a short conversation he carried on.

"Now at the beginning of July 1997, Eliza suddenly upped sticks and disappeared. She left her job and abandoned the house she was living in. Several extraordinary things happened around this time. She took Max out of school having told them he was going to live with his father. Now we know this wasn't Tom Bryant, but as we have been unable to establish who the boy's actual father was, we can't discount the fact that this may have been the case. As yet, no one's come forward, despite all the publicity and we've followed up every possible lead but hit a dead end."

"Sounds a bit dodgy to me," said Matt. "I take it this is the point where the boy disappears off the radar?"

"Um my thoughts exactly," said Mason. "I have a very bad feeling about the fate of young Max but nothing concrete to back up my suspicions. Around this same time, one of the partners at the firm where Eliza worked as a solicitor dropped dead in front of her; details in the folder," Mason once more tapped the file in front of Matt. "So, Eliza took compassionate leave, only she never went back. After she left, they discovered she'd stolen large amounts of money from several of her clients. She'd also allowed Ricky to live in a house that belonged to a deceased client. Someone tipped us lot off that Ricky was staying there; he was wanted for breaching his bail. Eliza was questioned but she denied all knowledge. There's a copy of the report in the file. None of Eleanor's wrongdoings were reported to the police as the company was concerned about its reputation. The two remaining partners, one of whom is now deceased and the other suffering from dementia, paid back the missing money. So, Eliza got off scot-free. We were given the information by Antonia Adebayo who worked in the offices at that time. She might agree to talk to you and her contact details are there." Once again Mason indicated the folder.

"So, like I say, Eliza just vanishes and we don't pick up her trail again until the year 2000, when she's working at a firm of solicitors around this area, Hillstanton, if I remember correctly. We have been unable to discover where she spent the interim years. At this time, she's calling herself Elizabeth Taylor. I know, I know," said Mason anticipating Matt's reaction. "We found her because a disciplinary tribunal struck her off after allegations of misconduct and dishonesty were proven against her. You can find all the details of the tribunal there in the file. She was also ordered to pay thousands of pounds in costs. She filed for bankruptcy, but we believe that Keith Kelly may have contributed financial help because she paid the fine. She and Keith had been in a relationship for a short time when the tribunal took place. He also helped her by allowing her to stay in his flat in London. Not long after this, she started using the name Eliza instead of Elizabeth and then of course she married Keith and became Eliza Kelly. And that, my son, brings you about up to speed. Fancy a pint?"

BBC Local News – Friday 10th July 1987

Police have named the 17-year-old girl who died on Wednesday during an end-of-term celebration at Leambridge County Grammar School, as Deborah White.

Deborah's body was discovered by another pupil in the swimming pool on the night of July 8th and, despite attempts to resuscitate her, she was pronounced dead at the scene. It is believed that the teenager got into difficulties after accidentally falling into the water.

Peter Jackson, Headteacher, released a statement expressing the profound shock and sadness felt by the whole school, and the wider community, on the death of a talented and immensely popular young lady, who, having just completed her A-levels, was looking forward to beginning her medical degree at Oxford University in September. He said that his thoughts, along with those of the Board of Governors, the staff and the pupils were with her family and friends at this very sad time.

~~~~~~

BBC Local News – Tuesday 28th July 1987

The funeral of 17-year-old Deborah White takes place today at 2:00 pm at St Peter's Church, Leambridge. The parents of the teenager have asked people attending the funeral to wear something bright, as they wish this to be a celebration of their daughter's life and a reflection of the light, she brought to the lives of everyone she met.

~~~~~~

Leambridge Chronicle – Thursday 16th July 1987

The parents of Deborah White, the teenager who tragically drowned just over a week ago in the swimming pool of her school, during end-of-term celebrations, have spoken of their gratitude to her friends and the staff of Leambridge Grammar for their kind thoughts, wishes and support at this terrible time.

They particularly expressed their thanks to Eleanor Cashmore, a close friend of their daughter's, who they called a hero for attempting to save Deborah's life by diving into the pool and supporting her fellow pupil until help arrived.

When interviewed, Eleanor said, "I don't feel like much of a hero. I just did what anyone would have done."

Asked about the events of the night, she told our reporter, "I had gone to use the toilets by the pool because I didn't think they would be as crowded as the others. I heard loud splashing noises whilst I was in the loo, so I looked in on the pool on my way out and there was Debbie lying face down with her clothes tangled all around her. I jumped in and tried to pull the clothing away from her face. I started shouting for help. It felt like ages before anyone came but I'm sure it was only minutes, and then loads of people were there helping to get her out of the water. I watched as they tried CPR, but I think I knew as soon as I saw her, just floating in the water, that she was dead. I'm certain she was dead before I got into the pool. It was horrible. I don't think I'll ever get over it."

~~~~~~
~~~~~~

BBC Radio 4

Series 2 – Episode 4 of Meet the Author with Edward Simmons – first broadcast April 2015

"Good evening and welcome to 'Meet the Author' with me Edward Simmons. Tonight, our first guest is Matt Dinsdale, renowned investigative journalist and author of the bestselling book 'An Innocent Man'. Good evening, Matt and welcome to the programme."

"Thank you very much, Edward, it's a pleasure to be here."

"So, your book Matt, 'An Innocent Man', currently top of the Sunday Times Best Seller List, is the account of your investigation into the murder of 8-year-old Sofia Dawson. Although this took place a number of years ago, I'm sure most of our listeners will be familiar with the case, but can you just give us some background information."

"Certainly, back in August 2010, the body of 8-year-old Sofia Dawson was found under a blanket in the garden shed of her family home. Sofia had been reported missing by her parents that afternoon. After going out to play, she failed to return home for her tea. Her body was discovered by the police later that evening. Without going into the whole story, her father was charged and then convicted of her murder. He was sentenced to life in prison with a minimum term of 15 years."

"And as a journalist, you were reporting on the case?"

"Yes, that's right. I was working for a local newspaper, and this was the first opportunity I had to work on a story with such public interest. Due to my local knowledge of the area, I was asked by several national newspapers to provide background information which I did, and I also received by-lines for some of the interviews I conducted with people who had a connection to the Dawson family. It was quite a coup for me."

"So, you had an interest in the case from day one and, as I understand it, you were never entirely convinced of Mr Dawson's guilt. So much so, that after the trial you continued with your own investigation, through which you unearthed new evidence that, as again I'm sure our listeners are aware, had startling consequences. Can you tell us what motivated you to continue your investigation?

Did you discover something in your background interviews that alerted you to the possibility that the case against Philip Dawson was flawed?"

"Well yes and no. There was no Eureka moment, but some red flags were certainly raised. Nothing substantial and certainly nothing concrete that I could approach the authorities with but enough, let's say niggles for want of a better word, that I couldn't quite let it go. As my wife would tell you I became slightly obsessed!" Laughter from the interviewer and interviewee. "And without wanting to sound too pious, I felt morally obligated to ascertain whether or not an innocent man had gone to prison."

"Can you explain with a little more detail?"

"Um, well, it's difficult to put into words, it was more just feelings, but for example, Sharon Dawson's reactions appeared wrong to me. They seemed a little bit off. Everything she said appeared to have been rehearsed. I have discovered through my line of work that it's virtually impossible for someone, especially someone who has been through a traumatic experience, to give the exact same account of the events every time they speak about it, to use exactly the same language and same order in every re-telling. People get confused, they miss bits out and they add bits later as they remember more.

Yet Sharon didn't change a single thing, not the words she used or the order in which she gave testimony. From her very first interview with the police up until she gave evidence in court, not once did she deviate from, what I was by that time calling, her script! Whereas Philip was absolutely devastated by what had happened and was completely unable to give a clear, lucid account of events. Because he was incoherent with grief, the man basically had a nervous breakdown, this was seen as a sign of his guilt and that didn't make sense to me. I didn't understand how being devastated over his only child's murder could be an indicator of his culpability."

"I'm right in saying, am I, that Mr Dawson didn't give evidence during his trial?"

"That's correct, yes. His barrister deemed him too emotionally unstable to withstand questioning from the prosecution, but with Sharon Dawson making such a credible witness, I felt that may have been a mistake on the defence team's part."

"Please explain."

"Well, there's no denying that Sharon's testimony was fundamental to the prosecution's case, they had very little else to go on. There was no physical evidence to link Phil, forensics were limited because obviously, all concerned parties lived together. So, the police relied heavily on Sharon's version of events and that's all the jury really had to go on. Despite the fact that Philip Dawson was presented as an upstanding citizen with no history of violence, his defence team could not prove his innocence. There was no evidence to show that he wasn't responsible. The whole case against him was almost too perfect if you see what I mean. From my point of view, I felt he was being set up."

"As was ultimately proven to be the case."

"Yes, Sharon and her policeman boyfriend had completely manipulated the whole situation."

"I don't want to give away too much as I'm sure you would much prefer for people to buy your book..."

"Oh absolutely!" More laughter.

"But even people familiar with the case are probably not aware of just how much you were involved with what happened next. Evidence uncovered by you ultimately led to Mr Dawson's conviction being overturned, his subsequent release from prison, the sensational arrest of Sharon Dawson and her lover DC Ian Hartwell, both of whom are currently on remand awaiting trial, charged not only with Sofia's murder but numerous other offences such as the falsifying of records, perjury, perverting the course of justice, etc. and an investigation into West Sussex Police Force's handling of the case. Which part of all of that are you, yourself, most proud of?"

"I've never really thought about it in that way. I mean at the end of the day a little girl lost her life in the most awful circumstances and a family has been completely torn apart by it all."

"Yes of course, a terrible tragedy occurred, and I am in no way diminishing that, but the fact that an innocent man is free, and the true guilty parties will be punished in due course must give you some sense of satisfaction."

"Oh yes, it certainly does, but I didn't do any of it on my own. A lot of people were involved. To be honest, I'm grateful I found someone who listened to me. It was fortuitous that when I first contacted the police with my suspicions about Sharon's testimony, I was directed to Superintendent Trevor Harrison. He took me seriously from the very start. If he hadn't, Phil would probably still be in prison, and I certainly wouldn't be sitting here."

"And isn't he also responsible for the overhauling of police procedures, after you highlighted the flaw which had enabled Hartwell to manipulate evidence, in order to cover up his guilt in the crime?"

"Yes, thanks to Trevor, systems have now been put in place to ensure no tampering like that performed by Hartwell can ever happen again."

"Something we should all be grateful for. Talking of gratitude, both Philip Dawson and his family have been very public in their praise of you. Could you give us an insight into why you never believed him capable of harming his daughter? I know you've already told us you felt he was set up but why did you feel that so strongly?"

"Again, it's hard to answer that as it was more of a feeling than anything else, but also out of everybody I spoke to not one person, not one single person, said a negative thing about Phil. They all told me, whether they were close to him or just an acquaintance, how he was a hard-working family man, a caring and devoted father. How Sofia was the light of his life. They all stated categorically that they could not believe he harmed his daughter. Also, during my interviews and background checks, I discovered him to be a very honest and open person and as silly as it sounds to make a judgement about someone who, at that moment in time, I had never actually even spoken to in person, I just couldn't believe that, for one, he could have committed such a heinous crime and for two, that he could have lied about it for so long. He just didn't seem capable of doing either.

"Sharon, on the other hand, was described to me as being the polar opposite of her husband. I was told consistently that she was a cold, unemotional and manipulative person. People were confounded when Philip was charged, and the thought hit me very early on, that if it was Sharon facing prosecution then people wouldn't have been anywhere near as shocked."

"Did you not think that maybe it had been an accident and Philip had never meant to harm his daughter, but after things had gone so far his only choice was to cover it up?"

"No, that didn't even cross my mind. Sofia's death was definitely no accident but even if it had been, Phil is just not the sort of person who can maintain a deception of that extent."

"Right, I see and finally, before we finish Matt, could you give our audience a taste of the new evidence that you found? Something that had been missed in the original investigation maybe. Something that proved to you that Sharon Dawson was lying about the events that had taken place."

"Well, I think the blanket was what first alerted me."

"The blanket that Sofia's body was wrapped in?"

"Yes. Sharon kept referring to it as Sofia's favourite blanket. She was insistent that Sofia had had it for years and that she couldn't sleep without it on her bed. Philip knew nothing about the blanket. When it was shown to him, he denied ever seeing it before. He told detectives that his daughter had a teddy bear that she took to bed with her every night, and this was backed up by other family members and the babysitter. No one else mentioned a blanket. It niggled away at me. Why was it so important to Sharon that the police knew the blanket was old? So, I investigated, and it turned out that this particular blanket had only been on the market for a couple of weeks before Sofia died. When the investigation was reopened, CCTV footage was discovered showing Hartwell purchasing the blanket. We believe that he brought it as a gift for Sofia."

"Fascinating! Thank you very much for that, Matt. So, listeners if that has piqued your interest then 'An Innocent Man' is available to buy from all retail outlets or from Matt's own website, where you will also find details of his other books written following the conclusion of several of his investigations. So Matt, what's next for you? You've published a number of articles lately, but will we soon see another book? Are you investigating anything at the moment?"

"No, nothing at the moment. I've just finished a book tour in the UK and will be travelling to the US shortly to begin a tour over there, so I'm a bit too busy right now to research something new. I need to find something that interests me, or as my wife would say, obsesses me, and so far, nothing has caught my eye. Well, that's not strictly true, something has but as it's an ongoing investigation, I think I need to wait for the outcome before I get too involved."

"Matt Dinsdale, thank you very much for coming in and talking to us."

"Thank you for having me."

"I'm certain that whatever you turn to next will have us all gripped just the same as 'An Innocent Man' has and I look forward to having you back on the programme to discuss it."

"Thank you very much, Edward. It's been a pleasure."

"After the news, we will be talking to actress and comedienne Jennifer Lewis about her upcoming autobiography."

~~~~~~

"And that," said Amy to Marcus as the recording came to an end, "is who Mason thinks we should meet with. Mason says he is a sound guy. He's met him a few times through his old boss, who is the Trevor Harrison that Dinsdale mentions in that interview. Matt Dinsdale apparently finds Eliza intriguing and he's interested in researching her background and her previous personas. According to Mason, he would appreciate my view of her as a person and any input I can give him about her life with Dad. What do you think? Should I meet with him?"
~~~~~~

4

Amy had chosen to meet Matt on a weekday morning at a quiet cafe in a side street off from the town centre. When Matt arrived, only a couple of tables were taken, and it was obvious that none of the cafe's current customers was Amy. He ordered a coffee at the counter and then took a seat at a table with a view of the entrance. As time passed, he began to think that he might have been stood up but when the waiter came to take his empty cup, he decided to hang on a bit longer and ordered himself a second drink. Five minutes later, the door swung open and a tallish woman with blonde hair swept up into a ponytail came through the door. Matt was certain that she must be Amy. He stood up and she smiled nervously at him as she came over.

"Matthew Dinsdale, I presume?"

"Please, call me Matt. I only get called Matthew when I'm in trouble."

Taking off her coat, Amy gave her order to the waiter and sat herself down facing Matt.

"I have to confess," she said, "that I almost bailed on you. I'm really nervous that I'm making a mistake in talking to you." Her cheeks turned red as she hurried on, anxious to get her point of view across before he could interrupt her.

"As I'm sure you can imagine we have been hounded by the press over the last year or so. They were unbearable when Dad first died. They camped outside our house and followed us, tailed us. We ended up sending the kids to stay with my husband's parents, it got so bad. We had to change all our phone numbers and have a police guard because journalists were phoning us and knocking on the door at all hours of the day and night, offering us ridiculously high sums of money to sell 'our story', to 'dish the dirt' on Zac. Then, when we wouldn't cooperate, they just made stuff up. They stalked all my relatives. They approached everyone who'd ever had any contact with Dad or with any member of his family. It was relentless. Poor Dad was trashed but we were advised not to respond. We were told that our best course of action was to stay quiet. Not to even attempt to defend him. It was so hard." She shook her head angrily and Matt could hear the bitterness in her voice. "Then it all died down," she continued, "only to erupt again when Eliza did a runner. The press were only really interested in sordid details so they could print sensational headlines to entice readers. We had no control over what they printed."

Amy paused for breath and Matt attempted to speak but she shook her head and put her hand up to stop him. Matt understood that he needed to let her finish what she wanted to say. He was certain that she had been fretting since she'd first agreed to meet with him and that it was vitally important to her that she got him to understand where she was coming from.

"DI Mason assures me," Amy continued, "that's not the kind of writing you do. You're not a tabloid journalist looking to besmirch my father. He said that you would approach the issues deferentially and sensitively. Before I speak with you, I need to know that's true. I've read some of your work and I agree with how Mason describes your writing, but I need to know what you are hoping to achieve with this book as regards my father. Although I'm sure you won't want to admit it, are you just trying to gain from our misery?"

Matt again tried to break in and say something, but Amy still wasn't finished.

"I have absolutely no intention of contributing to the grief that people who were close to my father are going through. I won't be a part of something that continues to promote the lies that have already been told about him. All I am really interested in is justice for my father and to exonerate him, clearing his name. Ever since Eliza has been accused of his murder, I've been waiting for the untruths that she told about him to be corrected in the press, but of course, nothing of the sort has happened." Amy was getting visibly upset now, her eyes filling up. "They just keep perpetuating the lies," she continued tearfully "and the public is still convinced that he was an abuser, a violent man, and that simply isn't true."

She finally stopped her tirade as a waitress brought her order to the table and Matt took the opportunity to speak for the first time since Amy had sat down. Leaning across the table towards her he spoke softly.

"Firstly, I would like to offer you my most sincere condolences on the loss of your father. I cannot begin to imagine what it must be like for you to lose him under the most horrific of circumstances, and all that you have had to deal with since. It must have been unbearable trying to come to terms with what your brother had done but then to discover that it was your stepmother and not your brother who was responsible! Well, I'm not even going to pretend that I have any idea what that must have been like for you. And I can guarantee you that I have no interest in adding to your own or your family's grief. As to whether your father was an abuser or not, I have no preconceived conceptions, but I promise you I will tell the truth about what I find. I'm not going to lie to you; if I find proof that he was violent towards Eliza then I will write about it." Seeing the look of horror on Amy's face, Matt hurried on. "But I also promise that if I uncover no evidence at all of any aggression on your father's part, I will make that very clear in what I write. I know it sounds corny, but I am only interested in writing the truth. I think the story is sensational enough without the need to embellish it. Does that sound fair?"

Amy nodded and Matt continued in an effort to reassure her. "I admit I have a morbid fascination with the case but that is only because of the behaviour of Eliza. To begin with, after your father died, to the general public she appeared to be a devoted wife and mother, which as we now know couldn't have been further from the truth. I would like to discover the real Eliza, the woman who murdered her husband and framed her son. That to me is the story, not your dad. If it's any consolation, from what I've researched so far, I only see your father as a victim. I've spoken to a number of people who knew your father personally and I have to say I believe you are telling the truth about him being a non-violent man. Nobody I have spoken to has given the slightest hint that he was anything other than a genuinely decent human being. I believe there is no better way to clear his name than to tell his side of the story and you are the person who is best placed to do that."

Amy nodded her thanks to him as she mopped her eyes with a paper napkin. Matt reached into his laptop bag and pulled out a couple of copies of books that he had written including 'An Innocent Man'. Setting them down on the table in front of Amy, he said,

"I brought these along so you could take them away and read them. They will show you my writing style, and how I conduct interviews with the victim's family members, people in a similar situation to yourself. Hopefully, they will help dispel your fears."

Amy gave a little laugh. "Actually, as I mentioned before, I've read both of these and almost all of your other work," she confessed. "Some I'd read before Mason told me of your interest in Dad. I've also watched or listened to lots of your interviews."

"So, you've been stalking me!" said Matt jokingly.

"To be honest, I thoroughly enjoyed the books and so did Marcus, my husband. But how you've written other people's stories doesn't necessarily mean you will treat our story in the same way, and that's the reason I wanted to meet you in person before I agreed to participate. I had to convey to you how imperative it is to me and my family that you don't just do a hatchet job on my dad. I'm pleased to say you've reassured me about that in what you've said here today. So, yes, I do agree to be interviewed."

Matt let out a sigh of relief. "Thank you," he said.

"So, what happens now?" asked Amy.

"Well, first of all, we need to decide where the interview should take place, where you would feel most comfortable talking. For some of my interviewees that has been in their own home, some prefer to come to me, others prefer a public space. That decision will be entirely yours."

Seeing Amy trying to determine which option she'd prefer he carried on quickly.

"You don't have to choose straight away. We can sort that out later. As regards the actual interview, to start with I'll be asking for some background information on your father, the usual bio-type stuff. You know, where he was born, his career, his family, how did he meet your Mum? I already know a lot about him from the usual sources, the internet, interviews he did, articles he contributed to or that have been written about him. But in my experience, personal perspectives are always better. They have so much more depth. I'd like you to tell me about your childhood. What was it like growing up with a famous father? Then we'll move on to how Eliza came into his life. I'm hoping you'll be willing to give me some background on her as information about her is sparse."

Amy shook her head, "I don't know much I'm afraid and I'm not sure what I know is true."

"Doesn't matter," continued Matt. "You'd be surprised at how much you'll be able to tell me. Again, I'll need the usual details. How she and your father met. What their relationship was like from your perspective. We'll talk about your own relationship with her and how you saw her relationship with other family members. I'd like your opinion of her as a stepmother, and also as a mother to Zac. I'll warn you now, we will discuss some very personal stuff. Other people I've interviewed have likened it to a therapy session but without the therapist. I appreciate that after everything that's happened, talking about Eliza might be disturbing for you, but I'm after as much detail as you can give me. She really is a fascinating character." Matt saw Amy wince. "Sorry," he said, "poor choice of words. But let me explain why I said that. This case caught my attention from the very beginning. The age of your brother…"

"Half-brother," said Amy.

"Of course, half-brother," Matt corrected himself. "It was his age that caught my attention. I couldn't believe that such a young child could be capable of causing such harm. So, I carried out some research and I discovered that child killers are not as uncommon as you might think and that got me excited." This time it was Matt that winced when he realised what he'd said.

'Come on Matt,' he thought to himself, *'for someone who is supposed to be a word smith you're making a pig's ear of this.'* He decided honesty was the best policy.

"I'm making a pig's ear of this," he told Amy. "I don't want to offend you in any way, but I have to be honest. It's true, the story excited me from the moment I first heard about it. A nine-year-old boy killing his father *is* an exciting story for a journalist."

He looked up to see how Amy was reacting and taking heart from the fact that she was nodding, he carried on. "I was already thinking along the lines of a book that would be based on children who kill their parents. And then, the news broke that the police now believed that Eliza was the culprit and that she was on the run. Even the manner in which she'd fled, still making time to empty the house. From my perspective, it was a fascinating affair. A mother who willingly allowed her son to take the blame for her crime. A son she then completely abandons. How could she do that? Why did she do that? I was eagerly awaiting her arrest. I needed the case to go to trial to get the answers I was looking for. But as you well know, she wasn't arrested. She seemed to have disappeared off the face of the Earth. Then my friend Trevor, who has close connections to DI Mason, told me that the case was being wound down. The police were not optimistic about finding Eliza any time soon. That's when I decided to try to find answers myself. When I start to obsess over a story that's when I know I can write a good book, and I was obsessed with this case."

"I'd like those questions answered too!" said Amy.

"I'm sure," said Matt. "I promise to keep you apprised of what I uncover, and I'll allow you to read everything before it's published. That is if it ever gets published. There are no guarantees you know."

He handed Amy his business card.

"When you're ready, give me a ring and we'll arrange a suitable time and place for the interview. Could I ask that you bring along photographs or anything else that you think might be relevant to show me? Visual aids can really help unlock memories and with your permission, there might be some items I would like to publish, like a wedding photograph, that sort of thing. Also, if possible, could you put together a list of other people who knew Eliza and your dad and who might be willing to talk to me?"

"I'll see what I can do," promised Amy.

Interview with Dale White

(Extract taken from 'The Evil Underneath; the true story of the murder of Keith Kelly', as told by award-winning author, Matt Dinsdale)

My name is Dale White, and I am the younger brother of Debbie White who drowned in her school's swimming pool in July 1987. I was 14 years old at the time. I remember the night it happened. I woke up when the police came around. They took my parents to the hospital and my aunt came to sit with me. I didn't go back to bed.

It was later in the morning when my parents returned and broke the news to me that Debbie had died. It didn't sink in at first.

The next few days are a bit of a blur. I remember lots of people coming in and out of the house. There was no routine. We ate some meals together but mostly I ate on my own. I didn't go to school. Friends and relatives took turns staying with us. My parents were devastated. I remember my mum spent a lot of time in bed. The funeral was really hard. I haven't retained many memories of it. I know we all wore something brightly coloured in memory of Debbie. She was such a bright and bubbly girl.

My strongest memories are of the fun we had together. You asked me what I remember about Eleanor. I remember her being around the house a lot after Debbie died but I don't remember seeing her before that. She was supposedly one of Debbie's best friends, but I'm certain I had never seen her before the accident. Debbie had lots of friends, most of whom she had grown up with. They were familiar to all of us. Sammy, Danielle, Christine and Julie to name just a few. Sammy was her best friend. They did everything together. But I really don't remember seeing Eleanor until after Debbie had died and as far as I know Mum and Dad felt the same. They were obviously grateful to her because she tried so hard to save Debbie and I think that's why they let her in when she kept turning up at the door. They also asked her to do a reading at Debbie's funeral. Including her on the day was their way of saying thank you for what she'd done.

We assumed that once the funeral was over, she would stop coming round to visit but if anything, she came more often. My mum said later that she felt Eleanor deliberately came round to upset her. She would say things, knowing that they would set my mum off and make her cry. And she was obsessed with Debbie. She would ask to go up to Debbie's room and once my nan caught her in Debbie's bed. It was all a bit creepy. She wanted to borrow some of Debbie's clothes, but my mum said no. Then a couple of weeks later, one of the local papers had her photo in it, because she'd won a bravery award or something and she was wearing Debbie's favourite jacket in the photo. My mum was convinced it was Debbie's. She was positive it had been in Debbie's wardrobe because she had contemplated burying her in it. She searched everywhere but the jacket was no longer in our house. Eleanor had definitely stolen it. That was the final straw as far as my parents were concerned. My dad said there was something not right with the girl. The next time she turned up at the door my dad told her she was no longer welcome, and I never saw her again.

5

Amy mulled over where it would be best to conduct her interview with Matt and ruled out her own home. The house originally belonged to Amy's mother who inherited it from her parents. It had been their family home, the one Amy and her brother Adam grew up in and the one her father stayed living in after her mother died. He also lived there with Eliza when they were first married. There were too many memories associated with the house, Amy decided, some really good and some really bad.

Although she knew it was inevitable that reliving all that had happened to her recently would be upsetting, she believed it would be easier if she wasn't surrounded by reminders and memories of both the parents she had lost. She also dismissed the idea of meeting in a public place. She was certain that getting upset and crying in front of Matt would be difficult enough without doing so in front of the world at large.

Matt suggested they meet at his house where he had an office, but she didn't feel comfortable with that. She felt she didn't know him well enough. So, they settled on the neutral territory of an office at Matt's publishers. No distractions and no interruptions. And that's where she found herself now. Sipping on a very bitter coffee delivered by a disgruntled young girl who, Amy deduced, was probably on work experience and had been expecting far grander assignments than coffee making.

Matt explained to Amy that he would be recording the interview as well as taking notes. He also asked her to try to tell him about the events that had happened without prejudice.

"What do you mean?" she asked.

"I know it's going to be very difficult because I appreciate how much you must hate Eliza," said Matt, "but I want you to be honest. Tell me what your impressions of her were when you first met her without the revulsion that you must currently feel impacting on those memories."

"I'll do my best," said Amy. "But if you want me to be honest, I have to confess, I disliked her from the moment I met her. Before we start," she said rummaging inside the large shoulder bag that was hanging off the side of her chair, "these are for you."

She pulled a manilla folder and a large brown envelope from inside the bag. She passed the envelope across the table to him first.

"Feel free to use any of the photographs in there," she told him, "I've cleared it with all the people who appear in them, except obviously Eliza. I've also written the names of people, their relationship with Dad and the date the photo was taken on the back of each one. Then in this folder are the names of all the people I've been in contact with who have agreed to speak to you. Can I just run through the list with you quickly, so I can explain who they are and why I think you should talk to them?"

Matt nodded. "Please do," he said sounding amused. "I'm not used to such efficiency."

Amy shot him a look to see if he was being sarcastic, but she didn't think he was.

"To start with there's my Uncle John and Aunt Maggie. They are Dad's only living relatives. John is, or rather was, Dad's older brother. He's 5 or 6 years older I think but he certainly remembers Dad being born. He can give you so much more information about Dad's childhood than I can and about my parents' relationship. He'll also be able to tell you about how Dad's career started. Obviously, they both met Eliza, but they didn't take to her, so they hardly saw her, but I'll let them explain all that to you.

"I've included Kath and Terry Lomas. They were my parents' closest friends, and they are more like Aunty and Uncle to me and Adam. They are probably the people who had the most dealings with Dad and Eliza as a couple. I know for a fact that Kath is very keen to talk to you and give you her opinion of Eliza," Amy gave Matt a grin. "Kath is quite a character. She certainly calls a spade a spade and I think you'll enjoy meeting her.

"Dad's solicitor, Tony Philips, is also a family friend and so he will be able to talk about Dad from both a personal and a professional perspective, which I think might be quite useful to you."

Matt couldn't help but be impressed by how much thought Amy had put into this list.

"Now, as well as Dad's agent, Marsha Scott-Williams, I've also included people who Dad worked with. People from both in front of and behind the camera and people who worked with him on everything from soap operas to Shakespeare. I've spoken to them all, to explain who you are and why you'll be contacting them. As you can imagine, after all the rubbish that has been written about Dad, they are wary of who they talk to. As well as about Dad, Marsha will be a good person to talk to about Eliza as she had a few dealings with her, none of them particularly pleasant. Right, I think that's it." Amy passed the folder over to Matt. "So how do we do this? Where do you want me to begin?"

While Amy had been taking him through her list, Matt sifted through the photographs from the envelope and spread them out on the table in front of him.

"Before we start can I just say, Wow and thank you," said Matt. "I don't think anyone has ever put as much effort into providing me with contacts to talk to and these photos are perfect."

Amy beamed back at him. She'd always been a sucker for praise.

"Right, we really should be getting started. The best way to do this is for you to just talk to me," Matt advised her. "Start with telling me about your father, about your childhood. What was it like growing up with a famous parent? What was life like after your mum died? Then we can build up to Eliza and you can tell me what's happened to you over the last couple of years. If I need to clarify something or if there's a question I want to ask, then I'll stop you, but other than that, I'd like you to just tell it in your own way. In your own words."

Amy nodded, took a deep breath and began. She talked about how happy her childhood was and how devoted her mother and father were to each other and to their family.

"I know it's easy to look back and only remember the good times, especially after losing my mother and what happened with Dad, but my childhood really was idyllic.

"We lived in the same farmhouse that my mother grew up in. My mum inherited it from her parents who died before me and my brother

Adam were born. They'd been in their 40s when they had my mum and had never expected to have children. My mum told me it made her sad that they missed out on being grandparents as they would have adored having grandchildren. I fully understand how she felt now, knowing how much my mum has missed and what a fantastic grandmother she would have been. It also makes losing Dad all the more devastating as he was an amazing grandad. Sorry, I'm going off topic.

"When her parents died, Mum sold the farm but kept the house and that's where we all lived as a family, although Dad also kept a flat in London, to be near his work. He would stay at the flat during the week when he was filming and come home at weekends or whenever he had a break.

"So, Adam and I had the best of both worlds. We lived in a house surrounded by the most glorious countryside where we were free to roam, situated not far from the seaside, where we spent loads of time, but we also had access to the heart of London and all there is to see and do there. Oh, and later on, Dad bought an apartment in Spain where we spent most of our summer holidays. We were incredibly lucky.

"Like I say, I had a really happy childhood. I remember my parents being besotted with each other to the point of embarrassment. Unlike my friends' parents, they were not afraid to be demonstrative with each other. They would kiss each other hello and goodbye and they held hands whenever they were out walking. There was always music playing in the house and I would often walk into a room to find Mum and Dad dancing together. It's those memories I think about when I'm really sad. It reminds me of how happy they were; how much they meant to each other."

"How did your parents meet?" asked Matt.

"At a gig of a local band. They danced together and went for a drink afterwards. They had a couple of dates after that, but Mum told me she wasn't sure about him," Amy smiled as she continued. "He was a bit full of himself, being an actor, albeit a struggling one. He was only doing local theatre at the time. He hadn't broken into television yet. She was contemplating breaking up with him but then one of her horses developed colic on a night when she'd agreed to go out with him. When he arrived to pick her up and she told him the reason as to why she couldn't go, he stayed to help with the horse. The only way for a horse to survive colic is for it to stay upright. It's best to keep walking them around so that they can't lie down. Dad ended up staying all night helping Mum. Between them they kept the horse moving and when the vet came back out and gave the all-clear both of them cried. That's when Mum said she knew that he was the right man for her. Dad always said he was sure they wouldn't have stayed together if the horse had died."

"What was it like growing up with a famous father?" Matt asked.

"That's a bit hard to answer," said Amy. "Seeing as how I didn't know any different. I suppose when Dad first started appearing regularly on the telly, there was some kudos attached to it at school, but that soon wore off. Mostly, I remember being embarrassed about it. You know the kids at school used to tease me and Adam if Dad's character did something silly, which he often did! Or they would take the mickey if he kissed someone on screen. It could all be a bit awkward really. But then there were a lot of perks too. We got to do fun things that perhaps weren't available to other kids. You know, like we went to film premiers and we met some famous people that sort of thing. But Dad wasn't that famous. It wasn't like he was a major film star and Mum shied away from publicity as much as she could. I mean she would go to award ceremonies and premiers and things like that with him, but she never really enjoyed them. Not like Eliza. My Uncle Terry used to say that Eliza would go to the opening of a crisp packet! Eliza and Mum were total opposites. Mum certainly never courted fame. We never had to do any of those awful photo shoots for the celebrity magazines that Eliza forced on Dad and Zac. Don't get me wrong, my mum loved to socialise and she would use any excuse to throw a party, but most of my parents' friends had nothing to do with show business.

"On the whole, I would say my parents kept both Adam and me pretty grounded. We always felt very loved, and we never went without anything, but I also don't think we were particularly spoilt. I don't know what else to tell you. It was all normal and boring, I'm afraid. Nothing sensational or traumatic happened during my upbringing. I left home to go to university, which is where I met my husband, Marcus, and we got married just before Mum was diagnosed. She died in 1998 and of course that changed everything."

Amy talked for a while about losing her mum and how difficult it had been for the whole family, especially her father.

"When Mum died, he fell to pieces. Marcus and I were living in Upton so we weren't too far away, and we tried to spend as much time with him as we could. Adam was at Uni but spent all his holidays with Dad. It wasn't a good time for any of us. Poor Dad had to take a break from work. He was very depressed. I'd go round some days, and it was obvious he'd struggled to even get out of bed. He'd make an effort, but it was very hard for him. I'd notice things like he'd have shaved, but only one-half of his face. It was so sad. We were all grieving. We had a lot of help; friends and family, people rallied around us, you know how it is. As time went on, we gradually started to pull ourselves together. Tried to get back to a bit of normality. Dad returned to work, which I think helped him a lot.

"When I got pregnant with Rory he was over the moon. He really tried to be there for all of us, but I could tell he was lonely. It was different for me; I had Marcus and was starting my family. Adam finished Uni and went travelling. As I said, we all tried to include him as much as possible, but he still went home to an empty house every night.

"Dad must have been a widower for 6 maybe 7 years when he met Eliza. He'd been on a few dates before then but nothing serious. Nothing that lasted more than a few weeks. He had a lot of friends who were women. Friends he could ask to be his plus one for social functions, but there was no romance between them. Then all of a sudden, he started mentioning a name. It was very noticeable that this 'Eliza' kept cropping up in conversation. He began to mention her more and more often. It was "Eliza thinks this", "Eliza agrees with me", and "Eliza says that".

I was pleased for him. I thought it was about time he met someone else. I mean he'd been on his own for a long time by then. I was very keen to learn all I could about his new lady friend, but Dad was a bit cagey. He told me they'd met at a hotel where she was working behind the bar. They had felt an immediate connection. He told me a lot about how much he liked her and how wonderful she was, but he told me very little of substance about her. If I asked questions like has she been married? Does she have kids? He would deflect and not give a straight answer.

"Everything I learnt about their relationship came piecemeal. Then he let slip that she was staying in his London flat. I was a little taken aback. Things seemed to have progressed very quickly, and I couldn't help but express my concern. He assured me it wasn't like that. His exact description was that she had "fallen on hard times" and he was just being a good friend and helping her out by letting her stay. Gradually, he revealed more of the story behind her moving in. She was a solicitor who had been working at a firm owned by a father and son. The son had been stealing from the company and, this is where I have heard so many different versions both from Dad and from Eliza herself, that I have no idea what's true, either Eliza took the blame for the sake of the father to spare him having to sack his son or else the son framed Eliza. I'm really not sure what actually happened but she ended up barred for life from practising and she had to pay a huge fine. I actually think my dad might have paid this for her. The outcome was that she was bankrupt and blacklisted.

"This wasn't the only part of her life where the story changed numerous times. For example, when they first met, I know for a fact that Dad told me she was working behind the bar in a hotel in Bathem where he was filming The Whitchurch Murders. He said the bar work was only temporary to tide her over until she found something better. However, when I first met Eliza, she told me she had been managing the hotel and was only behind the bar that night because they were short-staffed. Then, when she met my dad's brother and his wife for the first time, she told my Aunt Maggie that she had been a guest at the hotel when she and Dad met. And that was what Eliza was like. She never told you the same thing twice. And she lied. She constantly lied or exaggerated, and it used to really piss me off. Sorry to swear. As my Gran used to say, 'That woman couldn't lie straight in bed!' To say Granny disliked Eliza would be an understatement. She certainly made her feelings known, but that's a whole other story.

"Going back to the solicitor's business, it was weird. The story kept changing and I was so intrigued to know what had actually happened that I tried some detective work of my own, although it felt wrong going behind Dad's back to investigate his new wife. I didn't get very far as none of the firms that I contacted had ever had an Eliza Taylor working for them. I came to a dead end.

"I used to get very het up over her barefaced lies but if I took her to task, it only upset my dad. Marcus used to tell me to let it go. 'What does it matter?' he'd say. 'Where's the harm?' But I felt it was wrong. I thought there was a lot about her past she was hiding. I'm not just saying that in hindsight. Marcus will tell you it bothered me from the start.

"Anyway, I'm jumping ahead. Despite my dad saying he was just being a good friend by letting Eliza stay in the flat, you could tell he was smitten with her and as you can imagine, I was very keen to meet the woman who had swept him off his feet. But Dad had filming commitments in America, and he had to fly out before we had time to arrange a get-together. He didn't know exactly how long he'd be gone, but he told me he would introduce me to Eliza as soon as he got back. That all sounds normal, doesn't it? So, imagine how I felt when the next time I heard from Dad he was ringing me from Los Angeles, as pissed as a fart, to tell me that he and Eliza had gotten married. I thought it was some sort of joke, but I couldn't see what was funny. Dad drank, but he very rarely got drunk, so I thought it must be a silly prank that he thought was amusing because he was so pissed. I was dumbstruck. I don't remember exactly what I said but it was something banal like 'I didn't even know Eliza was joining you over there.' He just laughed and said he would explain everything when he got home. He sounded hurt by my lack of enthusiasm so when he asked me if I was going to congratulate him, I did, but I wasn't happy for them. Adam phoned me within the hour. He'd received a similar call. He was working in Australia, but he talked to Dad a lot on Skype, and he probably knew more about Eliza than I did, but he was as shocked as I was. We didn't know what to make of it. I mean we wanted to support our dad and if he had met someone special then we were happy for him, but why the rush? Why get married so quickly? Were they in fact married or was it just a joke?

"I expected Dad to call me the next day basically to apologise for making such an ass of himself. But I didn't hear from him. I tried getting hold of him over the next few days, but he didn't answer and didn't call back. When I finally managed to speak to him, he apologised saying he'd been busy filming, but I think we both knew he had been avoiding me. He told me Eliza was back in London and that he would be returning to the UK in two weeks, which coincided nicely with

Adam coming home for a visit. On his return, Dad said he would be moving Eliza down to live in the farmhouse with him. When Adam heard about this, he messaged me and asked if he could stay with me. He didn't like the idea of sharing the house with the newlyweds, especially as he had yet to meet the wife!

"Adam and I had a few days together before Dad came home and we spent a fair amount of time discussing the situation. We both admitted to feeling hurt and maybe even a little betrayed that Dad had married a woman that he hadn't even introduced us to. I think any child in our situation, no matter how old they are, would feel the same. We were also worried that they had taken such a big step having only known each other for such a short time. However, we acknowledged that they were both adults and entitled to live their lives how they pleased. Dad had been alone for such a long time, and he wasn't suited to being single. All Adam and I wanted was for him to be happy and enjoy life. We had seen him at his lowest when Mum died, and it was heartbreaking. He'd done a really good job of pulling himself together, but you could tell that he was still sad and incredibly lonely. The change in his demeanour when Eliza entered his life was profound. What right did we have to deny him such happiness? Not that either of us ever would. We both agreed that we would do everything in our power to welcome Eliza into our family. If Dad was happy then we were happy for both of them. Ha, it's hard now to remember that we ever felt that way!"

Amy paused for a moment and Matt could tell she was gathering her thoughts and deciding the best way to continue.

"If I could tell you that my relationship with Eliza deteriorated over a period of time, I think I would feel better about myself. But there is no point in talking to you and not being completely honest. I didn't like Eliza from the very first moment I met her.

"Dad invited all of us round for a meal but only Adam and I went. Marcus and I agreed that having the kids there would have made a difficult situation more stressful. They would be constantly demanding my attention and that would make it harder for me to relax. I was already starting to feel nervous. I'm not sure what bothered me more, that I wouldn't like Eliza or that she wouldn't like me.

"In my head, I had built up a picture of Eliza. I don't mean what she looked like, although Dad had always waxed lyrical about her looks, but more the sort of person she would be. The sort of woman my dad would be attracted to. I wasn't expecting her to be an exact replica of my mum. Nothing like that. But I assumed there would be similar personality traits between them. As the time to meet grew nearer, I started to experience real butterflies. I anticipated there would be some awkwardness to start with. I was expecting Eliza to be quite shy and maybe even a little abashed, given the fact that she had basically eloped with my dad. Of course, she was nothing of the sort."

Matt broke in for a moment. "Take yourself back to that first meeting," he said. "Try and remember exactly what your first impression was upon seeing her. What was your first conversation like?"

"I suppose the very first thing that struck me was her age. Dad had told me that Eliza was younger than him, but he hadn't said just how much younger. I thought he was talking about a couple of years difference between them, and it turned out that she was only five years older than me! That was a shock I have to say. She was definitely attractive, not stunningly beautiful, but still very pretty. She was impeccably groomed and immaculately dressed. I suppose looking back I would say I was a little intimidated by her appearance at that first meeting.

"She oozed self-confidence. She greeted both Adam and me cordially enough but there was an underlying air of contempt. Like she was looking down on us. It wasn't just me who felt that. Adam picked up on it too. The only person who seemed oblivious to it was my dad.

"The next thing that really stood out for me was her voice. It's hard to explain but it sounded false, as if she was putting it on. It was very breathy and to me, she put emphasis on the wrong words and her pauses, which she used for dramatic effect, were in the wrong places. She sounded like a really bad actress, a cockney trying to talk posh, and her choice of words was so over the top. Everything was either 'divine' or 'to die for'. I lost count of how many times she said 'fabulous darling' when she was talking to me. I found her voice grating from the first time I heard it, and my opinion never changed. When I got to know her better and we had a few run-ins, her posh accent would slip without her noticing, and there was a definite South London twang. I found that very amusing.

"It's hard to remember exactly how I felt but there was a definite sense of, 'What on earth does she see in my dad?' and, 'What on earth does he see in her?' I couldn't for the life of me fathom what the attraction was between them.

"You know when I look back and remember what Mum was like and how good she and Dad were together, I find it impossible to understand what Dad ever saw in Eliza. I know I'm reflecting on the difference between them, but I think it's important to make it clear how much I disliked Eliza from the start, and how I never got used to the fact that she was the person my dad had chosen to marry and spend the rest of his life with. Maybe there was a side to her that Dad knew, and I just never got to see. Well not just me but everyone else too. Nobody that I know who met her liked her. So, what hold did she have over Dad? I mean all the men fancied her. To start with anyway. She was that sort of woman you know – what do they call it? A femme fatal. Poor Marcus was certainly bowled over by her to start with. But with women it was different. She gave off a really bad vibe and I think most women picked up on that. Men, like Marcus, would say women were jealous of her but that's not true. She was just horrible. I didn't take to her when Dad first introduced us and that's not because of the circumstances. I tried really hard for Dad's sake to like her, to get on with her, but she was just a nasty piece of work. There's no other way of putting it. She and Mum were chalk and cheese. Eliza was Mum's antithesis. Dad couldn't have picked anyone more different. Maybe that's what appealed to him, who knows? And of course, she was a lot younger than him so maybe it was an ego thing?

"The only man who didn't instantly fall under her spell was Adam. During that first meeting, she hardly looked in my direction, but she did try hard with Adam. Whereas she didn't ask me a single question about my life, she bombarded Adam with questions and appeared to find his answers fascinating. She overtly flirted with him but when it didn't have the desired effect, I think the penny dropped and from then on, she treated him with the same disdain as she did me. Adam's gay you see, and I think that made him immune to her charms.

"Anyway, to go back to that first meeting, Dad was understandably nervous. It was so important to him that Adam and I took to Eliza. He did nothing but sing her praises; I think in an attempt to show her in the best possible light. He told us how clever she was, how entertaining she could be. He said that to him she was the best thing since sliced bread. I lost count of the number of times he referred to himself as lucky. 'Lucky to have met her, lucky she said yes when he proposed, lucky that someone who could have their pick of men, chose him'. He said that all the men he'd introduced Eliza to were jealous of him. Most women would have modestly tried to play down these over-the-top compliments but to my surprise, Eliza joined in. She boasted that men had always found her attractive. It was a problem she had to put up with all her life. Poor dear! She also told us that all women apparently, especially those she had met when she joined Dad in America, were envious of her looks and her dress sense. She bragged about how they wanted to know who her stylist was and when she told them she dressed herself, they all begged her to help them."

Matt assumed the funny voice Amy had put on whilst speaking for Eliza was an imitation of the woman's speaking style. If Amy's representation was in any way accurate, then Eliza really did speak in an infuriating manner.

"It was all starting to get a bit nauseating. Adam and I both attempted to move the conversation on from 'how wonderful is Eliza' and talk about something, anything else, but neither of them was having it.

"We heard all about the wedding and if either of us was expecting some sort of apology for the way they rushed into it, keeping us completely in the dark, then we were left wanting. They seemed completely oblivious to the fact that Adam or I might feel hurt or offended at being left out of their plans. Dad's behaviour around Eliza was also weird. He fussed about her as if she was some fragile object. Constantly checking if she was comfortable. Was she too hot? Too cold? Hungry? Thirsty? The way he was acting annoyed me, but it got to Eliza too and she snapped at him a few times.

"Also, she was quite derogatory when she spoke about him. I thought that very telling. If she was confident and comfortable enough to have a go at Dad in front of us at our very first meeting, then how did she treat him when they were alone? It certainly showed that she couldn't be worried about what sort of impression she was making.

"So, from my point of view, this first meeting was not going well and I could tell from Adam's face that he felt the same. Dad had cooked a meal for us and when we sat down at the table to eat, I realised what a mistake we had made by not meeting on more neutral territory. We had shared so many Sunday dinners, celebratory meals, so many Christmas dinners at this table with Mum and now this horrible woman was sitting in what used to be Mum's chair. I didn't want anyone to see that I was getting upset because I didn't want to have to explain why.

"To keep the conversation moving, I plied Eliza with questions. Her answers were conceited and pretentious but annoyingly she avoided giving away much about her past. She definitely mentioned she'd been married once before but I don't recall if she mentioned having a son. The police were asking me about it recently, but I honestly can't remember. I know Dad told me at a later date, that Eliza had a child whom she had no contact with, but I don't think Eliza ever said anything directly to me about it. I must have asked about children but infuriatingly I can't remember her response, and neither can Adam, which isn't surprising considering how much he drank!

"The conversation was drying up. I was running out of questions and those I did ask received very curt answers. Eliza didn't help. She didn't ask me a single thing. Neither Dad nor Adam was contributing to the conversation. It was a very uncomfortable meal. I was tempted to start drinking and order a taxi home. I had refused any alcohol up to that point making the excuse that I was driving but in reality, I didn't risk loosening my tongue. Adam wasn't so bothered and had been drinking steadily. I could tell he was struggling not to be rude to Eliza now. He was becoming more and more sarcastic. I noticed that Eliza also wasn't drinking, and I mentioned it and that's when she broke the news that she was in fact… pregnant!

"There was a deafening silence as Adam and I struggled to take in this latest unexpected announcement. Talk about dropping a bombshell. We both looked at Dad for confirmation, but he didn't need to say anything, the sheepish look on his face said it all. Neither of us could bring ourselves to congratulate them. Adam's immediate reaction was to ask how on earth that could be possible, seeing as Dad had had the snip and, understandably, both Dad and Eliza took offence at his tone. It crossed my mind that the baby might not be Dad's but in answer to Adam's question, Dad told us he had had himself checked and his vasectomy had failed. *What a way to start a relationship*, I thought to myself, h*aving to check that you haven't been cheated on!'* Still, it explained the rushed wedding and Dad being so attentive to Eliza's wellbeing.

"As if the day hadn't been bad enough, things deteriorated rather rapidly from that point. It was definitely time to leave before things were said that would later be regretted. Pointedly telling Eliza not to get up, I practically shoved Adam out the door, so he had no chance to say anything rude to her. Dad came out to the car with us, but we didn't speak about Eliza or the baby. I had no idea what to say about it all.

"Dad didn't offer me a goodbye hug which was most unusual and a sure sign of how upset with us he was. Before I got in the car, I asked him when he would be collecting his two dogs. I always looked after them at my house when he was away because they were both rescue dogs and they got really distressed if they had to go back into kennels. Dad had taken them on after Mum died and often credited them with keeping him going on days when he couldn't see a point to it all. He loved those dogs to bits and normally would pick them up as soon as he came home. Now he looked embarrassed.

'I've been meaning to talk to you about that,' he said. 'I was wondering if you could keep hold of them?'

'Of course,' I replied. 'How long for?'

'Indefinitely,' he said. 'Eliza is terrified of dogs. She hates them.'

"I climbed into the car and slammed the door. That for me was the final straw. What an awful way to end a horrendous day. Dad waved as we drove off but neither Adam nor I acknowledged it. We no longer cared if we were acting like kids instead of adults. We both instinctively knew that our relationship with our dad was broken."

This seemed to Matt to be a good time to take a break. It was unmistakable that Amy was upset and struggling to hold back tears. He suggested they go out for a coffee rather than risk another cup made by the work-experience girl. Amy agreed, saying she could do with some fresh air, and they left the building.

Matt purchased a couple of lattes from a kiosk, and they sat on a bench overlooking the river.

"Do I come across like a petulant child in the way I talk about Eliza?" Amy asked. "Only, I don't want to appear like a spoilt brat in your book."

"Not at all," said Matt. "To be honest it's Eliza who comes across as a spoilt brat. She sounds atrocious."

"I promise I'm telling the truth," Amy affirmed. "I've got no reason to lie. There's no need for me to paint a bad picture of her, is there? She's already done that for herself. She is wanted for murder after all!"

"Oh, I don't doubt your honesty," said Matt. "It's just hard to believe that she behaved that way during her first meeting with you and Adam. Most women would want to make a good impression on their partner's children. I suppose because she had already married your dad it wasn't such an important issue."

"That was Eliza, through and through. She didn't care what anyone thought about her and if you didn't interest her, she couldn't be bothered with you. I have no good memories from that first meeting except perhaps watching her attempt at flirting with Adam. There's never been much humour in my dealings with Eliza but seeing the look on her face when the penny dropped was priceless."

Think Edith, Think

How can this be happening? He was supposed to die. They promised. "There's been too much damage for him to make a full recovery and there's every possibility he won't pull through."

That's what the consultant said. I tried hard to look sad because I knew that was what they all expected.

Next thing they're sending him home! And now he's showing real signs of improvement, and I can't allow that. What the fuck. Can you imagine if I used that word in front of him? It would give him another stroke. Maybe that's what I should do. Dance around his bed shouting "Fuck. Cunt. Fucking Cunt. Fucking Bastard" over and over again.

I know I caused the first one. When I told him I knew who he really was. I knew who he was to me. Keeled right over straight in front of me. He lay there looking at me with his glassy eyes and his mouth opening and closing like a goldfish. Cunt. Bastard. Why didn't he die right there, right then?

Well, he has to go. I'm not going back to having to live by his rules. Not now. I can't. I've got a plan. Had one for ages. I've even got the stuff I need. Just been waiting for the right time. And I think the right time is just around the corner.

6

Matt and Amy took a little walk around the neighbourhood to allow them to finish their coffee before they returned to the office.

"Right," said Amy taking up from where she'd left off. "So, after that disastrous first meeting with Eliza, I didn't want Adam to fly back to Australia without having patched things up with Dad. Although Adam had woken up contrite for the way he behaved at the farmhouse, he was still angry. I thought it best if the two of them were able to talk one-on-one, and asking Dad to come over because his dogs were missing him seemed the best way of avoiding extending the invite to Eliza due to her being terrified of dogs.

"When Dad arrived, Marcus was still out walking the dogs with Rory. I went to make coffee leaving Dad and Adam alone in the front room to talk. When I came back into the room, Dad was waving a piece of paper at Adam. It was the letter from the clinic; the proof that his vasectomy had failed. He'd obviously come prepared for a fight. I didn't look at the letter, but I think Adam did. The atmosphere felt very tense between us, which was such an alien feeling in our family.

"Fortunately, it wasn't long before Marcus returned and the dogs, sensing Dad's presence, came bounding into the room. Dad was soon on the floor wrestling with the dogs and a very excited Rory. The noise woke Olivia from her nap, and she too joined in, squealing in delight at the sight of her grandad. The mood lifted and it felt a bit more normal. But in reality, nothing had changed. Adam and I were still reeling from the hasty marriage and the announcement that had been made the day before. We were both so disappointed that Eliza wasn't at all like we assumed she would be; as they say, 'never assume anything'. Dad was also disappointed that the initial meeting had gone so badly. I don't think for the life of him, he could work out why it had all gone so wrong, but he certainly wasn't putting the blame on Eliza.

"We didn't exactly kiss and make up but at least we were talking. Dad asked if we could all get together again before Adam returned to Australia. He said Eliza was excited to meet with my children, which I doubted very much. To my horror, I realised that she was now their step-grandmother! We agreed that we would go out the following Sunday for dinner a couple of days before Adam's flight back to Oz.

"For me, the following gathering turned out to be harder than the first. I found it far more stressful. The addition of two noisy young children added to the tension. I was on tenterhooks in case Adam upset the apple cart. Marcus was completely enamoured with Eliza, which irritated me beyond measure. To make things worse for me, Eliza seemed to have the knack of undermining my self-confidence. She wasn't subtle in her approach, but she managed to leave me no course for retaliation. She made me feel stupid and ignorant even in areas where normally I felt confident. That day she was just as rude and self-absorbed as she had been the week before and Dad was still fussing around her like an old woman.

"Still, if not exactly an enjoyable occasion at least we got through it without killing each other – ouch that was an unfortunate turn of phrase to use! Dad and Adam appeared to have made up, which is what I wanted to happen before Adam had to leave.

"Then the next morning everything exploded once again. Adam needed to pick up some stuff from his room at the farmhouse, so I drove him over. We didn't announce we were calling around, which in hindsight was rude, but it was our home, and we were used to walking in whenever we wanted. I opened the back door calling 'Hello!' to Dad, like I always did, only to be met by a very angry Eliza who demanded to know what on earth I thought I was doing just walking into her house. I could feel the anger radiating from Adam who was standing just behind me and before I could say anything, he pushed past me. He squared up to her and told her in no uncertain terms that this was his home, and he would come and go as he pleased. Eliza's reply was along the lines of 'This was your home but neither of you live here anymore. I'm your father's wife and I will not allow you to just walk in whenever it takes your fancy.'

"To be fair to Eliza, I could see things from her point of view. What if she had been naked? Or she and Dad had been – well you know! I was about to apologise to her when we were interrupted by a man coming in from outside carrying a clipboard and a tape measure. Turns out he was there to give an estimate on turning Mum's vegetable garden into a swimming pool. I swear Adam went purple. I think the builder sensed there was about to be trouble because he hurriedly left saying he would drop his quote off later. It dawned on me then that Dad had not explained his living arrangements to Eliza, and I tried to say this to Adam before he kicked off again, but he was too angry to listen. Both he and Eliza started shouting at each other. There was a lot of 'How dare you?' and 'Who do you think you are?' Neither of them was listening to each other or to me. And that's what Dad walked in on!

"Adam and Eliza started shouting at him too, whilst I hastily explained what had happened. Dad told them both to shut up so he could explain. Like a wimp, I said it would be best if Adam and I left but Adam was having none of it. He wanted to be the one who put Eliza straight. Because she was now quiet and before Dad had a chance to speak, he jumped in, telling Eliza that the farmhouse wasn't Dad's but his – well actually mine and his.

"He smugly explained that the house had belonged solely to our mother and when she died, she had left it to us and that we allowed Dad to live there. I could feel Dad bristle when Adam used the word 'allow'. That wasn't really the case. I don't want to be disloyal to my brother, but he was being an arse. Vindictively, he told Eliza that under no circumstances would he allow any alterations to be made to his home.

"It's safe to say that was the moment that any chance of Adam and Eliza ever getting on with each other evaporated.

"It seemed a wise time to leave and once again, I found myself shoving Adam out of the door. So, I wasn't a party to the conversation that followed between Dad and Eliza, but it can't have been good, because Dad arrived at my house a short time later in a foul temper and he and Adam had the biggest row. It was awful to witness because I'd never seen them fight before. They'd fallen out occasionally when Adam as a teenager tried pushing the boundaries, but other than that, they got on really well. Now, however, they were both so angry I was concerned that it might turn physical.

"Dad had a go at Adam for telling Eliza about the house situation when he should have left Dad to do it, and Adam rightly defended himself saying how was he supposed to know she hadn't been made aware? Adam told Dad exactly what he thought of Eliza and that I felt the same way as him. Although being the coward I am, I was annoyed at Adam for dragging me into the argument, I couldn't deny it. Dad was really upset; not sad upset but fuming upset. He told us how disappointed he was in us and how he assumed we would want him to be happy. He said we had let him down. That we were acting like spoilt brats and that Eliza was overwrought. He said if anything happened to the baby, it would be our fault and then he stormed off. I was devastated. I had no clue as to how to make any of this better. The next day, Adam flew back to Australia without seeing Dad and making up. The predicament hit all three of us extremely hard and none of us knew how to make things right between us.

"Over the next few weeks, Dad introduced Eliza to family and friends like Kath and Terry. From the feedback I received, it's safe to say the general consensus was, 'What on earth does Keith see in her?'

"Gradually Dad and I made up. In truth, with his dogs living at my house and him wanting to see them, he had to make the first move. Actually, that's a little unfair, he also wanted to see his grandchildren whom he doted on. It was difficult to start with but over time, we thawed. Not having to see Eliza helped with that. I was busy with work and used the kids as a get-out clause from visiting her and of course, she wouldn't come to me because of the dogs. She would occasionally ring, but it was only ever to ask a favour, mostly small ones, like picking up some shopping for example. But other requests were bigger.

"She was having a Caesarean and she wanted me to take time off work to look after her when she first came home from hospital with the baby. I was puzzled as to why she would think to ask me in the first place, seeing as how she made it clear she didn't like me. Maybe it was a way for her to look down on me by treating me like a skivvy? I politely explained that as a teacher, I wasn't allowed time off in term time. I was very careful in my choice of words so as not to upset her, so I was annoyed when my dad commented that I could have let Eliza down gently and there was no need to be rude.

"These misconceptions of Dad's were happening a lot, and I was certain that Eliza was deliberately painting me as the bad guy. She was most definitely stirring. I gave up saying anything in my defence because I didn't want to seem petty, and Dad didn't take any notice anyway. As it was, she persuaded Dad to employ an au pair. Granny was incandescent! 'Who the bloody hell does she think she is? Mrs too-posh-to push!" The fact that Eliza had elected to have a Caesarean also didn't sit well with Granny.

"Granny was the one who informed me of Zac's arrival. 'The sprog has arrived,' she announced gloomily when she phoned me. 'It's a boy. They're calling it Zac. Your father tried to tell me that it arrived a month early, but it weighs over 10lb. If anything, it's overcooked. I said to him, 'That baby's not yours.'

'Oh dear, what did he say to that?' I asked.

'His usual, not now Mother, same as he always says. He'll have to face up to it someday. He rang me just before he left for the hospital to bring them home. I told him a baby that big could catch the bus home on its own!' Like I said, my Granny was a character.

"Marcus and I took the kids to meet Zac for the first time. Granny was there too. It was more than awkward. I had taken some presents which Eliza didn't even bother to open. Granny kept referring to Zac as a cuckoo. I knew exactly what she was doing and chose to stay out of it. At age 5, Rory was more gullible.

'Why are you calling him cuckoo?' he asked.

'Oh, it's just my cute nickname for him,' said Granny, all sweetness and light.

'But why cuckoo?' persisted Rory.

'Because that's what he is,' replied Granny, 'A cuckoo in the nest.'

"Everyone pointedly ignored this and then Rory asked, 'Will Zac call you GanGan?'

Which was what my children called her instead of Great Granny.

'Oh, I don't think so,' Granny responded. 'To save confusion all round it's probably best if he calls me Vi!'

"My grandmother's name was Violet Kelly. Granny also chose this occasion to inform Dad and Eliza that they were incorrectly spelling the baby's name.

'I assume it's short for Zachary?' she said. 'No, it's just Zac,' said Eliza.

'Then it should be spelt with an 'h' on the end,' said Granny.

'No,' said Eliza sharply. 'We want it to be unusual.'

'There's a world of difference between being unusual and being just plain wrong,' said Granny.

"After this exchange, whenever Granny had to write Zac's name, in a birthday card or whatever, she would always spell it with an 'h'.

"Despite Zac's birth, I still didn't see much of Eliza unless it was an unavoidable family function, and then I was usually just a bystander watching as she and Granny did battle with each other. Living in Australia meant that Adam didn't have to deal with Eliza either. He and Dad had started Skyping again and I think they repaired their relationship by mutually agreeing not to discuss Eliza at all. Adam acknowledged Zac's birth. He sent presents when required. But that was the extent of his involvement."

"What was your dad's reaction to his new son? Was he hands-on?" Matt asked.

"Oh yes, he was very hands-on. He was over the moon. Very happy. I didn't actually see him with Zac that much but when I did, he was so good with him. I know he was involved with all aspects of looking after him. He changed nappies and bathed him. He would tell me all about it when he came round to visit. He would sometimes bring Zac with him when he visited, to give Eliza a break. He was very proud of Zac, and I think Zac was good for him. He used to tell me Zac kept him young."

"And how did *you* get on with Zac?" queried Matt.

"This is again going to make me sound like an awful person, but I'm determined to be honest. I didn't like Zac. I mean, don't misunderstand me, I didn't feel like that about him when he was first born. My dislike of him is something that developed over time. As a baby, he was cute in the way that babies always are and although I didn't see him often, I enjoyed having cuddles and playing with him. But as he got older. Well! I mean I'm a teacher and I admit that I've had some children in my classes that I haven't liked as much as others. But I can honestly say that I've never actively disliked a child as much as I did Zac. Usually, no matter how unruly or disruptive a child is, you can find something positive to say about them, but I can't think of one good quality that Zac possessed. As a toddler, he was a thug, a bully.

He enjoyed hurting other children, especially mine, and breaking things. He was rude, obnoxious and spoilt. That sounds so harsh, doesn't it, but it's true. I didn't see a lot of him, but whenever I did, his behaviour was atrocious, and it got worse each time I saw him."

"I'm surprised that your dad spoilt him or tolerated his bad behaviour. From what you've told me about your own upbringing he doesn't sound like that sort of parent," said Matt.

"And you're absolutely right, he wasn't. Adam and I wouldn't have got away with half the stuff Zac did. Don't get me wrong, Dad tried very, very hard to correct Zac's bad behaviour. He was certainly embarrassed by it. The problem was Eliza. I know I blame Eliza for everything bad, but she was a terrible parent. Possibly the worst I've ever encountered. When you get a chance to talk to other people, you'll discover I'm not the only one who thinks that. In my opinion, she spoilt Zac because she was lazy, and it meant an easier life for her. To be fair, she was on her own with him a lot because Dad worked away so much, but instead of routine and discipline, she let him do what he liked and bought him everything he wanted.

"As Zac got older, he developed a very bad temper which made his behaviour worse. That really bothered Dad and at the time of his death, I know he had been trying to find help for Zac, seeking professional advice. He wanted to know how he could teach Zac to control his temper, but he was also worried that there might be something psychologically wrong with him. Eliza, on the other hand, was adamant there was nothing wrong. Dad discussed it with me, and I know he talked to Kath about it too. It's why when we first heard what happened to Dad, what Zac had supposedly done, none of the family was particularly surprised. Looking back at that time, if it had been any other 9-year-old I would have doubted their ability to carry out an attack like that, but because it was Zac it was entirely plausible. Sorry, I'm moving ahead again.

"Understandably, having discovered the situation regarding the farmhouse, Eliza wanted to move to a new home. I don't blame her for that at all; I'd have felt the same way. So, Dad put his London flat on the market. He didn't need it anymore as he rarely had work in the city and it would fetch a fair price, so it made perfect sense. I assumed the flat had sold for a lot more than I had imagined it would because they moved into a massive house in an exclusive part of Brigholme. House prices there were and still are extortionate. Of course, I later discovered that Dad had also taken out a hefty mortgage. Not that that was any of my business. The move certainly made Eliza happy and when Eliza was happy so was Dad.

"I can't really tell you much about Eliza at that time because once they moved away, I saw even less of her."

"But you still saw your dad?" enquired Matt.

"Oh yes," answered Amy. "But I saw him less than I had been because he always seemed to be working. Still, whenever he could spare the time, he would visit. His dogs had both passed away, but he still very much enjoyed spending time with his grandchildren."

"What about Zac? Did you see much of him?" asked Matt. "No not really," Amy told him. "Eliza enrolled Zac in every after-school club and weekend activity group going. I'm sure it was so she didn't have to spend too much time with him. Therefore, he was very rarely available to accompany Dad on what was now his fairly infrequent visits. Dad, I imagine parroting Eliza, was always boasting how skilful Zac was at everything he did. He was destined to be the youngest Wimbledon champion, the next Tom Daley or a future winner of MasterChef. Zac in the flesh was a very different kettle of fish. He obviously had no interest in spending time with me or his cousins. He came across as rude and sullen and it was hard to imagine him enthusiastic about anything. Eventually, Dad just stopped bringing him.

"It wasn't until after Dad died and I reflected on those years that I realised how little Dad actually shared with me about his home life. He very rarely spoke about Eliza or Zac. He'd answer questions but not volunteer much information. He seemed happy enough. I wouldn't say he was as infatuated with Eliza as he had once been, but it's normal for feelings to die down a bit after you've spent a lot of time together, isn't it? He certainly wasn't critical of her. He never complained, not to me anyway. He shared his anxieties regarding Zac and these increased as Zac got older. I was aware that he often looked tired, but he was still working hard, and he was getting on in years. Sorry, I'm jumping ahead yet again.

"Once Eliza moved away, I'm fairly certain I didn't see her again until Granny died. It was a very difficult time for me, and I didn't handle it at all well. Eliza and I had a disagreement over whether or not she had visited Granny on the day she died. I was certain that Eliza was lying, which was silly of me, and then I fell out with her again because she inferred that my grandmother had been going senile and that's why she had overdosed on insulin. Anyway, that's all water under the bridge now.

"Then we had the reading of Granny's will. Eliza was furious to discover that not only had Granny left money to Adam and me, but to my children too. However, she had left nothing for Zac despite him also being her grandchild. Eliza had assumed that Granny's estate- that sounds rather grand, Granny wasn't badly off but she wasn't what you could consider wealthy. Anyway, Eliza assumed Granny's estate would be split equally between Dad and Uncle John. Finding out that wasn't the case, and others were to benefit too, sent her over the edge. She accused Adam and I of stealing from Dad and Zac saying, as if we hadn't received enough already with the farmhouse.

"By this time, Adam had met Pascal and decided to make his life in Australia. He needed money to buy a property there and Marcus and I needed a bigger home, so we had the farmhouse valued and paid Adam for his share and moved in ourselves. According to Kath, Eliza was really pissed off about this, but I couldn't understand why. She and Dad had their beautiful house. And now she was pissed off because we were beneficiaries of Granny's, but it wasn't as if we were receiving life-changing amounts of money and again, I couldn't see what her problem was.

"Adam and Pascal made it back for Granny's funeral which, fortunately, went off without a hitch. I'd been worried that Eliza might say something to Adam to upset him, but she didn't. Then just after we held the funeral, out of the blue, Eliza turned up at the farmhouse. The whole encounter was weird. Firstly, our dogs, who were still young and, to say the least, boisterous, were outside and began jumping all over her as she climbed out of her car. She didn't appear to be frightened of them as she kicked and batted them away.

"Then she launched into a verbal attack on me before she had even crossed the threshold. She just started on me, as if we had been in the middle of an argument that I hadn't been party to.

"It was the same complaint she had made after the reading of Granny's will. She accused Adam and me of stealing from Dad and my children from stealing from Zac. She demanded that I give Zac the equivalent of what my children had received out of my own inheritance. She told me not to expect a single penny when Dad died. She had made sure that all of his money would go to her and Zac. All the time she was shouting this, she was jabbing at me with her finger, and I was backing away from her. She was calling me all the names under the sun. She said I had been nothing but trouble and I was a spoilt brat who needed to grow up and live in the real world. It was surreal. She was so angry; I thought she was going to hit me. The dogs were going mental, barking at her and jumping up but it didn't faze her. She certainly didn't come across as 'terrified' of them. I didn't react immediately. I was too shocked. But then I got really angry too. How dare she come into my house and attack me! How dare she try and intimidate me in my own home. I shouted back at her and told her to get out. I told her I didn't give a monkey's- although I used stronger language, about Dad's money, but if she thought I would give money to Zac, then she had another think coming.

'Just leave me alone!' I screamed at her and to my surprise, she turned on her heels and left. I was shaken. It all ended as quickly as it started. I didn't know what to think. Where had that come from? What was the meaning behind it?

"The meaning became obvious when I later received a call from my dad telling me that due to my treatment of Eliza after she had tried so hard to make amends with me, he no longer wanted to see me and was cutting me out of his life!"

7

Amy had to take a break after explaining to Matt how her argument with Eliza culminated in her father cutting her out of his life. She became upset, and it had taken her a while to get her emotions under control. Matt left her alone to compose herself whilst he went out and bought some lunch for them, thinking it unlikely Amy would want to eat out whilst she was so upset. When he returned, she was calm again.

"Do you know what?" she said. "For ages now lots of people have advocated that I go for counselling. Both Kath and Marcus have been adamant that it would be beneficial to me, and help me to process my emotions. Even DI Mason wanted me to seek help through Victim Support and I've avoided it. I honestly thought I was okay and that I didn't need any help. But talking through everything with you has shown me that I have an awful lot of unresolved issues; emotions that I haven't yet released and definitely wounds that haven't healed. I am finding this cathartic, and I think now might be the right time to speak to a professional."

"I told you when we first met," said Matt. "Being interviewed by me is like therapy without the therapist."

After they had eaten, Amy continued to tell her story.

"So, after that call from Dad, I was a complete mix of emotions. One minute I was really upset, but the next I was furious. I was angry with myself for how I had let Eliza manipulate events, but I was far angrier with my dad for both believing her lies and for choosing her over me and my children. Because cutting me out of his life meant cutting the kids out too and I thought that was so unfair. No matter what he thought of me or what he presumed I'd done, the children didn't deserve to suffer for it. They adored their grandad and would miss him terribly. For me, having only just lost Granny, I felt like I was now also grieving for Dad. He might as well have died. If only we could see into the future!

"The problem was that neither of us was prepared to make the first move towards a reconciliation. We were both too stubborn. I definitely inherited my pigheadedness from Dad. Marcus, Kath and Terry stepped in to attempt to heal the rift between us and after a couple of months, we agreed to a meeting at Kath's house. Kath basically knocked our heads together, telling us that life was too short for this nonsense; again, if only we could see into the future! She advised us to forget all that had gone on previously between us and to count that day as a fresh start. She asked, what did it matter if Eliza and I didn't get on? We hardly ever saw each other anyway so why worry if we never saw each other at all? Kath said that as an outsider looking in, she would suggest that the most sensible course of action would be to carry on as we had been doing. Nothing had to change. We should just agree that I never had to see Eliza but also that I never criticised her to Dad. Of course, she was right. I rarely saw Eliza and had no problem with never seeing her at all. Dad admitted that he had been devastated by our fall-out and that he was happy not to even mention Eliza's name in front of me if that meant we could move on and get past this quarrel. So, we literally kissed and made up and I didn't see Eliza in person again until after Dad died.

"I'm so glad that we made peace with each other when we did because it wasn't long after this that he was diagnosed with his heart condition and had his operation. I saw quite a bit of him while he was recuperating. I don't think Eliza was the best nurse or very sympathetic towards him. And then, of course, she murdered him!

8

Matt wanted to interview Keith's long-term friends Kath and Terry Lomas separately, certainly to begin with. He wanted to have their individual perspectives on both Keith and Eliza's characters and their relationship together, rather than a collaboration. Luckily, Kath completely understood his reasoning when he contacted her to explain that he would like to interview her first, without her husband. She suggested that he come over to the house on a Saturday afternoon whilst Terry was playing his weekly round of golf.

Kath and Terry had known Keith and his first wife Angela for years and they continued to be close to Keith and his children after Angela died. They had played a huge supporting role in Amy's life for the last few years.

The Lomases home turned out to be a picturesque, thatched, chocolate box cottage situated close to the edge of a small village. The village was quintessentially English and completely unspoilt. Unsightly new housing estates had yet to sprout up on the surrounding farmland.

Matt parked on the other side of the road and stood for a while taking in the view, rolls of sweeping countryside. It was breathtakingly beautiful. The access to the cottage was via a wooden bridge over a poetic babbling brook that meandered its way along the front of all the houses on that side of the village. The cottage was double-fronted and getting to the front door required walking a narrow, winding path that cut through the traditional cottage garden, brimming with a colourful variety of plants, most of which Matt couldn't identify. The house and its setting exuded such tranquil charm that Matt felt a dash of envy. The ambience was in contrast to the noisy street that was home to his family.

"*Not so much fun living here in the Winter though,*" he thought to himself, trying to imagine a snow plough or gritter lorry negotiating the narrow lanes. Kath and Terry's cottage was exactly the kind of place that American and Japanese tourists rave about and will pay a fortune for the opportunity to get off the tour bus and take photographs.

Kath opened the door and invited him into a small hallway.

"I thought we'd sit out in the garden whilst the weather's so lovely," she said, and he followed her towards the rear of the cottage.

Through an open doorway, he caught a glimpse of a sitting room exactly how he imagined it would look, taking in the beams and the open fireplace. Kath led him into what was an extended kitchen/diner that stretched across the whole back of the house with bi-folding doors onto decking. The fittings were modern and the room was very light and airy. His surprise obviously showed as she grinned at him and said,

"There was no way I could live with the pokey little kitchen that was here when we bought the place."

Matt told her how lucky she was to live in such a stunning house, and she agreed.

"Do you know, Eliza was so envious of our kitchen that she had an almost identical one installed in her and Keith's home, even used the same company for the folding doors."

Kath offered him a choice of beverages and having made his decision, she ushered him outside to a very comfortable seating area. Again, the view was stunning, miles and miles of countryside with only the odd farm building here and there and miniature dots of white sheep. Matt spent some time savouring it before he unpacked his notepad. He was grateful for the shade of a large canopy as the day was turning out very warm. Although, with the interviewee's permission, Matt always recorded his interviews, he still liked to make notes of his observations. He documented facial reactions and other tell-tale signs that gave him more of an insight as to what the interviewee was actually thinking whilst they were talking.

So, in this peaceful, placid environment Matt asked his opening question,

"What did you think of Eliza?" and then very nearly spat out the mouthful of chilled homemade lemonade he'd just taken when Kath replied,

"She was a first-class bitch, an out-and-out cunt!"

He was shocked that this mild-mannered, middle-class woman sitting outside her perfect house in her immaculate garden came out with such foul language.

Kath immediately started to laugh, "I'm sorry," she said, "but that's exactly what I thought of her from our very first introduction."

During the course of the interview, Matt discovered that Kath was the retired headmistress of a large secondary school and despite her mild demeanour, she was actually a very tough, no-nonsense sort of person. Matt found her witty, amusing and extremely insightful. She apologised every time she swore, which she did a lot, explaining that when you are dealing with hormone-filled teenagers, volatile parents and teachers teetering on the edge of nervous breakdowns, you learned very quickly that straight-talking honesty was the only policy.

Matt decided that perhaps the best way to start the interview would be for Kath to tell him about her friendship with Keith and his first wife Angela, so he asked Kath how they met.

"Well, it was the men who met first," said Kath. "One of the first things Terry did when we moved into the area was to join the nearest golf club and that's where he met Keith. They have a shared love of sport and started going to football matches together too. After a while, they thought it would be a good idea if we wives met and so we went out for a meal one Saturday evening. Angela and I hit it off straight away and going out as a foursome once or twice a month became a regular date. Our children are around the same age, and it naturally progressed into barbecues at each other's houses and parties for birthdays, that sort of thing. As two families we would go on holiday together twice a year. The Kellys had a villa in Spain, which we would visit for two weeks in the summer and in the winter, we went to our skiing lodge at Chamonix in France.

Over the years we made friends with other couples and our social group got bigger, but we have always been closest to Keith and Angela. It was awful when Angela died. Keith went to pieces, and we did our best to support him and the children. It took a long time for him to start taking an interest in socialising again and when he did it was hard for all of us. We were acutely aware of the empty chair that should have been occupied by Angela."

Kath, briefed beforehand by Amy, had photos ready for Matt to look at and it was obvious to see that the two families had been very close. There were snaps from various holidays, birthday parties and Christmas parties. Some were taken with large social groups and others of just the two families.

"I have 3 boys as you can see," said Kath holding up a photograph of three teenage boys who were only a couple of years apart in age. "They're obviously adults now," she continued. "Amy and Adam could be their cousins, they're all so close. All three of my lads have been extremely supportive and protective, especially of Amy. She's the sister they never had. They make me very proud," she said, smiling.

"Were you surprised when Keith started dating Eliza?" Matt asked.

"Well, it was a bit odd. You see he never really told us about her. He mentioned this woman he had met whilst he was filming The Whitchurch Murders, but he never let on that he was actually dating her. I know Amy had teased him about it because he constantly talked about this woman "Eliza", but to start with he was adamant that they were just friends. Even when she moved into his flat, he still insisted they weren't an item. Personally, I thought that was a shame as he was obviously keen on her, and it was about time that he met someone new. And then the next thing we know he's gone and married her. We were stunned. It was unlike Keith to be so impulsive, so secretive.

"After Angela died, Keith struggled with making any big decisions and would often consult Terry and me about how he should handle a situation. This sudden wedding to a woman he hardly knew was completely out of character. He hadn't even mentioned that Eliza would be joining him in the States. I know that people can get carried away on holiday, but they don't usually do something as dramatic as getting married. I suspected there had to be something more behind their actions, that it hadn't just happened on the spur of the moment, and of course, the announcement of the pregnancy proved me right. A shotgun wedding!

"As Keith's friends we wanted to be supportive and obviously we were curious to meet his new bride, so we began to pester for an introduction from the moment Keith came home. But Keith seemed reluctant for us to meet. He kept prevaricating. Later, after I met her, I decided that his reluctance had stemmed from embarrassment. Partly because she was so much younger than him; she was nearer our children's age than our own, but mainly because she was pregnant. He thought we would disapprove. Which we didn't. We were bemused that it had happened and very surprised, but it wasn't our business to interfere.

"Of course, knowing and loving Angela as we did it was always going to be tricky for us to accept someone new in her place. But I made it clear to Keith from the get-go that I would never consider Eliza a replacement for Angela because no one could ever replace her. Eliza was just a new chapter in Keith's life. I think that helped. Terry was worried that I would be predisposed to dislike Eliza because Angela was one of my best friends, but I honestly don't think that was the case. I knew that Eliza was going to be completely different to Angela and that on its own should have made it easier to accept her. It would have been a lot harder if she had been at all similar to Angela in age or personality.

"I advised Keith that it would probably be best to first meet Eliza when we were socialising as a group. It's quite a large group and I thought that would be less intimidating for her than just meeting us as a couple, knowing that we were possibly Keith's closest friends. As it happened, friends of ours were celebrating their 40th wedding anniversary at the Golf Club and Keith agreed to bring Eliza along."

"You told me earlier that you considered her a first-class bitch from the very first moment of meeting her," Matt interjected - he was too embarrassed to say out loud the other description that Kath had used. "Why was that?"

Kath smirked, well aware that he had avoided repeating that certain word.

"Because that's how she acted," replied Kath. "I didn't expect her to be humble, but I was expecting her to make an effort. I anticipated that she would be polite, gracious and sensitive to the fact that this was potentially a very difficult situation for those of us who had been close to Angela. That wasn't how she was at all. Instead, she acted like she was granting us a huge favour by agreeing to meet us and she was plainly disinterested in getting to know us.

"When Keith introduced her to me personally, my impression was that everything about her seemed false, a little off. She was so over the top, with her mannerisms, her accent, and the way she interacted with Keith. I suppose she was the antithesis of the sort of woman I imagined Keith would be attracted to. She was certainly the complete opposite of Angela. She did most of the talking and she was boastful and conceited. She told a lot of stories about herself that were hard to believe. I can't know for sure that she was making things up but that's how it felt. And even if the things she spoke about had occurred, then she had to be exaggerating the truth. It was all overblown and excessive.

"For someone who you would assume wanted to make a good first impression, she was also extraordinarily rude and personal about the other guests, commenting on the other women's dress sense and making unkind remarks about people's looks. It was a strange way for her to behave in front of people she'd never met before. I found it quite childish. We are a close-knit group and if you insult one of us, you're going to upset the rest. I, for one, was a little cold towards her when she made these unpleasant comments, but she didn't seem to notice. Of course, once I got to know her, I discovered that she always behaved this way. She put down everyone she came into contact with.

"Afterwards, when we got home, I talked to Terry about her and the way she had behaved. He excused it saying she was probably suffering from nerves and compensating for being overanxious. But I didn't agree. Nothing about her behaviour betrayed nerves or anxiety. I would have expected someone in her situation to want to impress her new partner's closest friends, and from my point of view, Eliza had made no attempt to impress us whatsoever. I instinctively knew I was never going to like her, but I promised Terry, I would at least give her the benefit of the doubt for Keith's sake.

"However, the more we got to know her, the less I liked her, and Terry's opinion of her soon became the same as mine. We both felt that she wasn't the right person for Keith, but it wasn't our place to say anything to him about it. Also, I think we were both pretty certain that the relationship wouldn't last, and we wouldn't have to tolerate her for that long."

"How would you describe her character?" asked Matt.

"She was the rudest, most selfish, self-centred, arrogant person I have ever known. I don't remember a single time when she voluntarily helped someone out or paid someone a compliment. She enjoyed putting people down and got a kick out of making people feel uncomfortable. She tried her best to be intimidating; admittedly it didn't work on me, but I could see the effect she had on others, especially Amy. She was unpleasant, nasty even. I would call her personality toxic. I honestly can't think of one single positive characteristic. She was a despicable individual. And I can assure you that's how I felt before she murdered Keith. Imagine what I feel about her now!"

Kath slammed her glass down on the table, unable to hide her fury.

"It's clear that you never liked her," said Matt. "But could you possibly give some examples of what it was about her that you disliked the most?"

"That's put me on the spot a bit. I should have thought about this beforehand so I could give the best answer," Kath admitted. "Erm, let me think. Well for starters there's her ridiculous accent. It was so put on, so fake. Nobody talks like that. It was somewhere between the Queen and Mae West. I think she thought that she sounded posh and sexy, but it was like she was a really bad actress who kept forgetting the character she was supposed to be playing. Or a member of the jet set with a throat condition. She would start off with this really accentuated speech, but the more she spoke the less she remembered how she wanted to sound. And when she was drunk or angry her accent would slip, and she would revert to her origins - South London I would hazard a guess. It wasn't just the accent that was annoying, it was the way in which she spoke. Whenever she was describing something, it was so over the top. Everything was sublime, divine, glorious, superb, heavenly; all a bit much when you're talking about a shepherd's pie! She was the queen of the superlative adjective."

Matt remembered Amy making a similar observation about the way Eliza spoke.

"Eliza was so full of herself it was tiresome." Kath was getting into her stride now. "She, however, never tired of telling us how brilliant she was at everything. It got my goat so much that I made it my personal mission to point out every time I came across something that she wasn't brilliant at. If she wasn't good at something she either just wouldn't do it, like cooking, or she would take herself off and learn to perfect it before letting anyone see her attempt it again.

"For example, when she first came skiing with us, she was rubbish. Despite her telling us that she had been on numerous divine, heavenly, superb, etc, skiing holidays, it was obvious that she had never put on a pair of skis before in her life. There she was all kitted out in brand new expensive gear and then she couldn't work out how to put on her skis. She insisted that she didn't need to start on the nursery or practice slopes and instead, she came out with us.

"After falling on her arse more times than she stood upright she blamed it on her ankle which apparently, she had broken years before but was now playing her up. She then spent the rest of the holiday at the lodge, mostly shouting at Keith. I would have been far more sympathetic to her if she just admitted that she was inexperienced. However, when we went again two years later, she was surprisingly good, so I complimented her. Keith laughed and said she should be an expert by now after the amount of money she had spent learning on the dry ski slopes back home. Eliza was furious with him for disclosing that.

"She was the same with regards to Zac, so full of just how wonderful he was. I mean it was constant. Just a never-ending list of his abilities and achievements. The problem was that the real Zac had nothing in common with the one she consistently harped on about and it was apparent that she knew that.

"The way she talked about him was not the way she spoke to him. She would say the most awful things to his face, always putting him down. I accused her of child abuse once, having witnessed the way she spoke to him and the horrific names she called him. She just laughed and said she was toughening him up, preparing him for life. But when she was talking about him to someone else, it was as if he was the Messiah.

"I remember one time she was busy telling me and some other friends how so 'superbly', 'magnificently', 'splendidly' well Zac had done on a school report. She mentioned that the headteacher had written on it personally because it was the most 'outstandingly, amazingly, exquisite' report the Head had ever encountered. Eliza didn't like it when I pointed out that during my years as the Head of a school, I always wrote a handwritten comment on every single child's school report, each time one was issued. It was compulsory. An inherent part of my job. Ignoring me she went on to say that the class teacher had called Zac 'a very interesting character, full of imagination'. I told her that was teacher speak for 'spoilt brat and compulsive liar', we're just not allowed to write it like that as apparently, it upsets the parents. It's safe to say I pissed her off.

"I do think it was fortunate that Zac was a boy. I don't think Eliza would have coped well with having a daughter. I think as a girl got older, Eliza would have felt compelled to compete with her. She would have struggled to have a healthy relationship with Zac, let alone a younger, potentially prettier version of herself. I'm sure that's why she did her best to alienate Amy. She didn't like the competition."

Puzzled, Matt asked Kath to clarify the point she was trying to make.

"Oh, I don't mean with Keith's affections," said Kath. "Although Eliza objected to Keith spending time with Amy, I believe that was for a different reason which I'll explain in a minute. No, I mean in social settings, Eliza always had to be the centre of attention.

"For some reason, beyond my comprehension, she managed to enchant men. Especially initially, before they got to know her better. Eliza was never happier than when she was surrounded by adoring men. It didn't bother Keith. He wasn't at all jealous. I think he was rather proud to have ensnared such a 'trophy' wife.

"However, if you introduce a younger, prettier woman into the group, then the attention on Eliza is diluted and she hated that. Especially if it was Amy, who was often at our social gatherings, despite Eliza's attempts to prevent her from being invited. Amy's such a sweet-natured person. She hasn't got a clue how attractive she is. Well, you've met her. You know how gorgeous she is."

Matt was unsure what an appropriate response to this statement would be, so he just gave a non-committal grunt. "Why did Eliza object to Keith spending time with Amy?" he asked.

"Well, I don't think it was so much Amy, as Rory and Olivia that Eliza objected to Keith spending time with," Kath disclosed. "Keith doted on his grandchildren. Although they were older than Zac, it wasn't by much, and Eliza saw them as competition to Keith and Zac's relationship. Also, as was often the case with Eliza, it was about money. She had never recovered from the revelation that the farmhouse didn't belong to Keith. She was jealous that Amy and Adam had inherited it.

"Then when Violet, Keith's Mum, died and left money not only to Amy and Adam but to Rory and Olivia too, and yet excluded Zac completely, that was the final straw as far as Eliza was concerned. She'd obviously expected that Violet would split things 50/50 between Keith and his brother John. I'm sure if she could have found a way to coerce Violet into disinheriting John she would have done so. Amy told me that after the will had been read, Eliza stormed out without speaking to anyone. I'm convinced it's because of the will that she contrived the huge argument that she and Amy had after Violet's funeral. She wanted Amy completely out of Keith's life. As far as she was concerned, she'd already managed to drive a wedge between Adam and Keith; she was unaware that they were back on speaking terms, and now she wanted to do the same with Amy's family. She wanted to ensure that neither his children nor his grandchildren would benefit if something happened to Keith. She wanted it all left to her and Zac."

"Was this the argument that led to Keith telling Amy he didn't want to see her again?" asked Matt. "Amy told me about that and about the fact that you helped her, and her father reconcile."

"Yes, it was that argument," Kath replied. "It was so stupid of Keith to react the way he did, to believe everything Eliza told him. But Amy was just as bad. Terry spoke to Keith about it, and I talked to Amy and eventually, we managed to get them to meet.

"After that, things between them seemed much better. I'm sure it's because they both agreed to leave Eliza out of their relationship. In the same way that Keith already did with Adam. I don't think Amy had been seeing that much of Eliza anyway. It was only because of Violet's death that they were forced to spend time in each other's company.

"To be fair none of us saw much of Eliza anymore. Keith was so busy with work that they were hardly ever available for social functions, and if they were, Keith tended to come on his own. He made excuses for Eliza, but I think the truth was that Eliza had expected all of Keith's friends to be in showbiz. She was disappointed to discover that our group was comprised of normal, boring, everyday people and she soon dropped us.

"I suspected that Eliza had made new friends; ones closer to her in age. Zac was in school and with all his hundreds of after-school clubs and activities, I thought Eliza must have met people more suited to her than us old fogies, but apparently not. According to Keith, she had no friends or any sort of social life. I know it bothered him. The only person she ever spent time with other than Keith was Ricky, who she'd apparently known since she was little. I only met him a couple of times, one of which he was high. I expressed concern to Keith about the wisdom of a drug addict being around Zac, but Keith didn't see the harm. Apparently, Eliza had previously been responsible for helping Ricky get clean but he'd recently relapsed and she was helping him try again. Saint Eliza according to Keith's version of events."

They took a short break to enable Kath to replenish the refreshments. Whilst inside the house, she'd obviously been considering what to tell him next as she commenced talking before she'd even retaken her seat.

"The way Eliza treated Keith irritated me too," she began. "When they were first together, she claimed he was absolutely, totally, positively, unquestionably, perfect but it wasn't long before she was trying to change him. She made him cut his hair differently to try and hide the fact that he was losing it and what she got him to dress in was hilarious. A man of his age should not wear skinny jeans, there should, in fact, be a law against it. But Eliza told Keith that they made him look younger and so he took to wearing them to please her. She also made him wear shoes with lifts, so he looked taller than her. It was all a bit pathetic on Keith's part actually and really, I should have been more cross with him about it than her. I took her to task about it and she told me she was only trying to 'improve' him. If they were so perfect for each other, as she would have had us believe, then why did he need improving?

"But changing the way he looked was not the least of it, she started to attack him personally, verbally not physically. She would contradict him when he was speaking or talk over him. When we went out for the evening, she would tell silly little stories about him to deliberately undermine him. She criticised him constantly either for something he did or for something he didn't do. It was all very awkward and unnecessary. I found myself getting cross with Keith for not standing up for himself, but I think she had seriously begun to undermine his self-confidence."

"Why do you think her attitude to him changed so radically?" asked Matt.

"In my opinion," Kath replied, "it was because she'd realised, he wasn't as wealthy as she had believed him to be. The most important thing in the world to Eliza was money. Although it was a long time after Keith's role in Prospect Road, you have to remember that when Eliza met him, he was filming The Whitchurch Murders and about to start filming the second season of That's Not Fair, in the States. She considered him to still have a very successful career.

"The truth was that Keith's only really well-paid job, and his only regular one during his whole acting career, was playing Jeff Walker in Prospect Road, which as I say had finished years before. Since then, his work had been hit and miss and the roles he had taken were far less well paid. Don't get me wrong, he wasn't a starving actor by any means, and he subsidized his income by doing after-dinner speaking and hosting corporate events, but each year the parts he auditioned for got smaller, as did the amount of money he was offered.

"Things didn't always work out in his favour either. The network cancelled That's Not Fair, so there was no third series. Keith did return to theatre but none of the productions he appeared in made it to the West End. Also, theatre treated him the same as television, the parts and the money got smaller. It isn't unusual, it's what happens to all actors as they age and it's worse for women than it is for men. I don't think Eliza understood that when she married Keith. I think she assumed that she had married someone like Michael Caine, when in reality she had married a relatively successful actor reaching the end of his career.

"Since they'd been together, she'd also discovered that the impressive property he lived in didn't belong to him and that he didn't have as much disposable income as she had imagined. Not only that, but I'm certain she expected she would be living a very glamorous lifestyle with showbiz parties every weekend, attending film premiers and socialising with stars of stage and screen. Again, she was to be seriously disappointed. Keith was no longer a big enough name to be invited to parties or premiers and he had no relationship with the current celebrities. He did have friends in show business, he was a popular guy, but they were of a similar age and status to him and as such of no interest to Eliza.

"So, the lifestyle was not what she thought it would be. One of the celebrity magazines did a photo shoot with them when Zac arrived and then again, a smaller piece when they finished modernising the house, but other than that, despite Eliza's attempts to seduce them, the media showed no interest in them as a couple.

"All of this was a massive blow to Eliza and her ego. By the time she realised her mistake it was too late; she was married with a child. The change in the way she treated Keith was, in my opinion, punishment because she felt he had misled her. She didn't give up though. She pushed Keith to try out for every part going and to accept every job offered and made sure that they attended any invitation they received. It's possible she contemplated leaving him, but I think a divorce would have left her too short financially for her to consider it a feasible option."

Kath stopped talking, citing the need for a short "comfort break" as she referred to it. On her return she carried on with her explanation of why Eliza's treatment of Keith and his family annoyed her so much.

"She was cruel in her remarks about Amy and Adam, but it was the disparaging remarks she made about Angela that really infuriated me. More than once she and I got into a shouting match with my telling her to "Just shut the fuck up". I think she got a lot of pleasure from pushing my buttons until she got a reaction and, try as I might to control myself and rise above it, I always ended up losing my temper with her.

"I also detested the way she used subterfuge to force Keith to change his mind if he'd denied her something she wanted. She was so manipulative and would play on any weakness. For example, Angela's diagnosis was totally unexpected and before we had chance to come to terms with it, she died. We had no warning she was ill until it was too late. Keith was traumatised by the events. Inevitably he was petrified of losing another loved one and Eliza capitalised on this. I'll give you afor instance. A group of us were enjoying a meal out when halfway through the evening, Eliza asked for silence and once everyone had complied, she announced that "they" believed, based on her symptoms, that she was suffering from either Multiple Sclerosis or a brain tumour. Understandably, the group expressed shock and horror at this dreadful news. I happened to be sitting opposite Keith, so I saw his reaction. The blood drained from his face. He was clearly hearing this information for the first time too.

"Knowing Eliza fairly well by then and based on past experience of her "announcements" I was certain she was either lying about or exaggerating the diagnosis. So, whereas the others were expressing their sympathy, I began to ask questions. First of all, who were the "they" who had made this diagnosis? What tests had been done? The "they" turned out to be her regular doctor and she reluctantly admitted, whilst scowling at me, that she had so far had no tests, and no specialist referral had been made. This enabled the group to make up their own minds about the veracity of her diagnosis. I could see how badly affected Keith had been by her disclosure and how shaken he still was, so to lighten the mood, I mentioned that her symptoms could also be indicative of syphilis. There were a few stifled giggles before Terry diplomatically changed the subject.

"The point I want to make here isn't so much about the lie, it's her taking advantage of Keith's susceptibility. You see, she didn't just do this once but several times. As well as MS and a brain tumour, she also had leukaemia, Parkinson's, a suspected malignant lump on her boob, Motor Neurones and they're just the ones I remember. Each time Keith would go into a complete state of panic, and Terry and I would have to point out that, with no tests and no referral to a specialist, then she couldn't possibly have received a positive diagnosis.

"It was irritating that Keith could be so gullible and not see that her symptoms always coincided with him rejecting one of her endless demands, and that she always made a rapid recovery once he had acquiesced. What happened to Angela had left him so traumatised, that he was too scared not to take Eliza's hypochondria seriously in case she was genuinely grievously ill. Understandable but very annoying."

"Was Eliza a good liar?" asked Matt.

"I wouldn't necessarily say that she was a good liar, but she was certainly an outrageous one," replied Kath. "She would tell the most ridiculous, unbelievable stories that were so full of holes, and yet she expected us all to believe what she said as if it was gospel. It was almost as if she was seeing how far she could go before she was challenged. I like a challenge, so I used to try to catch her out whenever possible, but Keith on the other hand, more often than not, believed her."

Kath stopped for a moment and questioned Matt as to whether he was aware that Eliza had been disbarred from practising as a solicitor, and whether he would be speaking to Keith's agent. He answered affirmatively to both.

"In which case," she said, "I won't say too much about Keith's career, but it became apparent to Terry and I, as I'm sure it did to everyone close to him, that Keith was having money problems.

"Although it wasn't my place to, I objected to the way Eliza spent and wasted Keith's money. This had always been a problem, but it seemed the more Keith stressed about their financial situation, the more she spent. It wouldn't have been so bad if she contributed to the coffers, but she had yet to find successful employment. In fact, she spent more money on courses, etc, that would give her the necessary qualifications for jobs she never obtained, than she ever earned. She hadn't returned to the workplace since having Zac and he was now in school full time. We had never got to the bottom of exactly why Eliza was disbarred but she was/is an intelligent woman who was capable of doing so many things.

"I'm not denying that she tried to find work, but she was only interested in something if it was a bit different. She never attempted, for example, to apply for an office job, which she'd have walked all over, even though they were desperate for money. She seemed to consider such work to be beneath her. She attempted and failed to get both acting and modelling work. She even tried to get Marsha, Keith's agent, to sign Zac, but nothing came of it. So, she decided on photography. If she couldn't be a success in front of the camera, then she would do so behind one. A very expensive course later and with vast amounts spent on the latest photographic equipment, she discovered that photography wasn't something she excelled at.

"Next, she did a year's training to be a teacher. This was probably the most normal career path she undertook. Unfortunately, after only a single term of work experience, she was dismissed from the school for aggressive behaviour towards the pupils, and therefore kicked off the course.

"She then spent a fortune qualifying to be some sort of lifestyle coach; she paid for training in several areas such as counselling, hypnosis, acupuncture. She studied to be a nutritionist, a yoga instructor and a Reiki masseuse. I'm sure there were other specialities too, but I can't remember them. Each course cost a small fortune, but it all came to nothing. She rented a room at a private clinic and paid up front for a whole year, but she gave up using it after a couple of months. In the world according to Eliza, the other therapists were so intimidated by her impressive skills, they paid the gardener to mow the lawn outside her room every time she met with a client! Yet another impossible to prove true or false story, despite the fact this gardening sabotage supposedly took place in January, not a month renowned for lawn mowing.

"As she no longer had the clinic from which to run her practice, she spent an exorbitant amount of money converting a room at home into a therapy room; which was only used a couple of times before she ceased seeing clients at home. This time, in the world according to Eliza, one of her clients had not been happy with the treatment they received and had become aggressive, and Eliza had acted to defend herself. The police were called but it was Eliza who received the caution not the client. Make up your own mind about who became aggressive.

"So, like I said a lot of money was spent but at the end of it all Eliza still didn't have an income. It wouldn't have mattered so much if Eliza was good with money, if she stuck to some sort of budget. But Eliza is possibly the most materialistic person I have ever met. It was important to her that you knew how much something cost, how much she had spent; she needed to prove to people that she was well off, that money was no object for her. She hated it if one of our group purchased something that she didn't have. She would rush to purchase one herself as soon as possible, but of course it had to be bigger and better. She couldn't bear the thought of people having more disposable income than her.

"To begin with, this didn't bother me. I found it irritating, like when she copied our kitchen, but it wasn't any of my business what she did with money. But once Keith opened up to Terry and, then eventually to me, about the financial difficulties he was experiencing, Eliza's constant spending on unnecessary items started to grate. There was poor old Keith working all hours to try and keep them afloat and she would book them yet another expensive foreign holiday or buy a new sofa when there was nothing wrong with the old one, she just fancied a different colour.

"There were savings they could have made too. Zac was being privately educated and the fees were extortionate. In an attempt to save money, Keith advocated sending him to a state school, but Eliza would have none of it and Zac stayed where he was. Then there were all the activities Zac attended outside of school. All the clubs she enrolled him in. I'm certain Eliza tried to fill all of his free time, so she didn't have to look after him herself. Whatever the reason, they were a huge drain on Keith's income.

"It was the same regarding household expenditure. The amount that was spent on eating out was astronomical but as Eliza refused to cook, and with Keith being away from home so much, there was little Keith could do about it. He would moan about how much Eliza spent but he seemed unable to curb her habits. To be honest, I'm not sure he even tried. And then there's the amount of stuff she bought for that kid; it was obscene. As soon as something new came on the market, she had to buy it for him, even if he wasn't particularly interested in it. They probably could have paid off half their mortgage just by selling the toys and games that had never been played with.

"So, it was no wonder that Keith's stress levels were rising. Despite being desperate for money there was, up till then, one area of television work that Keith had refused to contemplate, Reality TV. He had always said that would be scraping the bottom of the barrel and tantamount to a career killer. It shows the level of his desperation that he now auditioned for one of these shows. Before being accepted, he was required to have a medical examination and that was how his heart problem was detected. This condition required an operation and precluded him from taking part in the series. Eliza was fuming."

At this point Kath's husband, Terry, returned from his round of golf and Matt considered it a good place to stop this first discussion. He thanked Kath for her time, and they arranged a date for a second interview, as well as a date for a first interview with Terry.

Driving home, Matt went over the interview in his mind. Between talking with Amy and now with Kath, he felt he was beginning to build up an authentic picture of Eliza.

9

Matt assumed that finding people still living in that particular area of Leambridge who could remember Betty and Edith O'Reilly would be problematic, as so many years had passed, and the area had undergone numerous renovations over that period. The Leambridge of today was very different to the Leambridge of the 1980s and '90s when the O'Reilly women had lived there.

However, it didn't prove to be as arduous as he had expected. Matt often started his searches at local churches because they proved to be invaluable sources of information. So, his first port of call was to St Peter's Methodist Church, in the aptly-named Church Road. Here he met Martin Roberts, a churchwarden, who not only remembered Betty but also told Matt that he knew of a lady who had been a close friend. He was naturally reluctant to give Matt this lady's details, but he very kindly took Matt's business card and promised to call once he had spoken with the woman. He was as good as his word and called Matt a few days later to say that the lady's name was Peggy Dixon and although she was willing to talk with him, she was understandably wary of meeting a strange man on her own. So, Martin asked if Matt would mind meeting her at the church so that he could be present as well. Matt readily agreed and arrangements were made for a mutually convenient date and time.

Usually, Matt would have taken Trevor with him to meet Mrs Dixon. Trevor's calm and reassuring manner was inestimable in interviews such as this. All his years within the police force dealing with the general public had given him the ability to act as a calming presence in any situation. Unfortunately, Trevor wasn't available as he was attending a security conference somewhere up North, having recently been asked to join a government funded committee, tasked with looking into how best to safeguard the public from the threat of terror attacks at outdoor venues. Trevor had always been a very active man. His motto as he grew older was "use it or lose it" and the thought of his looming retirement had terrified him. So, unlike many of his contemporaries who had taken early retirement, Trevor hung on as long as he could. Inevitably though, age caught up with him and he had to leave the job he so loved. Long before he was forced to retire, he signed himself up to as many different committees and organisations as he could; all of which appreciated his abilities and his experience.

Taking into account what Mr Roberts had said and understanding that Mrs Dixon might find talking to a man she didn't know a little intimidating, and with Trevor being unavailable, Matt decided to call Amy instead, to see if she would be willing to accompany him. Amy, like Trevor, had a calming demeanour and Matt was hopeful that the presence of another female would put the elderly lady at ease.

Amy was very interested in how the book was progressing and had been extremely obliging with background information regarding Edith and her father, but Matt was unsure if she would be willing to go so far as to attend an interview with him. To his pleasant surprise, Amy was delighted to be asked.

Matt collected her from her house and during the drive to Leambridge, she questioned him about how he carried out his work and what she could expect to happen during the course of the day. She asked whether she would be able to participate in the interview. For example, if she felt that he had missed an opportunity to gain useful information, would it bother him if she interrupted with a question of her own? She was worried that she might mess things up. She'd also brought along her own notebook and had already listed some potential questions. She read these out to Matt, secretly hoping, he assumed, to have come up with something that he hadn't already thought of. Amused at her enthusiasm, he told her to "Fill her boots" and do whatever she felt comfortable with.

At St Peter's they were met by Mr Roberts who led them through to a small meeting room. Peggy was already there, sitting at a table with a cup of tea in front of her. She stood as they entered and shook their hands. She was a tiny woman with permed grey hair and huge glasses that gave her an owl-like appearance. After the introductions had been made and Martin had offered Amy and Matt refreshments, which they both declined, they all sat down. Amy took the chair nearest to Peggy and Matt sat a little further back, discretely setting his phone to record.

Amy, Matt soon realised, was a born natural. She began chatting away to Peggy about how beautiful the church was and what unusual weather they were experiencing for the time of year. Matt let them chat without interruption, as he could see Peggy visibly beginning to relax. He felt extremely pleased with himself for having had the idea to bring Amy along. Gradually, Amy introduced questions regarding Peggy's friendship with Betty, and Peggy responded happily, explaining how the two of them had met and what they liked to do together. Matt only interjected occasionally to ask Peggy to clarify certain points. There was a lot of unnecessary information but neither Amy nor Matt stopped the flow. Like Matt, Amy instinctively understood that sometimes you can obtain more information from letting someone just talk rather than from asking specific questions.

Time was running on, and Amy needed to get back to her family. There was still a lot of ground to cover, and Matt was wondering how to ask for a second meeting when Peggy suggested that they visit her at her home the following week, as she had some photographs of Betty that might be of interest. A day and time were agreed, and they said their goodbyes. Peggy became a little tearful as they exited the church, explaining that she still missed her friend and talking about her brought back a lot of painful memories. Amy stopped and gave Peggy a hug which went down really well with the little old lady, and Matt once more congratulated himself on having asked Amy to accompany him.

"*Watch out Trevor*," he thought. "*You've got competition!*"

10

The following is an interview with Marsha Scott-Williams, Keith Kelly's agent.

I was Keith Kelly's Agent, and also his friend, for over twenty years. Before signing with me, Keith had mainly worked in theatre. Prospect Road was already hugely popular when he auditioned on a whim for the role of Jeff Walker, never expecting to get the part. To his astonishment, the audition was successful, and so then he found himself in need of an agent who understood television. My agency was recommended by several cast members already signed to me.

Keith and I not only had an excellent working relationship for many years but also a true friendship; not something I shared with many of my clients. Like so many who knew and loved him, I was devastated by his death, and the subsequent defamation of his character, initiated by his wife, with the propaganda then circulated by the media.

Knowing Keith as well as I did and for as long as I had, I refuse to entertain the notion that he was anything other than a hardworking, down to earth, family man. I don't believe there to be an ounce of truth to Eliza's accusations and will do anything in my power to support his family and clear his name, which is why I'm talking to you now.

Unlike many of his peers, Keith did not have a large ego that needed constant massaging. He was as happy doing charity work for free as he was hosting a lucrative corporate event. He deservedly gained a reputation for being easy to work with and was genuinely liked within the whole industry, and believe me that made him unique. He didn't cause me a spot of bother in all the years I worked with him, up until he met and married Eliza, and then the problems were caused by her and not him.

My first meeting with Eliza was a baptism of fire. Keith had only just notified me of his marriage. I hadn't even realised he was seeing someone. He called me from the States where he was filming That's Not Fair. Firstly, to give me the news of his nuptials and secondly to say that his new wife was back in the UK and would like to meet with me. I thought it odd that she would want to see me without Keith but as I was intrigued to meet this 'surprise' wife I agreed.

The meeting got off to a bad start. In this business, you get used to pushy people, but she was on a whole new level. No one intimidates me; I wouldn't be able to do this job if that was the case, but that was certainly her intention. Without bothering with any pleasantries, or even giving me time to congratulate her on her recent wedding, she began to list for me the television programmes she believed that she and Keith should be booked on, such as GMTV and Jonathon Ross. This was followed by a list of publications that she would be willing to do interviews with. For a moment, I was dumbfounded. I actually believed it to be some sort of set-up. I expected the door to fling open and Keith to appear, then we'd all laugh about how I'd fallen for the joke. How on earth could this presumptuous, brash individual be Keith's partner of choice? Surely it had to be an act. Unfortunately, it was neither an act nor a joke. She was deadly serious.

Trying to keep my temper for Keith's sake, I politely informed her that promotion was a job for a publicist, not an agent.

"Well get me Keith's publicist then!" she demanded.

I didn't speak. I just sat in silence giving her my best 'hard stare'. Eventually she cracked and asked for the publicist's details.

"Keith doesn't have one," I replied. "He's never needed one. He's not that sort of artist. And before you get too carried away and cause him any embarrassment, I should warn you that your chances of getting a slot on programmes such as Jonathon Ross are nil. Even if they were interested in talking to Keith – which they wouldn't be, because he's not a big enough name to warrant an appearance for no reason, and he's not currently appearing in anything mainstream or a newly released film - they would have absolutely no interest in you whatsoever. Let me put you straight, Keith may have a small supporting role in a relatively successful American Sitcom but that doesn't mean he's a big star. He hasn't ever been that big a star. Not even when he was appearing in Prospect Road.

Eliza then subjected me to another ten-minute harangue, insisting it must be my fault he wasn't a bigger name. Why had I never secured him a starring role in a blockbuster movie? Why was Keith doing so much theatre work when film and television paid much better? Why had I allowed his character to be killed off in Prospect Road so that there was no opening for his return? To be fair to me, I had made this point to Keith at the time he was negotiating his departure with the producers, but Keith was adamant he was done with Jeff and never wanted to play him again.

After this tirade, I no longer cared about Keith's feelings. "If Keith has a problem with the way I have handled his career, then Keith needs to speak to me about it," I told her. I then asked her to leave as I had another appointment.

I contacted Keith and tore him off a strip. I told him how disappointing it was to learn that he was so unhappy with my work from his wife rather than from him. It was apparent Keith hadn't the faintest inkling of what Eliza had said to me, and it certainly wasn't a conversation he condoned. He was contrite, extremely apologetic. He assured me he would speak to Eliza and that nothing like this would happen again. Still fuming from my encounter with her, I told him in no uncertain terms that if Eliza set foot in my office again, I would have her escorted off the premises by security.

Fortunately, Eliza's intrusion caused no permanent damage to my and Keith's relationship, but that didn't stop me from being surprised when a short time later he asked for my help in arranging a screen test for Eliza, as she wanted to break into acting. Having made him acutely aware of my dislike for her, I was perplexed when he also asked if I would be willing to take her on as a client. I immediately refused to do the latter. I wouldn't touch anyone with no training or experience. As for the former, I personally did not think that Eliza had any aptitude for acting and therefore a screen test would be a waste of time. Keith wasn't to be put off telling me he was certain Eliza would "Nail it", so, refusing to get involved personally, I gave him some names and contact numbers and left him to it.

Keith arranged for Eliza to have a photographic and video session with a cameraman friend of his, and then somehow managed to persuade a casting director, with whom we were both acquainted, to look over it. Obviously, I wasn't there so I can't testify to exactly what happened, but when I next saw the said casting director, I asked for her opinion of Eliza. The feedback was entirely negative. According to her, Eliza was not at all photogenic and had zero acting talent. Apparently, she had informed Eliza straight away that she was not suited to be in front of a camera. She was incredulous at the way Eliza reacted to her verdict. Having already been rude and overbearing at the beginning of the interview, on receiving this unfavourable judgement, Eliza threw a massive tantrum, which included sweeping items from a desk to the floor and had then stormed out leaving Keith to apologise for her behaviour. As my acquaintance said to me, and I agreed with her, it was a good job that Keith was so well liked within the industry, otherwise Eliza's behaviour could have cost him work.

Undeterred by her negative review, Eliza took to phoning my agency every other day to see if there was work for her. Keith had obviously neglected to inform her we had refused her as a client. I had to ask him to put her right as her calls were an inconvenience. I could hear the reluctance as he promised to "Have a word."

This wasn't the only time I had to speak to Keith regarding Eliza. I got word from a friend of mine who runs a modelling agency that Eliza had tried to use my name to secure herself an audition. Apparently, I was "Highly recommending" her to them. Fuming, I called Keith and told him that if Eliza used my name again to try and open doors for her, I would sue. Once more, he was apologetic and promised to speak to Eliza but again I could hear the dread in his voice. I wouldn't say Keith was the most masculine of men, but Eliza certainly appeared to have him utterly under her thumb.

Not long after this, we received the news that there would be no third series of That's Not Fair. Ostensibly, the network had been disappointed by the drop in ratings between the end of the first season and the end of the second season. I must admit this was a blow as both Keith and I had expected it to run for several series.

However, Keith, being his usual pragmatic self, had soon secured a role in a theatre production that would be touring the North for at least 3 months.

On account of his time in Prospect Road, Keith was able to command a reasonable fee for work outside of acting, such as Nightclub and Supermarket openings, after-dinner speaking or hosting of corporate and social events. He was one of my most sought-after clients for this type of work. He had also secured some well-paid supporting roles in various television dramas and sitcoms, such as That's Not Fair. But as he got older, the supporting roles became smaller. He now played the part of the father of a lead character or a grumpy employer, that sort of thing. So not exactly a walk-on part, but not particularly well paid or regular either. He continued working in theatre, but here also, the roles were smaller and not especially rewarding financially. Nothing he appeared in was successful enough to secure a long run, although his portrayal of Falstaff at Stratford received renowned reviews.

It was around this time that he stopped doing the charity work that he had so loved, and my understanding is that Eliza pressurised him into not committing his time to anything that didn't pay. This was when I first became aware that he was having financial difficulties.

It was also at this time that he asked my advice on how to find acting work for his and Eliza's son, Zac. Unlike with Eliza, this time I was willing to help him as I knew his older children and, more fool me, I assumed that Zac would be of a similar nature. Finding work for his son could be a way to help Keith financially. With this in mind, I arranged for Zac to have a session with another casting director friend of mine who worked on a prime-time drama show set in a school. What was a perfect opportunity turned into an absolute disaster! The feedback was as negative as Eliza's. The boy was apparently surly, uncommunicative, and lacking in both ability and charisma. It seems he had nothing in common with his older siblings, or his father for that matter!

As time went on, it became harder to find roles suitable for Keith. Work was drying up across the board. As he was no longer a household name, he stopped being asked to appear on panel shows or host events. I knew he had really hit rock bottom when he approached me about auditioning for one of the Reality TV shows. He'd always insisted he would never stoop that low. As part of the auditioning process, he was required to have a full medical examination and that was when it was discovered that he needed treatment for a heart condition.

When he was well enough to return to work, we had an honest and frank discussion. He understood that the work was just not available to him, but he informed me he couldn't possibly afford to retire. His royalties and his pension were not enough to cover his outgoings. With a view to saving him some money, it was agreed that I would no longer officially be his agent, but as a friend I would continue to put his name forward for suitable roles. As I've said before, Keith was a pragmatic sort of person and he immediately found work speaking at events run by the U3A. He also began talking in front of groups like the WI. All of this work was low paid, but he was busy every day of the week.

The very last time I saw Keith was when I happened to bump into him in town just a couple of weeks before he died. I was in a rush so I couldn't stop but I was shocked at how old and ill he looked. I determined that I would try and find him some work and had potentially secured him a part in a detective series when we received the horrendous news. It was a terrible shock. Such an awful thing to happen to such a lovely man. And of course, with all the melodrama surrounding his death, it turns out Eliza was a much better actress than any of us gave her credit for.

11

When Matt and Amy turned up at Peggy's bungalow at the appointed time, they were greeted like old friends. The bungalow was small and situated in a cul-de-sac of identical bungalows. The only difference between them was that some had obviously been extended into the loft space and now sported dormer windows. Peggy's bungalow appeared not to have been altered since it was first built but it was well maintained.

Peggy ushered them through to the living room where the majority of the space was taken up by a large, soft pink, three-piece suite. The mantle shelf, above the fireplace housing an electric fire, was crammed with figurines, mostly shepherds holding crooks and shepherdesses with flouncy bonnets and lambs at their feet. There was a shelving unit with knick-knacks and ornaments filling every available space. To Matt it felt a little claustrophobic, not helped by the fact that the central heating was turned up high and the electric fire was on, despite the day being relatively clement. Whilst Amy went off to help Peggy make some tea, Matt surreptitiously removed his jacket and rolled up his shirt sleeves in a vain attempt to cool down.

When the women returned, Amy bearing a tea tray with an old-fashioned China tea service, and Peggy with a selection of cakes on a tiered cake stand, Matt was instantly taken back to being a small child having Sunday afternoon tea with his grandmother and great aunts. His grandmother's house had always been overheated too.

After the tea was poured and handed around alongside cakes placed on matching China side plates, complete with linen napkins, Peggy opened a drawer at the bottom of the shelving unit and removed a couple of photo albums. She handed them to Amy who made the appropriate noises over photographs of Peggy's wedding, her children and her grandchildren. Matt began to wonder if Peggy had forgotten who they were and why they were there, but to remind her seemed rude. After what seemed to Matt like an eternity, Amy eventually asked Peggy if she had a photograph of Betty she could see. Peggy turned through several pages of the album before stopping and removing a couple of photographs from between the cellophane. Amy studied them for a moment before passing them across to Matt.

The photographs had been taken on a day trip to the seaside, so Peggy informed them. It was easy to spot Peggy wearing a cotton sundress and large floppy hat. Betty, on the other hand, wore a long coat and an old-fashioned hat, and again Matt was reminded of his Great Aunts. The photograph could have been of a mother and daughter. Although Peggy was a couple of years older than Betty, she appeared far more youthful and vibrant in the photograph. Betty looked sullen, as if unhappy at having her picture taken. Matt could see instantly why Edith might have been embarrassed about her mother. It was like looking at someone from the 1950s, not the mid '90s.

12

Note from author of 'The Evil Underneath,' Matt Dinsdale:
The following is an amalgamation of the notes taken from various interviews with Peggy Dixon, (lifelong friend of Edith's mother) so that the information she gives appears in chronological order.

I've known Betty since we were little girls. Her father was the minister of my family church, and her mum ran the Sunday School. I was a couple of years older than her, and my mum told me I needed to look after her because she was a little bit slow. I know that there are different names for things these days, but when I was growing up that was how we referred to people with learning difficulties.

The family moved away when Betty was about 13 but we stayed in touch by sending letters to each other. We were pen pals which was a popular thing in those days. I've still got some of her letters. Her spelling is awful, but her handwriting is neat. I suppose I always felt a bit sorry for her. Her parents were so strict. Her father was very much a hell and damnation type of preacher and, although I was quite young, I do remember that a lot of his sermons centred around Jezebels and fallen women and that God was always watching and would know if you sinned. To be honest, I enjoyed going to church much more once he left, the new vicar wasn't anywhere near as sanctimonious.

Anyway, once I left school, Betty and I started to lose touch. My life was very different to hers. Remember this was the sixties and I left school and went out to work. I wore make-up and miniskirts. Poor Betty didn't have any of that. Her dad didn't want her to get a job, so she stayed at home helping her mum out with household chores and things to do with the church. Her dad wouldn't allow her to wear fashionable clothes. She wore plain skirts (always below the knee) and blouses, never anything colourful or with a pattern, and always flat shoes, never heels. She wore her hair up in a bun and never used make-up. We would occasionally meet up on a Saturday, as we were only a bus ride away from each other, and I took her to one of those department stores once, as a treat for her birthday. It was one of those places where girls in the cosmetics department would let you experiment with testers and would help you choose and apply make-up. I just wanted Betty to see what a difference a bit of eyeshadow and lippy could make to her appearance, but she wouldn't have any of it. She got very distressed telling me that according to her dad, make-up was only worn by wicked girls.

"That must mean I'm very wicked," I teased her. "Because I wear make-up all the time." And we had a bit of a laugh about it, but I could tell she was really upset, so I never tried to do anything like that again.

As time went on, I started to find it a bit awkward meeting with her. We had less and less in common and nothing to talk about. Then I met Jim, and I spent all my free time with him. I did ask her to be a bridesmaid at my wedding, but she made up some excuse as to why she couldn't. I can't remember what it was she said, but I do remember at the time thinking it was because her dad wouldn't let her. I must have been married 2, maybe 3 years, when her mum died. Betty was in her early twenties. She didn't tell me herself. She hadn't even told me her mum was ill. It was cancer that took her, and apparently Ruth had been poorly for quite some time, but Betty never let on. By then we were only exchanging birthday and Christmas cards. I'd put a letter in with mine just giving her all my news and sometimes she would write back but not very often.

It was my mum who heard about Ruth passing. I think someone from church told her. I rang Betty to offer my condolences. I felt so bad for her because I knew that while her mum was incapacitated, not only would she have been caring for her, but she would also have been running the house and helping her dad out with the Church, basically doing everything her mum had done. I also knew that her dad would expect her to carry on doing that now her mum was dead and that's exactly what happened.

Mum and I, and a few others that remembered the family from their time at our church, went to Ruth's funeral and that was the last time I saw or heard from Betty until after she had the baby.

Now that really was a bolt out of the blue. As far as I was aware, Betty had never even had a boyfriend let alone a fiancé, so when she appeared on my doorstep with a sweet 6-month-old baby girl, I could only assume she was looking after her for someone else. I was so surprised when she told me that the baby was hers and that the father had died before they had had a chance to marry, but they had been engaged. I didn't really believe her. Betty had never been a good liar, and I assumed she'd fallen pregnant by accident and the father either wouldn't or couldn't (i.e., he was married) get involved. We didn't have easy access to abortions in those days and even if we had, Betty's religious beliefs would never have allowed her to get rid of the baby.

Betty was besotted with her baby girl, and I honestly believe it was the best thing that ever happened to her. I had never seen her so happy. It never even crossed my mind that she might have been raped or abused. I know it's hard to believe now, but they were much simpler days and women like me were sheltered from the darker side of life. I was simply too naïve to think anything bad might have happened to Betty. I just accepted what she told me, and we never spoke about it again; that is until after her father died and I discovered the horrible truth.

13

Continued - Note from the author of 'The Evil Underneath,' Matt Dinsdale: *The following is an amalgamation of the notes taken from various interviews with Peggy Dixon, (lifelong friend of Edith's mother) so that the information she gives appears in chronological order.*

I started to see more of Betty again after Edith was born. I don't think she had any other friends around her own age and because I'd had children of my own, she used to lean on me for help and advice as regards Edith. Also, I have to admit to being a little concerned about how well Betty could cope with a child. Although she was now in her mid-twenties, she behaved more like a 15-year-old. It was kind of a relief to know that her dad was there to lend a helping hand. Her home life carried on as it had before. She and Edith lived with her father and Betty took care of them both, looked after the house and helped out with the Church. I'm not sure what they told people at church about Edith's father, but it was obviously accepted because otherwise, as an unwed mother, Betty would have been ostracised.

Betty coped surprisingly well while Edith was a baby. She had a tendency to treat her like a doll. She loved dressing her up and showing her off. But as Edith got older, the problems started. Although she was a polite, well-behaved girl in company, I think at home Edith ran them ragged. She was as sharp as a tack. I remember her rolling her eyes at something her mother said when she was only about 3 years old. According to Betty, Edith had a wicked temper and would have massive tantrums if she didn't get her own way. It was surprising to learn that Edith clashed so often with her grandfather. When we were growing up, we were all terrified of him as he was such a harsh, no-nonsense man, and we would never have dreamed of answering him back; his word was law. However, according to Betty, Edith had no fear of him, and Betty was forever trying to keep the peace between them. She confessed to me that she wasn't sure what she was most afraid of, John hurting Edith or Edith hurting John. That was a remarkable thing to say when Edith was only 5 years old! It's funny but Edith only seemed to misbehave at home. I did wonder if Betty exaggerated sometimes. I witnessed the odd tantrum, but they were nothing out of the ordinary and Edith's school reports were excellent. She really was super smart, and she loved school, which was a blessing for Betty who was so proud of her little girl, but it also meant that Edith could literally run rings round her mother and I'm sure she did so from a very early age. It must have been difficult for John too. Edith wasn't the push-over that Betty was and that must have been anathema to him.

So, life still wasn't treating Betty very kindly but then as horrible as it is to say, things did get better for a little while after her father died. Although obviously that was such a tragic thing to happen and the shock to Betty was enormous. I'll tell you how shocked she was – her hair turned white overnight! It all happened when he was home alone, and I don't think Betty ever forgave herself for not being there. To be fair it probably wouldn't have happened if she had been at home, but that's life isn't it. The only time Betty ever stayed away from home was when she went on a church retreat, which she did once a year, every year, right from when she was a little girl. That year they had gone to North Yorkshire, I believe. Edith was away too. She'd gone abroad with the school. Italy maybe? I can't remember. But John had not been well. He'd had a stroke, and it affected his movement and his speech. I'd been over to the house a couple of times since he'd come out of hospital and the change in him was quite profound. He wasn't as sharp in his mind or with his tongue! They investigated the fire and told Betty afterwards that they thought he'd started cooking his supper and then forgot about it and went to bed. That's where they found him, in his bed. The smoke had obviously got to him first, which would have been a blessing.

The police met Betty off the bus the next morning and broke the news to her. The whole house was destroyed and everything in it. She had nothing, only the clothes she had with her. She was utterly devastated, and the police didn't want her to be on her own. As she had no family, she got them to ring me, and they brought her round to mine. She and Edith ended up staying with us until things got sorted and they got their own little house not that far away from here. I don't think Betty wanted to go back to where she'd been living, all those memories and she knew this area of course having lived here before.

When the fire happened, Edith still had another week of her holiday left and Betty didn't want to spoil it for her, so she knew nothing about it until she got back. I have to say she took the news very well. I knew her relationship with her grandad hadn't been that good, but she certainly wasn't outwardly upset at his passing. Nor did she seem too bothered that they had lost the house and everything in it. She was really interested in the fire though and what it had done to him. Wanted all the gory details. Weird kid. My Jim always said there was something not quite right about her. When they lived with us for those few months, my kids said she gave them the creeps.

So, the two of them moved into their new house and for the first time ever, Betty was free to do what she pleased, but Betty being Betty not that much changed. She certainly never went wild. There were no nights out and definitely no men! She still dressed very conservatively and mostly kept to herself, only really mixing with people from church. I suppose that's the only sort of life she knew, and it was what she was comfortable with. She always looked at least twenty years older than she actually was. She left her hair white after the fire, never bothering to colour it, and with her dowdy dress sense and, not meaning to be rude, her plain face, you would have mistaken her for being in her fifties not her thirties. I know for a fact that Edith tried to pass her off as her nan rather than her mum when she went to the first parents' evening at Edith's new school. Betty was rather upset by that!

Betty also struggled for money. She was always short of cash. I know that alongside getting the tuition for free with Edith's scholarship, I'll tell you about that in a minute, there was a grant to cover things like uniform, but I don't think it was anywhere near enough and Edith always seemed to need something new. Up until then most of Edith's clothes had come from jumble sales. Jumble sales were very popular back then, but you don't see them nowadays! But when she started at that posh school, second-hand would no longer do for Edith.

Betty ended up working about three cleaning jobs and making cakes for people on the side to earn a bit extra. She was an excellent baker and also incredibly talented when it came to decorating cakes. She made Wedding and Christening cakes for people at church, and she was always in demand. At Christmas time, she was rushed off her feet with orders for Christmas cakes and mince pies. It was a lucrative little earner for her, and she enjoyed doing it. I introduced her to our Sharon. Sharon's my son Adrian's wife. She owns a tea shop in town and Betty started making cakes for Sharon too, for her to sell in her shop. Sharon would also take in orders for her. When Sharon had a vacancy, Betty started working in the tea shop full-time. She really loved that job, and she was very good at it. She got on so well with the customers. It was great to see her mixing happily with so many different people. Working there brought her out of her shell a little bit, although she was still painfully shy outside of the cafe. I know Sharon was pleased she had employed her. This should have been a time when Betty was really happy, but Edith spoiled that for her.

Through her hard work, Edith won a scholarship to Foxford and although she continued to do well with her schoolwork, she didn't seem to make any friends there. I don't think it helped her being on a scholarship. I mean nearly all the other girls- did I mention it was an all-girls school? - came from wealthy backgrounds and I can only assume that they looked down on Edith or that Edith felt she didn't come up to their standards. We all know how bitchy teenage girls can be. Our Tracey had a right old time with bullies when she was at school. Well, whatever the reason, Edith started hanging around after school with kids from the local council estate instead. I mean, I'm not passing judgement on council estates, but this particular group of yobbos were notorious in the area for causing trouble. Everything from robbing local shops to setting fire to cars. And then that Ricky she'd been friends with at primary school, reappeared on the scene.

Betty had been hoping that, as he had been fostered out of the area, and then they themselves had moved, then Edith wouldn't get to see him anymore. Betty was convinced that he was a bad influence on Edith, but I think it was more likely the other way round. I met him a couple of times and he was a nice enough lad but, in a way, he reminded me of Betty. He wasn't that bright, and I think it was easy for Edith to manipulate him, just like she did with her mother. Anyway, Edith would stay out till all hours and come back stinking of smoke and alcohol. Betty was beside herself. She didn't know what to do. She tried setting curfews, but Edith just ignored them and Betty completely lost control; not that she'd ever had much as far as Edith was concerned. Betty was so ashamed of Edith's behaviour and so intimidated by her that she didn't seek help from anywhere. Who could have helped anyway? Certainly not me. There was no way Edith would listen to me. And that girl was so clever. Her schoolwork never suffered, and she always behaved like butter wouldn't melt, in front of other people. When the vicar confronted her about her no longer attending church, she told him it was only temporary whilst she devoted time to her studies, but she never went back and the vicar chastised Betty for pushing her daughter too hard with her schoolwork!

It was obvious that Betty was scared of Edith. As the girl grew older, both Sharon and I were aware that Edith was perhaps physically hurting her, but Betty would never admit to it. And it never felt right to push the issue. Just as Betty's life should have been getting easier, Edith was making it a living nightmare. I think Betty blamed the way that Edith had come to be in the world as to why she behaved so badly, and I have to say that I agree with her. You see Betty shared a secret with me that first night at mine, after the fire that had killed her dad, when she was still in such a state of shock. Neither of us could sleep so we sat up talking and she had asked me if I thought God could be punishing her father for what he had done. I asked her what she meant by that. Surely the man had devoted his life to God and there was nothing to punish him for.

And that's when she confessed to me that not only had she taken her mother's place within the home but also in her father's bed. Her father was Edith's father! I had no idea. I was speechless. Nothing like that had even crossed my mind. I did promise her that for both her own and for Edith's sake I wouldn't tell anyone, and I never have until now. Not even my Jim. But then after everything I have learned about Edith and what she has done, I feel the time is right to share Betty's secret, because like her I think it might be the reason why Edith has turned out the way she has.

14

Continued - Note from the author of 'The Evil Underneath,' Matt Dinsdale: *The following is an amalgamation of the notes taken from various interviews with Peggy Dixon, (lifelong friend of Edith's mother) so that the information she gives appears in chronological order.*

Sorry to take a little break there but talking about what happened between Betty and her father is rather upsetting. Right, where was I? Oh yes, well things did become easier for Betty once Edith left that posh school. Edith did extremely well in her O Levels but instead of staying on in the 6th form there, she decided to sit her A Levels at a more local school, albeit one with an excellent reputation. I think she wanted to get away from those snobby girls.

For her 16th birthday, Edith asked Betty to pay for her to have her name changed by deed poll. She changed it from Edith O'Reilly to Eleanor Cashmore. I think she had always hated her Christian name. She considered it old-fashioned, which I suppose it was for her generation. She had been named after her maternal grandmother who Betty had adored. I also think Edith considered her surname to be a bit beneath her, a bit too common. Going to that exclusive all-girls school hadn't done her any favours in that respect. So, a new name, a new school and a completely fresh start did seem to make a difference to Edith and her behaviour. I wouldn't say their home life was perfect, but Edith did seem to treat her mother a little better. Let's say she was kinder to her. The only time she really got vexed was when Betty forgot to use her new name. This happened often as poor Betty struggled to get used to calling her daughter Eleanor, and whenever she talked to me about her, she always referred to her as Edith. If it's okay with you, I'll carry on calling her Edith while I talk to you because it's what I'm used to.

Edith passed her A levels with top marks and got accepted at Oxford to study Law. Betty was over the moon. She was so proud of Edith, rightly so because it was a tremendous achievement. Betty didn't see very much of Edith once she went to university. She hardly ever came home for a visit, and more often than not, she made plans to spend the holidays with friends elsewhere. To be honest, who could blame her? Life at home would seem very mundane to an outgoing young girl. It upset Betty that she and Edith weren't close, but at the same time, it was a consolation to know that Edith finally had friends she was comfortable with. Betty never visited Edith on campus. Jim and I offered a few times to take her but there never seemed a convenient time that suited us and Edith. In the end, I stopped offering. It was plain to see that Edith didn't want to be paid a visit by her mother.

However, when it came to graduation time and Edith began to come up with reasons as to why Betty shouldn't attend, I felt I had to step in. Betty was so hurt at the thought of not being able to share such an important landmark in her daughter's life. Betty's birthday was a few months before graduation, and I knew Edith was calling in to see her, so I arranged to be there at the same time. When Betty left the room for a moment, I'm afraid I gave Edith a piece of my mind, and by the time Betty came back, Edith had agreed to Jim and I taking Betty to Oxford for the day. It made me smile when Edith told Betty her birthday present was a ticket to the graduation. Clever cow, making it seem as if that had been her intention all along and she had only put her mother off so as to make it a birthday surprise.

Then, as fate would have it, Betty never got to see Edith graduate. She died just after her birthday. So sad! Broke my heart!

15

Continued - Note from the author of 'The Evil Underneath,' Matt Dinsdale: *The following is an amalgamation of the notes taken from various interviews with Peggy Dixon, (lifelong friend of Edith's mother) so that the information she gives appears in chronological order.*

I remember the events around Betty's death really well. I first became concerned about her because I'd been trying to get hold of her for a couple of days, but she wasn't answering her phone, which was really unusual. She'd told me that as she'd worked the previous Saturday and Sunday at the café, her days off would be Tuesday and Wednesday that week. I knew she would be catching up on washing and housework on Tuesday, but I thought she might like to meet me in town on Wednesday for a spot of lunch, so I tried phoning her. I think it was probably around 4 or 5 pm on Tuesday afternoon when I first tried. I was surprised when she didn't answer but thought she'd probably popped to the local shop. I left a message for her to call me back and when she didn't, which was most unlike her! I tried once or twice more before I went to bed. I thought she probably wasn't feeling well and had gone to bed early.

When she didn't call me back the next morning and she still wasn't answering her phone, I started to become worried. I called Sharon at the cafe to see if she had heard from her or if she knew if Betty had been feeling unwell on Monday, but Sharon said she'd been fine on Monday and as far as she was aware, she would be back to work on Thursday. That's when I decided I'd better go and check up on her. I took the bus because I don't drive, and Jim was at work. The stop for Betty's house was just past where she lived, so the bus drove past it before it dropped me off. I always tried to get a window seat on that side of the bus, because if she knew I was coming Betty would wave at me out her front room window. That day, the curtains were still drawn so I was certain that she must be ill and decided to pick up some chicken soup from the shop at the bottom of her road before I called round. I was pretty certain that she would be too unwell to answer the door, but I knocked anyway before I used my key. She had given me one when she first got the house in case she ever locked herself out.

I found her in her favourite chair in the front room. She looked like she was asleep, but I could sense that she was gone. I did go to check but as soon as I touched her, I knew for sure. She was stone cold. I was so shocked that I burst into tears. Poor Betty, I thought to myself, what could have happened? I thought it might have been a heart attack or a stroke, but she looked so peaceful. Then I noticed her insulin kit was out on the little table next to her armchair and not in the fridge where she usually kept it, so I assumed she might have had an episode. They didn't happen very often. She managed the condition really well; especially for someone like her. I suppose if you've been diabetic since you were little then it becomes second nature.

As I leant over her, I caught a whiff of Edith's perfume. Edith wore a very expensive perfume with a powerful, distinctive scent. She never wore anything else, and Betty always tried to find enough money to buy her a bottle for her birthday and for Christmas. Sorry, I'm rambling again.

After I pulled myself together, I phoned 999. I explained to the lady on the phone what had happened, and she told me she would send someone straight around. Whilst I was waiting, I went upstairs and got a blanket off the bed. I know it sounds stupid, but Betty hated being cold. Covering her over, I could really smell Edith's perfume. It was as if Edith had been hugging Betty, but that was unlikely; Edith wasn't a hugger, and she was in Oxford!

A policeman soon arrived, followed very shortly after by an ambulance. The paramedics confirmed that Betty had been dead for some time so any treatment by them was unnecessary. As they left, the policeman was on his radio arranging for Betty's body to be collected. The policeman was so nice and kind, checking that I was okay. He told me he needed to ask some questions and suggested we go into the kitchen because they would be arriving shortly to take Betty away, and it would probably be better for me not to be in the room. I asked if she would be going to the funeral home, but he said she would go to the mortuary at the hospital first as they would need to do a post-mortem because it was an unexpected death.

I asked him if I could make a cup of tea and he said he didn't see why not but if I showed him where everything was, he would make it. He put sugar in mine, even though I'd told him I didn't take sugar. Sharon told me afterwards it would have been for the shock. I was surprised that I had to tidy up some paperwork that was scattered across the top of the kitchen table before we could sit and drink our tea. I said to the policeman what with that and the dirty cups in the sink, it was most unlike Betty. I mean she had that compulsive obsessive thingamajig. She couldn't abide mess. She must have been feeling unwell to not put the paperwork away or at least put it in a neat pile, and I'd never known her to leave a single teaspoon unwashed. To myself, I also wondered who on earth she had round for a cup of tea, because as far as I knew only myself or Edith went in the house. I'm certain she didn't even know the name of her neighbours, let alone be comfortable enough to invite them in for a cuppa. When, once, one of her neighbours had taken a parcel in for her, she asked me to go and collect it from them because she was too shy to speak to them. Sorry, I'm rambling again.

While we drank our tea, the policeman asked me to explain how I came to find Betty in her house, so I told him about not being able to get hold of her on the phone and about having to use my key to get in. He asked about Betty's next of kin and I told him there was only Edith, who I didn't have a contact number for, but he could get hold of her at the university. He then asked if there was anyone who could come and pick me up and I told him everyone was busy at work so I would get the bus, and that's when he offered to run me home. Wasn't that kind of him? It got a few net curtains twitching, I can tell you – me being brought home in a police car. It wasn't long before Jean across the road came running over to find out what had happened. I have to say that for once I didn't really mind that she was so nosey, because she stayed with me until Jim got home, and it was nice to have the company.

The next morning, the same policeman telephoned me at home. He'd rung the university he told me, but they'd never heard of an Edith O'Reilly. Of course, silly old me, I'd forgotten about Edith changing her name. I apologised to him and explained the situation and he was so nice about it and told me not to worry. I asked him if, when he got hold of Edith/Eleanor, would he mind asking her to get in touch with me and he said he would. I wanted to let Edith know I was willing to help in any way I could with funeral arrangements and the like. I mean, it's a lot to expect a young girl to do on her own isn't it, and she had no one else. I was the closest thing to family she had.

Under the circumstances, I expected Edith to pop around to see me rather than ring. But as the days went by, I didn't hear from her at all. Then the days turned into a couple of weeks, and I started to get concerned about the funeral arrangements. People from the church were also asking me when it was going to be, and I felt bad that I couldn't give them any information. I tried to contact Edith through the university, I even remembered to use her new name, but I could only leave a message asking her to call me and she never did. Sharon said the term had ended and Edith had probably left the university, bearing in mind she was soon to graduate. Sharon thought Edith would most likely be staying at Betty's house now that it belonged to her. That made sense, and so Sharon and I called around there. And what a surprise we got. No, Edith wasn't living there, but there was a For Sale sign in the front garden, and the house was empty. All the furniture was gone! I couldn't believe it. Sharon and I just stood there not knowing what to do. Sharon said she was surprised that Edith had been able to act so quickly as it was unlikely that probate had been granted yet.

My main worry was about the funeral and how was I going to be able to get in touch with Edith now? Sharon suggested we call the Estate Agents to see if they could give us a forwarding address for Edith but, because we weren't family, all they would do was pass on a message. It was the same when Sharon managed to track down the funeral home that Betty had been sent to. Although, they did inform us that Betty had already been cremated and that they were in possession of her ashes. They told Sharon they would ask Edith to contact us when she came to collect her mother's remains. I have to say this news was devastating. Finding out that she had already been cremated, I felt like poor Betty had been let down yet again. It was obvious she hadn't had a proper funeral because none of her friends were there. Not only me and my family but people from the church, and customers from the cafe had all wanted a chance to say goodbye to her and we had been denied that. I was fuming. If that little madam ever bothered to get in touch, and I wasn't holding my breath, I would certainly let her know exactly what I thought of her.

So, I believed that was an end to it. Our vicar suggested we hold a service of remembrance for Betty, which we did, and it was lovely. So many people came. Betty would have been thrilled. I was a little put out that I would never know what Betty had died of, but as Jim pointed out what did that matter really?

Then about two weeks after we held the memorial service, I got a phone call from Edith, right out of the blue. She didn't give me a chance to talk. All she said was that the funeral home was giving her grief about not collecting the ashes and that as she was away and would not be coming back to the area any time in the foreseeable future, she had given her permission for me to go and collect them myself, and I could do what I liked with them. Before I had a chance to say anything, she put the phone down. I was flabbergasted. How strange was that? What sort of a daughter was she? But I couldn't bear the thought of Betty being all alone and unloved, so that's when Jim and I came to an agreement. We went and collected Betty, and we put her in our China cabinet and that's where she still is! She'd laugh at that. She'd love the fact that she's treated as well as my prized porcelain.

Jim and I have a joint plot in the churchyard. Obviously, Jim's there now, under the elm tree, waiting for me, and I visit him all the time for a chat. When my turn comes, I know our children and grandchildren won't forget us and they will visit on special occasions, leaving fresh flowers and keeping our grave tidy, all that sort of thing. I wanted the same for Betty, and Jim and I agreed that she could be buried with us. So, when I go, I've left instructions for her to be put in my coffin with me, it's the very least I can do for her. If I had died before Jim, he would have made sure she was placed beside me. I just can't bear the thought of her being alone for eternity.

You asked me why I thought Edith had been in the house just before Betty died, despite her telling the police that she hadn't seen her Mum since her birthday. Well, first of all, the smell of her perfume. Like I said she wore a strong scent, but not strong enough to still be hanging around all those weeks later. I'm not a big believer in signs from above, so when I thought about it sensibly later on, I wondered if maybe Betty kept a bottle herself, to remind her of Edith. You hear of people doing that sort of thing don't you? Although, usually after someone has died. But then Betty was a funny old thing!

Secondly, the paperwork strewn about the kitchen table. It was so unlike Betty to leave things in a mess. Same with the cups in the sink. I suppose if she was feeling ill, she might have left them while she went for a sit-down but, knowing her like I did, I'd have been far more likely to find her dead at the kitchen sink when there were dirty cups that needed washing, rather than sitting peacefully in an armchair. Sometimes when you know someone really well, you just get a feeling when things are out of place don't you? And that's what I felt. But how do you explain that to someone else? Especially someone like that policeman who didn't know the first thing about Betty. He would just see me as a silly old woman, wouldn't he? I spoke to Jim, and our Adrian and Sharon about it, but they thought I was reading too much into it. It was odd though that the papers on the table were all to do with money. The deeds of her house were there, a copy of her will, her life insurance policy and her bank statements. Why those items in particular? And then with all that happened afterwards with the house and poor Betty's ashes, you can see why I was a bit suspicious can't you?

~~~~~~
~~~~~~

Although they kept in touch with Peggy after this, especially Amy, it was the last proper sit-down interview they held.

Naturally, Peggy got upset when she related to them how she had found her best friend dead in her chair, and she got quite agitated when discussing Betty's funeral, or rather lack of one. Amy, too, seemed to have been considerably affected, and it was she who asked Peggy to explain again why she thought Edith might have been to visit her mother shortly before her death.

Matt waited until the two of them were in the car driving home before he raised the issue with Amy. By this time, she was noticeably pale, and he assumed Edith's heartless treatment of her mother after her death had really affected Amy, perhaps stirring up memories of her own father's death. When he asked her if that was what was wrong, Amy told him that although it had been difficult to listen to, it wasn't the reason why she was upset. When Matt asked her to explain what she meant, she turned to him and said:

"If you swapped the teacups in the kitchen sink for sherry glasses, Peggy could have been describing exactly the way in which I discovered my grandmother's body, and the state of her house when I found her dead in her armchair; from an apparent insulin overdose!"

16

The following is a statement from Sharon Dixon, Peggy's daughter-in-law and Betty's employer.

I was introduced to Betty O'Reilly by my mother-in-law. I run a tea shop in Leambridge High Street and was looking for someone who could bake cakes for me after the lady I had been using retired. Betty had been making Wedding, Christening and Birthday cakes for people for years and Peggy showed me some photographs as examples of what she could do, and I have to say I was very impressed.

I asked Betty to make cakes weekly for me to sell from the café, and I also took in orders for her from customers who wanted cakes for special occasions. When I had a vacancy come up in the tea shop, I offered it to her, and she started working full-time for me and did so up until she died. She was a lovely woman. A little limited mentally, but hard-working and extremely loyal. She never said very much, she wasn't chatty or a gossip, but as I got to know her better, she opened up more. She liked to talk about her grandmother, and I got the impression that the only love she had ever experienced within her family came from 'Granny Edie'. It was obviously a special relationship because she named her daughter after her. She told me that her granny always called her special because she had been born with the cord wrapped around her neck and she had come out blue. They thought she was dead but when Granny Edie held her and rubbed her and blew in her face, she started to breathe. Granny Edie called it a miracle. I think that explains why she was mentally challenged. I think she was starved of oxygen at birth.

One thing about Betty was that she worshipped her daughter. She talked about her all the time. But, although I didn't see very much of her, I'm afraid I never took to the girl. I thought she was vile and to me their relationship was toxic. Betty would never have a bad word said against Edith, but I could tell she feared her own daughter. Sometimes, she would show up at work with bruises or burn marks on her arms. Every time I asked her what had happened, she had an excuse. Always blaming herself for being clumsy and banging into things or accidentally pouring hot water over her arm! I shared my concerns with Peggy who told me she was given the same excuses and that these incidents were happening a lot less now than they used to. If she had been married, I think we would all have assumed she had an abusive husband. As it stood, the only person who could have inflicted that sort of harm on her was Edith, but Betty would never admit to it. Edith was all sweetness and light in front of me, but I caught her out a couple of times when she didn't realise I was there, and the way she spoke to her mother was disgusting. You wouldn't talk to a dog the way she talked to Betty.

After Edith went to university, Betty seemed happier. There were no fresh bruises, and she was far chattier and forthcoming. I know she was exceptionally proud of Edith. She would tell all our customers about her clever daughter who had gone to university. It was such a shame that she never got to go to Edith's graduation, it was something she was so looking forward to.

I know that Peggy struggled to come to terms with Betty's death and for a long time she couldn't accept that it was an accident but, in all honesty, I think it probably was. Like I said, Betty was not the sharpest tool in the box and there were a number of instances at work where she hadn't got her insulin levels right, and I had had to intervene, so it's something I can imagine happening.

I think what really upset Peggy was the way Edith treated her mother after her death. When Peggy didn't hear from Edith, I drove her to Betty's house where I had assumed Edith would be living. Finding that it had been cleared out, and was already up for sale was a real shock to Peggy. Understandably, Peggy was very concerned that she might miss Betty's funeral, so in a last-ditch attempt to track Edith down, I contacted the hospital where I knew Betty would have been taken, and someone there took pity on me and kindly gave me the name of the funeral home who had collected Betty's body. I contacted the home but of course, because I wasn't a relative, they wouldn't give me any information or contact details for Edith. I explained the situation, that we were just trying to get details of when the funeral was to take place as no one had been given any information, and the woman there took pity on me too. She explained that Betty had already been cremated and that they were still in possession of her ashes. She told me she couldn't promise anything, but that when Edith came to collect the ashes, she would be sure to tell her that we would appreciate a chance to say goodbye, so maybe we could be there when she scattered them.

Peggy was naturally devastated by this news. Finding out that her friend had been cremated with no proper funeral. I mean what daughter arranges a funeral and doesn't invite anyone? I think that's what's behind Peggy's accusations. But Edith always was a strange fish. I wouldn't be surprised if she was on the autistic spectrum. She certainly doesn't consider other people's feelings. Peggy's such a good soul though. She arranged a memorial service for Betty, which lots of people attended. I told her what a good friend she was, but she just said it was the least she could do. And then Peggy got the call from Edith about Betty's ashes. Just goes to show that my impression of Edith was right. She's a vile person.

PART FOUR

Shit! Shit! Shit! Think Edith, think.

What a time for the idiots in accounts to finally discover a discrepancy. After all the times I've messed around why did they have to uncover this one right at this moment? Why now? I've got too much else going on to be able to think straight.

Shit! Shit! Shit!

I've got no way to pay this back. What am I going to do? They'll report me. It's theft. It'll be a police matter.

Think Edith, think.

I can't afford for the police to be involved. They'll discover what happened at home. I need to sort that mess out first.

Shit! Shit! Shit!

I just need some time. Just a bit of time so I can work this out. Just give me a fucking break.

Think Edith, think.

It's her I need to distract. Now that's an idea. That could work. Think Edith, think.

1

After Amy's revelation in the car regarding the similarities between Betty's death and that of her own grandmother, Matt was intrigued to hear the whole story. So, he asked Amy if he could interview her again like he had before.

"But this time I would like to concentrate solely on your grandmother," he told her.

Knowing Matt so much better now, Amy agreed to call round to his house the following Wednesday afternoon whilst his wife, Jasmine, was at work and before he had to pick his daughters up from school.

They took coffee through to his study and knowing what to expect, Amy waited until Matt had switched his phone to record before she began.

"My dad's mum, Granny Kelly as we called her, was an amazing woman. She was ferociously independent, a very strong character but she was also incredibly loving, hugely generous and absolutely devoted to her sons and their families. She called my mum and my Aunt Maggie the daughters she never had. As her only grandchildren, Adam and I were spoilt rotten by her. Her husband, my grandfather, had died when her two boys were quite young, and she raised them on her own. She had lots of men friends that she called her 'beaus' or her 'suitors'. They were all completely enthralled by her, and she was proposed to on a regular basis, but she always declined. She told me, when I was older, that after my grandad died, she promised herself she would never again have to pick up any man's dirty underwear from her own bedroom floor. She also used to tell me I needed a different boyfriend for each day of the week and two on a Sunday. She tried to talk me out of marrying Marcus as young as I did. It wasn't that she had anything against him, she was, in fact, devoted to him, it was just that she felt I was giving up my freedom much too early.

"Whenever I visited her, there would invariably be one of her doting followers there carrying out repair work on her house or dropping off shopping. She treated these men abysmally, always castigating them for not doing a good enough job or for not acting quickly enough. She never compensated them for any money they spent on her, and they were lucky if she so much as made them a cup of tea, but still they'd come back for more.

"Granny always spoke her mind but she somehow managed to avoid offending people. She had a knack of getting on with people whatever their social status. Marcus always said she'd have made a good Royal; she certainly expected to be treated like one! She was on speaking terms with everyone in the village, they all loved her. She was such a personality, a force of nature. I adored her and we were incredibly close. She was my rock when my mum died.

"She was immensely proud of both her sons. Of Uncle John's success in the business world. He was the CEO of a large and extremely profitable marketing company before he retired, and obviously my dad's acting career. My dad and Uncle John were complete opposites. Granny said John took after his father, who was a staid and steady character, and my dad, being of a more unconventional nature, took after her. But the brothers were incredibly close. My Uncle and my Granny both supported Dad at the beginning of his career, helping him out financially and attending all his 'first nights', dragging along as many friends as they could. Granny kept scrap books filled with every review that was written about my dad's performances, and Adam and I would spend hours looking through them when we were younger."

Amy paused for a moment and then said to Matt,

"I think Uncle John must have those scrap books now. I'll ask him for you as they could be helpful." Then picking up on what she had been saying, she continued, "Granny was also my and Adam's biggest cheerleader. She supported us whatever we chose to do. Because of the generation she was a part of, Adam had been a little nervous about coming out to her. But he needn't have worried. When he told her he was gay, she hugged him and said, "Of course you are darling." She had obviously known for some time and wasn't at all fazed.

"When Mum died, although she was as devastated as the rest of us, it was Granny who took on the role of looking after us. She saw us through our darkest moments. For Granny, Mum's death upset the natural order, no child should go before a parent, and she considered my mum one of her children.

"In the aftermath of Dad's marriage to Eliza, Granny was a godsend. She refused to kowtow to Eliza or be intimidated by her, but she tolerated her for Dad's sake. She acted as my safety barrier against Eliza. Granny's death left an enormous hole in my life. Without her, there was no buffer between Eliza and myself and my relationship with Dad suffered as a result."

Amy had to stop for a moment to wipe her eyes.

"Every time I talk about Mum and then have to move on to talking about Eliza, it kills me," she told Matt.

"Do you want to take a break?" he asked.

"No," said Amy. "I'm just still so angry with Dad for bringing Eliza into our lives. Is that a terrible thing to admit? Talking about Granny reminds me of how well she got on with Mum, which only underscores how much she and Eliza clashed. Eliza upset Granny so many times. Not that Granny ever let it show that she was hurt; she wouldn't give Eliza the satisfaction. But I knew. That's why it's so upsetting that I still believe Eliza was the last person to see Granny alive. Granny would have wanted to spend her last hours with anyone but her! Sorry, I'm okay to carry on now I've had a rant.

"Granny was away on a cruise, paid for by one of her many beaus when Dad moved Eliza into the farmhouse. In fact, by the time Granny got to meet Eliza, she was nearing the end of her pregnancy. I was the one who had picked Granny up to take her to meet her new daughter-in-law. She confided in me her deep disappointment on hearing of both the marriage and the pregnancy. "Marry in haste, repent at leisure," she said. She was adamant that the baby couldn't be Dad's even after I told her Dad had proof. I purposely hadn't given Granny my opinion of Eliza, as I thought it only fair she make up her own mind, but I think my avoidance on the subject must have been telling. As I've said, Granny was a formidable character and on the rare occasion she took a dislike to someone she could be brutal, and of course that's exactly what happened when she met Eliza. They clashed. Neither of them was willing to play second fiddle to the other.

"Eliza immediately put Granny's back up by treating her like an old woman. We all knew it was best to pretend that Granny was at least 20 years younger than she actually was, but Eliza obviously hadn't received the memo! Granny, for her part, took exception to the way Eliza spoke. Unlike Adam and I, who were too polite to comment, Granny went in with both guns blazing.

'Why on earth are you talking like that?" she queried Eliza, "are you ill? Do you have asthma? Is that why you're breathing funny?'

"She also took the mickey out of the words Eliza used. When Dad asked about her cruise, Granny answered,

'Oh, darling it was absolutely fabulous, simply divine, totally to die for.'

"Eliza tried to insult Granny, but Granny was more than a match for her and just flung a worse insult back. When Eliza was rude, then Granny was ruder. Dad was flustered and embarrassed by the way they were both behaving, but I thoroughly enjoyed the exchanges between them. It was like watching two master craftsmen at work. Granny was convinced that Dad would soon come to his senses and see Eliza for who she really was. She was frustrated by his continuing infatuation. That Granny disliked Eliza helped me a lot. I felt less guilty about my own feelings towards Dad's new wife.

"Despite having Type 1 Diabetes, Granny had always enjoyed good health. She was very aware of the many problems she might possibly face due to her condition, and she took great pains to look after herself properly. Therefore, it was an enormous shock when she died of an insulin overdose. She died at home, and I was the one who found her.

"Granny had phoned me earlier in the day and asked if I was free to go round as Eliza had just called her to say she was going to be paying a visit, and Granny didn't feel up to entertaining Eliza by herself. I had something to do, I've forgotten what it was, but told her I would get round there as soon as I could. By the time I eventually arrived, I assumed Eliza had already left because her car wasn't there.

"Initially, I thought Granny had fallen asleep in her chair but when I went to wake her, I realised she was gone. It can't have happened much before I arrived as she was still warm, and it upset me that I had missed being with her during her final moments by such a short space of time.

"Like Peggy said when she told us about finding Betty, I thought Granny must have suffered a stroke or a heart attack, but whatever the cause, she had passed peacefully. There was no sign that she had been distressed or in pain, which was a blessing. I thought that Granny and Eliza must have been going through some of Granny's paperwork, whilst they enjoyed a glass of sherry because the box file that Granny kept her bills in was out. So, when Dad and Eliza arrived together, I was disconcerted when Eliza told me I was mistaken. She hadn't phoned Granny. She hadn't called round. It wasn't her that had drunk the sherry. She said it must have been one of Granny's friends. She stated Granny had been getting confused a lot lately but then that was to be expected of someone her age. She implied that Granny was going senile. I was certain that Eliza was lying about not being there, but I couldn't fathom why. Why lie? Discovering later that Granny had in fact died from an insulin overdose was a huge shock to me because like I said, Granny had been managing her condition all her life. It was so unlike her to make such a silly mistake. It was something I struggled to come to terms with and I said so to everyone. Eliza reiterated that Granny had been, as she put it 'Losing her marbles'. But that simply wasn't true. I saw Granny more often than anyone else and she was still as sharp as a pin.

"As I mentioned before, I didn't cope well with Granny's sudden death. I couldn't shake my belief that Eliza had been with Granny just before she died, and I got it into my head that Eliza had encouraged Granny to change her will. Why else was that folder out? I mentioned my concerns to Marcus, and to Kath, but they both felt I was being paranoid. Why would Eliza lie about being there? What would be the point? Why would she be trying to get Granny to amend her will? What could she gain, when Dad was going to inherit anyway? They both reminded me that no one was capable of forcing Granny to do anything she didn't want to do. I realised they were right and tried to forget my misgivings and then when Granny's will was read, it was obvious that Eliza had not been party to Granny's wishes before she died. Her reaction to Granny's bequests left no doubt that Eliza had not been an influence in any decisions."

2

During Amy's interview regarding the details of her grandmother's death, she had disclosed that she discussed her initial suspicions that Eliza was lying with Marcus and with Kath, both of whom had treated her allegation with skepticism. Matt thought it would be good to get Kath's point of view, so he called her.

"Hi, sorry to trouble you. If you're not busy I wondered if you could answer a question for me?"

"Sure, go ahead," said Kath. "You're only disturbing the ironing, so fire away."

"Amy told me she thought Eliza lied about seeing Violet just before she died. She also feels Eliza may have been trying to influence Violet regarding her will. Do you think that's possible?"

"Um, well, that's a tricky one to answer. Amy is adamant that Violet called her on the day she died to say Eliza was calling in to see her, and as she didn't want to be on her own with her, she asked Amy to go round as well. Now Amy has no reason to lie about that. According to Amy, there was clear evidence, unmistakable evidence, that Violet had received a visitor prior to Amy arriving, and she was convinced it was Eliza. She said she could still smell her perfume."

"Smell her perfume?" queried Matt. He'd heard mention of Eliza's perfume before. Was it Peggy? He'd have to check through his notes when he finished this call.

"Yes, Eliza always wore the same distinctive scent, and she smothered herself in it. So much so, that the aroma would linger long after she left a room. Amy was convinced that Eliza had been there that day, but Eliza strenuously denied it. Not just visiting but she denied even making a call to Violet. Eliza blamed Violet becoming senile for the misunderstanding. I don't think that was necessarily true but it's hard to deny that someone of Violet's age could easily have been confused. It was one of those awkward situations where it didn't really matter whether it was true or not, but Amy got a real bee in her bonnet about it.

"She was certain Eliza had been there to persuade her granny to change her will. I don't know why she got that idea in her head but, try as we might, we couldn't get her to see that Eliza had no need to do that. She and Keith would inherit half of everything. At that time, we all assumed that only Keith and John would inherit. Also, Violet was in such rude health it wasn't as if she was expected to die any time soon.

"I think a combination of factors were affecting Amy's emotions and she was desperate to have a reason to blame Eliza. I don't think Amy even knew what she was blaming her for, lying? Manipulating Violet? Maybe even being responsible for Violet's death?

"She was overcome with grief, and she needed to lash out. Having already lost her mother, she had now lost her beloved granny too and, in a sense, lost her dad. He certainly wasn't the same as the father she had known before Eliza entered their lives and she absolutely blamed Eliza for that."

3

Amy had readily agreed to Matt's request that she accompany him on a trip to gather some background information on Eliza. She had thoroughly enjoyed their recent excursions. Matt informed her that the agenda for the day comprised a tour of Eliza's high school, a meeting with some of her classmates and a meeting with a probation officer who had had dealings with Ricky Kerr.

"We can also do a tour of the neighbourhood that Ricky and Eliza grew up in," Matt told her.

However, two days before the trip, Matt contacted her to say he could no longer make it. Something urgent had cropped up that he had to attend to, but rather than cancel the scheduled meetings, he had asked Trevor to go in his place. Matt must have sensed Amy was about to back out, as he reassured her that Trevor was a very nice man, and she had nothing to worry about. He also told her that it was about time she met Trevor, anyway, seeing how involved in the research she had become and how Trevor was also collaborating with him on the book.

Amy had heard a lot about Trevor from DI Mason who, when he had first introduced the idea that Amy should meet with Matt, told her how his ex-boss and good friend, Trevor, worked with the author. It was obvious that Mason held Trevor in high esteem, and he assured Amy that his friend would not be working with Matt if he suspected the author was in any way a charlatan. Mason had also told her that Trevor was a retired Chief Superintendent, which sounded like a very senior position to Amy and didn't help her with her anxiety about spending a day with him. Then having had a very brief and to-the-point conversation with Trevor, when he'd called to discuss the arrangements for the day, Amy felt that her suspicion that he might be rather severe and officious appeared to have been confirmed. It didn't take long, however, on meeting the man in person, to realise that he was in fact the complete opposite of what she had expected.

Trevor greeted her with what she now considered to be the standard greeting anyone meeting her for the first time made. He offered his sincere condolences on the death of her father. Amy thanked him, thinking that would be an end of it, but then Trevor told her that he had in fact met her father on a number of occasions. Both he and her dad had taken part in the same annual charity golf tournament. Not only that, but a few times they had been partnered up together. Trevor went on to tell her how much he had liked her dad. He had found him to be charming, intelligent and exceedingly entertaining. He also revealed that he had met her mum a couple of times, who according to Trevor was a 'wonderful woman', before adding that Amy looked just like her. Nothing he said could have made Amy happier and she instantly relaxed.

From then on, the day, although busy, was plain sailing. Amy found herself really enjoying Trevor's company. He was extremely knowledgeable on a variety of subjects but in no way was he boring or overbearing. He was also incredibly solicitous, very gentlemanly in an old-fashioned sort of way, but one which Amy thoroughly appreciated. His manners reminding her greatly of her dad and his attitude towards women.

They travelled first to Croyston. They hadn't expected to see much, knowing that the house Edith grew up in had been destroyed by fire. It turned out to be impossible to work out where the house might have once stood. The whole area had undergone major regeneration, and all the properties were newbuilds. The Primary school Edith had attended had also either been replaced or modernized, they couldn't tell which. It was the same story when they went looking for Ricky Kerr's childhood home. It had vanished without trace.

From there they moved on to Leambridge, stopping on the way at a pub for lunch. The pub traded off the claim that King John had supposedly spent the night there before riding off to meet with his rebel Barons for the signing of the Magna Carta. Although doubting this claim, due to the location of the pub, it did enable Trevor to indulge in one of his many passions, history. He gave Amy a step-by-step guide as to how and why the Magna Carta came about and Amy was more than happy to listen, as Trevor explained why it was still significant to this day.

After an enjoyable lunch, they drove to the outskirts of Leambridge where Amy and Matt had met with Peggy Dixon. On arriving at Foxford School which Edith had attended on scholarship, they were met and given a guided tour of the school by the current headmistress, Mrs Stevens. Amy could see how Eliza might have felt inferior here. It was a beautiful building, set in stunning grounds and everything about it screamed money, and old money at that. The 'Girls' as the head referred to the pupils, (it was still an all-girls school), wore, what Amy considered to be, an outdated uniform of long brown skirts, white blouses and striped blazers with sensible brown lace-up shoes. The uniform would not have appeared out of place a century before.

"All that's missing is the straw boater," Amy whispered to Trevor, who grinned back at her.

The headmistress finished the tour by showing them several display cabinets containing a variety of gold and silver trophies. Peering in for a closer look, Amy wasn't surprised to see cups for sports such as lacrosse; all very Enid Blyton she thought to herself. They were then served coffee in the Headmistress's office where Mrs Stevens had thoughtfully set out on the coffee table, photograph albums from the time Edith attended the school. It was hard to tell much detail from these photographs that were taken of every form at the beginning of each year; row after row of seated girls all dressed identically. But there was a numbered guide listing the name of each girl on each seat, which enabled them to identify Edith in every photograph and in every single one, for each different year as she progressed through the school, she had the same sullen look on her face.

Mrs Stevens then shared a brief account of Edith's academic record. The star pupil had excelled in every subject except sport and even then, her results were good if not outstanding. She had studied all the sciences and several languages, including Latin. Whilst Mrs Stevens was still running through a list of Edith's academic achievements, there was a knock and another, older, woman entered the room. She was introduced as Miss Burrell who was a retired Maths teacher, and now a Governor of the school. She had also been Edith's form tutor during her second year. Mrs Stevens excused herself and left them to chat with Miss Burrell. This turned out to be a bit of a waste of time as all the woman did was go over the same academic achievements and reiterate the fact that Edith had not been a troublesome pupil.

However, she did offer a nugget of interest. Apparently, during that 2nd year, several items had gone missing from the form room. Girls had lost personal belongings and small amounts of money. Although she could never prove it, Miss Burrell was convinced that Edith was the thief. However, when Amy questioned her, she couldn't remember any of the other teachers mentioning a problem of that nature regarding Edith personally.

Having thanked both the women for their time and having reassured Mrs Stevens jokingly that they would ensure the forthcoming book would portray the school in a good light, and not as a training ground for murderesses, they left for a meeting with Mr Elder, who had been one of Ricky Kerr's many probation officers.

As with the school, Trevor and Amy came away from their meeting with Mr Elder not knowing much more about Ricky than they had beforehand. Most of what he told them he read from the notes in front of him, all of which Trevor was already acquainted with from reading the police reports, although it was new information to Amy.

Up until the age of 11, Ricky had lived with his alcoholic mother and four older brothers, all of whom had criminal records. His father had died in prison whilst serving life for murder. Social services had been involved with Ricky since he was born but it had never been deemed necessary to remove him from his family home. Although not an ideal upbringing, he was no more neglected or abused than any other child being brought up on that estate at that time.

Life had changed for Ricky after an arson attack, believed to have been committed by a rival gang, wiped out almost his entire family. Ricky had only survived because he was away from home at the time. After the fire, he was initially sent to live with his grandmother, but she struggled to cope with his behaviour. He was truant more often than he attended school, and having already been in trouble for petty crimes, these now increased both in number and severity. He was taken into care at the age of 12, and spent time at various foster homes, all of which he ran away from. By the age of 14, he was spending months at a time in young offenders' institutions for breaking and entering, taking and driving away and one longer stint for GBH. By the time he was in his twenties, he was a convicted drug addict and a career criminal. Mr Elder's tone made it clear, that to him, Ricky was just one more Scaghead he had dealt with in a long line of Scagheads.

Travelling to their next appointment, Amy expressed disappointment that they had learnt so little, but Trevor reassured her that the day had been well worthwhile. If nothing else, just for the background details.

"You'd be amazed how much information we've actually uncovered," said Trevor. He then proposed that they both get together again in the near future to go over their notes. He explained that they needed to do this before they started to forget the little details or certain feelings they'd experienced, which could prove vital to telling the story. They could put together a comprehensive report of the day's findings for Matt whilst it was all still fresh in their minds.

"We will both have picked up on different things and have different opinions on what we saw and heard," he told her. "Just our individual descriptions of the school will give Matt a better insight. For example, you commented on the uniform, whereas I hadn't even noticed it. Also, I could show you the information on the police enquiry that Mason passed on to me as you haven't had access to that yet."

"Okay," said Amy. "Sounds like a good idea.

"Do you know," she continued, her thoughts returning to their visit to the school, "I wasn't at all surprised to learn from Miss Burrell that Eliza was a thief."

"It's that sort of information that we have to be careful about," said Trevor.

"How do you mean?" asked Amy.

"Well, that was the teacher's opinion," replied Trevor. "She had no evidence. She wasn't basing what she told us on fact; it was just her assumption. Also, how do we know that she suspected Eliza at the time and it's not something that she has only 'suspected' since she's learnt of the terrible things Eliza has done? People don't like to think they've been duped. They like to believe they saw bad in someone early on before that person committed a crime or was found guilty of committing a crime. How many times have you heard a neighbour, teacher or work colleague of a convicted killer say when interviewed, 'I always knew there was something wrong with him,' or 'I could tell he was evil from the moment I met him,' and yet even with their apparent discernment they still allowed the said 'evil' person to babysit their children, and they never thought to pass on their concerns to anyone in authority."

"That's very true," agreed Amy. "The number of people, especially on social media, who suddenly knew that my dad was a wife beater, or that Zac was the 'devil's child' having never had dealings with either of them. I shouldn't be so quick to judge, not when I've experienced the other side of the denunciation."

"Don't blame yourself," said Trevor. "We're all guilty of it. It's human nature. And anyway, chances are high that Eliza was the thief."

"Wasn't that probation officer a dry stick?" said Amy.

"Years of dealing with that side of society will do that to you," said Trevor. "Day after day of dealing with the lowest of the low will suck the humour out of anyone. I've seen it happen in the Force too. Some people just lose all sense of feeling. They start off enthusiastic and by the end they have lost any empathy they once had. At least in the Force there is more variety to the job, allowing most officers to retain some sense of humour, albeit a warped one."

"Yes, I suppose so," said Amy. "It's the same with teaching. You start off convinced you are going to make a difference to each and every child. Give them the best education possible. Then after years of broken pencils, playground fights, government cuts and unteachable math's programmes, you just give in. It becomes a job like any other and you're as eager as the children for the bell to ring at the end of the day."

"So, you're a teacher, are you? What age group do you teach?" asked Trevor.

"Primary," answered Amy. "And I was a teacher. I worked at the local primary school but after what happened to Dad, I wasn't able to face going back. I didn't want to deal with the staff's well-meant sympathy or the pupil's and their parent's inappropriate questions. Despite what I said before, I do love teaching and I do miss it. I will need to work again soon if for no other reason than the money. But I resigned from the local school and when I go back, I'll probably head further afield, where hopefully no one will make a connection between me and Dad."

They drove on in silence for a little while, Trevor making a mental note to speak to Matt about making some sort of financial recompense to Amy for her contribution to the book. Amy then broke the silence.

"Talking of connections, it's a bit of a coincidence that both Eliza and Ricky's childhood homes were destroyed by fire. I'm not jumping to any conclusions," she hurried on. "I can't possibly see how or why they would be related. It's just an unusual connection that they have. Maybe it's one of the reasons why they remained close."

"Mm," said Trevor. "I don't really believe in coincidence but you're right. I can't see how they could be connected."

Their next appointment was with three women who had all attended Foxford and were in the same year as Eliza. The meeting had been arranged at a café, set in the grounds of a local stately home. As Trevor drove them through the impressive wrought iron gates and up the long sweeping tree-lined drive towards the house, Amy was thinking how appropriate the setting was for the meeting. The surroundings were reminiscent of the private school they had visited that morning.

The three women were easy to spot amongst the many visitors milling around the converted barn which housed both the cafe and a gift shop. Facially, they looked very different from each other, but they were dressed almost identically in skinny jeans tucked into knee-length boots and waxed jackets. Their mannerisms and their accents were eerily similar. They had that air of superiority about them inherent in the privileged. Amy again thought how out of place Eliza must have felt when she first started at Foxford, coming from her lower-class background and being thrust into the heart of this elite group of girls.

Introductions had been made and refreshments ordered, English breakfast tea for Trevor, an ordinary latte for Amy and a chai tea latte with oat milk, a lemon balm tea and a rooibos tea respectively. Amy, having never even heard of rooibos but assuming it to be a plant of some kind, reflected how the order emphasised the difference between herself and Trevor and the women they were here to talk to. Once again, Amy thought how difficult it must have been for Eliza encountering the likes of these women for the first time.

To begin with, the three women, Sophia, Lulu and Grace, talked amongst themselves, ignoring Amy and Trevor completely. Although it was obvious that they had kept in touch with each other over the years, it was apparent that it had been a while since they had last met up in person. Amy was fascinated by the way they spoke. It was like another language. But it was a language she had heard before, because it was how Eliza had spoken. They used lots of abbreviations that, for the life of her, Amy couldn't work out the meaning of. She guessed that BTB was a person, and that Ab Dab was a place. There were an awful lot of 'Yars' and 'Totes'. It also made for compelling listening. Amy was staggered to hear that Hugo's recently purchased polo pony, which was considered an 'absolute bargain', had actually cost the equivalent of her and Marcus' first house. It was amusing to discover that Suki's recent Botox disaster had left her unable to move her eyebrows.

As fascinating as this all was, Amy started to grow impatient with their behaviour. It was tantamount to rude. Just as she was contemplating breaking into their chirping, Trevor cleared his throat.

"Ladies," he said, "I'm afraid that Mrs McDonald and I have a very tight schedule."

Amy knew this was untrue as this meeting was the last of the day.

"So, as you can imagine," continued Trevor, "our time is precious. Would it be possible for you to catch up on your gossip after we have finished questioning you?" Although Trevor spoke mildly there was a definite hint of censure in his voice and Amy thought he had intentionally used the word 'questioning' to make it appear more like a police interview than an informal chat.

The women were immediately apologetic.

"So, so sorry," said Lulu. "Got carried away. Forgot we were here to talk about Edith."

"I was wondering," said Amy, taking the opportunity to get the conversation on the right track. "Did you know of Eliza Kelly before she hit the headlines? Were you aware that she was the Edith you went to school with?"

All three women shook their heads in unison, but it was Grace who spoke.

"No, absolutely not. Not a clue. We never saw or heard from Edith after she left Foxford. If I remember rightly, she left before the start of sixth form?" She turned to the others for affirmation.

"Yes, I'm sure that's right," confirmed Lulu.

"Well, I met Eliza once," continued Grace. "It was at a charity auction. Some benefit event to save the dolphins or whales or some sea creature. Her husband, that actor, the chap she murdered – Keith, was it? He was the auctioneer. Frightfully good at it he was. Very entertaining."

Trevor gave Amy a wry look and she gave a short shake of her head in return, to let him know she didn't want him to enlighten the women as to her relationship to Keith.

"I only met her briefly," Grace told them, "But I certainly didn't recognise her, and I would say she didn't recognise me either."

"Didn't she change her name after she left Foxford? I think someone told me that or I read it somewhere, but it wasn't Eliza it was something else," asked Sophia.

"She's changed her name several times," said Trevor.

"Can you tell us what Edith was like at school?" asked Amy.

"I didn't know her that well," said Lulu. "We shared some of the same classes, but I never sat next to her. I'm not sure I ever even had a proper conversation with her. Just the odd word here and there."

"We worked with her once, didn't we Grace?" said Sophia. "Do you remember, we had to do that Chemistry project with her and Amber Wheaton?"

"Oh gosh, yar," replied Grace. "I remember. She was ghastly."

"In what way?" asked Amy.

"So, so bossy. I mean she was terribly clever, I'm not denying that, but she tried to treat us like her minions. The whole thing was a nightmare. I made Bozzy promise we'd never have to team up with her again."

"Bozzy?" queried Trevor.

"Our chemistry teacher, Miss Boswell," explained Grace. There then followed a discussion about how standoffish and rude Edith was.

"Was she ever bullied?" asked Amy trying again to steer the conversation back in the right direction. "You know because she was on a scholarship?"

"Oh, you know how nasty an all-girls school can be," said Lulu. "I'm certain we tried. I remember her wearing clothes that were way too big for her. I'm sure we would have teased her about that." It didn't seem to bother Lulu that she was admitting to the fact that Edith had most likely been bullied by herself and the other girls at the school.

"I clearly remember that she told us her parents were dead and that she lived with her granny but then it turned out her granny was actually her mum," pitched in Grace. "Do you remember Soph? Wasn't it Babs who announced it on the hockey pitch? And then Edith attacked her with her hockey stick. She gave Babs a concussion and two black eyes!"

"Yar, I remember that," said Sophia. "Didn't she also take on Ruby Nuttall?"

"Ruby Nuttall?" interrupted Trevor. "As in Colin Nuttall's daughter?"

"That's right," said Sophia. "Foxford was a popular place for criminals to send their offspring. I remember Ruby being driven to school by her bodyguard. The rest of us were dropped off by the au pair. We were all scared of Ruby. She was a real hard case. She and Edith went at it one day in the dining hall. I don't know what caused it, but it took both Miss Schwartz and Miss Evans to separate them. I don't think there was any more trouble between them after that though. So, Edith must have won the fight."

"Colin Nuttall?" Amy looked at Trevor for an answer.

"Local villain," said Trevor. "High up the food chain."

"So, did Edith get into a lot of trouble at school?" asked Amy. "Did she start a lot of fights?"

"Oh no, not at all. Just those couple of fights really. She mostly kept to herself. She won loads of awards. She really was frightfully clever," said Grace.

"I do remember Miss Burrell once accused her of stealing," said Sophia, causing Amy to throw a glance over to Trevor.

"That must have been in Year 2," said Grace. "If it was Miss Burrell."

"Edith was furious. She threatened to sue Miss Burrell for slander. Said she was being picked on because she was on a scholarship. It was all pretty tense. The Head had to get involved."

"Do you think she was stealing?" asked Amy.

"Oh yes, absolutely." All three women agreed.

"She definitely stole £10 off me," said Sophia. "No doubt about it. But of course, I couldn't prove it and after what happened with Babs, I was too scared to confront her."

"We just learnt to keep things locked away or out of her reach," said Lulu.

"It did stop though, didn't it?" said Grace. "I don't remember it being a problem by the third year."

"Well, she had that horrendous boyfriend by then. I'm sure he was either buying stuff or stealing it for her. She started turning up at school in expensive shoes and with designer bags. You must remember that bloke. He kept trying to sell drugs to us outside the gates. Bozzy called the police on him that time. Don't you remember?" asked Sophia.

"Oh yar. I *do* remember him. He had ginger hair. Used to pick Edith up on his motorbike after school," said Grace.

"She thought she was so cool being picked up by a bloke on a bike, but he was really seedy. Not what one would call a catch," Sophia added.

"Sounds like Ricky," Amy said to Trevor.

Amy was struggling to think of any other questions.

"Did you ever go to Edith's house after school or invite her over to yours? Or invite her to Birthday parties, that sort of thing?" she asked.

All three women shook their heads.

"We really didn't know her that well," Lulu answered for all of them.

"Did she have any close friends that you know of? Could you give us the name of someone she was close to, that we can get in touch with?"

"There really wasn't anyone," Lulu seemed to have become spokesperson for the group.

"Like we told you Edith kept herself to herself."

"But she must have had a least one friend?" pressed Amy.

"I know it looks bad," said Lulu. "It looks like we were horrible to her but honestly it was the other way round. She was an awful girl. She would say really terrible things to you. Call you the vilest names. Do you remember how she tormented Jess Ryan?" Lulu turned to the other two who both nodded solemnly. "Jess Ryan would be the first to admit she was a little overweight, but Edith tortured her. She called her names like Fatty and Miss Piggy. It sounds harmless now, but it wasn't. Every time Edith went near Jess she would make pig noises at her. Jess stopped eating lunch in the dining room to avoid Edith, but wherever she tried to eat, Edith would seek her out and persecute her. It got worse and worse. She stopped eating at school altogether in the end. We would try to step in. We never left Jess on her own if we could help it, but Edith got to her all the same. In the end, Jess attempted to take her own life. It was terrible. Her parents took her out of school, and she spent time in a private clinic. I've kept in touch with her, and she still has a problem with food. Because of Edith, she has spent her life battling with anorexia."

After that, neither Amy nor Trevor felt that they would get any more from the meeting and they departed leaving the women to continue their catch up. Amy was sure the rest of the school friends' time together would be spent bad mouthing the Edith they had known and sharing their surprise at discovering her transformation into Eliza Kelly.

Back in the car, Amy thought about what Trevor had said regarding them getting together to compare notes. She had been about to propose meeting one evening at a pub but then she had a change of heart.

"Why don't you come for lunch on Sunday, so that we can discuss what we've learnt today?" she asked. "It's Marcus' turn to cook and he's a dab hand in the kitchen, only don't tell him I said that."

"Oh, I wouldn't want to impose," said Trevor.

"You wouldn't be," assured Amy. "Marcus loves cooking for people. The more the merrier as far as he's concerned. And we could put together that comprehensive account you were on about, ready to give to Matt."

"It's very kind of you to offer," said Trevor, "but I've left JR alone a lot this week. Normally, Mrs T would pop in and see him but she's away visiting her nephew. I daredn't leave him again or his sulking will get out of hand!"

"JR?" questioned Amy, wondering if this was Trevor's partner. He hadn't mentioned he lived with someone, but they hadn't discussed personal stuff much.

"My dog," explained Trevor. "He's lovely but needy. He's a Jack Russell, hence the name JR."

"Clever," said Amy, "I like it. Is he sociable? I mean is he good with other dogs?"

"Oh yes. He loves other dogs, cats, rabbits and humans, especially humans. Most unusual for a Jack Russell apparently."

"Well in that case bring him along with you. We have two border collies, Flo and Jet; short for Flotsam and Jetsam, and they'd love to meet him, as would my daughter Olivia; she's nuts about animals. Currently, she wants to be a vet."

"Brilliant names," said Trevor. "For your dogs I mean. Although I like the name Olivia too," he added hastily. "Well, if you're sure it's okay then both JR and I would love to accept your kind invitation. I'll tell you what, if it's not alright by your husband or something crops up between now and then, just give me a bell. I won't be offended. Promise." He handed her his business card. "You can reach me on the numbers on there."

"Lovely," said Amy. "If you can get to us for about half twelve, as lunch will be around one o'clock and then we can spend the afternoon going over what happened today."

"Will do," said Trevor.

"Dad used to have a Jack Russell you know. A Jack Russell and a black lab. Marcus and I took them both on when Dad got together with Eliza because she didn't like dogs. They were both quite old by then, so we didn't have them long, but they really missed Dad and he really missed them. Another reason for me to dislike Eliza."

"What did your dad call his Jack Russell?" asked Trevor.

"Um, not sure I should say really," said Amy. "You might be offended. The lab was called Gus."

"Offended? Why would I be offended?" Trevor was puzzled.

"Trevor," said Amy laughing. "His name was Trevor!" and the Trevor in the car burst out laughing too.

4

Having enjoyed her day out with Trevor, Amy was thrilled when Matt asked her to accompany him on his visit to Tom Bryant. The interviews they conducted together with Peggy Dixon went extremely well, and Matt praised Amy for her ability to coax information from Peggy. He told her she had a natural talent for putting people at ease which made her an excellent interviewer. Amy, on the other hand, was impressed by the way Matt worked. She had expected him to be an interrogator but instead he was very calm and relaxed, so much so that by the end of the first session Peggy was treating them both like old friends. Matt feigned interest in some of Peggy's more mundane stories because he knew they would eventually lead to something juicier. He was an excellent flatterer and extremely empathetic. It was the complete antithesis of Amy's preconception of how he would conduct himself. Amy enjoyed all the subsequent meetings, especially the car journeys to and from the interviews. She made sure to pack plenty of snacks, (a hangover from taking children on long drives), and Matt entertained her with anecdotes from his career. It was amazing what you could learn over a shared bag of jelly babies. But for Amy the very best bit of all was uncovering Eliza's past - with the icing on the cake being the discovery of the skeletons in her closet.

That Saturday morning Matt picked her up early which suited Amy down to ground. It meant Marcus was left playing taxi driver for the children, dropping them at and collecting them from their various activities and he was also lumbered with the food shopping. It felt good to be doing something different. Something with a little more kudos than the usual run-of-the-mill mundane family Saturday. She felt much more at ease with Matt now. Any awkwardness or nervousness evaporated over their recent shared time together, and they were now comfortable enough to tease each other. They chatted happily during the car journey. Matt told Amy that he deliberately asked her and not Trevor to accompany him on this particular meeting because, he explained, he felt that as she had known Eliza in person, she would be able to share some of her experiences with Tom, which in turn might help to gain his trust. People, Matt told her, were often wary of talking to journalists under any circumstances, but Tom was likely to be extra sensitive as to how he might be portrayed. He would worry about being made to look a fool and that could mean he held back from being entirely open with them. Matt made it clear to Amy that getting Tom to unwind would be paramount to a good interview. The fact that she herself had witnessed the worse side of Eliza meant she would be able to sympathise with Tom, which would be invaluable in helping him retell his experiences. Amy was thrilled to be specifically chosen over Trevor. She felt it justified her accompanying Matt even though she had very little experience of this type of work.

Tom Bryant lived in what Matt would have described as a Manor House in a picturesque English village. The village itself was almost identical to the one that was home to Amy even though they were set in different counties. Tom greeted them at the door and then escorted them through to a sitting room that was very pleasingly decorated with cream walls and primrose yellow curtains. Cushions made from the same fabric as the curtains adorned the two immaculate cream leather sofas and accompanying well-padded armchairs. There were landscape paintings on the walls that looked like originals and obviously depicted the local area. The room was spacious, helped by the fact that there was minimal furniture. A large bay window, aided by additional side windows, allowed light to flood into the room. The focal point was a large working fireplace which currently housed a flower arrangement set in a wicker basket. The décor made Amy think of springtime, reminding her of Easter and primroses. It was the sort of room, she thought, that looked simple, but in fact a lot of hard work and planning had gone in to achieving the result. She also knew that it was a style she herself could never accomplish.

Whilst they waited for tea to be served by Tom's wife, Lizzie, they exchanged the usual small talk and pleasantries about the weather and then both Matt and Amy complimented the couple on their house.

"I inherited it from my parents," said Tom. "It was a little dated when we took it over, so we've had a lot of work done. I can't take any credit for the remodelling though; that's all down to Lizzie."

"Oh," exclaimed Amy. "I inherited my house too. My mum left it to me and my brother. Dad lived there for a while but when he moved out, my husband and I decided to make it our family home; so I bought my brother out."

"Yes, I had to buy my sister out," replied Tom.

There followed a brief discussion about the complexities of inheritance that Matt felt completely unqualified to join, but then Lizzie excused herself, saying she had things to be getting on with in the kitchen.

"Right," said Matt, "if it's okay with you, Tom- you don't mind if I call you Tom, do you? I think it's easier in these situations to be less formal, so alright if we use our Christian names?"

"Yes, that's absolutely fine," Tom replied.

"So, I think it would probably be best if you just start from the beginning. You know from when you first met Edith…"

"Hang on," Tom interrupted, "do you mind if I refer to her as Eleanor? I noticed that Mrs Macdonald- I'm sorry, I mean Amy. I noticed that Amy referred to her as Eliza earlier and just now you called her Edith. I've only ever known her as Eleanor, and I think talking about her using a different name would just be confusing."

"Of course," said Matt. "To be honest with you it's something my team and I have been struggling with." He looked over to where Amy was perched on the edge of her armchair, trying very hard to keep the crumbs from a homemade scone on the bone china plate she was balancing. She blushed a little at being referred to as part of Matt's team. Amy nodded her agreement, her mouth too full to answer.

"Anyway," continued Matt, "what I'd really like you to do is to tell us the story of you and Eleanor in your own words. Amy or I might occasionally stop you to ask a question but otherwise you just tell it your way. Both Amy and I will be making notes, but I'll also be recording the conversation if that's alright with you?"

"Yes, that's fine," replied Tom.

"Oh, and also," said Matt, "I know this will be really difficult but if you could tell the story as it happened without hindsight. They say, 'hindsight's a wonderful thing', but in this instance it will be a hindrance."

"Sorry I'm not quite with you," said Tom.

"Well, when Edith, sorry, I mean Eleanor, told you she was pregnant, you didn't doubt that the baby was yours did you? But subsequently you found out that you weren't Max's father. Like I say, I know it's hard, but I need you to remember how you felt at the time these events were happening and not how you feel about them now, knowing what you know."

"Well, I'll try my best," said Tom frowning, "but if you think I'm telling things from a later perspective as opposed to when it happened, just let me know."

"Brilliant," said Matt, "so if you could start from when you first met Eleanor."

"I first met Eleanor through my girlfriend at the time, Rachel Tomlinson," Tom began. "Well, actually Rachel was far more than just a girlfriend, she was my fiancée. Rachel was at Oxford University studying for a degree in modern languages and Eleanor, who was there reading law, was one of her housemates. There were three other students sharing the house. Two boys and another girl, Sabine something? She was German or Austrian, I think? I only remember the boys as Tim and Ethan, possibly Elliot? I can't remember their surnames, but you should be able to trace them via the university. Anyway, as housemates they all got on, but they weren't that close. They didn't have a lot in common. They all came from very different backgrounds and as far as I recall, they were all studying something different. Rachel had originally intended to share a flat with a friend she made during first year but then her friend dropped out of university. Rachel couldn't afford the accommodation by herself and didn't feel comfortable sharing such a confined space with just one other person she didn't know, so she opted to do a house share with more people instead.

"I travelled a lot with my job. Still do. Back then I could be away for one week or for as much as 6 weeks, but it was never really any longer than that and I would stay with Rachel at her university digs whenever I was back in the UK during term time. You know what it's like when you're young and in love, when you want to spend every possible moment together. During her first year living in the house, we spent most of our time in her room and I had very little to do with the other housemates, apart from a quick hello when passing in the hallway or on the odd occasion when we would end up cooking at the same time; but Rachel and I rarely socialised with them."

"And how did you meet Rachel?" asked Amy.

"We came from the same village," explained Tom. "Our families were close friends. We went to school together, although I was a couple of years older than her. Basically, we grew up together. We started dating when she was 17 and we got engaged a year later on her 18th birthday. Our families were delighted. They both helped us financially with the wedding, which was booked to take place a couple of months after Rachel's graduation. Unfortunately, Rachel died in a cycling accident before she finished university. It's very much because of Rachel and what happened to her, that Eleanor and I ended up getting married."

"You're doing great but please don't jump too far ahead," Matt reminded Tom.

"Right, yes of course." Tom took a deep breath and continued, "Out of all the people living in the house Rachel got on with Eleanor the best and by the end of the first year of living together, they were becoming quite good friends. They went to the local pub together every week to take part in the pub quiz. Eleanor had no family and would stay at the university at the end of each semester. By the time the second Christmas came around, Rachel, being the kind and sympathetic soul that she was, couldn't bear the thought of anyone being alone over the festive period and so she invited Eleanor to go home with her for the holidays. Eleanor declined to spend Christmas Day with the family but joined them in time for New Year. My parents held an annual New Year's Eve party, and that year Eleanor came along with Rachel and her parents. That's the first time I really started to get to know Eleanor. I'm not sure I'd even had a proper conversation with her before that night, but we got chatting and discovered that we had an awful lot in common. After that, whenever I went to stay in Oxford, the three of us would spend time together."

"What sort of things did you have in common?" Amy was genuinely curious because Eliza had a lot of shared interests with her father when they first got together. Although she seemed to lose interest in them once they had been married for a while.

"Well," said Tom, "we had a shared love of astronomy. On a couple of occasions, we went out into the countryside at night with my telescope to watch an event. Rachel didn't come with us as she had no interest in watching a meteor shower or whatever it was we were going to view. We also both enjoyed trying to complete the Times crossword and would help each other out solving clues. She got into the habit of saving the crossword if she couldn't finish it, so I could help her with it when I next visited. But I think it was the shared love of Rugby Union that really cemented our friendship. Not being sexist, but at the time it was very unusual for a girl to know much about the sport, let alone follow it. I was astounded to discover she was as big a Harlequins fan as I was. She knew everything there was to know about the team and even bought me tickets to a match as a birthday present. Also, I inherited a love of opera from my father, who was a patron of the Royal Opera House, and as such had access at certain times to a Grand Tier box. Very occasionally, when there was a performance that my father was unable to attend, he would allow me to go in his stead and as Rachel abhorred opera, I asked Eleanor to accompany me. To be fair, I think it was the grandeur of the occasion that was the appeal for Eleanor. She loved dressing up and mingling with the rich and the famous. So, as you can imagine, the more I got to know Eleanor, the easier it was to spend time with her. Rachel got a part-time job at the local cinema and on the nights she was working, Eleanor and I would spend the time together. It was totally innocent. We had just become really good friends."

"But that must have changed at some point?" suggested Matt.

"Yes," admitted Tom reluctantly. "It changed when Rachel went back home for a weekend not long before she died. Her grandmother was turning 80 and there was a huge family gathering on the Saturday to celebrate the special occasion. Friends and family were coming from all over the country and Rachel returned home on the Friday to give her Mum a hand with the preparations. Normally, I would have accompanied her, but I was flying out to Germany with work on the Saturday afternoon, so it made more sense for me to stay in Oxford before catching my flight from Heathrow. On the Friday night, Eleanor and I went to the local for a couple of drinks. I don't remember drinking in excess, but I must have done because I have no memory of what happened that night, but when I woke up the next morning, I was in bed with Eleanor in her room. The trail of clothing from the door to the bed painted an exact picture of what happened. Both Eleanor and I were guilt-stricken. We were both devastated that we had betrayed Rachel, and we made a pact that morning to never mention the incident again. We agreed it was a stupid drunken mistake. Her memory of the night seemed as hazy as mine. I was so grateful that Eleanor felt the same way about what had happened as I did. She was just as contrite as I was. Rachel was the woman I wanted to spend the rest of my life with, but I knew she would not be able to forgive me for cheating on her, no matter what the circumstances. Eleanor understood exactly. She didn't want to lose a good friend over what was a regrettable drunken one- night stand.

"After a couple of awkward hours, I left the house for the airport. Whilst I was away, I worried that Eleanor might renege on our pact and say something to Rachel, but whenever I spoke to Rachel on the phone, everything seemed fine between us. Going to stay at the house for the first time after that night was nerve-wracking, and I found it really hard to act naturally. I must have nearly given the game away as Rachel queried whether I was coming down with something. I blamed pressure at work as to why I was not my usual self. Eleanor, on the other hand, was a consummate actress and Rachel genuinely didn't seem to suspect a thing. I was only with them for a few days and then I had to fly back to Germany, and the next time I came home I was far more relaxed. As time went on, I was able to put what had transpired between myself and Eleanor behind me and my friendship with her carried on as it had done before without any awkwardness between us."

"So, am I right in thinking that Max was a result of this one-night stand?" asked Matt.

Tom nodded.

"When did she tell you about the pregnancy?" asked Amy.

Tom sighed, obviously finding this part of his story difficult to tell.

"Another opportunity arose to attend a performance at the Royal Opera House, and I invited Eleanor. It was during the interval that evening that she broke the news to me of the pregnancy. I was shocked. My initial reaction was denial, but the dates fit and one thing you couldn't accuse Eleanor of was being promiscuous. I wasn't aware that she had ever had a boyfriend since I had known her. She never stayed out overnight or brought anyone back to the house as far as I knew and I'm sure Rachel would have told me if that had happened. As I had no recollection of the night we spent together, I had no idea if I had used protection, but the evidence seemed to suggest not! I'm ashamed to say I didn't behave very well to begin with. All I could think about was how this was going to affect my life and what I could do in the way of damage limitation. I offered to pay for an abortion which horrified Eleanor. She told me that although she had lapsed, she was a Catholic and under no circumstances would she be getting rid of the child."

"She was never a Catholic!" Amy exclaimed. "Sorry, ignore me. Carry on."

"She was adamant that her keeping the baby would have no impact on me at all," Tom told them. "She said she would tell Rachel she didn't know who the father was. We argued a lot, shouting back and forth at one another. I'm not proud of what I said to her or how I made her feel. I really upset her, and she said she wished she'd never told me. She'd only done so because she thought it was unfair for me not to know that I had fathered a child. I told her that I wished she'd never told me, too. Ignorance is bliss, so they say. She said we were both too emotional to discuss the situation sensibly and suggested we talk again in a few days when I had had a chance to think things through and calm down. She reassured me again that she didn't want to do anything that would jeopardise my relationship with Rachel, and I have to say I believed her. I spent the next week in a total pit of misery. I didn't have a clue what I was going to do. If I'm honest, I was hoping that Eleanor would change her mind about an abortion. But I knew if she was determined to keep it, then I needed to step up, if only financially. By the end of the week when I met Eleanor in secret, we came to an arrangement, whereby I would discretely support her financially and she would never reveal that I was the baby's father. I gave her a sum of money there and then to seal the deal. Looking back, it was all very shabby and like I say, not my finest moment. I was so grateful that I was again having to go away with work so that I would not be around when Rachel inevitably discovered the pregnancy's existence. It had been difficult enough for me to act myself after that shameful night, but this was a whole new level."

"And how did Rachel react when she found out? She must have wondered who the father was," said Amy.

"Well, that's just it, she never did find out. Only a few days after I arrived back in Germany, I received a phone call from my father informing me of Rachel's accident," said Tom.

"What sort of accident?" asked Matt.

"She was knocked off her bike down some country road. It was a hit-and-run. The front wheel of her bike was buckled, and it was surmised from the damage that she had been clipped by a car. They couldn't be sure, but they felt it was quite a while before anyone found her. The road was hardly used, you see. After the phone call, I went to pieces. My dad had been clear about the fact that Rachel was in a serious condition. My boss was brilliant. He booked me on the next flight home and my dad met me at the airport and drove me straight to the hospital. Rachel was on a life support machine. She had serious head injuries. Her parents and her brother were at her bedside when I arrived, and her brother told me the doctors were not hopeful of a recovery.

"After a few days on life support, the doctors pronounced Rachel brain dead and I stayed along with her family after they'd turned the machine off until she died. It was surreal. I can't put into words the grief that I felt. It was compounded by guilt. I felt guilty for cheating on Rachel. I felt guilty for the way I had reacted when Eleanor broke the news of the baby to me. I felt guilty for buying Eleanor off. To me, it felt like I was responsible for Rachel's accident. Her dying was my punishment. I fell into a deep depression. I couldn't function. The people at work were supportive, giving me as much time off as I needed. My parents were brilliant and did their best to look after me, believing that grief had overwhelmed me, and I couldn't be honest with them and tell them of my guilt. The only person I could discuss my true feelings with was Eleanor and I have to say she was incredible. I was staying in the cottage that had belonged to my grandparents; it's where I always stayed when I went back to visit my parents, and Eleanor would visit me there. She didn't smother me with affection, but she allowed me to talk, to get everything off my chest. She persuaded me I was in no way to blame for either the accident or Rachel's death. Instead, she got me looking at the situation in a different light. Through no fault of mine, Rachel was gone and there was nothing I could do to change that. I needed to think about myself and my future."

Tom paused as Lizzie came into the room to offer more refreshments. Whilst Amy gave her a hand to collect the dirty cups and take them back to the kitchen, which was another elegantly styled room, she thought back to the statement she recently read of Mason's meeting with Eliza in the hospital, the morning after her father's death. Eliza had used very similar words to the ones Tom remembered her using on him after Rachel died. "What's happened has happened and it can't be changed. You have to think of yourself and move on." The words had stuck with Amy when she'd read them because it was such an awful and unusual thing for someone to say so soon after losing their partner.

On her return to the lounge, the two men, who were discussing the recent terror attack in Turkey, ceased their conversation and as soon as she sat down, Tom immediately picked up where he had left off. '*He's finding this really difficult,*' thought Amy, seeing the look of pain etched on Tom's face. '*He just wants to get this bit over with.*' She made the decision not to interrupt him again unless absolutely necessary.

"Instead of wondering how I could face a future without Rachel, Eleanor got me thinking about the future I could have with the child she was carrying," Tom told them. "It's impossible to explain exactly what went on between Eleanor and me during those days and weeks. For me, it was an extremely dark time, but I ended up convinced that I could expunge my guilt by taking responsibility for my actions, and before I had a chance to really understand what I was doing, I had proposed to Eleanor, and she had accepted. It wasn't a happy time. Breaking the news to my parents was hard. They were naturally disappointed by my behaviour and couldn't really understand how I had been able to cheat on Rachel. I couldn't give them a satisfactory answer because I didn't know myself! My father was supportive of my decision to take responsibility, and I know my mother would not have been happy for me to have a child out of wedlock, but as far as they were concerned, the timing could not have been worse. My sister, Laura, was horrified that I was going to marry someone I hardly knew, and she repeatedly asked if I was certain the baby was mine. If I found telling my parents hard, you can imagine how difficult it was to tell Rachel's parents, but it was something I felt obligated to do. To say they were devastated would be somewhat of an understatement. I was supposed to have been unconditionally in love with their daughter. When I broke the news to them that I was marrying someone else, and the reason why, I think I broke their hearts all over again. We hadn't even reached the date set aside for my and Rachel's wedding, yet here I was announcing my intention to marry someone else, who was expecting my child. It drove a wedge between our two families that was irreparable and before the year was out, and much to my relief, Rachel's parents moved away from the village, up to Scotland, to be nearer their son and daughter-in-law and neither I nor my parents ever had contact with them again. So that was another reason for me to feel guilty, I had lost my parents two of their best friends.

"Fortunately for me, shortly after I had come clean to everybody, I went back to work overseas; Eleanor accompanied me and we got married there, with two work colleagues as witnesses, no family or friends. We didn't really celebrate it at all. It felt more like a business transaction than a wedding. Straight afterwards, Eleanor returned to the UK and stayed until she finished her exams and then she joined me, and our son Max was born whilst we were living in Germany.

"We were hardly living in married bliss. Really our marriage was doomed from the start. When it came down to it, we hardly knew each other. Sex between us before marriage had consisted of one drunken fumble that neither of us remembered, and we didn't consummate our union, if I can put it like that, until after Max was born, what with Eleanor being pregnant and having her exams to finish and me being severely depressed and grieving for Rachel. By the time we were both ready to be with each other in that way, we had gotten to know each other a lot better, and I don't think either of us liked what we discovered about the other. I don't know if having a child changed Eleanor or if the guilt that I tried to bury changed me, but after Max was born, it became obvious that we just weren't compatible. Eleanor no longer enjoyed any of the interests we shared when Rachel was alive. We never watched another Rugby match together; never attended another opera, I wasn't even permitted to play any of my opera CDs."

'*Exactly like with Dad*,' Amy thought, but she didn't say anything out loud and Tom continued uninterrupted.

"It was around this time that Eleanor's fixation with money started to get out of hand. She was obsessed with wealth or rather our lack of it. I know we both come from privileged backgrounds. I mean we were both privately educated and neither of us went without during our childhoods, but whereas I was determined to make my own way in the world, Eleanor wasn't prepared to make sacrifices. She found it impossible to live within our means and it frustrated her that I refused to use credit to purchase unnecessary items that we couldn't afford. We started to argue a lot, mostly about money. She couldn't comprehend my unwillingness to ask my parents for financial assistance. I struggled to understand her obsession with money. Maybe losing her parents at an early age had traumatised her and she needed the security that having money provides."

"What did she tell you about her childhood?" asked Matt.

"What did I know of her childhood?" queried Tom. "Very little really. She didn't like to talk about it much. I don't think she ever got over the shock of losing her parents in such horrific circumstances. She told me her father was a diplomat and both her parents were killed in a car bomb whilst he was serving in the Middle East. After that, she lived with her grandmother who, as I understand it, had rather Dickensian attitudes regarding the raising of children. Eleanor certainly gave me the impression that her childhood was not a happy one. Her grandmother was her only other living relative, apart from some distant druggy cousin who used to turn up from time to time."

"His name wasn't Ricky Kerr by any chance?" Amy was pretty sure what the answer would be.

"It was definitely Ricky, but I couldn't be sure about the surname. Have you met him?"

"Just a couple of times but I know he was around a lot when Eliza was married to my dad."

No one picked Amy up for using Eliza instead of Eleanor, it just wasn't worth it.

"He was actually involved in covering up Dad's murder. He's dead now. He died in police custody."

"I'm so sorry," said Tom, "I didn't know." He was silent for a few seconds and then "Oh God, sorry. That's really awkward. I'm not sorry he's dead, I'm sorry about your dad." Tom covered his face with his hand as if trying to brush away his comments.

"It's okay," said Amy, "if there's one thing I've learnt over the last few months, it's that it's impossible to say the right thing when you're discussing Eliza. I mean Eleanor. There see!" She smiled at Tom, and he smiled back. "Please, carry on. I'm sorry I interrupted you."

"Where was I? Oh yes. Well, with the arrival of Max, we suddenly had much bigger issues to face. Whereas I was besotted with the baby from the moment he was born, Eleanor struggled to bond with him at all. She didn't take to motherhood and back then there really wasn't much help for mothers with post-natal depression, which I'm certain was what she was suffering from. She had no interest in breastfeeding, which wasn't a problem, but she struggled even to give him a bottle or do any of the basic tasks such as changing his nappy. She didn't even enjoy holding him. I was the one who got up with him at night as I thought it was more important for her to get the sleep, even though I had work every day. She was unhappy staying at home with the baby and longed to start work herself. To be fair to her, she hadn't even been able to start a probationary period at a law firm since gaining her degree, let alone finish it. I tried to do as much as I could to help but juggling work and home life was hard and on top of that there was just so much arguing between us. It was exhausting for both of us, even without adding a new baby to the mix. Eleanor would have preferred it if I stayed home, and she went out to work but that was totally impracticable as I was the breadwinner. She was torn between her love of money and her hatred of being a stay-at-home mum.

"Considering how adamant she had been about keeping the baby, this all came as a huge shock to me. As I said, post-natal depression wasn't widely discussed, and I struggled to comprehend her behaviour towards the baby. Although this was the 1990s, it was still unusual for a bloke to do the majority of the childcare, and both my friends and my work colleagues thought our situation was odd.

My mum came to stay for a while to lend a hand and she soon understood that not only were we struggling with parenthood, but we were struggling with our marriage too. In an attempt to help by easing some of the pressure, she offered to pay for an au pair/nanny for the remaining couple of months we were in Germany. Eleanor nearly bit my mum's hand off. Considering she never normally had a good word to say about my parents and, for some reason, she especially despised my mother, she seemed genuinely grateful for my mum's offer of support. I was more reluctant as I didn't want to be beholden to my parents but, as I couldn't afford to pay for it myself, and seeing how happy at the prospect Eleanor was, I agreed. At this point, Eleanor and I also came to an understanding that on our return to the UK, she would start work. She wanted to employ an au pair or a full-time nanny, but I objected on the grounds that we could definitely not afford to do that, and when I refused point blank to ask my parents for any more help, it was agreed that we would send Max to a childminder and share his care at home between us.

"I thought that returning to the UK and setting up a home there together might be just what Eleanor and I needed to get back on track, but it didn't pan out like that. Eleanor started work with a firm of local solicitors and that did seem to make her happier. She certainly preferred to be out of the house. Max was a lovely baby, rarely causing us any trouble. He was exceptionally bright and, on the whole, very happy and content. As he grew older, Eleanor's relationship with him improved beyond measure, but unfortunately her relationship with me continued to deteriorate.

"She loved showing Max off and she wanted the best of everything for him. Now, not only did she spend what I regarded as obscene amounts of money on herself, but also on Max. She was still on probation, so her income was not that high and although I earned more than she did, it was a struggle every month to make all the necessary payments, especially as we now had a mortgage to pay. We had decided not to take my parents up on the offer of my grandparents' cottage, even though we could have both commuted easily from there. Me, because I wanted to be independent and Eleanor because it wasn't grand enough for her taste. Despite our lack of income, Eleanor insisted that Max be dressed in designer clothes; he had to have all the latest toys and attended every toddler class going. I mean she had him doing gymnastics, playing tennis, swimming. I tell you one of the funniest sights you'll ever see is an instructor trying to get a group of 2-year-olds to use a mini racquet to hit a ball over a net. Hilarious!

"Montessori schools were all the rage at the time and Eleanor was adamant that Max attend one, even though they charged extortionate fees compared to the childminder. Before I knew it, Max was enrolled and learning Japanese!

"Almost every argument we had, and there were a lot of them, was over money. Eleanor had a way of twisting everything, making me feel like a Scrooge who was depriving my child of life's necessities when in reality, I was just trying to get her to live within our means. She was so unreasonable. She refused to compromise. She would book trips abroad for every school holiday when prices were at their highest, just because she was trying to keep up with the snobby mothers at the Montessori, who had their own villas and skiing lodges. We just couldn't afford to compete in those sorts of circles. Nothing was ever good enough for Eleanor. She wanted a bigger house in a more desirable area, a fancier make of car, and in all honesty, a wealthier husband. We had absolutely nothing in common. The days of shared Times crosswords and the nights of star gazing felt like they happened to somebody else. We argued and bickered all the time. I'm not laying all of the blame on Eleanor, I was at fault too, but she went out of her way to undermine me and to make my life miserable. My friends didn't like her either; that's always telling, isn't it? Although I would still go for nights out with my male friends, Eleanor and I were no longer invited out as a couple, and it was made very clear to me that neither my friends nor their partners could tolerate her. The only good thing about my home life was Max."

At this point, Lizzie came in the room again and announced that lunch was ready. Matt was delighted. His stomach had been rumbling for some time and he was unsure what the eating arrangements would be. He had been waiting for the right time to suggest that they broke for lunch and had planned on taking Amy to the pub, inviting the Bryants to join them.

After enjoying delicious homemade quiches - Quiche Lorraine and a mushroom alternative in case they were vegetarian, with an accompanying salad, a fresh fruit tart and a shared bottle of wine, Amy, Matt and Tom returned to the sitting room. Amy, now convinced that Lizzie was some sort of domestic goddess, had offered to help her clear the kitchen, but Lizzie declined. Matt, who was worried he might nod off after the wine and good food, was grateful to hear Lizzie say she would bring coffee to them shortly. Sitting purposefully upright in his chair to help him stay awake, Matt switched his phone to record again as a signal for Tom to continue with his account.

"I was given a promotion which entailed spending more time abroad than in the UK, so Eleanor and I became even more distant from each other and by the time Max was three years old, our marriage had broken down completely," Tom explained. "Unless it was about Max or money, we no longer spoke to each other and even then, it wasn't so much speaking as shouting. It will come as no surprise to you, I'm sure, to learn that I met someone else. Lizzie was doing work experience at our Stockholm branch, and I fell head over heels in love with her from the moment I met her. My marriage to Eleanor was a failure. I was certain that Eleanor was just as unhappy as I was. I wanted to spend my future with Lizzie, so I broached the subject of separation with Eleanor. As our relationship was now so toxic, I expected her to make things difficult. I felt she hated me enough to inflict as much pain as possible. To my surprise though, she was really understanding and considerate. Obviously, she wanted to be compensated financially, I mean this is Eleanor we're talking about. Her main concern wasn't the fact that I had met someone new, but more about how much she would be entitled to as a settlement when we divorced.

"We actually discussed our separate futures as two adults. Eleanor disclosed that she found Marcham too small and suffocating. Now she had finished her probationary period, she would prefer to move further afield, and so she began applying for jobs in different areas and before long, she had secured a post in Dolford. Because I still worked away a fair bit of the time, it was decided that she would be Max's main carer, but we would have joint custody. Max would live with her but spend as much time with me as possible. Obviously, she was going to need somewhere to live, and I was keen to stay put as where we were living was conveniently close to my friends and my family. We decided to have the house valued and I would pay her half the purchase price for it. Typically for Eleanor, the house she wanted in Dolford was more expensive than she could afford. This might have been a sticking point in our separation, had it not been for my father stepping in and agreeing to give her the deposit, on the understanding that it be returned if she ever sold the property before Max reached the age of 18. With the help of solicitors, we managed to negotiate a settlement and a maintenance allowance that I would pay monthly. The amount of maintenance Eleanor requested from me was much higher than would normally be expected, but because she had been so obliging over the divorce, when I had expected her to make my life extremely difficult, especially as I was the one who cheated and wanted to put our marriage behind me so I could start my new life with Lizzie, I readily agreed. We were able to obtain a "quickie" divorce because of my infidelity and it was finalised before Max turned 4."

Tom paused for a moment before continuing,

"I wouldn't describe my and Eleanor's relationship as amicable after the divorce. We still argued a lot. She could be extremely unreasonable regarding my access to Max. From the start of the divorce negotiations, she accepted the fact that I wouldn't be able to stick to a regular schedule because of work taking me out of the country so often, and usually at short notice, but that didn't stop her from creating problems every time I wanted to see him. She intentionally made difficulties, and this was proven when it came to Lizzie and I arranging our wedding, but I'll leave Lizzie to explain about that. As time went on, the arguments between Eleanor and me grew worse; it was like when we were married all over again. Our arguments centred around Max and money, but mostly money. There always seemed to be a reason why she required a rise in her monthly allowance. I mostly managed to deflect these but at least once or twice a year, I would end up giving her a lump sum of money to help her out."

Again, Tom paused, seemingly lost in his memories. At that moment, Lizzie came into the room with a tray carrying the promised coffee. To give Tom a bit of a break and more time to rationalise his thoughts Amy suggested that Lizzie might like to give her impressions of Eleanor whilst they drank their coffees.

Tom zoned out whilst Lizzie answered questions put to her by Matt and by Amy. He took himself back to what was probably the worst argument he and Eleanor ever had which took place at his father's funeral.

During a reading being given by his uncle Charles, Tom became aware of a lot of commotion coming from the foyer at the back of the church. Along with most of the rest of the congregation, he turned his head to see who was disturbing the proceedings, just as the woman entering the chapel allowed the large, heavy wooden door to slam behind her. The click of her stiletto heels sounded out of place on the stone floor of the 17th century chapel. The woman, who was wearing a long black coat, and a black pillar box hat, complete with a net veil that obscured her face, continued halfway down the aisle before stopping and not bothering to lower her voice, instructed the mourners already seated to shuffle up the pew to allow her to sit. Tom's heart sank. As if the day wasn't going to be difficult enough to endure; that confident swagger and ability to disrupt the service without so much as a hint of apology could only mean one thing, Eleanor had arrived!

At the end of the service, Tom, along with Lizzie, Laura and the vicar stood in the foyer to receive condolences from the funeral goers.

"I can't believe Eleanor came," Laura whispered to Tom. "It's not like she got on with Pa, is it? When was the last time she even saw him? She never bothered to turn up to say farewell to Ma."

Tom felt Lizzie tense beside him as she reached for his hand and knew this signalled Eleanor's approach. Lizzie would not be concerned for herself; she was more than capable of handling Eleanor. No, she would be worried how he would react knowing that Eleanor was likely to say something inappropriate or spiteful.

As it was, all Eleanor said as she kissed him on the cheek was, "I need to talk to you. I'll see you back at the house." Tom sighed, one because he had hoped she would leave after the service and not attend the wake, and two because he knew the conversation was bound to be about money. Turned out he was right.

Back at the wake, whilst the guests tucked into the abundance of food and drink provided by a local catering firm, and began swapping anecdotes about his father, which became more embellished the more they drank, Tom did his very best to avoid Eleanor. Eventually, she managed to corner him in the kitchen and told him she needed to speak to him in private. As they moved into his father's study, Tom barely had a chance to close the door before she started on him, demanding to know why she hadn't been invited to the reading of the will.

Tom was confused. "Why on earth would you be?" he asked.

"Because," Eleanor replied acerbically, "I need to know what arrangements he left regarding paying for Max's education."

Tom was astounded. Ever since Eleanor had put Max's name down for an exclusive Prep school close to where she lived, she had been pestering him to contribute towards the fees. This he had refused to do on the grounds that it was her choice to send Max there, and Tom was already paying her twice as much as he was legally obligated to.

"Dad left no such arrangement as well you know," he told her. "Why in the world would you think he had?"

"Because," Eleanor repeated, this time severely sarcastically, "he contacted me not long before he died and told me he wanted to do something for his only grandson." She stressed the word 'only' which Tom knew was a dig that so far, his and Lizzie's attempt to start a family had been unsuccessful. They were about to embark on fertility tests; not that he would ever share such personal information with Eleanor.

"And?" Tom felt he had to ask even though he had already guessed what she was going to say.

"And," said Eleanor, "he offered to pay for Max's schooling until he turns 18."

"How exactly did he contact you to make this offer?" Tom asked matching her sarcasm.

"He called me at work," Eleanor replied smoothly. "He told me he didn't want you to know about it as you would try to stop him."

"You're lying," said Tom, "Dad would never go behind my back and there is no way he would offer you any financial assistance. He always said you were nothing more than a money grubber. Face it, Eleanor he didn't even like you. His biggest regret was that he had encouraged me to marry you."

"Think what you like," said Eleanor confidently. "He promised me he'd pay for Max's education, and I expect you to honour his wishes."

"Bollocks!" replied Tom aware that he was raising his voice but not caring. "Where's the evidence, Eleanor? If Dad had, and we both know he didn't, but if he had made an agreement with you, he would have put it in writing. He was meticulous, you know that better than anyone. When he got his diagnosis, getting his financial affairs in order was a priority to him. If he had wanted to make such a provision for Max, firstly, he would have spoken to me about it, not you, and secondly, he would have received advice from his solicitor and then he would have added it as a codicil to his will. But," now Tom was really shouting, "but, he would never, ever have made an arrangement with you behind my back. He wouldn't have even known how to get in touch with you."

"Believe what you want," Eleanor shouted back. "It's not my fault if he didn't inform you of his intentions. Even if all I have is a verbal agreement, I expect you to honour it. You know he would expect you to."

"Are you out of your mind?"

Both Tom and Eleanor turned as Laura entered the room.

"You might want to keep your voices down as the whole of the village can hear you, let alone the guests. And Tom's right, Eleanor. You are talking bollocks!"

"Well of course you'd agree with him," Eleanor spat back. "You two make me sick. Here you are rolling in money, but you're too mean to give your only son and only nephew a decent education. I mean it's not like you two have ever been deprived of anything is it?"

"And neither have you or Max," Tom retaliated. "If Max goes without then that's down to you and your mismanagement of your finances!"

"Oh, come on Tom, your father was a very wealthy man. Surely, you can spare enough of your inheritance to cover Max's school fees."

"That's not the point Eleanor," Tom began.

Laura interrupted, "Even if Tom is willing, I'm not. You are not going to get a penny of my father's money. You are not entitled to anything, Eleanor. You've bled Tom dry for years and enough is enough. Max will get his share in the fullness of time. Now if you don't mind, Tom needs to come and speak with the people who have had the decency to come and pay their respects to my father's memory, rather than to steal from him."

"You sanctimonious bitch!" screamed Eleanor, launching herself at Laura, who stood impassive until Eleanor came within reach, then drew back her hand and slapped her ex-sister-in-law hard across her face. Eleanor stopped in her tracks, putting her hand to her stinging cheek, unable to believe that Laura had the audacity to hit her. By now a number of the guests were standing in the doorway rubbernecking. Mustering as much *dignity as she could, Eleanor made her way out of the room calling out to Tom over her shoulder, "You'll be hearing from my solicitor."*

"I've always wanted to do that," Laura smiled up at her brother as she took his arm and led him from the room.

"Is that okay with you Tom?"

Tom looked up at Laura, "Sorry, is what okay?" he said.

"I said I'd get the photos of Max to show Matt and Amy, if you don't mind. You were miles away; is everything alright?"

"Yes, of course, fetch the photos, good idea," said Tom. "Sorry, I was just remembering that awful argument between Eleanor, Laura and me at Dad's funeral."

"Oh, what argument was that?" asked Matt.

"Well," said Tom and he recounted what had taken place. "After that," he continued, "I did my best to avoid Eleanor.

"With her moving away and my working abroad, I was seeing less and less of Max, and if arrangements were made for us to have him to stay, they were conducted by Lizzie, who was also the one who collected him and dropped him back. It was just easier that way, as it avoided all the arguments. The cost of Max's education was not raised again but I knew it was only a matter of time. I actually don't think I saw or spoke to Eleanor again until the results of the DNA test came back."

Before he could elaborate any further, Lizzie returned to the room clutching a photo album and some photo frames in her arms. She dumped the frames on the floor in front of Matt and passed the album to Amy.

"Oh goodness," exclaimed Amy. "He's gorgeous. Just look at that ginger hair!"

"I know," said Lizzie. "Everyone used to comment on it and on his curls."

"His colouring definitely came from Eleanor's side," said Tom. "All of my family are blonde and blue eyed."

"Was Eleanor ginger when you knew her?" asked Amy. She felt a little awkward using the term ginger, certain that you were supposed to use another term these days, but she had no idea how else to describe the colour.

"No, she was blonde too, but that cousin of hers that we were talking about earlier, Ricky. He was a copper top."

Amy was certain that the term Tom had used was also no longer PC.

"Getting back to what you were saying, Tom," Matt wasn't really interested in looking at the photographs, he was more interested in getting Tom's story. "Can you explain why you felt you needed a DNA test?"

"Yes of course," said Tom. "Lizzie and I had been trying for a family for quite some time without success and we decided to seek professional help. We were both sent for tests which I thought was unnecessary as, no disrespect to Lizzie, but you know, I had already fathered a child. So, when the tests came back, saying that Lizzie was fine, but the problem lay with me, I was shocked. The results showed that I had a very low sperm count. Not really what a bloke wants to hear! I was also told that this would have always been the case so the chance of me being able to impregnate anyone, although not impossible, was very slim. Once Lizzie and I had been reassured that this problem didn't rule out our chances of becoming parents, my mind obviously turned to Max. I wasn't ready to entertain the possibility that he might not be mine and concentrated instead on what the specialist had said about it not being impossible for me to have got someone pregnant.

"However, once our IVF attempt proved successful and we knew the twins were on the way, the knowledge that I might not be Max's father played more and more heavily on my mind. Although I didn't act on the information, my doubts started to plague me. I kept going back to the fact that I had no memory of that night Max was supposedly conceived. How strange it was that I was so drunk after just one or two drinks. That had never happened to me before or since. It was like a fog was lifting and I began to see things more clearly. The way the clothes were spread out on the bedroom floor suddenly seemed very staged. The fact that I was in Eleanor's bed when I had never even gone into her room before. Things just seemed off! And then Eleanor's behaviour after Rachel died. The more I thought about it, the more I understood how Eleanor had manipulated me during my grieving, the rushed marriage. It very much looked like she had intentionally set out to trap me. Maybe she had been trying to take me away from Rachel before Rachel died. It would explain all those interests we had in common which she then actively despised once we were married.

"I mean, don't get me wrong, I don't and didn't think for one moment that she was responsible for Rachel's accident, but I do think she took advantage of it. Had she played me? Did she know I wasn't Max's father from the outset? But why would she do that? I already knew the answer – money! Money was the only thing Eleanor cared about. She had always intended to use Max to extract money from me. In fact, I had already given her money for the baby before we married.

"I began to think deeply about it all. When she first met me, I would have appeared extremely affluent. I had a good job and obviously came from a wealthy background. Seeing my ancestral home, so to speak, when she came to my parents' New Year's Eve party, would have confirmed that. When I proposed, it must have been the icing on the cake. She must have thought she was set for life and our marriage had failed because I wasn't as rich as she had assumed. I didn't act on any of these suspicions. I certainly didn't say anything to Eleanor. I didn't even talk them through with Lizzie. In the cold light of day, I thought I was being absurd, but at night the dark thoughts plagued me. No one likes to think they've been played.

"Then, when the twins were a year old, Eleanor was causing problems about Max attending their birthday party, and I made a throw-away comment to Lizzie about how annoying it would be to discover that Max really wasn't mine, and we had been putting up with Eleanor for all these years unnecessarily. 'Think how much money we would have saved,' I told her half-jokingly. Then it all came out and I told her of my concerns, all those dark thoughts that had kept me awake at night and that's when she suggested we do a DNA test. If nothing else, it would give me peace of mind. DNA tests had become popular and more available thanks to that awful Jeremy Kyle chap. So that's what we did. Obviously, I didn't mention anything to Eleanor about it. Why rock the boat unless I had to? We tested Max when he was staying with us one weekend. We made it into a game so as not to freak him out. Then we sent the samples off for testing at a private clinic. The results proved conclusively that I was not Max's father.

"Even though deep down I was expecting that to be the case, the news still hit me like a ton of bricks. I was devastated. It was as if I'd been told Max had died. The feelings I had were akin to grief. I mean I loved Max just as much as I always had but something fundamental had changed. He was the literal cuckoo in the nest. He wasn't mine. He belonged to someone else. After the initial shock passed, then those other nasty thoughts raised their heads again. Had Eleanor known all along? Had I been played for a fool? I grew more and more angry at the thought that I had been Eleanor's patsy. In hindsight, I should have waited until I was calmer before I challenged Eleanor but then again, I'm not sure if I ever would have calmed down.

"I went to see her on my own, arranging to meet her on neutral territory whilst Max was at school. Both Lizzie and Laura offered to go with me to ensure things didn't get out of hand, but I refused. This was something I wanted to have out with Eleanor by myself. I felt humiliated enough and didn't want anyone to witness the humiliation I was sure would come. I confronted Eleanor with my fertility test results and lo and behold, she tried to convince me that Max must have been that one in a million, just as I had wanted to believe myself when I first found out. I then showed her the proof from the DNA test. Oh, my goodness, how her demeanour changed. She went from being calm and reassuring to enraged in a nanosecond. She was fuming, absolutely fuming. I don't think I have ever seen her so furious, and I had experienced her losing her temper numerous times. How dare I have the audacity to have her child tested behind her back? That's exactly the point I told her – he's your child but not mine. It occurred to me straight away that she had referred to Max as 'hers' and not 'ours'. I can't recall exactly what words were exchanged between us, but it got out of hand very quickly. So much so that the landlord of the pub came over a couple of times asking us to keep the noise down. I think he was also checking on Eleanor's welfare, but if he had any idea of what she was capable of, he should have been checking if I was okay.

"I demanded Eleanor tell me who the father was, and she swore she had no idea; if Max wasn't mine, she said, then he must be another Jesus; an immaculate conception! Nothing I said got her to change her story. She was adamant that I was the only possible father.

"She accused me of trying to get out of my responsibility to Max because I no longer needed him now I had the twins. She also tried to lay the blame on Lizzie, saying that she must have faked the DNA result because she didn't want competition for her children. I told her she was more than welcome to have the test done herself.

"We were at an impasse. I made it clear to her that I had no intention of contributing any more money for Max's upbringing, knowing that this would hurt her more than anything else. I was right. If that was the case, she said, then I was no longer entitled to see him. Although I couldn't imagine not having Max in my life, I was so angry with Eleanor, that I told her I would take her to court if necessary. If I couldn't see him then I wanted to be reimbursed for all the money I had laid out for him. She told me I didn't stand a chance in hell and with that she stormed off.

"Basically, I cut my nose off to spite my face because I knew that unless I paid up, Eleanor would never allow me access to Max. When I got home Lizzie was furious with me. She loved Max as much as I did and didn't want to lose him. I told Lizzie I was going to need a bit of time to calm down but then I'd get back in touch with Eleanor. I was certain that for the right amount of money, an agreement could be reached but before I could do that, something happened that made me rethink my situation."

Tom asked if they could take a break at this point, and they once more stopped for refreshments.

"So," said Matt after what he felt was hopefully a long enough time for Tom to be ready to start again, "what happened to make you rethink?" Time was moving on and Matt would really like to hear the end of the story before he and Amy had to leave.

Tom took the hint and, sitting forward in his chair, his hands resting on his knees, continued with his tale,

"I was out running. I tend to run most evenings; I always have done. It's a way of keeping fit and it helps me clear my mind. Anyway, I was out running one night. It wasn't that late, probably around 7:30ish – just starting to get dark, when I heard a car approaching. Because it's all countryside around here there are no pavements, and I have to run in the road. I always run towards the oncoming traffic, so drivers have plenty of time to see me. I dress sensibly too. Be seen, be safe has always been my motto.

"As I say, it was just starting to get dark but there is no way the driver of the car couldn't have seen me, unless he wasn't looking at the road. Well, that must have been the case, because I swear it was like he deliberately swerved his car towards me. I leapt out the way and he drove past without stopping. I didn't get a good look at the driver but good enough to see it was a man. Then, before I knew it, the same car was coming up behind me, and once again, I had to jump out of the way. It was obviously being driven by an idiot who'd taken offence at the names I had called him the first time.

"I tried to get a better look at the driver and make a note of the license plate, but all I saw was that he had bright ginger hair and the car made off before I could see more than that it was an 05 plate. I was cross with myself that I didn't clock the make or model of the car, but it all happened so quickly. I wasn't even sure of the colour. I was fuming. What a stupid thing for the driver to do, I could have ended up seriously hurt. I considered ringing the Police but with the limited amount of information I had, I felt I would be wasting their time. I carried on with my run, watching and listening very carefully in case the lunatic decided to have another go at running me over, but he never came back.

"Although I only caught a fleeting glimpse of him, I thought I recognised the driver, but I couldn't place him. Was it someone I knew pratting around? If I could work out who it was, I would give him a piece of my mind. I decided not to mention anything to Lizzie as I didn't want to worry her, but I did talk to my running friends about it in case they experienced something similar, and to make them aware there was the possibility that a driver with a grudge against runners was in the area. One of these friends, someone I've known for years, jokingly said it was probably Eleanor trying to bump me off so she could inherit some money. Everyone laughed because they all knew what Eleanor was like about money. And it was then that it came to me who the driver reminded me of – it was Eleanor's cousin.

"Now don't get me wrong," Tom added hastily, "I know how paranoid that sounds and just because the bloke had ginger hair, it didn't mean it was Ricky. Also, I'm not saying that someone was trying to bump me off. No, that's not what I was thinking; I was thinking more about Eleanor and how she would benefit if anything happened to me. Obviously, being my ex, she didn't stand to gain anything personally by my demise, but as things currently stood, Max did. I was his father. It was my name on his birth certificate. As far as the law was concerned, he was my son and if anything happened to me, he would be entitled to a share of my estate. And that did worry me. What if something happened to me before Max reached his majority? Any money he was entitled to would go directly to Eleanor and I couldn't stand the thought that she might get her hands on my hard-earned money, a payout from my death. And something could easily happen to me;– accidents happen all the time, I could keel over with a heart attack. Lizzie and the twins would be well taken care of, and they had the DNA test to prove that Max wasn't mine, but I knew Eleanor was devious enough to get around that. She would pretend that we had an agreement. Look at how she lied to try to get money from my dad's estate!

"It really bothered me, and I had an overwhelming need to get the problem sorted out, so I went to my solicitor to ask his advice. Having explained my predicament to him, he recommended that I get my name removed from the birth certificate, that way there would be no legal claim on my estate. And as for Max, I could leave some money in trust for him to inherit at an age I specified. I know how this makes me look. As if I'm as obsessed with money as Eleanor. But in truth she had played me for so long, taking money she wasn't entitled to and making my life a misery to boot, that I couldn't bear to leave her with the opportunity to do the same to my family after I was gone."

"Didn't you have to have Eleanor's consent for that to happen? To get the birth certificate amended?" asked Matt. "How on earth did you get her to agree to that?"

"With money, of course." It was Lizzie who had answered his question, and it was obvious from her tone that she had not been happy with the arrangement. "As if she hadn't already appropriated so much that she wasn't entitled to."

"It was worth it," said Tom. "Once my name was removed, Eleanor no longer had a hold over me with regards to Max. I was so relieved."

"How much money did you pay her? If you don't mind me asking?"

"A lot!" replied Lizzie and Matt decided that as it was obviously still a sore subject it would be best to leave it there.

"Did you also make arrangements to continue to see Max?" asked Amy deliberately trying to move the conversation on.

"Well, that was the plan," replied Tom, "but I had a contract starting in Saudi and Lizzie and the twins were joining me. It was originally only supposed to be for 3 months and being happy at having received her payment, Eleanor assured me that we could come to some arrangement, whereby I could start seeing Max again on my return. The Saudi job over ran and we ended up staying for almost a year. I tried several times to contact Eleanor to explain the situation, but she changed all her contact numbers, and I couldn't reach her. I phoned her work, but they told me she had left.

"When we got back to the UK, I went to see her, but she was no longer living at that address. No one could tell me where she had gone. The school would only tell me that Max was no longer a pupil there. I spoke to my solicitor to see what I could do, but because I'd insisted on having my name removed as Max's father, I had no legal rights to any information.

"The only thing the solicitor managed to ascertain was that the house she had been living in had been repossessed which meant the money my father had given her as a deposit would never be recovered. Not that I was bothered about that, I just wanted to find them. Neither Eleanor nor Max could be classed as a missing person, they had just moved, so there was no point going to the police.

"I swear I did everything I could possibly think of to find them, but they had disappeared without a trace. I'm still hoping that one day Max will get in touch, you know, like when adopted kids go looking for their birth parents. I would just like the opportunity to explain my side of the story to him. It would be nice to be able to tell him that I didn't abandon him completely, which is how it must have seemed to him at the time and that I did try my best to find him. Maybe he bears too strong a grudge to come looking for me."

"Oh, I don't think that could be true," said Amy reassuringly. "I'm sure now he's grown up he'll just remember the good times with you. In my experience six-year-olds don't hold grudges for very long."

"They do if their mother constantly drips poison," replied Tom gloomily.

"Do you have any idea who his real father might be?" Matt asked.

"No, like I told the police," Tom replied, "there was never another man on the scene. Believe me, I've thought about it a lot over the years. I'm surprised and a little concerned that even after all the news coverage and the appeals for information, Max hasn't been located. You will let me know if you do manage to find him, won't you?"

"Of course," Amy rushed to console him. "I promise that you will be one of the first to know of any information we uncover."

"Thank you," said Tom. "It would just be so good to see him again."

Both Amy and Matt could see how upset Tom now was and they came to an unspoken agreement. It was unlikely that he had anything else of use to tell them and it was getting late, so they thanked the couple profusely for their time and their hospitality and making the excuse of still facing a long drive home, they took their leave.

Neither of them spoke much for the first part of the journey, both lost in their own thoughts. Matt was trying to put himself in Tom's shoes wondering what it would be like to discover that a child you were raising as your own, turned out not to be yours at all. He had to take his hat off to Tom, Matt wasn't sure he would have handled it so well. Matt assumed that Amy was upset by everything she had heard today and that was why she was so quiet.

It would have surprised him to discover that actually Amy was thinking about the similarities in Tom's marriage to Eleanor to that of her father's to Eliza. As when Peggy had talked about the circumstances surrounding Betty's death and Amy had been astounded that the scenario was almost identical to that of her grandmother's death, now Amy could see a connection between Max's conception and Zac's. The chances of Tom being Max's father had been slim because of his low sperm count, and the chances of her father getting Eliza pregnant had also been slim because he had had a vasectomy. Both she and Adam had challenged her father about it, asking how it was possible that Zac was his. But their father reassured them. He too had been concerned so he got himself tested and the results came back showing that the vasectomy had failed, and that he was more than capable of fathering a child.

After listening to Tom today, Amy was now beset with doubt. Had Eliza managed to fool her father like she had fooled Tom? Had her father really got himself tested or had he just said that to satisfy her and Adam? Although she had a feeling, he had shown her a letter as proof. Still, would it be possible to request a DNA test on Zac? To find out definitively. She was his half- sister after all. Or was she? Amy knew she needed to talk her worries over with someone and she decided to speak to Kath in the morning as she was the one person Amy could trust to give an unbiased opinion.

Needing to distract herself from her current thoughts Amy turned to Matt.

"I've been thinking," she said.

"Uh oh," said Matt, "did it hurt?"

"Very funny," said Amy. "This name business with Eliza, Eleanor, etc. I think when we are talking about her, you and I and Trevor of course, we should call her Edith. Edith must be a name she disliked because she changed it as soon as she legally could at 16, and it's the only name she never chose for herself. I like the idea of calling her by a name she hated."

"Okaaay?" said Matt not sure where this had come from or where it was going.

"Also," said Amy, "the other night my kids were looking at what their names meant. You know, Olivia is derived from olive meaning peace, which was quite amusing considering how many fights she starts, and Rory means red king apparently. Well, I asked them to look up Edith and it means 'fighting for money', and if that's not an appropriate name after what we learnt about her today, then I don't know what is."

"I agree," said Matt. "From now on we will refer to her as Edith. What does Amy mean by the way?"

"Beloved," said Amy smugly. "Marcus means anything to do with the planet Mars, bit boring but Marcus liked it, and Trevor means 'large settlement' which was disappointing. I expected it to be something like 'man of steel'.

"And Matt?" Matt had to ask.

"Don't know," said Amy. "We never looked it up."

"That's a lie," Matt turned and grinned at her. "If you looked up Trevor then you definitely looked up Matthew."

"It means 'gift from God'," said Amy begrudgingly.

"I knew it," laughed Matt. "Jasmine will be so pleased she's right. She always says I think I'm God's gift."

At that, they both burst out laughing, glad to ease some of the tension of the day.

5

The following is an interview conducted with Tom Bryant's wife, Lizzie.

"Eleanor is possibly the most obnoxious person I have ever met in my life. She was incredibly difficult to deal with on every level. She considered herself to be above everyone else and everything always had to be about her. She consistently tried to put me down, to undermine me at every possible opportunity. I'm certain she wanted me out of the picture because she found Tom easier to manipulate if I wasn't around, but I was not intimidated by her and I was determined to be part of Max's life as much as I was Tom's.

As far as I was concerned, they came as a package. Tom is my soul mate, and I knew from the moment I met him I wanted to spend the rest of my life with him, I fell in love with Max the very first time I met him too.

"Max was adorable. So cute and clever. It broke my heart when we lost touch with him, and I don't think Tom has ever gotten over it. He was crushed to discover that Max wasn't his; as was I, but I think we both were able to move on from that. As Tom says, we couldn't just stop loving the boy. He was our family, and we would and did do everything we possibly could to make him happy. Losing him has left a huge hole in both our lives.

"It's hard to explain exactly how Eleanor tried to undermine me. If I said she always criticised, never complimented, does that make sense? I think using this method enabled her to dominate people. I'm trying to think of an example. Everything I can think of just sounds petty now, but then Eleanor was very petty. For instance, rather than greet me with 'Hello' she would say 'Oh, aren't you short!' I was good at deflecting though and my answer would be something like 'Same height as I've always been.'

"Sorry, that's an extremely bad example. How can I explain it? She always tried to make you feel like you were lacking in some way. She would criticise your appearance and the way you were dressed. She'd say things like, 'You know, yellow isn't really a good colour for you.' Like I said, it sounds petty now, but that's what every conversation I ever had with her was like.

"But my relationship with Max was amazing. He made it so easy to love him and I did, as if he was my own. It was just Eleanor who made life difficult. Like I said she was impossible to deal with.

"As I think Tom explained, we couldn't have Max every other weekend like normal couples with joint custody, because we never knew too much in advance when Tom was going to be working away, or for how long he would be gone. So, it was important for us to have Max stay for as long as possible whenever Tom was home. But Eleanor always had an excuse as to why either Max couldn't come on the dates that we wanted him, or he had to return home early. Sometimes when we had arranged to collect him, they wouldn't be at home when we arrived, and Eleanor would pretend she had forgotten we were having him. It was very unfair on both us and Max.

"Tom and I tried very hard not to involve Max in any disputes with Eleanor but sometimes it was unavoidable. There were a couple of times whilst he was staying with us that Tom had to fly off for a few days because of work and I kept Max with me rather than sending him back to his mum. It was risky, because for some reason, Eleanor was incredibly jealous of my relationship with Max, and she would have kicked up a stink if she was aware that I was looking after him on my own. Max was a very bright child, and I think he understood the dynamics. I'm certain he never said a word to his Mum about these occasions because she never had a go at me.

"I worried about the effect Eleanor and Tom arguing every time they saw each other had on Max. As time went on, the arguments between them got worse. They could be quite heated, and I felt it wasn't good for Max to witness them being so awful to each other. After the huge argument at Edward's- that's Tom's dad's funeral, I took over picking Max up from Eleanor and dropping him back to her. That way she and Tom didn't have any contact. She hardly acknowledged my existence, which I considered healthier for Max than being party to his mummy and daddy screaming at each other.

"But I think it was Eleanor's pettiness that got to me most. She would always send Max in really awful, old, tatty clothes and anything new I returned him in would never be seen by us again. Same with toys. This happened to friends of mine who were stepparents and so I followed their advice and kept a whole wardrobe for him at our house. I'd change his clothes as soon as he arrived and put the outfit that he'd arrived in to one side, so it was ready to return him home in. And I always sent him back in the car with a book or a cheap toy to play with for the same reason. This really did annoy Eleanor, who would make snide comments about us being cheapskates, but it was water off a duck's back to us. Tom and I preferred to spend quality time with Max rather than shower him with expensive toys, which was Eleanor's preferred parenting style. She once boasted to me that when she and Max received a home visit from his teacher before he started school, the teacher commented that he had more toys at home than they did in the classroom. I'm not sure the teacher meant it as a compliment!

"Max really enjoyed spending time with us. We would plan special days out, but he was happy enough just walking in the woods. I'm certain Eleanor never really spent any quality time with him. She enrolled him in every class going and I'm sure this was to avoid having to amuse him herself. Although, she was also super competitive about him, so that might have been a reason behind it. She was convinced that he was the best at everything he did. I mean, there was no denying he was clever, but not a child prodigy as Eleanor would have you believe. You could guarantee she would tell you that the instructor of every class he ever joined was convinced that Max was the best pupil they had ever had. I remember Eleanor telling me once that Max's karate moves were so incredible that to see them would make me weep! I mean, really, who talks like that?

"But I was never concerned about how Eleanor treated Max. No, not at all. I'm not saying she didn't love him in her own way. Eleanor struggled with emotions, and her constant bigging up of Max was her way of showing him she loved him. She could be very hard on him. I do think he was a little scared of upsetting her because she was strict, and she could be scathing, but I'm certain she was never physical with him. I mean we never saw any bruises or anything at all like that. I think Tom and I would have been aware from his demeanour if something bad was happening at home, don't you think? He was a quiet child and shy with people he didn't know but that's not unusual, is it? The most I could say is that he wet the bed for longer than I would have considered normal, which could have been for any number of reasons. Maybe it was due to his parents splitting up or the relationship between them after the divorce. Personally, I think it was probably just one of those things.

"Eleanor tried to cause difficulties with our wedding, just as I knew she would. But I was wise to her by then. I told Tom of my concerns, but he said I was being silly, so I proved to him that I was right. I got in touch with Eleanor and gave her a bogus date for our big day, saying obviously we would need to have Max that weekend. She told me that Max wasn't available that weekend, some tennis tournament or something. Tom was convinced it was just a coincidence, but I knew better. I gave her another date. 'No problem,' she told me. Then just two days beforehand, she rang to say Max was ill! Now Tom had to believe me. We let Eleanor assume that we had gone ahead with the wedding but in fact it was planned for the next time we were due to have Max. I'd already had him fitted for his suit and he was our ring bearer. Eleanor was fuming when Max went home full of what a wonderful time he'd had when Dad and Izzie - that's what he called me - got married. She couldn't have a go because we had done nothing wrong, but she did spitefully make it very difficult for us to see Max for the next few months. It probably didn't help that I gave Max a slice of wedding cake to give to his mum when he got home!

6

Amy spent a sleepless night after the meeting with Tom. So many different things ran through her mind and try as she might, she could not switch off from them. She mulled over the correlation she had sensed between Max's conception and Zac's. She could vividly recall the look on Eliza's face, when Adam questioned how their father had managed to get her pregnant having previously had the 'snip'. Her father had immediately become extremely defensive; straight away telling them he had proof that his vasectomy had failed. It obviously bothered him. So much so that the next day, at Amy's house, without Eliza present, he had waved a piece of paper at them – proof from a private clinic regarding his failed vasectomy, but try as she might, Amy could not remember actually looking at the paper in his hand. It had been a very strained conversation. Her father, in no mood to deal with the distress he had caused his offspring, had left almost immediately.

Also, something was bothering Amy about Tom being led to believe that Ricky was Edith's cousin. Amy was determined to call her Edith from now on, even if she was only thinking about the woman and not actually having a spoken conversation regarding her. She knew for definite that Ricky was not related to Edith, and so for some reason, Tom had been deceived, but for the life of her, she couldn't fathom out why.

Something also niggled about the photos she had seen of Max, but she couldn't quite put her finger on it. Then there were the similarities between Betty's and Violet's deaths; was the way in which they both died just coincidence?

Having spent most of the night tossing and turning, nagged by doubt, Amy knew she would have to do something. She decided that to start with she would tackle the predicament regarding Zac. Her first course of action in the morning would be to try to track down this notification her father had received from the clinic, to discover what it actually said. She also needed to speak to Kath and ask her advice. Having formed a plan, she finally fell asleep.

~~~~~~

All of Keith's paperwork had been sent to his solicitor after his death to enable probate. On its completion, this paperwork had been returned to Amy as next of kin, because by then Eliza had long since disappeared off the radar. Amy had been dismayed when it arrived. When she agreed to accept it, she assumed it would consist of a couple of files of bills and bank statements, but instead several medium-sized cardboard boxes were deposited in her kitchen by the courier. Every bit of paper that her father had ever handled seemed to be inside those boxes. A quick look through had revealed everything from golf fixtures to party invites, scripts to car insurance documents. Unable to face sorting through it all at that moment, but unwilling to throw any of it away without checking it first, Amy had asked Marcus to store it up in the loft.

Certain that the notorious letter from the clinic would be dwelling inside one of those boxes, Sunday morning found Amy sitting on the attic floor sorting each box one by one. She pulled out handfuls of paper at a time and, having leafed through them, discarded them into piles on top of the beams until the box was empty. Then she shoved the piles back into their original box before pulling the next one in line forwards. She tried very hard not to get distracted but every now and then something would catch her attention, like a drawing to her dad from one of the kids, or a birthday card he had kept that her mum had sent him. She was surprised Eliza allowed him to keep these mementos but perhaps she was unaware of their existence.

Inevitably, it was inside the last box that Amy finally unearthed what she was looking for. Tidying up the mess she had made as best she could, she took the letter downstairs and into the study. Sitting at the desk, she picked up the landline and rang Kath. It was cathartic talking through with her mum's friend all that Tom had told them. Kath listened without interruption.

"Fucking hell," said Kath when she was totally up to speed. "That's a lot to take in. That poor man. Sounds like Eliza treated him as badly as she treated your father. Obviously not quite so badly as she didn't kill him!"
~~~~~~

"There's the possibility she attempted to. Or at least that she tried to have him killed."

"Oh, you mean the car and the Ricky look-alike? Well, we certainly wouldn't put it past her, would we?"

Amy now felt the time was right to express the doubts she was having over whether Zac was actually her half-brother.

"I found the letter from the clinic this morning. I've got it in front of me," she told Kath. "I've checked the clinic out whilst I've been on the phone to you. It really exists and they're still in business. It's the same name and the address as on the letterhead. The thing is, I don't think this letter is genuine."

"Why not?" asked Kath.

"Well, for starters the logo on the letterhead is different to the logo on the website."

"I don't think that proves it's a forgery," said Kath a little sarcastically. "Logos are updated all the time."

"True," said Amy, "but that's not all. From the look of their website, they're a swanky outfit. It's a private clinic; no NHS, paying customers only. So, you would think they would address the issue in a more professional way rather than saying: We regret to inform you that you are not firing blanks but rather live bullets."

Kath laughed, "Possibly, maybe they felt they knew your father well enough to dispense with formalities," she said. "You know what your dad was like, always call me Keith, never Mr Kelly."

"So, in that case why did they use the term spermatozoa instead of sperm and how come they've spelt it wrong?"

"How do you know they've spelt it wrong?" Kath was intrigued.

"I've been helping Olivia with her biology homework," said Amy, "plus I am a teacher, remember?" Amy sounded slightly offended.

"Fair enough," said Kath. "But I'm still not sure that's enough to say it's not genuine."

"Well maybe the name of the consultant will convince you," said Amy. "A fertility specialist called Mr Bates!" She held the phone away from her ear as Kath shrieked with laughter.

"I thought I'd give them a ring tomorrow morning to see if they can shed some light. If nothing else, I can find out if Mr Bates is a real doctor. Oh, one other thing. I think I need to tell Peggy about Max. I think she should know that if Betty had lived, she would have been a grandmother long before Zac arrived. What do you think?"

"I think you're right," said Kath. "When Max is found, it's bound to hit the news and I think Peggy should be told about him, so it doesn't come as a shock."

~~~~~~

On Monday morning, Amy hurried through the necessary chores, tidying up after the kids, gathering up dirty clothes and putting a wash on, washing up the breakfast pots; never enough to fill the dishwasher but too much to leave until later. Then she made herself a well-earned cup of tea and picked up her phone to make a call.

"Hi Peggy, it's Amy. How are you?"

"Oh, hello Amy. How lovely to hear from you. I'm very well thank you, how are you? How's the family?"

Amy quickly updated Peggy on how Marcus and the children were faring. In response, Peggy told her all about Sharon and the café. When Peggy paused for breath, Amy tried to intervene but before she was able to get a word in, Peggy began listing the latest achievements of her grandchildren. Trying to remain patient and adding the appropriate oohs and aahs, Amy eventually managed to bring the conversation around to the reason for her call.

"I have some news for you regarding Betty," she told the old lady.

"What's that then love?"

Amy thought it best to dive straight in. Peggy's hearing wasn't that great, and she had a habit of interrupting. Amy didn't want her to misunderstand what she was being told.

"Do you remember telling me how much Betty would have loved being a grandmother?" Amy asked.

"Oh, she really would have, she would have spoilt that… Zac, was it? She would have spoilt him rotten you know. That's if Edith would
~~~~~~

have let her have anything to do with him. You know how horrible Edith could be to Betty and-"

"We've just found out that Edith had another boy, Peggy. Betty would have been a grandma twice over." Amy felt she had no choice but to interrupt as once Peggy got into her stride bad mouthing Edith, there would be no stopping her. "She had a child with her first husband. A son called Max. He was born in 1991."

"Well, goodness me!" exclaimed Peggy. "I never thought that one would be interested in having any children, let alone two. How old is- did you say Max? How old is Max now then? Where's he live? What's he doing?"

Having sought the advice of Kath before making the call, Amy kept her answers as simple as possible. She told Peggy how they had found out about Max from Tom, then how Tom had discovered he wasn't Max's father, and she finished by explaining how he had come to lose contact with the child. Thankfully, Peggy easily got the gist of what had happened.

"So, Edith conned him into thinking the boy was his, did she? Sounds like something she'd do. And no one's been able to find this Max then?"

"No," said Amy, "unfortunately nobody has come forward with any information about him, but we are still hopeful we will track him down."

"I'm positive you will," said Peggy. "Poor Betty, she'd have made such a lovely grandmother," she added sorrowfully. "She'd have worshipped both those boys."

"I'm sure," said Amy. She always felt a little uncomfortable discussing Zac with Peggy so she decided to bring the call to an end before Peggy could ask after him.

"Well, I really must go. I'm sorry if this news has upset you. I just thought you should know."

"Thanks, darling. Yeah, I am a little upset. It's sad that Betty never got to meet either of her grandchildren. Perhaps when you find Max, I could meet with him and tell him all about her."

"That's a really nice idea," said Amy.

"Well, thanks for ringing, Pet. I'll make myself a cup of tea and then go and tell Betty all about her grandson called Max. What a surprise."

"Oh, just before you go, Peggy, I've got a quick question."

"What's that love?"

"I know you told us that Betty never wore make up, but did she ever dye her hair?"

"Oh no darling, she would never have done that."

"And her hair definitely wasn't ginger, and neither was Edith's?"

"No love, both of them had what I would call mousy brown hair. Well Betty did until after her dad died. Then it went pure white, but she never dyed it, not even then. Why do you ask?"

Amy remembered now that Peggy had told them that the shock of the fire which killed her father had turned Betty's hair white overnight.

"No real reason just wondering," she said. "I don't suppose either of Betty's parents had ginger-coloured hair?"

"Well yes, actually, now that you mention it, Betty's dad was ginger. It was a real deep copper colour."

"Oh gosh, really. Okay well thanks very much, take care now and I'll be in touch again soon."

Hanging up, Amy smiled at the thought of the little old lady, with a cup of tea perched on her lap, talking to the cherished urn that stood safely in the cabinet alongside the best China.

The next call Amy made was to the clinic.

~~~~~~

Speaking to Kath on the phone later that morning Amy vented her frustration.

"I mean I understand about patient confidentiality and all that, really I do, but I don't know how many times I had to explain that Dad was dead before the blonde bimbo got the message."

"Now, now," said Kath, "you don't know she was blonde."
~~~~~~

"Yes, I do," said Amy. "Her photo is on the website. 'Our efficient receptionist Stacey is on hand to deal with any queries you may have,' Amy quoted. Efficient my arse, she just wanted rid of me. Apparently, I will need to send a death certificate and several hundred proofs of my identity, including blood from my first born."

"I don't know what's giving it away, but I can tell you're a little upset," said Kath.

"I just want them to resend me the letter they sent Dad, that's all. I want to know if it's the same as the copy I have. It seems so stupid to have to jump through all these hoops for one piece of paper."

"Patient confidentiality is there for a reason," said Kath calmly, "and it's a very good one. Why don't you ring Mason? Tell him what's happened and why you want it and I bet he'll sort it out for you. It's totally different if the police request information."

"Don't you think he'll be a bit too busy to help me?" asked Amy. "It doesn't seem that important."

"Of course, it's important," said Kath. "Not only for your peace of mind, but also for the case they're building against Eliza. And while you're at it you could ask him about getting Zac's DNA tested. They must have both Zac's and your dad's DNA on file because of… well you know, after what happened. I'd be surprised if they haven't already tested, which makes me think you've got nothing to worry about because if your dad wasn't Zac's dad, then they would have told you. One quick call to Mason could clear the whole matter up for you."

"Yeah, I suppose you're right," sighed Amy.

"Of course, I'm right. I'm always right," replied Kath.

~~~~~~

Amy was thrown to hear a curt "Mason". She hadn't expected the DI to answer his own phone, even though next to the number on the card he had given her it said it was his direct line.

"Hello?" he sounded impatient.
~~~~~~

"Hello there," although she had been told several times to call him Mike, Amy couldn't bring herself to do it. "It's Amy, Amy McDonald."

"Oh, hi Amy, what can I do for you?"

The Evil Underneath

Extract from the book The Evil Underneath
– written by Matt Dinsdale

Although, to my knowledge, Edith has never undergone a psychiatric assessment, after speaking with both psychiatrists and psychologists, personally I am of the opinion that she is a psychopathic narcissist. Her character and behaviours fit with the traits of someone with a personality disorder of that nature. For example:

- She has a grandiose sense of self-importance
- She needs constant praise and attention
- She has a sense of entitlement
- She exploits others without guilt or shame
- She frequently demeans, intimidates, bullies or belittles others
- She has troubled relationships
- She has a complete lack of empathy

However, you could also say she is a Narcissistic Sociopath as this term is used to describe someone who manipulates and harms others for their own personal gain. Whether her personality traits are down to nature or nurture, we will never know, but I can confidently define Edith as a truly iniquitous person. Someone wicked, nefarious and immoral.

For the purpose of writing this book, I have interviewed numerous people from all the different aspects of Edith's life, starting with her early years and continuing up until her disappearance. Obtaining an unbiased opinion of her was always going to be difficult because the subjects of my interviews were familiar with her implication in the murder of Keith Kelly. I did my best to counter this negative bias by asking people to describe their first meeting with Edith and what their initial impression of her was.

From these interviews, the overwhelming impression gained is that nobody liked her. Even if at that initial introduction the dislike was not instantaneous or the interaction too short to form an opinion, it was never very long until Edith said or did something to offend. In an attempt to add some form of balance to people's assessment of Edith's personality, I asked each individual to tell me something positive about her, something good about her character. Not one person was able to give me an immediate answer. Most gave it a lot of thought, some asking if they could come back to me at a later date, but nothing positive ever came to light. It was also extremely rare that someone described a positive experience they had shared with Edith and if they did, it had happened at the beginning of their relationship. A small minority referred to the Edith they encountered as evil, but no one suggested they had prior knowledge of what she could be capable of. The majority of those who took an instant dislike to Edith were women. Men seemed to find her charming on introduction and only subsequently discovered her more negative traits.

When necessary, she appears to be able to show herself in a positive light, otherwise, she could never have married not just once but twice. Maintaining a facade in close relationships is extremely difficult but it is something she managed for a short time in her first marriage and, as far as I can tell, for a much longer period in her second marriage. I came to the conclusion that she found it far easier to manipulate her second husband than she did her first, but this is only conjecture on my part.

Edith also managed to sustain one relationship from her childhood, with Ricky Kerr. Not having had the opportunity to interview him and with very few people having intimate knowledge of him, it is impossible to judge either his character or how the relationship between them worked.

7

Trevor had attended several enjoyable Sunday lunches with the McDonald family, where Marcus had cooked and cleared away, whilst he and Amy collated their notes and finalised research ready to pass on to Matt. This Sunday, however, was slightly different because Matt was joining them. Matt's wife, Jasmine, had taken the girls to visit her parents for the weekend and, on hearing that he would be alone, Amy invited him to come and join them for lunch.

Arriving at the same time as Trevor, Matt was amused at how comfortable the self-proclaimed loner was inside the McDonald's home. He watched in surprise as his normally introverted friend kissed Amy on both cheeks when she opened the door to them and was then warmly greeted by Marcus to whom he handed over a bottle of fine wine. Rory came bounding down the stairs eager to discuss the latest signing made by their shared favourite football team, whilst Olivia begged Trevor for help with her history homework. Even the dogs joined in the enthusiastic welcome, once they had run around the kitchen a few times with JR. Matt might have been tempted to make a wisecrack had he not seen the look of pure joy on Trevor's face. Instead, he held back, quite moved by the scene playing out in front of him.

Amy informed them both she had some news to share with them but not until after they'd eaten. Her excitement was palpable. Trevor had a good idea of what it was regarding but he kept schtum so as not to spoil her enjoyment. It was quite some time later before they were actually able to settle into the study and begin work. After lunch, Trevor, as promised, helped Olivia with her homework whilst the others took the dogs for a walk. Matt offered to clear the kitchen, but Marcus insisted he was quite happy to do it so the three of them could get on.

Matt and Trevor were looking at something on the computer when Amy pushed the door open with her foot and carried in tray of coffee. The men were treated to the sound of Marcus singing "I'm Every

Woman" at the top of his voice. Setting the tray down, Amy gave an apologetic shrug as she closed the door on the noise.

"Eclectic taste in music, my hubby," she grinned. "Sounds like it's going to be a disco afternoon."

~~~~~~

The first order of business was to go through the itinerary for Trevor and Amy's visit to Dolford the following Wednesday. Matt, once again busy elsewhere, was designating the two of them to interview Antonia Adebayo, who had worked at the Solicitor's Mitchell, Ruddick and Jones at the same time as Edith, and Reg Hargreaves who had lived next door to Edith and Max.

Matt had been given Antonia's contact details by DI Mason, but they had been put in touch with Reg after Trevor previously paid the area a visit. He put up notices in some of the shops and the local library asking anyone who had been living in Abbey Road between 1995 and 1997 to contact them. It was a long shot as the road was small and the houses popular with first-time buyers, so people frequently moved in and out. As luck would have it, Trevor was contacted by Stephen Hargreaves whose father, Reg, had actually lived at number 32, right next door to Edith during those two years. Although now living in a residential home, Stephen assured Trevor that Reg's memory was sound, and he had a good recollection of 'the stuck-up cow and the wee young bairn.'

"So, what's this news then?" Matt asked Amy when they had finalised the questions to be asked during the interviews.

"Do you remember after we visited Tom Bryant, and I felt there were similarities between Max's conception and Zac's?" asked Amy.

"Not really," admitted Matt.

"Well, no I'm not sure I voiced it at the time," said Amy. "But when Tom was telling us about finding out Max wasn't his, it just made me think of when Adam and I found out Edith was pregnant. Dad had a vasectomy you see, after Adam was born, years before he met Edith. Did I tell you that?" She didn't stop to wait for a reply. "So, as you can
~~~~~~

imagine, finding out he was going to be a father again came as quite a surprise."

"It would," agreed Matt.

"Adam and I were worried that Dad was being played for a fool and we told him of our concerns. But he had already had himself checked. He'd had the same thoughts himself, that the baby couldn't be his. So, he'd gone to a clinic and had a test done. Turns out his vasectomy had failed. He had the results to prove it."

"I remember you telling me about that," said Matt. "So, what's the news?"

"Patience," said Trevor. "Let her tell it her way."

"Thanks, Trevor," said Amy gratefully. "Well after we'd been to see Tom, I got this nagging feeling, so I went searching through Dad's paperwork and I found the letter; the one from the clinic regarding Dad's test results. This time when I looked at it a few things didn't add up and I suspected it might be fake. I'm not certain that I actually looked at it when Dad first showed it to us and if Adam did, I don't expect he studied it. We were all a bit emotionally charged at the time, to say the least. So, I didn't pick up on anything back then but now looking at it closely it felt wrong."

"What?" said Matt. "Really?"

"Yes, I checked on the internet and the clinic still exists. The letterhead's similar but not exactly the same, although as Kath said, that doesn't prove anything. But it was the language that was used that seemed wrong, the terminology and there was a spelling mistake and… well," Amy paused unsure whether to continue. "Well…?" said Matt.

"Well, the name of the specialist was Mr Bates," Amy blurted out. She waited. She couldn't look at Trevor as he gave an amused snort. Still she waited. It took Matt a while.

"Oh, I get it," he said.

"Finally," teased Amy. "Anyway, I tried phoning the clinic, but they wouldn't give me any information, so Kath suggested I ask DI Mason to help. Which I did. At the same time, I also asked him if it would be possible to check Dad and Zac's DNA, if it hadn't already been done; just to make sure. Just for peace of mind."

"Oh Amy, I had no idea," said Matt. "And I take it you've got the results?"

"Yep," Amy confirmed. "Here's the letter from the clinic that was in with my dad's paperwork," she said, placing a piece of paper in front of Matt. "And here's the original that the clinic held on file. The one Mike obtained for me," she said, placing a second sheet next to the first with a dramatic flourish.

Trevor thought this was the first time he had heard Amy refer to Mason as Mike and he saw it as a good sign that she was feeling less intimidated by the detective.

"Oh, wow," said Matt. "Share," demanded Trevor.

"They're completely different. The original letter, the one held by the clinic, actually says that the vasectomy was a success, and it tells Keith he is 100% infertile."

"Goodness," said Trevor and so as not to give away that this information was not new to him, "And the DNA test?"

"Well," said Amy. "It's that that's taken the time. It turns out it was never done originally because no one saw any need. However, I can now confirm," she paused for effect, "that," she continued then paused again, "I am in no way related to Zac; he is not my father's son."

"Really?" Matt was astounded.

"Really," said Amy "And that's not all," she hurried on, "I actually know who Zac's real- I mean biological father is."

This was news to Trevor. "So, who is it?" he asked intrigued.

"Ricky Kerr," replied Amy. "They ran Zac's DNA through their database, and it matched with Ricky's."

Amy enjoyed the moment as the two men sat in stunned silence.

8

Antonia Adebayo's office was situated above a wedding dress shop in a side road near the top of the high street and accessed via a small side door. After climbing the three flights of steep, narrow stairs to reach her office, both Trevor and Amy were out of breath. Trevor waited a couple of minutes to get his breathing under control, at least enough to enable him to speak, before he knocked on the door.

"Come in," said a voice from inside.

The office space had been created from the eaves of the building and was tiny, just big enough for a desk, a couple of chairs and a rather neglected rubber plant, standing forlornly in a large green pot in the corner. The roof comprised exposed beams which sloped down to a small window, underneath which were untidy piles of files and folders. Extra light came from a skylight. On one of the walls sat two shelves. The top one was filled with precariously stacked books and the bottom held an assortment of mugs and jars. A kettle rested on a tray on the floor and plugged into an extension lead that, to Amy, seemed a little too overloaded with plugs to be considered safe.

Behind the desk sat a very attractive black woman whom Amy estimated to be in her mid-40s, who was currently on the phone. Putting her hand over the receiver Antonia apologised,

"This won't take long," she said. "Help yourself to tea or coffee," pointing to the kettle on the floor underneath the shelf of mugs. Trevor and Amy exchanged looks and Amy politely declined.

"I'm sorry, Mr Thompson," Antonia spoke into the phone, "miracles I can achieve but the impossible takes a little longer," she gave a girly giggle. "I'll see what I can do. Hopefully, it'll be ready by the end of the week."

Hanging up, she once more apologised whilst leaning across the desk to shake their hands. Amy could fully understand why the smartly dressed woman didn't come out from behind the desk to greet them; she wasn't sure there would be enough room for all three of them to stand in the limited space. Antonia indicated for them to take a seat which Trevor gratefully accepted, not only because his legs were aching after the climb, but also because since he entered the room, he had been unable to stand up straight for fear of banging his head on a beam.

For an awkward moment, no one said anything, until Amy attempting to break the ice, pointed to a gilt photo frame sitting pride of place on the desk, which contained a single photograph of a young adolescent male, grinning in cap and gown clutching a diploma.

"Your son?" asked Amy.

"Yes, that's Anthony," replied Antonia with pride. "He's a surgeon. He works at the Bristol Royal Infirmary. He's married now with children. They're my life." Divulging some personal information seemed to remind Antonia that these visitors were not clients.

"So, how can I help you?" she asked. "I've already spoken with the police but the gentleman on the phone, Matt, was it? Told me you're writing a book? I'm not sure how I can help you, and to be perfectly honest, I'm not a hundred percent comfortable with my name being associated with that woman. Not after what's she's done."

To avoid unnecessary confusion, Trevor and Amy had agreed beforehand that today they would refer to Edith as Eleanor, the name she had been using at the time that Ms Adebayo was acquainted with her.

"That's perfectly reasonable," said Trevor. "What we are really after is background information on Eleanor. We don't have to use your name at all if you don't want us to," he continued. "If there's something you tell us that we would like to quote in the book, we'll just refer to you as one of her colleagues. Would that be okay?"

"I suppose so," Antonia still sounded unsure. "It was quite a substantial firm. Hopefully, the workforce was big enough for me to remain anonymous."

"There's no need to worry," said Amy. "We will protect your identity, I promise."

"I'm sure I'm overthinking this," said Antonia. "It's unlikely that Eleanor remembers me, let alone my name. I doubt very much she knew it back then. I don't imagine she'll come seeking revenge for my talking to you about the time I worked with her. It's well over twenty years ago. I'm sorry, I'm being paranoid. It's just not in every job that your boss turns out to be a murderer. It leaves you a little discombobulated."

"Was she your boss?" asked Amy.

"Well, no not as such, although she was higher up than me obviously, I was only a junior at the time. I worked in the accounts department and had a supervisor. The Accounts Manager was in charge of the department, and he was my ultimate boss. Eleanor obviously had her own office, but she shared secretaries with the other solicitors. Her bosses would have been the three partners the firm was named for."

"Mitchell, Ruddick & Jones is that correct?" asked Amy.

"We always referred to it as MRJ," said Antonia, smiling as Amy stumbled over the name. "Otherwise, it was a bit of a mouthful."

"So, you didn't know Eleanor well then?" asked Amy returning the smile.

"Hardly," Antonia responded with a smirk. "Being in accounts meant I didn't really have anything to do with her. Eleanor was not the sort of person to acknowledge the existence of junior members of staff anyway unless it was to berate them. I know the secretaries and the receptionists had a terrible time with her. She treated them like they were her personal assistants, always sending them on errands like fetching her dry-cleaning or picking her up a sandwich. My friend Hannah, one of the receptionists, complained to Miss Ruddick about it because Eleanor was forever tasking her with something when Hannah should have been enjoying her lunch break.

Unfortunately, Hannah picked the wrong person to complain to. Miss Ruddick had a massive crush on Eleanor and so she didn't really do anything about it. She must have had a word with Eleanor though because she treated Hannah even worse afterwards."

"I don't suppose you're still in touch with Hannah?" asked Trevor.

"No, sorry. She got married and moved away," said Antonia.

"You said Miss Ruddick had a crush on Eleanor; was there anything going on between them?" asked Amy. "Were they having an affair?"

Antonia paused for a moment, thinking before she replied. "I really don't think so. I couldn't say for definite, but it didn't seem to have gone that far. Eleanor was definitely into men, that much was obvious, although she could have been bi of course. She certainly enjoyed the attention she got from Miss Ruddick. I think it's more likely that she strung the poor woman along. Miss Ruddick was old-fashioned, naïve, a bit immature, if you know what I mean. She always dressed in tweed skirts and twin sets. She talked as if she was still at boarding school. It was all 'jolly good' and 'bravo' and 'here, here.' It was clear that she fancied Eleanor. She would colour up as soon as Eleanor walked in a room. She would hang around the kitchen at lunchtime in order to invite Eleanor to eat her lunch with her in her office. You'd hear them giggling like a couple of schoolgirls. She died at work you know, Miss Ruddick, in her office. Eleanor was with her when she died."

Both Amy and Trevor sat up, keen to be enlightened especially as the details provided by Mason proved disappointingly scant.

"How did she die?" asked Amy.

"An allergic reaction," said Antonia. "She had a severe allergy to nuts. She made sure we all knew about it and knew where she kept her…" Antonia couldn't think of the word.

"EpiPen?" supplied Amy.

"That's it, EpiPen. She kept one in the first aid box and always had one in her bag."

"So, what happened when she died?" asked Amy.

"Well, I'm not sure exactly. I didn't see anything. First, we knew something was wrong was when we heard the shouting. The supervisor told us to stay where we were, and she went to see what was going on. Next thing we knew, an ambulance arrived. I watched them carry the body out on a stretcher. We knew she was dead because they'd covered her face with a blanket. We all got sent home early."

"Do you know any of the details?" asked Amy, trying not to sound impatient. "You said Eleanor was with her?"

"Well, I only know what Dave told me afterwards. He was one of the trainee solicitors. He heard Eleanor shouting for help from inside Miss Ruddick's office, so he ran in to see what the problem was, and Miss Ruddick was collapsed on the floor. Eleanor yelled at him to get the EpiPen from the kitchen, the one from the first aid box. Eleanor had used the one from Miss Ruddick's bag, but it apparently hadn't worked. Dave rushed to get it and said he saw Miss Ruddick's face when he handed the pen over, and it was all swollen and puffy. He said he thought she was already dead, but Eleanor used the pen thing on her and then one of the partners, I can't remember which one, started doing CPR. According to Dave, Eleanor was in shock. I know she took compassionate leave. She never came back. So, we never got to the bottom of the missing money."

"That sounds awful," said Amy. "What a terrible thing to happen."

"It was," agreed Antonia. "We were all upset by it. I didn't go to the funeral. None of us juniors were invited but I did contribute to the flowers the firm sent."

"Do you know the official cause of death?" asked Trevor, thinking it didn't really matter if she did or not because he'd get a copy of death certificate. There might be a coroner's report, or an inquest might have been held seeing as how the poor woman died at work.

"Well, it was anaphylactic shock, but I don't think they discovered what had triggered the attack," replied Antonia.

"Before we go into the details of the missing money, I don't suppose you have contact details for Dave, do you?" asked Amy, thinking how interesting it would be to hear from someone who had witnessed the event firsthand.

"Sorry," said Antonia. "I can't even remember his surname."

"Not to worry," said Trevor. He was hopeful he would be able to track both Dave and Hannah down if he could obtain a list of the firm's employees from that time.

"So, what about this missing money?" asked Amy.

"Well, it was the only time I had anything to do with Eleanor really. I discovered a discrepancy with one of Eleanor's accounts and I alerted my supervisor who took it up with Miss Ruddick. Personally, I'd have gone to someone else knowing how Miss Ruddick felt about Eleanor, but it wasn't up to me. I got called up to Miss Ruddick's office, because my supervisor had forgotten to take the statement, and Miss Ruddick asked me to go over what had happened."

When Antonia didn't continue Amy asked, "And what had happened exactly?"

"Sorry, I was just thinking back. Trying to remember it right. First off, I got a call from a local charity, something to do with cats I think, anyway they were calling regarding a rather large bequest left to them by one of their volunteers. This woman had died a few months back, but they still hadn't received notification of when the money would be transferred to them. Their benefactor had led them to believe they would be receiving £25,000. That was a lot of money back then."

"It's a lot of money now!" exclaimed Amy.

"Well, exactly and the representative from the charity was basically calling to chase it up. I looked up the client's file and discovered it was one of Eleanor's clients. The money had been set aside according to the paperwork, but I couldn't trace it. It hadn't been paid to the charity, but it wasn't in the bank either. That's when I alerted my supervisor as I didn't think, with the amount of money that was missing, I should ignore it like we normally did when there were inconsistencies with Eleanor's accounts."

"Were there a lot of inconsistencies?" asked Amy. Which was just what Trevor had been about to ask.

"More than there should have been," answered Antonia, "but Eleanor always seemed to have an excuse as to why the money was missing. It had only ever small amounts up till then which usually turned up after a few days. I think we all knew what she was doing. I certainly did. But because Miss Whelan - she was my supervisor - turned a blind eye, I didn't think it was my place to say anything."

"So, what did you think she was doing?" asked Amy.

"She was borrowing the money and then paying it back at a later date. Like I said, it had only been small amounts before. She wasn't supposed to do it obviously, it's illegal, but I think Miss Whelan took the attitude it wasn't harming anyone. But this was vastly different. It wasn't just a few hundred pounds, it was £25,000. So, like I was saying,

I flagged it up to Miss Whelan and rather than confront Eleanor - I think she was as scared of her as we were - she spoke to Miss Ruddick. And then I was called up to the office. I showed Miss Ruddick proof that the money had left the client's account but had not been paid to the designated charity. She asked me to check again to make sure that it hadn't just been sent somewhere else by mistake, but I was confident that the money was missing. She told me to leave it with her and that's what I did, and then the next day was the day she took ill and died, and I didn't even think about the missing money until a few days later."

"And what happened about it?" asked Amy.

"Well, it was never traced. I know that much because in the end Mr Mitchell and Mr Jones authorised the payment to be made to the charity from the company's own account. After we realised that Eleanor was never coming back, we went through all her clients' files and discovered a number that were missing money. Just a few hundred pounds here and there but it all added up. The company covered all the discrepancies."

"What, they didn't go to the police?" asked Trevor incredulously.

"No, they paid it all back themselves. I can't be sure, but I assume it's because of the firm's reputation. If they had gone to the police, and it had been made public that a solicitor from the firm had been stealing clients' money, the company's reputation would have suffered. This is a small town. They couldn't afford to lose clients."

9

It was a relief to leave the cramped office of Antonia Adebayo. Amy made Trevor go in front of her as they descended the narrow, steep steps so that if she stumbled, he would save her fall.

Once outside, Trevor steered Amy in the direction of The Kings Arms pub, where he had enjoyed a relatively decent lunch during his last visit to the town. They managed to secure a table in the corner of what was a surprisingly busy dining area for Wednesday lunch time. After choosing what to eat from the limited menu, Trevor went up to the bar to place their order. As he returned to the table with their drinks, his phone started ringing and after checking the caller ID, he dumped the call.

"It's only Mike," he said in answer to Amy's unspoken question. "He'll be wanting to arrange a night out at the pub. I'll call him back later."

"Oh, there's-" Amy, seemingly about to say something regarding Mike, changed her mind and said instead, "That was a very interesting talk we just had with Antonia, wasn't it? Very enlightening."

"I thought so too," agreed Trevor. "There are certainly a few things to look into. In fact, I've a couple of questions for Mike when I call him back. He might know something more of that Sue Ruddick's death. You know how I feel about coincidences; and Edith being alone in the office with the woman just before she died feels like a heck of a coincidence."

"I agree," said Amy. "I feel exactly the same."

Trevor, suddenly serious said, "I've been meaning to ask you all day. How do you feel about finding out that Zac's not your brother?"

"Half-brother," replied Amy automatically before it dawned on her that she would never have to stress that point again. "To be honest, I feel relieved. Pure relief. I hadn't realised up until Mike gave me the news just how guilty I'd been feeling. Although I didn't have a relationship with him as such, I still felt terrible guilt about him being left all alone in that unit. I couldn't face visiting him though. I know he didn't actually kill Dad, but he was involved. He did stab Dad and for some reason, I just couldn't get past that, still can't. But that didn't stop me feeling like a terrible person for not seeing him, especially as his Mum abandoned him. I mean, at the end of the day he has no one and he's still just a little boy.

"Even if they tell him the truth about Ricky, it doesn't change the fact that he's all alone. Both his biological dad and the man he called dad are dead. It's a horrible situation. Terrible. Knowing I have no responsibility towards him whatsoever has lifted a huge weight from me. I'm sorry if that makes me a bad person."

"It doesn't make you a bad person at all," Trevor reassured her. "All of those feelings are entirely natural." Then to lighten the atmosphere, he added, "And look at you; you're turning into a proper investigator. And I never would have guessed in a million years that Ricky and Edith ever slept together. Did that shock you?"

"Completely," said Amy. "I was stunned when Mike told me that Zac and Ricky's DNA were a match. I know I didn't know Ricky well, but he seems like the last person you'd expect Edith to have a sexual relationship with."

"Nowt as queer as folk," said Trevor.

Their food arrived and Amy distributed the cutlery and sauces between them. She picked up her knife and fork but before she began to eat, she said,

"That wasn't the only strange thing Mike revealed. I've wanted to talk to you about, well about another coincidence in a way. I'm sure it's just me reading too much into something but it's been niggling away at me ever since Matt and I visited Tom. It stood out to me in the same way that the similarities between Max and Zac's conception did and look what that's uncovered! I'd tried to put it to the back of my mind but then, with what Mike told me, it's got me thinking again."

Amy paused for a moment.

"I'm not sure how to put it into words. It seems very complicated but in reality, it's simple."

"Just tell me the best you can," encouraged Trevor.

"Well, when Mike rang and told me Ricky was Zac's dad he made the comment: '*I suppose we could have guessed from the colour of Zac's hair.*' I had no idea what he was on about and said as much. I think Mike thought I was trying to be funny in some way. '*You know,*' he said, *because of Zac being a carrot top.*' Now, I'm certain that's not the way to describe a red head but that wasn't my issue. I didn't get what Mike was saying because Zac has black hair. He has never been ginger. I said as much to Mike. That's when he told me that Edith had admitted to dyeing Zac's hair, would you believe?"

"What!" said Trevor. "Why?"

"She told Mike that Zac's school was holding a fund-raising event, and the children were allowed to dress up as a favourite character. Zac had wanted to go as Harry Potter but because of his – to use Mike's terminology "carrot" coloured hair, he thought his friends would tease him saying he looked like Ron Weasley instead."

Amy stopped to check that Trevor understood the references. "It's okay," he assured her, "I'm a huge fan of both the books and the films."

"Of course, you are," said Amy smiling at him. "So, Edith told Mike she dyed Zac's hair black so he would look more like Harry. Mike had to ask Edith about it, I'm assuming, because it showed up in the forensic results that Zac's hair had been dyed."

"I admit it's odd, but it is a plausible explanation," said Trevor. "So why is this such a problem for you?"

"Because," said Amy, drawing a deep breath, "if Zac's natural hair colour is red, then Edith has been dyeing it since he was born! Mike seemed to think Edith dyed it just for that one occasion, but Zac always had black hair. I admit I haven't seen him in person over the last couple of years, but Dad was always showing me photos and Zac's hair was the same colour as I'd always known it, black. Zac's never had red hair. Don't you think that's strange?

"I struggle to believe that Dad agreed to Edith doing something so unnecessary. He wouldn't have cared what colour Zac's hair was. I know Edith was always dyeing her own hair as well as using those coloured contact lenses. She had different coloured eyes every time I saw her. I couldn't tell you what her natural eye colour or her natural hair colour is. But I don't understand why you would dye a child's hair and why you would start doing it at such an early age. I mean seriously, she must have started to dye it when Zac was first born. That's just not right. It's downright weird. I just can't see Dad going along with it. And even if he did, it's such an odd thing to do, I'm certain he would have mentioned it to me.

"The only way it makes sense, as far as I'm concerned, is if Dad didn't have a clue she was dyeing it either. I mean it would have been possible for Edith to hide it from him because he was away so much, but she would have had to bribe Zac to keep quiet."

"I still don't get," Trevor started to say and then, "Oh right, Ricky was a redhead. You think she was trying to hide who Zac's father really was?"

"Exactly," said Amy. "Ricky had proper ginger hair. Unmistakable. And if you see what Zac looks like now, his hair is the identical colour to his biological father's. I checked with Mike, and he showed me a picture of Zac taken only a few weeks ago. Now stay with me, hear me out. Max also had the same hair colour. I've looked into it, and for a child to have red hair they must have, for the sake of simplicity, let's call it red hair DNA from both parents. But that isn't the same as saying both parents have to have red hair. A parent could have a recessive red hair gene; that is they don't have red hair themselves, but they could have hidden red hair DNA. So, they could be a red hair DNA carrier."

"I understand what you're getting at," said Trevor. "You think there's a possibility that Ricky could be Max's father too?"

"Precisely," said Amy. "As I said, Edith was always dyeing her own hair and that got me thinking maybe she was a natural red head. So, the last time I spoke to Peggy, I checked with her that Edith wasn't born with ginger coloured hair. Peggy confirmed that neither Edith nor Betty ever had red hair, but that Edith's grandfather/father did."

Amy gave an involuntary shudder after using that description for the man.

"He was a proper redhead. He too had copper coloured hair just like Ricky. So, that means that Edith carries the red hair gene."

"Maybe Edith's dad was Ricky's dad too," said Trevor only half joking.

Amy shuddered again.

"It's a huge coincidence though, isn't it? Edith had two children by Ricky and manages to convince two different males that they are the father. I know it's highly unlikely, but…"

"It is a leap," admitted Trevor. "But at this moment in time, I wouldn't rule anything out."

10

The second interview of the day was with Reg Hargreaves, who had been Edith's next-door neighbour. He was currently living in a private residential home that turned out to be a converted Victorian town house just on the outskirts of the town centre.

Amy's only previous experience of a care home was the state-run old people's home, that she took her class of primary school children carol singing to every Christmas, with its gloomy interior and a very distinctive smell of urine pervading the building. So, she was pleasantly surprised to find herself standing in the rather grand entrance hall of Abbotsbury Lodge, where all she could detect was a faint aroma of pine disinfectant. The silver-haired lady sitting at the reception desk looked old enough to be one of the residents. Trevor introduced them both and asked where they could find Reg who should be expecting them.

"Oh, our Reg is ever so excited you've come to visit," she told them. "He's waiting for you in the day room." And she gave them directions by pointing to the door opposite them.

The day room was a large sitting room with a high ceiling and a wide bay window. The lone occupant stood in the bay which looked out over the immaculately kept garden.

"You've come at the perfect time," the respectable looking gentleman informed them in a surprisingly strong northern accent, after they had shaken hands. "They've all gone into town because it's market day so hopefully we should have the room to ourselves for a good while."

Still thinking back to her previous experience, Amy was delighted to discover that Reg appeared to be in full possession of his faculties. The residents at her local home had either slept through the whole session or displayed varying degrees of senility. It had been a little intimidating for the children to be approached by these individuals. Having researched the benefits of the older and younger generation interacting with each other, any hopes Amy harboured of establishing regular contact between the two groups, evaporated when she was faced with the reality.

'How different if the local home had been like this one,' she thought, unable to ignore the contrast between the State run and privately run homes.

She turned her attention back to Reg who was busy discussing Newcastle's latest match and their position in the league with Trevor. Visibly eyeing Amy up and down, Reg said,

"I really hope now tha' some of the fellas get back before you have to leave. They're gonna be so envious of me entertaining such a lovely wee lassie as you."

To Amy's annoyance, she felt herself blush.

Trevor took control of this interview as Reg did not seem to be able to take Amy seriously, believing she had accompanied Trevor purely to take the notes. Amy tried hard not to be offended; it was a generational thing after all. Reg had already mentioned several times that he was 95 years old. She was impressed by his mental capacity, his recall and immaculate appearance which helped her forgive his chauvinism.

Max, according to Reg, had been a lovely little boy, well-mannered and extremely well-behaved. Although, they hadn't had that much to do with him, Reg and his wife, Avril, had stepped in on the odd occasion to look after Max when Edith had been let down by her child minder.

Reg clearly remembered collecting Max from his private school and bringing him home to their house to wait until his mother finished work. They would give him fizzy pop and chocolate biscuits as a treat. Reg recalled a time when Avril had given the boy a jam doughnut and some of the jam had squirted down the front of his white school shirt. Max got himself in such a state, terrified of what his mother's reaction would be, that Avril wrapped him in one of Reg's shirts while she washed the stain out of his school shirt, so his mother would be none the wiser.

After some probing by Trevor, Reg admitted that both he and his wife, who had died from a stroke several years previously, 'God bless her', had worried about whether or not Max was being physically abused by Edith. They were certain of the verbal abuse because they could hear it through the walls.

"She always acted like butter would'na melt when she were out of the house," Reg told them. "But behind closed doors she used to screech at him like a fishwife. Some of the names she called the wee bairn."

"Did you not mention it to anyone?" Amy tried hard to keep from sounding judgemental.

"Ah, I know hinny, but it wasn't the done thing back then. You didn't interfere. The boy seemed happy and healthy, and you know sticks and stones and all that. If we'd been certain that she was hitting him, we definitely would have rung the social."

"So, you don't think Eleanor was hitting him?" asked Trevor, seeking clarification.

"Oh, I'm sure she probably gave him the odd tap but he were such a good boy, she'd have no need to do more than that," said Reg, sounding convincing but Amy wasn't convinced.

"There was one time," continued Reg, "only a couple of days before they left, when Avril heard some noises that worried her."

"What sort of noises?" Trevor enquired, not trusting Amy to ask dispassionately.

"Well, it were a Friday night. I remember because I came home from playing darts. I played for the Kings Arms do you know it?"

"We just had lunch there," replied Trevor.

"Aye well it's a bit more upmarket these days. It was more a straw on the floor type of establishment when I frequented it."

Amy really wanted to hurry him along, but she remained silent.

"When I got home, Avril was in a bit of a state because she thought something must have happened next door. She'd heard Eleanor shouting and then a lot of banging. After that, it went quiet. She went and knocked on the door to see if everything was alright like, but she got no answer. She came back home and then next thing she knew, Eleanor was leaving the house, but she didn't have the laddie with her.

So, Avril went back round and knocked again but no one came to the door. She called through the letter box, but Max didn't answer. When she heard Eleanor come home, she went round again although it was getting late by then. Eleanor answered the door and Avril asked if everything were alright because of the banging and such she'd heard earlier. Avril told me Eleanor acted like she didn't have a clue what she was on about, but she apologised saying the television must have been up loud.

"When Avril asked after Max, Eleanor told her he weren't there. He'd been picked up by his dad cos he was going to spend a few days at his house. So, like I say, Avril were in a state when I got back from the pub, because firstly Eleanor had apologised, when normally she would just have told Avril to mind her own beeswax, and secondly because she had seen Max go into the house with Eleanor earlier, but she hadn't seen him leave. She certainly hadn't seen his dad arrive.

"Now, don't get the wrong impression, my Avril wasn't a curtain twitcher like, but she did keep an eye out as to what cars came and went in case anyone was burgled. She was high up in the Neighbourhood Watch was my Avril," Reg told them proudly. "Always going to meetings and the like."

Amy had an image of a little white-haired, bespectacled lady sitting in a rocking chair by a window, clasping binoculars and jotting down number plates.

"So why does that particular night stick in your mind, Reg?" asked Trevor.

"Well, that was the start of all the funny business," replied Reg. "It were only a couple of days after that I caught her next door," he used his thumb to indicate next door, "early in the morning, digging up the bloody garden. So, I asks her what she's doing, and she tells me it's so as she can get some sort of swing thing put there before Max got home from his Da's as a surprise for him. And, sure enough, next thing you know there's a couple of blokes fitting this… well, I don't know what you'd call it. It were like something you'd find in play park. Swings, slides, climbing frame the whole shebang. Then," Reg continued in disbelief. "Then, before we even see the lad using it, they've disappeared. There's a bloke with a white van emptying out the house. I said to him, 'What the ruddy hell do you think you're doing?' And he tells me he's clearing the house out cos she's buggered off abroad. I asks him if the kiddie had gone with her or whether he were with his Da? But the bloke didn't know. Said he was just being paid to clear the house out. He took all the furniture, even the fitted kitchen cupboards. He literally took everything, bar the kitchen ruddy sink! Now that's not usual, is it? He left that monstrosity in the garden though. It were too big to move I'd wager.

"The Jackson's, who were the new people that moved in, were chuffed it were there. They got the house for a bargain price what with it being repossessed by the bank, like. They were a lovely family. Had a couple of kiddies who were always out in the garden playing on that thing so at least it weren't wasted.

"It must have cost a bob or two. Fancy her spending all that money and the kiddie never playing on it, not once. What I don't get is that she must have known she were moving when she got it. Most peculiar."

It was apparent to Trevor that Reg was getting tired, running out of steam.

"Before we leave you in peace, Reg," he said. "Did you ever find out where Eleanor had gone? Did you see Max again? Did Eleanor ever come back to visit the house or the area?"

"That's a lot of questions," said Reg in mock complaint, "but there's a simple answer to all of 'em. No!"

For Trevor, saying goodbye to Reg involved a handshake. For Amy, it comprised two sloppy kisses and a pat on the bum.

~~~~~~

As they closed the gate behind them, Trevor asked,

"Do you mind if we detour past the house where Edith used to live before we start on our way back?"

"I don't mind," said Amy. "But I thought you took photos when you were here last?"

"Yes, I did," said Trevor. "This is just to take a quick look at something."
~~~~~~

Amy didn't bother to ask what as she was sure Trevor would fill her in on his thinking, eventually.

There was nothing outstanding about the semi-detached property that had once been home to Edith and Max. Just an ordinary house in an ordinary street. They parked the car and then walked down the side of the property. Trevor jumped up to see over the fence. He repeated this two or three times. Amy was curious to know what he was looking at. There was no way she would see over the fence, even if she was to jump up. But before she could ask him, Trevor said tersely,

"Let's get back to the car."

Yanking his phone out of his pocket, he pressed the screen a couple of times and then putting the phone to his ear set off at such speed that Amy struggled to keep up. His face was grim. She was about to ask him what was wrong when his call was answered, and he stopped dead.

"Mike," said Trevor. "You're not going to like this, but I think I might have found out what happened to the boy. Yes, Max. I think I know where you can find him."

Amy pulled up just short of where Trevor was standing, unable to take another step, as the realisation of what he was saying hit her.

Trevor finished his call and strode over to her. "I'm so, so sorry," he said contritely, unsure of what to do as Amy stood doubled over on the pavement.

Amy, now certain she wasn't going to vomit but still feeling nauseous, forced herself to stand upright taking deep breaths as she did so.

"I just didn't think." Trevor was full of remorse. He wanted to hug Amy but wasn't sure if that would be appropriate.

"It's okay," said Amy. "I feel such a fool. Talk about overreacting. How embarrassing. Don't suppose I could have a hug?" she asked.

Trevor immediately folded his arms around her, and she rested her head on his shoulder.

"You think Edith killed Max and buried him in the garden," she stated, it wasn't a question.

"It's the most logical explanation," said Trevor. "How about we go and grab a cup of tea, or something stronger if you prefer, and we'll discuss it."

11

Try as he might, Trevor just could not bring himself to make a decision. Several silk scarves in various shades of blue lay displayed on the counter in front of him, artfully arranged by the initially enthusiastic sales assistant. Although no chink appeared in her sunny smile which revealed her perfectly white, even teeth, that matched absolutely with her impeccable attire and immaculate make-up, Trevor could sense the woman was struggling to maintain a cheerful disposition.

'And who can blame her?' he thought.

He had been standing at the counter for what felt like several hours unable to make a choice between the options presented before him.

"Just pick a blue one," his sister had instructed him when he had sought her advice over Skype.

It had sounded so simple. The problem was he had never realised exactly how many shades of blue were in existence. He had anticipated having to choose between light or dark blue and of course, he'd heard of navy blue and possibly even French blue. But in her eagerness to please, and possibly because he was currently the only customer, the shop assistant had gathered every blue scarf that the store carried, naming each individual hue as she fanned them out in front of him. Periwinkle, Ultramarine, Savoy, Baby and Powder had been followed by blues named after places such as Argentinian Blue, Egyptian Blue, Spanish Blue and even Uranium Blue.

When she then began to set out another pile of patterned scarves, Trevor had been so overwhelmed by the choice that he had become paralysed, unable to single one out. Trying to be helpful the assistant had asked about the colouring of the lady he was purchasing for. Having to admit that he had never met the woman in question just added to his anxiety. Detecting that the up-until-now, extremely obliging assistant was losing the will to live, Trevor, despite the eye-watering price, selected three of the items before him. Periwinkle (a light blue), Bluebonnet (a bright blue) and Midnight (a dark blue).

Surely, the recipient of the gift would be delighted by at least one of them.

Panicking that all his choices were plain, he hurriedly asked to exchange the bright blue for one from the other pile. The one he selected was patterned with little dogs that looked remarkably like JR. The assistant, who had returned to her usual buoyant manner upon realising that she was to make commission on three items rather than one, willingly obliged and offered to gift wrap them for him at no extra charge.

Trevor found himself in this predicament due to his having accepted Amy's invitation to join the family for Christmas dinner. To be fair, he hadn't so much accepted as Amy had refused to take "no" for an answer.

Over the time they had spent together Amy had elicited a fair amount of personal information from Trevor; mostly without him even realising just how much he had divulged. Normally a reticent person, unwilling to talk about himself, Trevor begrudgingly acknowledged that Amy's subtle interrogation skills would make her an excellent investigator. Over a number of Sunday lunches and a fair few car journeys, Trevor had disclosed that he had never married. He then unwittingly revealed one of his innermost secrets, that his first love had spurned his proposal on the grounds that she was in love with his best friend, and that the rejection had deterred him from ever asking anyone else. To get over his disappointment he had thrown himself into his job and although he had enjoyed many relationships, any serious girlfriends, whom he might possibly have considered taking the leap with, had been put off by the long hours he worked and his inability to switch off; to leave work at work.

His dedication had paid off and he had enjoyed an immensely successful career; but now that he was retired, he had to admit that a part of him regretted not having anyone to share his life with. His biggest regret was not having had children. He was conscious of the fact that meeting Amy and her family had filled a void that up until then he hadn't been aware existed and now, he couldn't contemplate his life without them. That said, he had still tried his hardest to wriggle out of the invitation to join in with their Christmas festivities, once Amy had informed him that Kath and Terry and Kath's sister Sylvia would also be joining them.

"You can't back out now," Amy had declared. "That would leave us with an uneven number which would mess up my place settings." And she absolutely refused to entertain the idea that he would prefer to stay home on his own. Normally he would spend Christmas with his sister and her family but this year they were all spending the festive season in Australia, visiting his niece's in-laws.

Being an organised person, Trevor had already sorted his Christmas presents for Amy, Marcus, Rory and Olivia. He was extremely pleased with what he had managed to acquire for each of them. Once he knew about the extra guests, he felt it only polite to include them in his gift giving.

He was already acquainted with the Lomases, who as well as often being invited to the Mcdonalds' Sunday lunches, had also been part of the Charity golf tournament circuit where Trevor had met Amy's father, Keith. Finding Kath and Terry an appropriate Christmas present had been simple because he had a contact in the golfing fraternity, but when it came to Kath's sister, Trevor came unstuck. He hadn't wanted to ask Amy because he was certain she would tell him not to buy anything at all. But he couldn't turn up empty-handed. A voucher seemed too impersonal but all of his other ideas, such as perfume, seemed too intimate and anyway, he wouldn't know where to begin with regards to what sort of fragrance to purchase. Hence, the conversation with his sister, seeking her advice whilst she enjoyed the sunshine on the other side of the world.

"A Hermes scarf," she told him. "Every woman of a certain age loves a Hermes scarf."

Now that his ordeal was over, Trevor relaxed and thanking the sales assistant profusely for her patience, he scooped up his beautifully wrapped purchases and left the store a happy man.

12

Monty's enthusiastic greeting was the balm that Mason needed after such a heavy day. As soon as the dog had finished his dinner, Mason slipped on his lead and the two of them headed out to walk along the cliff tops overlooking the bay.

Once they reached the top, Mason left Monty to his futile rabbit hunt and stood staring out to the horizon. The fresh salty air was clean and pure, and Mason drew in deep restorative breaths. He needed to rid himself of the noxious feeling that had sat within him ever since the child's remains had been unearthed in the back garden of 30 Abbey Road, Dolford.

This morning, about five minutes after he arrived at his office, he received the call he had been expecting from Martha Daniels, confirming what he already knew; they had found the missing boy, Max O'Reilly. Leah suggested the use of Edith's birth surname for the boy whose father was unknown. She reasoned that at least that way he would have a genuine surname and not just something Edith had made up.

As expected, Martha hadn't been able to provide much in the way of any extra detail due to the decomposition of the remains, but she estimated that the child had been around 6 years old at the time of his death, which fitted with the last known sighting of Max. That meant the boy had lain buried under concrete undisturbed for over twenty years. After so much time, Mason was unsurprised by the lack of forensic evidence or by Martha's inability to establish the exact cause of death. But she had ascertained that the boy had been subjected to a violent attack, during which he had sustained numerous injuries many of them severe enough to cause death.

Mason had felt sickened reading through the report of her findings that Martha emailed to him directly after their telephone conversation. So did the rest of the original investigating team when he pulled as many of them as were available away from their current cases and into a hastily organised meeting. From the hardened, experienced coppers down to the fresh, as yet unsullied newbies, they all felt the same outrage that so far Edith O'Reilly had escaped justice. They were all, especially Mason, frustrated at their inability so far to apprehend the depraved woman responsible for murdering her own child. Because there was no doubt in the room that the person responsible for the boy's demise had been his own mother.

After the meeting, Mason felt it only right to send Leah to Hornby to break the news to Tom and Lizzie Bryant. He notified the couple before the search commenced because he didn't want them to hear about it via the media, but he felt it only right that they be notified in person that Max had been found. He knew they would both be devastated by the news having held out hope that Max would be found alive and well. Mason had also called Trevor and asked him to break the news to Amy and to Matt. He promised to send all the relevant information across to Trevor so that it could be included in the book currently being written about Edith. Mason was still optimistic that publishing the book could aid them in locating the woman's whereabouts. There was every possibility that it would bring up new leads. Now, more than ever, he was determined to bring her in so that she could face justice.

Feeling a lot lighter than he had when he set out on his walk, Mason whistled to Monty and set off down the cliffs back towards home.

BBC News – 12th July 2016

BREAKING NEWS: Surrey Police today confirmed that officers have begun a search at the garden of a property in the Dolford area. They are refusing to give any further information at this time.

~~~~~~

BBC News – 14th July 2016

Police have now confirmed that the body discovered in the garden of a house in Abbey Road, Dolford is that of a child. A post-mortem is due to take place. A police spokesperson stated that there is no connection between the current owners of the property and the discovery of the body.

~~~~~~

The Sun – 30th August 2016

Police today released the identity of the body discovered in the garden of a property in Abbey Road, Dolford. The body is that of Max Cashmore, believed to have been aged 6 at the time of his death. In another dramatic twist police also announced that missing woman Eliza Kelly, already wanted for the murder of her husband Keith, is the mother of the boy and she is now also wanted on suspicion of his murder and unlawful burial. The body is believed to have lain undisturbed for over twenty years.

~~~~~~
~~~~~~

BBC News – 14th September 2016

A post-mortem carried out on the remains of Max Cashmore, whose body was discovered in a back garden in Dolford, has been unable to establish the actual cause of death. A police spokesperson has stated, however, that the boy sustained numerous severe injuries, all or any of which would have contributed to his death. His mother, Eliza Kelly, is wanted on suspicion of his murder.

~~~~~~

Daily Telegraph – 15th November 2016

An inquest was opened today into the death of Max Cashmore, the 6-year-old boy whose remains were discovered in the back garden of a house in Dolford. The coroner recorded the boy's name, date of birth and an estimated date of death in the year 1997, meaning the child was aged 6 at the time of his death.

The coroner confirmed that a post-mortem had been unable to establish cause of death. The inquest was adjourned to allow the police more time for their investigation. The police are asking members of the public for their help in establishing the whereabouts of the boy's mother, Eliza Kelly. She is wanted on suspicion of both his murder and that of her husband, Keith Kelly back in February 2015.

~~~~~~

13

Trevor, Matt and Amy were once more sitting in the study of Amy's farmhouse having enjoyed another superb Sunday lunch cooked by Marcus, who could currently be heard singing his heart out whilst he tackled the devastation he had caused in the kitchen. This week's music choice would appear to be Paul Simon, a choice approved of by both Matt and Trevor.

"So, it's definite then?" Amy asked Trevor. "Edith killed Max."

"No, not definite," replied Trevor. "But it's certainly beyond reasonable doubt."

"I hate the fact that she got away with it. Without anyone knowing what she'd done, for over twenty years her son lay buried in a back garden, and she just carried on with her life. My poor Dad had no idea what he married. I can't believe I spent time with that woman. I sat at the same table and shared meals with her." Amy picked up piles of paperwork off the desk and stacked them nosily together before slamming them down again.

"I feel sorry for Tom," said Matt. "He was so hopeful of being reunited with Max and now he knows that's never going to happen."

"What will happen to Max's remains now?" asked Amy "What do you mean?" replied Trevor.

"Well, who's going to be responsible for laying him to rest?" asked Amy. "He has no family who will claim him?"

"To be honest, I don't know," said Trevor. "When people have no money and no family the state takes care of the funeral so, I suppose, that's what will happen in this case."

"Would I be able to go?" asked Amy. "I hate the thought of no one being there for him. I'd like to pay my respects. I'm sure Tom and Lizzie would too."

"I'm not sure they would even be able to tell you when it was being carried out," Trevor informed her. "Give Mike a ring and ask him. He should be able to authorise them to tell you when and where the funeral will take place."

Having spent the night mulling it over, Amy had come up with a plan and the next morning she called Mike Mason to once more ask a favour of him.

After she'd explained why she was ringing, Mason told her it was a great idea, and he would see if he could get approval from those above him. He did warn her, however, that she might not be able to implement her plan for the foreseeable future.

14

Looking around at the detritus that only a few hours before had been an enchantingly decorated festive dining table, Trevor conceded that he was enjoying this Christmas so far. The food had been delicious and the company genial, particularly that of Kath's sister, Sylvia, who was seated next to him. And, even if he said so himself, he thought smugly, his gifts had been an outstanding success. Everyone was still sitting at the table, chatting away to each other, too full to contemplate moving. Trevor caught Amy's eye and raised his glass to her in a silent toast.

The sound of a rather loud snore made Trevor jump, and he turned to Sylvia in surprise.

"Did you think that was me?" she said laughing and she pointed to her lap where a contented JR was curled up fast asleep.

"I'm so sorry," said Trevor, worried. "Do you want me to get him down? He's a bugger. He sneaked up without me noticing."

"Oh no leave him be," said Sylvia. "I lost my Tilly only a few months ago and I miss her so much. I can't even contemplate replacing her yet. I'm not sure I ever will. They become such a huge part of your life these dogs, don't they?"

"Definitely," said Trevor. "I'd be lost without him."

"Well, if you ever need someone to look after him, I'd be more than happy to help out," Sylvia smiled at him. "While I've got your attention," she carried on, "I hope you don't think I'm rude, but I was wondering... Well, that is, if you don't think me too cheeky, I would just like to say that I would love to accompany you when you go to see Humphrey Charles. Only I'm a sucker for mediaeval history. And I watch all of his programmes on telly. I'd love to see him live."

Amy and Marcus's Christmas present to Trevor had been two tickets to see the renowned historian give a talk to accompany his latest book, at the Theatre Royal in Brigholme later that year.

"We got you two tickets in case you fancied taking someone from your local history group," Amy had told him.

"I'd be delighted if you'd join me," Trevor told Sylvia looking into her eyes and trying to determine if they were periwinkle blue or cornflower blue.

"Those two are getting on rather well," Kath whispered in Amy's ear, watching from the other side of the table as her sister covertly flirted with the lately retired police officer. "Well done, darling." She returned her attention to Amy. "Everything has been fucking brilliant. All yours and Marcus's hard work has really paid off. Your parents would be so proud of you."

"I must admit I've enjoyed today far more than I expected to," Amy told her. "I wanted to make it a good Christmas for everyone after all we've been through recently but at the same time it's hard not to miss the loved ones who aren't here, Mum, Dad, Granny, and it's such a shame Adam and Pascal couldn't make it."

"I know, darling, but you've done amazingly well. Look how far you've come since this time last year and how you've coped with all that's happened this year. It's certainly been a traumatic time."

Kath didn't need to go into detail, Amy was well- aware of what she was referring to. Finding out that her father was not Zac's dad, and then the discovery of Max's remains, and the knowledge that the same woman who murdered her father had killed her own child, was rather a lot to come to terms with.

"At least Tom and Lizzie have some closure now," added Kath.

"Yes, but not proper closure. I feel that until Edith is arrested none of us will ever have closure."

"Well, the book launch could help with that."

"Yes, hopefully. At least it keeps Edith in the public eye."

"How are you feeling about the book being out in the shops? Very excited I should imagine."

"I think I'm more nervous than excited," Amy confessed.

"Timing it to coincide with the second anniversary of losing your dad is genius. That should help tremendously with the publicity," said Kath.

"That was Matt's idea. It's all down to him. It's that side of it that makes me nervous. What if people see it as me trying to cash in on Dad's death? Well, that and the fact that I'm terrified it'll be a complete flop. Matt says he always feels the same whenever he publishes anything; doesn't matter if it's a book or a small article for the local paper. He always thinks it's rubbish, no-one will read it and if they do, they'll just criticise it."

"I'm sure no one will think you've published it just to make money," said Kath. "I think they'll understand your intention is to clear your father's name."

"Well, I've declined doing any of the publicity for 'The Evil Underneath'. I'm not sure I could cope with the hype or with answering people's preposterous questions. Anyway, I'm considering going back to work. Just part time to begin with. Harlestone Primary are looking for someone to cover maternity leave, starting after February half term. It's only three days a week as it's a job share and obviously it's temporary."

"That sounds ideal," said Kath. "A great way to ease yourself back in."

They both looked up as Trevor hauled himself to his feet with his glass in his hand.

"I'd like to propose a toast to our wonderful hosts," he told the seated guests. Then raising his glass in the air, he continued, "To Amy and Marcus, thank you so much for inviting me to join you today. Marcus, thank you for such excellent food and Amy, thank you for not helping in the kitchen." Everyone laughed. "No, seriously, Amy. Thank you so very much for all your hard work. Thank you both of you. The day has been magical."

"Hear, hear," said Terry. "Three cheers for the McDonalds."

Everyone cheered and toasted a delighted Marcus and a ferociously blushing Amy.

To Amy's surprise, Rory then stood up. Not one to draw attention to himself, Amy deduced that his glass was more likely to be filled with white wine than apple juice.

'*Still, it is Christmas,*' she thought.

"I would like to raise a toast to absent loved ones," he declared. Everyone raised their glasses once more and Amy felt herself welling up. Then Marcus noisily moved his chair back from the table and stood up, wobbling a little, with a full glass of red wine in his hand.

'*Uh oh, here we go,*' thought Amy to herself. Marcus was definitely more than a little worse for wear and she dreaded what he was about to say, knowing how embarrassing he could be when drunk.

"I would like to propose a toast to my wonderful wife," he smiled blearily across at the mortified Amy. "I'm so proud of her, not only for how she has coped with all the dreadful things that have happened over the last few years but also I'm so proud that she is soon to be a published author."

"Co-author," Amy corrected as everyone else raised their glass to her. Secretly she had been thrilled when Matt had insisted on naming both her and Trevor as co-authors rather than just contributors. It also meant she would be getting a percentage of the royalties.

'*That's if we actually sell any copies,*' she reminded herself.

"I would like to thank you all for being here to share this special day with us," Marcus carried on. "I know some of you have made great sacrifices to be here. Especially, the children, who agreed not to bring their mobile phones to the table."

Amy groaned. Marcus was in no hurry to sit down.

"And I can't thank Trevor enough for the most wonderful gifts."

"Hear, hear," Terry repeated, so loudly that Kath kicked him under the table.

"I can't wait to attend my cookery class weekend with Jodie Pigmont; she's my favourite celebrity chef," continued Marcus.

"I can't wait to see Sudden Death," Olivia chimed in.

Earlier, after opening the envelope given to her by Trevor, Olivia had emitted a high-pitched squeal and then proceeded to jump up and down on the spot before rushing over and flinging her arms around Trevor.

"Thank you so, so much," she said. "They're my favourite group. How did you know?"

"How could I not when you're playing their blasted music at full volume every time I visit," laughed Trevor.

Rory on the other hand had been rendered speechless on opening his envelope. Marcus had to ask him twice what he had received before Rory was able to say that he would be watching all Brigholme's home games that season from a private box.

"If your dad can't go with you as the accompanying adult, Rory, then I will," Trevor informed the delighted teenager.

Terry now took up the mantle and standing up to join Marcus he raised his glass in a toast to Trevor thanking him for arranging for himself and Kath to play 18 holes of golf with a PGA professional.

"I don't know how you've managed to arrange all this," he told Trevor.

"It's all those committees he sits on," said Marcus.

"It's not what you know, it's who you know," added Kath with a grin.

"And what you've done for Amy is incredible. Absolutely outstanding," added Marcus as he hiccupped and then succumbing to the amount of wine he had consumed, flopped back down onto his chair.

Sylvia leaned over to Trevor until their arms were brushing and said, "I absolutely adore my scarves. Blue is my favourite colour."

Trevor, much to his surprise, could feel himself blushing, not something that happened very often.

"I must confess I did seek help from my sister," he admitted.

"Well, your sister has excellent taste," Sylvia told him. "You've really spoilt me. You must let me cook a meal for you sometime as a thank you."

"I'd love to," said Trevor enthusiastically. '*Her eyes are definitely periwinkle blue,*' he declared to himself.

The couple jumped away from each other guiltily as they felt someone approach from behind. And then burst out in simultaneous laughter at their overreaction. Amy laughed too.

"What are you two whispering about?" she asked.

"I was just asking Trevor how on earth he found the time to track down all those clips of your father and how he managed to put everything together onto the DVD like that. He's so clever. I wouldn't know where to begin," lied Sylvia deflecting Amy away from her and Trevor's personal conversation. She knew her hostess well and if Amy got a sniff of the couple being interested in each other, she would take on the role of matchmaker. Sylvia got the feeling that she was going to have to take things slowly with Trevor. She didn't want to scare him off and she certainly didn't need Amy interfering, even if it was with the best of intentions.

"Again, I can't take the credit," Trevor answered. "I have a friend who works in TV production who owed me a favour."

"Well, I'm thrilled with it," Amy told him. "It's such a special gift, so thoughtful."

Amy hadn't opened her present at the same time as the others. Instead, she'd enjoyed watching the looks of amazement and disbelief on her children's faces, and then the faces of everyone else, as they opened their envelopes or packages, whilst she helped the excited dogs, whom Trevor had included in his gifts, open their presents of toys and treats. She left the small package Trevor handed to her sitting in her lap.

"What have you got, Mum?" Olivia asked.

"I don't know, I haven't opened mine yet, I was just enjoying everyone else's excitement," Amy replied.

Picking up the small package, she carefully undid the paper. Amy wasn't sure what she had been expecting but after what the others had received it certainly wasn't a DVD. There was no label on it, the cover was blank. Feeling a tad disappointed but trying not to show it she held it up for everyone to see.

"Read the menu inside," Trevor instructed her.

Opening up the case, Amy took out a piece of card and began to read it to herself.

"Oh my," she said.

"What is it, Mum?" asked Olivia impatiently.

"It's a compilation of all your Grandad's work. It's got a bit of everything on here. All the TV shows he appeared in. All the films. All the quiz shows. Oh goodness this is wonderful," Amy said reading further and turning the card over. "Oh wow, there's even his appearance on Wogan. I lost my copy of that. Do you remember Marcus? We had it on video, and you taped over it with some Rugby match."

"It was the Three Nations," said Marcus somewhat defensively.

"Trevor, this is amazing," said Amy, rising to her feet and picking her way through the mounds of discarded wrapping paper. Trevor stood as she approached his chair. "I don't know how to thank you," she said, her voice breaking as she gave him a massive hug. "Thank you so much. I think that's the nicest present I've ever received."

"What? Nicer than the lawnmower I got you?" asked Marcus, feigning hurt.

"Oh, only a tiny bit," Amy reassured him.

PART FIVE

Letter from inside the envelope that was attached to the journal.

June 2017, St Agnes Hospice, Inverness.

Amy,

If you are reading this, then I am dead. It is my intention to finish writing this before my illness becomes too debilitating. But whether completed or not, I am leaving instructions that this journal be sent to you along with a copy of my death certificate. How ironic that the same cancer that killed your mother will be responsible for my death too!

I would not blame you if you questioned the authenticity of my death. After all, you are aware of how much I like to deceive. But ask yourself this. With everything you have learnt about me do you imagine I would be so foolish as to commit a confession of my crimes to paper, if there was the slightest possibility that I could be discovered and punished?

So, why have I written my confession and arranged for it to be sent to you? Because, my dear stepdaughter, I read The Evil Underneath, for which you are credited as a co-author, and reluctantly I have to commend you for a job well done. However, I feel it is imperative to enlighten you on certain issues, correct some inaccuracies and reveal crimes I committed that you failed to uncover.

Consider this memoir my legacy for it will be studied by behavioural experts for years to come. Why? Because I am unique. You cannot compare me to any other killer in history. Unlike the majority of serial killers, I was not driven to kill for sexual gratification, nor do I suffer from a form of mental illness that drives me to kill, although obviously I'm a sociopath. I have never killed a stranger although some were merely acquaintances, but I am also guilty of familicide, and you can't get closer to home than that! Some of the murders were for financial gain, some for self-preservation and some simply the result of having lost my temper.

I have been killing people all my life and yet I have never been caught. If I leave no confession, then my true genius will never be known. And I do believe myself to be a genius. I have outwitted the most intelligent people at every turn. To have committed one murder and got away with it is an accomplishment, but to have committed as many as I have and remain at liberty is nothing short of miraculous. I refuse to go to my grave with my ingenuity unacknowledged and therefore I have written this testimony for you.

Press Release by Amy McDonald – Daughter of Keith Kelly

Article from The Daily Telegraph (Monday 10th July 2017)

Amy McDonald, daughter of the late actor Keith Kelly, today released an excerpt from what she claims is a confessional journal, written exclusively for her by the woman accused of her father's murder; his second wife Eliza Kelly.

According to a statement released by Ms McDonald alongside the accompanying paragraphs, (which have been published in their original format – seemingly written by Mrs Kelly's own hand), she received the document after Mrs Kelly left instructions on her death bed that they be handed to her stepdaughter.

When questioned, DCI Mason from West Sussex Police, who has been leading the investigation into Mr Kelly's death, confirmed that he is satisfied that Eliza Kelly is deceased. Rumours that she died of cancer in a hospice in Inverness, Scotland, have yet to be substantiated.

The release of this passage is the culmination of an incredible set of events which began when Mr Kelly's son Zac, who was aged only 9 at the time of the incident, was accused by his mother, Eliza Kelly, of the fatal stabbing of his father. Sometime later an extraordinary development occurred that saw Eliza herself accused of the murder, having framed her child. Before she could be apprehended however, she disappeared from the family home and was believed to have fled abroad under a new identity. During the subsequent investigation it was discovered that Eliza Kelly, having been born Edith Staples, used numerous aliases during her lifetime.

After Eliza absconded, Amy McDonald joined forces with awarding winning investigative journalist Matt Dinsdale in an effort to clear her father's name from allegations made against him by Eliza that he was an abuser. Together, with the help of retired DSI Trevor Harrison, they explored Eliza's childhood, and her life before meeting Keith Kelly.

In another bizarre twist in this tale their investigations led to the discovery of the body of another of Eliza's children, Max. The child had lain buried in the garden of the house he and his mother resided in in Dolford undisturbed for over twenty years!

The discovery of these remains opened up another murder investigation during which it was established that Max had last been seen in 1997, at which time Eliza was using the name Eleanor Cashmore.

This nefarious woman then disappeared off the radar only to resurface some years later at the time she began dating Keith Kelly.

After the death of Mr Kelly, despite a massive police investigation, the killer remained at large. That is until the receipt of this confession led police to the address where she had been staying at the time of her death.

Other astonishing discoveries uncovered by Matt and his team have been published in a book entitled The Evil Underneath, (*HarperCollins* 2017), including the real paternity of Eliza's two children.

Statement from Amy McDonald:

A few weeks ago, I received notification through a solicitor that Eliza Kelly had died. I was given a confession supposedly written by herself, in which she detailed not only the death of my father, but also a number of other murders she alleges she committed, including that of my grandmother.

I can confirm that this journal has been authenticated but I am not at liberty to discuss any of its contents, other than what I am releasing for publication today, due to an ongoing police investigation.

My hope is that the following excerpt will prove, once and for all, that my father was innocent of the allegations made by Eliza at the time of his death, therefore, ending the countless rumours and speculations that have continued to cause my family so much additional heartache on top of the unbearable loss of a beloved father, grandfather, brother and friend under the most horrific circumstances.

Excerpt from Eliza Kelly's Journal
– Released for publication by Amy McDonald, July 2017.

I despised your father, Amy. He betrayed me. I thought I was marrying an incredibly wealthy and successful actor – he certainly looked the part on paper, but he never lived up to the image.

If I hadn't been in such desperate straits when I met him, I might have thought twice about accepting his proposal, mostly due to the age difference. I can't deny he was devoted to me, completely besotted with me. He did his best to satisfy me, but I hated him for being so passive, so eager to please. Where he wanted me to see strength I saw only weakness, as in his willingness to ditch his own children in favour of me.

No matter how hard he tried to convince me otherwise though, I was aware he would never love me as much as he loved your mother and that he adored Adam and you and his grandchildren in a way that he could never adore Zac. I hate you and your brother for that. Life has been so easy for the two of you. You've never had to fight for anything. You have no idea what it is to struggle. I despise people like you.

So, when your father died, and I saw how much pain you were in, I relished it. I did everything I could to make that pain worse, (hence the hurried funeral – another way to hurt you). But more *satisfying than that was watching the desolation that the destruction of his reputation caused you. It gave me enormous pleasure to know how much those lies I told about him tormented you. It was pure bliss. And you were so naïve. You thought it would all stop once I was accused of your dad's murder. But it didn't, did it? The rumours just wouldn't go away. They became an indelible stain on your father's character. That's human nature for you, Amy. We always want to believe the worst of people. Your dad was just too good to be true, and so when I made those accusations, people leapt on the idea that underneath the good guy image was a wife beater, an abuser. And those stories that appeared in the Press as told by 'a source close to the family', or 'a friend of Eliza's'; do you remember those stories, Amy? The ones that corroborated the abuse. They were all planted by me and Ricky. Every single one of them. And just to rub salt into the wound, we got paid for them. The papers paid me to perpetuate the lies I told about Keith Kelly hitting me. Lies I used to cover up the fact that I had murdered him in a fit of rage! It's a crazy world, isn't it?*

"Wow," said Kath. "She really hated your guts didn't she!"

"I know," said Amy. "I feel quite lucky to be alive. I'm sure if she'd had the opportunity, she would have bumped me off, no problem. Poor Marcus has been quite disturbed by it all. He feels we've had a close brush with death."

The two women had met together to plan Keith Kelly's memorial and although Kath had already read Edith's whole confession, she had just re-read the part Amy intended to publish to familiarise herself with it once more.

"This is going to embarrass those who believed your dad *was* guilty of hitting her," said Kath.

"Exactly," said Amy. "That's why I want to publish it before we hold the memorial."

My first attempt at murder was so successful it resulted in the deaths of four people, well 5 if you include my grandfather. You didn't know that did you? Not for sure anyway. It was speculated about; both by yourselves and by the police. 'What a coincidence,' you all said. 'Ricky's family die in an arson attack and then a few weeks later Edith's grandfather dies in an accidental house fire.' So, you had your suspicions, didn't you? You may even have tried to find a connection, but you failed.

The first fire was deemed an attack by a rival gang against the notorious Kerr boys. It had all the hallmarks of a professional hit. Traces of accelerants were found in the hallway by the front door. A firework had been shoved through the letter box. The only survivor, a small boy, who was fortunate enough to have been spending the night at a friend's house and unfortunate enough to lose his entire family in one fell swoop.

The second fire could only have been accidental. An elderly man home alone. A pan left on the stove, forgotten about until it was too late, and the house was ablaze. A mother and her young daughter left homeless. All their possessions lost to the fire. Such a tragedy. So unusual to have two fatal fires so close together, both in time and proximity, but two completely different scenarios. And even when you found out about me and the various crimes I committed, you still couldn't bring yourself to believe that an 11-year-old girl could be responsible. At that age how could she have such knowledge? How could she be capable of such planning? But you all, as usual, underestimated me. It was actually incredibly easy; the only difficulty perhaps was convincing Ricky to play his part. That was why his family had to go first.

So why did I do it? To escape my perverted grandfather or should I say, my perverted father. Thanks to your book, Amy, it's not a secret anymore. The whole world knows they are one and the same person. But I refuse to be ashamed. And maybe it justifies all that followed. I am the unhappy result of an immoral union.

I wasn't very old when I began to suspect I wasn't being told the truth about my supposedly dead father. My imbecile of a mother couldn't even concoct a decent cover story. When asked to describe her fictional fiancée she could never remember what answers she had previously given. So sometimes his eyes were blue and other times they were brown. Sometimes he had black hair and other times he was blonde. She could provide no sensible reason as to why she had no photographs of him, nor could she explain his lack of family.

Now, if I was in her situation what a story I would have told. And, as I grew older, that's exactly what I did. When children at school asked about my father I would show them a photograph, one I had stolen from somewhere or other, where the man in question looked very dapper in his expensive suit. I made up stories about him to fit the way he looked. And although I am certain that no one believed me, not one of my stories could be disproved. Later, because she looked the part, I passed my mother off as my grandmother so that I could play at being an orphan. This enabled me to create elaborate scenarios for the way in which my beloved parents died. My favourite was that they were both spies and had been assassinated by a car bomb in Lebanon.

But I digress. The reason I killed my grandfather, or more accurately, the reason I arranged to have him killed, (I was not personally involved in the arson – I just orchestrated it), was because he appeared to be recovering from a stroke, which according to the doctors he should have died from. I should also be credited for instigating the stroke. I confronted him with my suspicions regarding my parentage and the hideous old man, unable to cope with a verbal attack from the product of his heinous behaviour, succumbed to a massive stroke. Instead of dying as the specialists predicted, he began to make a successful recovery, and I could not allow that to happen. I was no longer willing to tolerate his Dickensian ways, and my mother was never going to stand up to him or leave him. It was down to me to *find a way out of the situation and so I planned his death.*

Having done a fair amount of research, arson seemed the simplest way to achieve my goal. When I discovered that my school trip coincided with my mother's annual retreat weekend, the opportunity was too good to ignore. Ricky and I had often discussed how much better my life would be without my grandfather and his life without his alcoholic mother or his violent brothers. I began to share my plans with him, but he assumed they were pie in the sky. Imagine his shock when I put my plan for his family into action and it went off without a hitch. I had to get it done before I went away with the school, otherwise, he would miss his window of opportunity to repay the favour.

"This is incredible," said Matt as he turned the page. "I could almost feel sorry for her. Working out that your grandfather is your father at - how old was she - 11?"

Amy nodded.

"How horrible," he continued. "Then you read on, and you really don't feel sorry for her anymore."

The second murder I committed was not premeditated. I was 18 at the time and it only happened because the perfect opportunity to eliminate a problem presented itself. Let me give you some background information which will make the circumstances clearer for you.

As you are aware, at the age of 16, I reinvented myself. I had newfound confidence after discovering my ability to make money, seriously good money. This, in turn, enabled me to create a whole new persona. I was no longer solely dependent on my mother to provide for me, and for the first time in my life, I could have whatever I wanted. I could dress fashionably. I got myself a new name, started a new school and constructed a new back story for myself.

At my previous school, I'm ashamed to say that I was subjected to bullying because I didn't come from the same background as the other girls, and for a short while, I allowed them to intimidate me. Now I made myself a promise that I would never again feel inadequate or allow myself to be disparaged or belittled because of who I was or where I came from. Now I had the freedom to choose who I wanted to be. I was on a par with my peers and if I still had no friends that was through my own choice, and not because I had been deemed unworthy.

So how was I making money? Through prostitution. Not the seedy down a back alley or in the back of a bloke's car type of prostitution. No, it was more like I was an escort. Although, that title may be a little grand. It wasn't like 'Pretty Woman'. There was no going to the opera or polo matches, instead, it was second-rate hotel rooms or at the client's house. I didn't get an education in etiquette, but I did get an education in how to satisfy a man in bed.

My pimp was a woman in her 50s who would have been called a Madam if she had managed a brothel. Instead, she ran her business over the phone from her council flat. She was successful because she was discrete, and she made sure her girls were too. And she was good at matching girls to clients to suit their particular tastes.

She approached me one day when I was hanging out with Ricky and asked if I wanted to earn some money, and it started from there. I was always in demand because I looked like a schoolgirl. I mean technically I was a schoolgirl, but I could make myself look even younger than I actually was, about 12, and you may or may not be surprised to learn that an awful lot of men want to have sex with an underage girl.

Although prostitution was illegal, the benefit for my clients, if we happened to be caught by the police, was that I was actually above the age of consent, and the benefit for me was that I was less likely to be caught working in this way than if I worked the streets. Also, I wasn't exposed to the same dangers as the streetwalkers. Even so, I used Ricky, or if he was unavailable, one of his cronies, to ensure I got to my appointments and back home again safely. I never fully trusted clients and Ricky acted as my bodyguard. However, it was this arrangement that nearly got my extracurricular activities exposed to the whole school. Don't get me wrong; I was in no way ashamed of what I was doing, I just didn't want it to become common knowledge. Who would? It's not exactly the sort of thing you put on your application to Oxford.

Anyway, I'm getting off point again. The two years I spent studying for my A levels had gone by smoothly. I achieved really good grades despite what I was getting up to outside of school. After the final exams and just before we left to go our separate ways, the school organised an end-of-term ball. These events were similar to the Prom Nights that schools currently hold; that tacky Americanism hadn't made it across the Atlantic yet! But the idea was very similar, boys in black tie and girls in evening gowns. I had pretty much kept myself to myself whilst at school. I found it easier to be a loner than to try to fit in with the crowd. I didn't share their interests in music or popular culture. So, imagine my surprise to be invited to the ball by one of the most popular boys in 6th form. Not popular enough for me to remember his name all this time later though!

I really hadn't expected anyone to ask me, especially not one of the Elite, and I was secretly delighted. Unbeknownst to me, Debbie White not only had a massive crush on this boy, but unfortunately, her cousin was one of Ricky's cohorts who on occasion had acted as my bodyguard. This cousin had told her all about how I was making a living.

So, moving on to the night of the ball. I was all dressed up to the nines and I have to say for once I was thoroughly enjoying myself. However, it wasn't long before my evening was spoilt by Debbie. She cornered me as my date went to fetch refreshments. The silly girl threatened to expose what she knew about me to the boy who had brought me to the dance. I suppose you could say she wanted to tell my escort I was an escort! She honestly believed she could manipulate me into ditching my date and going home. She had no idea whom she was dealing with. Her audacity infuriated me. I told her to do her worst and moved away. She was shocked that I hadn't reacted in the way she expected, and so she took to following me and my partner wherever we went – to the bar, to the dance floor. Every time I turned around, she was there, smirking at me.

I found I could no longer relax and enjoy myself. My anger began to rise. How dare she spoil my evening? What gave her the right to ruin my reputation? What had I ever done to her? Sometime later I saw her leave the hall heading for the toilets and decided now was the time to bring the matter to an end by having a quiet word with her. Making my excuses to my date I went after her.

The queue for the ladies was huge and when she passed by the toilets without stopping, I followed. I wasn't sure where she was going but soon realised that she was heading to the swimming pool, obviously planning to use the toilets there. I have to say it was an inspired idea.

She was startled to find me standing waiting when she came out of the loo, but she wasn't scared. Why would she be? For two years I had purposely kept to myself. She considered me to be a timid little mouse. So, I certainly caught her off guard when I started to push her, telling her exactly what I would do to her if she breathed a word to anyone about me. We tussled for a bit but then I gave one hard shove and she fell backwards into the water. I wanted her to know I was serious. That I wasn't intimidated by her. I knew her to be an accomplished swimmer. I'd been in the pool with her on numerous occasions.

So, when she started shouting for me to help her, I assumed it was her silly attempt to get me to jump in and ruin my clothes and make-up too. I wasn't going to fall for that. I would wait for her to clamber out and then I would kick the living shit out of her.

Then realisation struck. She couldn't get out. Her ridiculously long velvet dress, complete with underskirts, once wet, had become so tremendously heavy that it was pulling her under the water. Remember this was the '80s and fashion had to be seen to be believed! The more she struggled, trying to get out of the dress, the more entangled in it she became. She was sinking deeper underwater, only occasionally managing to break the surface gasping for air. Each time she managed to get her lips above the water line she beseeched me to help her. Her panic was palpable. It was thrilling watching her fighting for her life. It seemed to last for hours, but in reality, it was probably only a matter of minutes.

I had no intention of doing anything other than stand and watch but then I heard voices approaching. Others had the same idea regarding the toilets. For a moment I hesitated and then I jumped in. By now Debbie was exhausted. She had no strength left to fight me off as I added my weight to that of the material that was pulling her down. I grabbed her long hair and yanked hard so that her head stayed underwater, but she was looking up at me. I actually saw the life leave her eyes. It was like a light going out. That was an incredible moment for me. I had never before had such an intense feeling of pleasure. It was so much better than sex!

As a group came into sight, I screamed for help. A couple of them jumped into the water and together we hauled Debbie to the side of the pool where hands were waiting to pull her out. I have to say she was a deadweight!! People started working on her as I too was helped from the pool. Others, alerted by all the shouting arrived and began to assist with the efforts to revive her. I collapsed on the floor as if I was exhausted, but I was actively avoiding answering the many questions being flung at me.

I suffered a few anxious moments fearing that Debbie might respond to their attempts to bring her round. Staying mute seemed my safest bet for the time being. I didn't want to say something that might incriminate me.

Someone helped me to a chair whilst another wrapped a blanket around me. I was surprised at how solicitously they treated me. I was fully prepared to defend myself against any accusations that I had harmed her. I assumed they would know we had been fighting. But they had no idea anything had gone on between us and instead of being blamed I was treated as a hero. They automatically assumed I had been trying to save her.

I reaffirmed this notion by saying that I was going to the toilets when I discovered her floating face down in the pool. And it escalated from there. The story got bigger in the telling and before I knew it, I was the person of the hour. The rescuer. The saviour. Even though Debbie had died! It was very strange.

The next few weeks were surreal. Her parents treated me like I was Debbie's best friend, much to the disgust of her true best friend. They even asked me to do the reading at her funeral. I was interviewed by the local TV and radio stations and my photograph appeared in the local newspaper alongside details of my good deed. Inside I was crying with laughter. People are so dumb. There I was being treated like a hero when I was, in fact, solely responsible for her death! I had drowned her! I had watched her die!

I got a real thrill out of seeing her parents grieve. Nothing could have prepared me for how extensive it was. It completely consumed them, and I was fascinated by it. It never occurred to me that people could have such strong feelings of love and loss, and it gave me a deep sense of satisfaction to know that I was responsible for the way they felt. I visited them at home a number of times to deliberately poke their grief so I could experience and enjoy their suffering. In the end, I think it got too much for them and they asked me to stay away. That hurt! How ungrateful!

Comment from Dale White - brother of Debbie White

"I can't believe she killed our Debbie and got away with it. I've got no idea how I'm going to explain this to my parents. To think that she got treated like a hero. Not just by us but by the whole community. I'm glad she's dead because I'm not sure I could control myself if I came into contact with her, but it's criminal that she never went to prison."

"Bloody hell," exclaimed Danny. "Talk about nutjob!"

"Well, I think this more than proves what she was capable of," said Leah.

"The bit where she describes watching Debbie die! All I can say is thank God she's dead," added Danny. "She can't hurt anyone else. She is definitely dead, isn't she?"

"Do you know Amy McDonald asked me the exact same thing a little while ago," answered Mason.

"She's definitely dead," confirmed Leah. "We got shown the bed she died in, the plot in the graveyard where she's buried."

"That doesn't prove anything," said Danny.

"No, but Sister Matilda, the Nun who looked after Edith at St Agnes' took a photograph of her. She couldn't believe that even if she had no family, someone as lovely as Edith, or Andrea as she was calling herself, had no friends that would miss her. She fully believed someone would come looking, so she took the photo so Edith could be identified. She just didn't think that it would be the Police who came in search of her."

"Andrea?" queried Danny.

"Yes, another name change," confirmed Mason. "She was calling herself Andrea Kent when she booked into the hospice."

"That's different," said Danny. "Not using a Christian name that starts with E."

"I assume it was deliberate as another way of making it harder for us to find her. She knew we would be more likely to take notice of names beginning with E and of course, with Ricky dead, she didn't have to worry about that anymore," said Mason.

"Sister Matilda also gave us a box with Edith's sole possessions. The contents were meagre, to say the least," Leah told Danny. "Hairbrushes, make-up, stuff like that. Nothing personal and nothing of value."

"We used hair from a brush to get the DNA match," added Mason.

"Poor Sister Matilda, she kept telling us how Edith had been so sweet and grateful for all the care she received. She told us over and over what a lovely lady she was. The boss nearly killed her when he explained exactly why we needed to ascertain that Andrea Kent was Edith O'Reilly," said Leah.

"I couldn't stand her talking about Edith as if she was some sort of saint," said Mason. "She needed to be put straight." Leah and Danny exchanged a look.

Until I saw my mother on that fateful last day, I wasn't sure I would actually go through with my intention to kill her. But then seeing her slumped in her chair, in her shabby clothes, with slobber running down her chin just reminded me of all the times she had embarrassed me, and I could feel myself getting angry. To be honest, she had given me very little choice from the moment she'd insisted on attending my graduation. I couldn't afford her to be there. Not when everyone believed me to be an orphan. Her turning up would have made the situation more than a little awkward; wouldn't you agree? Also, at that particular moment, it was imperative that I made a good impression on Tom – more about him later. He had already shown me immense sympathy after I gave him an elaborate story regarding my parents' untimely demise in the Middle East. The last thing I needed was for my mother to put in an appearance and prove me a liar. So, it was in my best interests for her to no longer exist for real, and on top of that, I would be her sole beneficiary, and the money would come in very handy.

It was so easy to do and knowing you to be a sensitive soul, Amy, if it makes you feel any better, it was completely painless for her and for me. An extra-large injection of insulin and she basically just fell asleep. Sound familiar? That's exactly what happened to your grandmother, isn't it? And I should know because I was there when that happened too! But more on that later. Let's stick to the timeline.

As soon as I was certain Mum was no longer breathing, I left the house and headed back to Oxford. I was able to act suitably shocked when the police contacted me the next day even though she had been found sooner than I expected. I thought it would be a few days before she was discovered. Not that it made any difference. I sorted everything out quickly. Had her cremated, put the house on the market, sold all the furniture and collected on the insurance. Again, sound familiar Amy? I admit it was a mistake not to hold a proper funeral for the benefit of her friends, especially Peggy. She was a bit of a pain up until I let her have Mum's ashes. It wasn't until I read your book that I realised Mum was so popular. I never took much notice of what was going on in her life. Also, until I read the book, it never crossed my mind that foul play had been suspected. Good old Peggy. Such a shame no one paid attention to her suspicions. Might have saved your grandmother, Amy – just kidding!

Extract from follow-up Interview with Peggy Dixon

I always knew there was something seriously wrong with Edith and I was right, wasn't I? I don't take any pleasure from it though. Same as I don't take pleasure from being right about her killing Betty. It never crossed my mind that she started that fire. And to think she killed her own little lad. No, she wasn't normal, we all knew that, but never in a million years did we think she was pure evil.

I have to say, you let me down, Amy, presuming that I staged that one-night stand with Tom to enable me to pass off the baby I was expecting as his. There's a slight flaw in your assumption. I wasn't pregnant when Tom and I allegedly spent the night together. Admittedly, it happened shortly afterwards so your mistake is understandable, but I feel if you were as clever as you think you are, you should have been able to work it out. I set Tom up because he rejected my advances.

It was after I accepted the invitation from Rachel to spend New Year with her and she took me along to the party at Tom's family home, or 'country pile' would be a more apt description, that I determined to take Tom away from Rachel. What had she, who'd never had to struggle for a single thing in her whole life, ever done to deserve the perfect marriage to the perfect man? How come she got the happy ever after? When I saw first-hand, the entitlement and privilege that this perfect couple enjoyed, I decided that I wanted that life to be mine. I despised Rachel. I wanted to destroy her and stealing Tom from her was the perfect way to achieve that. I could change her life and mine irrevocably in an instant. Shatter her dreams and make mine come true. And she deserved for it to happen because that insipid, naïve, silly little bitch, lived a charmed life.

Her parents doted on her; they paid for everything. She'd never known a moment's hardship. Good fortune just dropped into her lap without the slightest endeavour on her part. She was blessed with good looks, naturally pretty. And to make it worse she was soooo fucking nice. Sickly sweet, unbelievably kind and selfless. Everyone loved her. Everyone wanted to be her friend. On top of all that, she had this preppy, good-looking fiancé who treated her like a princess. It wasn't fair. It was my turn.

However, this proved far more challenging than expected. Tom seemed impervious to my charms. But I do like a challenge, so I set out to captivate him. Up until that time, I'd had nothing much to do with Tom, but I knew everything there was to know about him because the lovesick Rachel talked about him ad nauseam. I did my research and became an expert on all of his hobbies and interests which comprised some of the dullest activities on the planet, but no pain, no gain as they say.

All my hard work got me precisely nowhere. Despite spending so much time together and apparently having so much in common, Tom was only interested in a plutonic relationship. He was so in love with Rachel that the concept of a fling never crossed his mind, let alone ditching his fiancé for her captivating best friend.

It infuriated me. What was it about that innocuous little mouse that made her so much more attractive than me? I doubled my efforts in trying to seduce him. The first time he took me to the opera I was convinced I would succeed. I was bewitching, enchanting, provocative. Even though I say so myself, I looked stunning, mouth-wateringly shaggable. That evening men were literally dropping like flies at my feet, but the man I wanted to impress was indifferent. He even encouraged me to flirt with my admirers. So frustrating!

So, coming to the realisation that Tom would never leave Rachel for me I planned to entice Tom into bed with me, just once. Then I'd promise to keep it a secret between us until such a moment that revealing it would cause maximum damage; maybe Rachel's Hen Do or, as she'd asked me to be a bridesmaid, on the morning of her wedding. In my fantasy I would drop the bombshell whilst she preened in front of the mirror, in her perfect wedding dress, preparing herself for her perfect day. I was certain she wouldn't be able to cope with Tom's infidelity and when she inevitably called off the wedding, Tom would be mine. But try as I might, Tom remained immune to my seduction, and I was running out of time. The date of the wedding was fast approaching. I was left with no choice; if he wouldn't succumb willingly then I would have to force the issue.

So, I formed my plan. I got Ricky to obtain some Rohypnol for me to coincide with Rachel being away for a weekend. It was so easy to set Tom up, far too easy really. He was incapable after I doctored his drink. Completely unaware of what was happening. The look on his face when he woke up the next morning was priceless. I played along, pretending to be as upset as he was. We made promises of secrecy that I had no intention of keeping. Everything had gone exactly as I had planned.

Then things took a peculiar turn. I killed my Mum. I never expected it to affect me but subconsciously it must have done, because I went on a massive bender with Ricky. That's when I got pregnant. A huge mistake on my part, as was telling Ricky; that certainly came back to bite me! To start with Ricky was over the moon about becoming a father but once I explained the reality of the situation, the number one factor being that he would have to get clean, he soon came round to my way of thinking, that I should have an abortion. And that's where Tom came into it. The timing of setting him up couldn't have been more perfect. I was confident that as soon as he knew of the pregnancy, he would offer to pay me to get rid of the baby and that's exactly what he did. But not straight away.

What I hadn't anticipated was that he would question whether he was responsible. I'd expected guilt and contrition, but I got anger and denial, and it pissed me off. Entitled prick. So, I decided to make him sweat for a bit longer. I still had plenty of time. I could extort more money from him if I told him that I couldn't go through with the abortion and wanted to keep the baby. After extracting more money, I could have a sudden miscarriage (abortion) and that would be that. He was used to throwing money at a problem to make it go away, so why shouldn't I benefit? I gave him a week to think it over, mentioning Rachel's name just before we parted to reiterate exactly what he stood to lose. I suppose it was a form of blackmail but so what, he could afford it.

Just as I predicted, by the end of the week he capitulated and even handed over a wad of cash. That's when it occurred to me that having his child could be my meal ticket. The baby would tie Tom to me financially for life or at least for the next 18 years. Although I didn't particularly want to have the baby, I wasn't completely averse to the idea, especially as everything would be paid for.

So that was my new plan, and I fully intended to stick to it. I had absolutely no intention of killing Rachel. It really was purely accidental. It just so happened that we were on the same country road at the same time. Me driving Ricky in his car and her on her bike. I have no idea why she was there at that time; maybe it was fate? Anyway, you know that urge you get that compels you to stick your finger into an electric pencil sharpener or to touch the metal plate of an iron even though you know it's hot? Well, it was that overwhelming urge that caused me to give her bike a nudge, with the front end of the car, as I drove alongside her. Just a little bump to knock her off her bike. I fully expected, when I looked back in the rear-view mirror, to see her standing at the side of the road, brushing mud off her jeans and waving an angry fist in the air. I knew she wouldn't recognise me because as I said, it was Ricky's car I was driving. He was sitting in the passenger seat, too stoned to drive. He came to when he felt the car swerve and when he realised what I'd done, he shit a brick and made me turn round and go back to check on her.

As we drove slowly past the spot, we could see her lying motionless on the ground. She hadn't been wearing a cycling helmet, they weren't vogue back then, and I assumed she had hit her head and knocked herself out. She was probably just concussed. Ricky wanted us to stop and help her, but I kept on driving. I knew that his car wasn't kosher. It certainly wasn't in his name or insured. So far, we hadn't seen another vehicle but if someone else came along and took down the details of his car I explained to him, then he could end up in serious trouble. Besides, I said, she won't be that seriously *hurt, and someone will come along soon and stop to help her. I had no idea how wrong I was on both counts!*

Comment from Tom Bryant

"I feel sick. This is unbelievable. I always had an inkling I'd been played but I had no idea the extent she went to. I'm stunned. And the casual way she brushes off Rachel's death. It was an accident – she didn't mean it! This really hasn't sunk in yet. I can't even start to process it. I'm horrified. The impact that this deranged woman has had on my life.

Thank you for the warning. You say there's worse to come. I assume she goes into detail about Max. I'm not sure I want to keep reading but I know I have to. I need to know what happened to my poor little boy."

1997 was a challenging year for me. In the words of Her Majesty the Queen, it was my "annus horribilis". I committed two murders during that year, very close together and yet still managed to avoid detection. Although at times it felt as if my world was unravelling. There were moments when I was actually unsure about how to proceed but as usual, I managed to navigate my way through and come out a winner on the other side. Two events happening simultaneously caused me much anguish and ultimately led to the death of two individuals.

The first was the discovery by Tom that Max was not his biological child. The bastard, (Tom, not Max ha-ha), had carried out a DNA test behind my back, no doubt egged on by that bitch of a wife of his. Why pay out for Max now they had sprogs of their own? Because that's what happened. As soon as Tom found out the truth about Max, he cancelled my monthly allowance and ceased paying me a penny. Then he had the audacity to tell me he wanted to keep seeing the kid. According to him, it would be better for Max to continue contact. Bollocks to that! I made it very clear that if he wanted to spend time with Max, then he needed to pay for the privilege. Next thing I know he's off working somewhere for a few months, and will 'contact me' when he gets back to make arrangements regarding access to Max. At least that sounded like he was willing to pay. I did succeed in getting some money out of him before he left. He paid me for taking his name off Max's birth certificate. I invested this money in a major project (the second event), which was already in the planning stages.

This was my involvement in a rather ingenious plot to bring a large quantity of illegal drugs into the UK. Sometime before, Ricky had introduced me to acquaintances of his who had contacts high up in some Balkan drug trafficking organisation. These people were looking for investors. People who could provide untraceable amounts of money that would be repaid with interest once the drugs had successfully made it to the UK. I had already profited from taking part in several smaller deals and now I was given the option to invest in a 'once in a lifetime' transaction. This required the contribution of a huge sum of money, but the payback was colossal. It was too good an opportunity to miss. I didn't have sufficient personal funds, although I put in everything I possibly could, but in my position as a solicitor, I had access to large amounts of clients' money. I didn't see the harm in 'borrowing' from the deceased and paying back their estates upon receipt of my earnings. It would only be for a few weeks. At least that was how it was supposed to happen.

I heard the news on my car radio while driving home from work. The police had discovered a major drug haul after intercepting a consignment off the

Kent coast. I knew instinctively that it was the consignment I had put my money into, and as such I had lost the lot. Luckily, there had never been any contact between myself, and anyone involved in the scheme at any point during the transaction; Ricky had handled everything, so there was no way I could be connected with the haul. But that was small comfort compared to the amount of money I had lost, and that I now needed to recuperate by some means in order to return what I had borrowed before it was missed. Where on earth was I going to get my hands on the thousands of pounds that I had 'borrowed'?

Could the day have got any worse? I hear you ask. Yes, actually it could. A lot worse. Intending to take my bad mood out on Ricky, who had got me into this mess in the first place, I drove to the house he was staying in where I had left him looking after Max. It was the school holidays, and it was cheaper to leave Max with Ricky than it was to stick him in an Activity Club or with a childminder.

Now, I should explain about the house. It was owned by one of my recently deceased clients whose estate was going through probate. Ricky had urgently needed a place to stay because he had broken the conditions of his bail, by mixing with his Balkan associates, and was currently sought by the police. It made perfect sense for him to move into my client's house. He could easily stay there undetected until probate was completed, and ownership of the property passed to the beneficiaries of the estate. As long as the place was left in the same condition as when he moved in, no harm done.

Anyway, as I was telling you, I was fully geared-up to have a go at Ricky but walking into the living room I discovered him off his face on the sofa, surrounded by his drug paraphernalia and a tearful, frustrated Max demanding to know why Uncle Ricky was saying he was really his dad and not his uncle. I couldn't believe what Ricky had done. I had explicitly told him not to breathe a word to Max about what Tom had discovered. Having always known he was Max's real dad, Ricky couldn't see the harm in telling the boy the truth. Ricky envisioned Max being thrilled to discover his favourite uncle was actually his father, and then the three of us would sail off into the sunset and live happily ever after. Prat! I knew Max would take it badly. He was too young to understand, and as much as I'd always badmouthed Tom to him, the kid adored him. He was devoted to both Tom and his new Mrs. He loved spending time with them. I had patiently explained all this to Ricky and told him we would have to wait until Max was older and had got used to not having Tom around before we told him the truth. Ricky, it seemed, had chosen to ignore my warnings and taken matters into his own hands. Instead of facing the consequences of his actions, he'd used his usual trick of avoiding an unpleasant situation by getting high, leaving me to deal with the aftermath.

I slapped and kicked Ricky trying to raise him from his drug-induced stupor but to no avail. Max, usually so malleable, was acting up big time, unbelievably stroppy and uncooperative, even after I walloped him. I bundled him into the car where he continued with his pathetic cry of 'I want my Daddy' all the way home.

He played up all evening. He never once let up. He just wouldn't shut up about wanting to see his dad. It didn't matter what I said, how much I threatened him or how hard I hit him, he kept on and on. It drove me insane. He sent me over the edge. I don't really remember exactly what happened as the red mist descended. Judging by the state Max was in when I finished, I would say I definitely went over the top. When I got control of myself again, I was panting, and my fists hurt. I instantly knew he was dead. I think because of the silence as much as anything else. He was no longer whingeing. But there were also the tell-tale signs that I'd gone too far. It was obvious I had kicked his skull in and stomped on his face and there was a livid imprint to prove it.

Now, I know reading that bit will have upset you Amy, what with your 'sensitive nature' but I need to tell the truth. That's what a confession is all about, isn't it? Baring your soul, revealing the truth about yourself. I wasn't sorry. I know you'll struggle to believe that too, Amy but it's true. I wasn't sorry and I felt no guilt, no remorse. I was just so fucking angry. If only the stupid kid had shut his mouth when I told him to, none of this would have happened. It was so unnecessary. He had totally brought it on himself. Even at that moment, I was aware that people like you, Amy, so-called 'normal' people would be repulsed by my behaviour, but I can assure you I felt no revulsion at what I'd done, just incredible anger. I wasn't devastated by what had happened, just infuriated that my actions, my loss of control, had left me in this situation. It was an unwanted complication. If I'd just hit him the once, I could have gone through the proper channels and passed it off as an accident. But no, I'd beaten him to death. Anyway, even if it had been accidental, involving the authorities would likely lead to a post-mortem, which would show up historic injuries, so I'd still land in the shit.

I was furious. Now, on top of my financial problems, I was going to have to somehow dispose of this body. Because that's all it was to me now, a body. An inconvenience. I'd killed my only child but there was no point dwelling on the loss. I wasn't going to waste time grieving. I'm not sure I know how to grieve. I'd never loved Max. I've never loved anyone. I don't think I'm capable. It was unlikely that I would even miss him. In reality, my life was going to be so much easier without him. He no longer served any purpose since I received no financial compensation from him for living with me. He would just have been a drain on my resources, which at that moment in time were non-existent. I just needed to think of a way to get rid of him and quickly. It wouldn't be long before he started to decompose; he already stank because he'd soiled himself; which must have happened during the assault.

The thing was I was still really, really mad and whilst I felt like that I couldn't think straight. I shoved the body out of the way into a corner of the room and covered it with a blanket. Then I drove back over to see Ricky. He was still out of it, but he came to soon enough when I started to attack him. I was like a wild animal. I remember that feeling of being on the outside looking in on myself and I could see myself hissing and spitting at him whilst I punched and kicked and clawed and bit. Oh, it felt good. Getting rid of all that built-up tension. By the time I was spent, Ricky was curled up in a ball on the floor, pleading with me to stop. He thought I was going to kill him.

He'd often been on the receiving end of my fury, but I'd never attacked him like that before. I'd got rid of my rage, but I still didn't want to be around him.

I blamed him for causing me to harm Max and I certainly didn't want to have to tell him that his son was dead. He wouldn't be able to cope, especially knowing I was responsible. He was too fragile emotionally to trust to keep quiet, so it was better that he knew nothing. Still, he would need an explanation for the beating he'd just suffered. He would need a reason why I had attacked him so ferociously. Storming out I told him Max was in the hospital because he'd had an accident whilst Ricky was off his face. I told him he was lucky that Max hadn't died. I felt that was explanation enough.

At least Ricky was one problem that was easily dealt with. An anonymous call to the police tipping them off as to his whereabouts saw him automatically returned to prison, having first paid a visit to A and E. I was fairly confident he wouldn't grass me up with regards to his injuries and it can hardly have been a surprise for the police to discover a badly beaten drug addict.

I spent a sleepless night running different scenarios around in my head as to how to dispose of Max's body. The majority of ideas I had I discounted almost as quickly as I thought of them. It was imperative that his body not be found, or certainly not quickly, but every plan I came up with carried a high risk of discovery. I considered the classic 'dump the body at sea' method. But there were too many chances of being caught as I'd have to put the body in the car, drive to the coast, hire or steal a boat, get the body on the boat unseen and then throw it overboard. Then, even if I weighed the body down, I had no idea whether strong currents would bring it back to shore. It just wasn't plausible. The same went for dumping it in the canal. Too risky.

As I paced back and forth pondering what to do, I would occasionally kick the bundle in the corner hidden under the blanket just to vent my frustration. I can still remember that feeling of such intense anger. Stupid boy for causing me so much anxiety. I had the idea of concealing the body in some sort of bag and making sure it went in the dustbin lorry when it was making its rounds, but that ran the risk of discovery once it got to the landfill and taking it to the tip myself was a no go for obvious reasons. I daren't just dump the body in the woods because dog walkers always discover bodies left out like that, don't they? Same for burying him in a field, that's if I wasn't discovered digging the hole first. I was at a loss for a solution.

I arrived at work the following morning in a foul mood. I was still no closer to coming up with a foolproof plan for disposing of the body, despite a whole night of deliberating. I was exhausted from lack of sleep, and I ached from the beatings I'd doled out. So, the last thing I needed was to be met by the

Office Manager demanding an explanation as to how a squatter had managed to gain entry into one of my dead client's houses. I feigned ignorance and carried on to my office, but she followed me. According to the police, she informed me, the squatter, a convicted criminal, had told them that he had my permission to stay at the premises. The police were in her office waiting to speak to me. I was horrified. I couldn't believe Ricky had dropped me in it like that. What was he thinking? I tried to gather my thoughts as I followed her to her office.

Fortunately, I was able to act convincingly in front of the two police officers that this was all news to me. They showed me a mugshot of Ricky. It must have been an old one because there was no evidence of the previous night's beating. I confirmed I couldn't identify the individual. They mentioned the anonymous tip-off and how they'd discovered the man badly beaten. Were they sure he was squatting? I asked. Could he not have broken in somehow in an attempt to flee his attacker who then made the call to you? There could have easily been documentation with my signature on it lying around, I told them, it was my client's house after all. Could that be how he got my name? To my amazement, they happily adopted this explanation. I am constantly surprised by how utterly gullible people are.

However, I wasn't home free. Later that morning I was visited in my office by Sue, one of the firm's senior partners. Sue had an enormous crush on me which I often used to my advantage, but it had no effect that day. She came to tell me that some low-life little girl from the accounts department, who was obviously trying to make a name for herself, had discovered a discrepancy with one of my accounts. Something to do with a bequest to a Charity having not been paid. I knew exactly what she was on about, despite feigning ignorance. The bequest had been for £25,000 and I had appropriated it to add it to the pot for the drugs deal.

I often used money left to charities in my clients' wills for my own use. It was an easy way to take money without anyone realising. Previous amounts had only ever been of a few hundred pounds. Most times charities didn't even know that they were to be beneficiaries of someone's will. So, more often than not, I kept the money only bothering to pay it back if for some reason it was flagged up. Unfortunately, in this case, the client had made the charity aware of the sizeable donation they would be receiving and because it hadn't arrived, they had contacted the office. Hence why the young cretin in accounts had gone snooping.

Normally, I would have managed to fob Sue off with promises of looking into it, but in spite of her expressing concern at how tired I looked – I told her Max had kept me up all night, almost the truth! – she wasn't going to be put off. She was adamant that it needed to be sorted by the end of the week to avoid any legal action being taken by the charity. As if I didn't have enough on my plate with a dead body to dispose of and the worry that Ricky might further incriminate me, now I was supposed to find £25,000 by the end of the week! This was one of those extremely rare occasions where I actually felt a little panicky.

As luck would have it, a solution to one of my problems did present itself later on in the day. Whilst fixing my lunch in the kitchen, I overheard one of the secretaries discussing how she was having a swing set installed in her garden for her children. I know, riveting conversation, right! However, when she mentioned that they had to lay down a concrete base before the company would install the equipment it got me thinking. Telling her I was considering doing something similar in my garden for Max, she gave me all the details. It was almost as if it was meant to be as the company had a sale on.

As for the other problem, I just needed to find a way to buy myself some time. I think, *subconsciously, I had already decided I was going to flee, I just hadn't thought it all through yet.*

Trevor was struggling to digest all that he had just read.

"It's the way she's so cold when she discusses killing Max and her problems regarding the disposal of the body that gets me," he said. "The only emotion she expresses is anger."

"I know," said Amy. "It freaks me out. The way she blames Max himself and Ricky, but she admits no guilt on her part. I fully believe her when she says she felt no remorse."

"Evil, evil, woman," Trevor sighed and shook his head before returning to reading the pages in front of him.

I had to take a couple of days' break. I'm definitely reaching the end. I can only write so much before I become too fatigued to carry on. When I think of all the times I pretended to be ill to get my own way with your father, Amy and now I am really ill, so ill I'm dying. Ironic! One of the Nuns has seen me struggling to get this down on paper. She's offered for me to dictate it to her, and she'll do the writing to save my strength. I don't think that's a good idea, do you? Not so sure she would continue looking after me once I dictated how I killed my own father, mother and son. And now I'm about to confess to another murder albeit one that I didn't intend to commit.

Before that though, I wanted to say how impressed I was Amy, that you and your cohorts, not only worked out that I was responsible for Max's disappearance but also identified where the body was buried. The police hadn't even established he was missing until over twenty years later! So, good on you girl.

I was telling you about how I got rid of the body, wasn't I? You'll have to excuse me, the painkillers leave me a bit foggy.

Right, in order to do that we have to go back to the discussion about the swing set. I got in touch with the company, and they confirmed that they would be able to deliver and install within 2 days, so long as the foundations had been laid. Well, that part was easy. All they needed was a concrete base. I didn't even have to dig very deep as Max wasn't exactly large. I fetched several bags of that ready-mix stuff from the local DIY store, set my alarm and started digging early. I managed to get Max in situ before the nosey neighbour poked his head over the fence, and I had the whole job finished before 9:00 am. Not bad going, even if I say so myself.

The neighbour, Ralph, Reg, Roy whatever, was suitably satisfied with my explanation as to why I was carrying out the work and, with the swing set being installed two days later, everything tallied. How clever was that! Clever enough that Max lay undisturbed until you went poking. And the icing on the cake was that I paid for it all on the company credit card.

Now, back to that other matter of the missing £25,000. Well, actually it was a lot more than that, but at that point, it was only that particular donation that had aroused concern. I knew I had to act fast otherwise more misappropriated funds would be uncovered before I had a chance to disappear. As far as I knew, Sue was the only person the stupid accounts department had spoken to about their findings. So, if I could put Sue out of action for a few days it would give me time to sort things out and be on my way. I'd already instigated proceedings to enable me to change identity, and I just needed a couple of days to tie up loose ends and make arrangements to sell my stuff, so I had the money to disappear with.

An idea had come to me during the night. Sue had an allergy to nuts. I knew this because she constantly reminded everyone. Every time there was a birthday and people bought in cake, she would make a huge drama out of ascertaining whether the cake contained nuts. She made us all aware of the EpiPen that was kept in the first aid box in the kitchen, and the fact that she carried one in her bag at all times. So, I began to prepare. I purchased muffins, a syringe and peanut oil. I injected some oil into one of the muffins, putting a mark on the paper case, so I knew which one had been dosed. I had no idea how much to use. Too much and there was a good chance Sue would smell it before taking a bite. Too little and it might have no effect. I didn't know how severe her allergy was but suffice it to say a little bit of nut was likely to make her unwell, otherwise why all the drama? The next day I got into work early and took the EpiPen from the kitchen. I had been hoping to just empty it of the adrenalin or whatever was inside, but I couldn't get into it. Instead, I injected it into a sponge and then replaced it in the first aid box. Part one of my plan was completed. Quite often, Sue and I would share a coffee break around mid-morning. That day I buzzed her just before 11:00 am to say I was making coffee did she want one? Of course, she did. I made coffee and took it to her office along with the pack of muffins, making sure that I shut the office door behind me.

We sat at the small table in her office, just like we always did, and I gave her the doctored muffin. I swear she only took one bite before she started to wheeze. She asked if they contained nuts and I said of course not; pointing to the packaging, they're just chocolate. Her condition deteriorated rapidly. In no time at all she was struggling to breathe and unable to talk. She stood up, sending the mugs crashing to the floor. I was worried the noise would alert someone. She grabbed at her bag, and I took it from her and pulled out the EpiPen from inside. The look of relief on her face, silly cow. I approached her as if I was going to administer the drug but instead, I shoved more of the cake into her mouth. To this day I don't know why I did that. Maybe I just wanted to ensure she didn't make a quick recovery which would destroy all my hard work, or maybe I was fascinated by what was happening and wanted to see it through to the end. She tried to spit out the contents of her mouth all the while struggling for air. I pinched her nose and within seconds she collapsed on the floor.

It was a very different death to those I'd witnessed previously. It was nothing like watching Debbie drown or my Mum drift away. I have to say Sue looked repulsive. Her eyes were red and bulging, her eyelids so swollen that they were just slits. Her lips had swelled to three times their normal size. In fact, her whole face had swollen up so much she was unrecognisable. I watched to see if the light left her eyes, but it was impossible to tell. I checked for a pulse and as soon as I was certain she was dead, I started to yell for help, while at the same time lifting her skirt and stabbing her leg with the EpiPen. I verified that she was still dead and that the administering of the Pen had not led to a miraculous recovery. And then I really started to shout, screaming for help at the top of my voice, making sure I sounded panic-stricken. As the door opened, I screeched that the EpiPen wasn't working. "Fetch the one from the first aid box!" I yelled. The next minute, the room was full of people all trying to help. Someone handed me the second Pen and I injected Sue's leg again. It would have looked authentic to the bystanders, but I knew the Pen was empty. Having announced that she was dead, I moved away and let others try to revive her with CPR and call for an ambulance. I was well aware that they were wasting their time.

I pretended to be in shock and, just like after Debbie died, it worked in my favour. I was helped to a chair, and someone passed me a mug of sweet tea. The paramedics arrived and confirmed that Sue had died. There was an awkward time after they took her body away where people wandered around unsure of what to do. I was questioned as to what had occurred and I explained how she'd taken ill after eating the muffin, and how it had all happened so quickly. The packaging was examined, someone even took a bite of one of the remaining muffins and it was confirmed that the muffins did not contain nuts. I had scooped most of the doctored muffin out of Sue's mouth with a tissue and stuffed it in my pocket before calling for help. I obviously hadn't managed to get all of it, but I was hopeful that the remains would never be tested. Even if they were, I should be long gone before the results were ready. It was a risk, but I didn't have many options. Everyone had a theory.

Rather than suffer being questioned more closely, I pretended to break down. I started to cry and loudly blamed myself for Sue's death. Immediately contrite, everyone began to assure me it wasn't my fault and I'd done all I could. They praised me for my quick reactions. Someone offered to drive me home, but I told them I wanted to be alone, and I left. I never went back. I called in sick the next day saying the doctor had signed me off for at least two weeks. The Office Manager was so sympathetic it was sickening. She said she'd let me know the details of the funeral, but I was long gone before the family had time to arrange one.

Extract from a follow-up interview with Ms Adebayo

I'm in shock. She murdered Miss Ruddick while we were all in the building. It happened right under our noses, and no one had a clue. I watched them carry Miss Ruddick out on a stretcher and I watched Eleanor leave. She was distraught. She was sobbing and shaking. I just can't get my head around it. I'm also upset about how she describes me. I wasn't trying to make a name for myself, I was just doing my job!

I'm getting so tired now. Writing is becoming a real struggle. I need to hurry it up.

So where did I run away to? Spain of course. The Costa del Sol. Isn't that where all good criminals disappear? By then the loophole regarding the extradition of criminals had been plugged but it was still a relatively safe place for me to hide, especially with my new identity. Besides, I didn't have enough money to travel too far afield. I'd already sold all my possessions to enable me to get this far.

When I arrived, I was in dire need of funds and so I had no alternative but to return to prostitution as a quick and easy means of making money. Although again what I did would be classed more as escort work than prostitution. I didn't enjoy going back to it, but my choices were limited. It was a way of making good money relatively quickly. The majority of my clients were elderly men which made the job even less enjoyable. It's not a part of my life I wish to dwell on.

After a few months, I had a couple of well-heeled clients in my sights, lined up as potential sugar daddies. Men who would pay handsomely for exclusivity. Basically, I would become the mistress and maybe even eventually the wife. That was the plan. Unfortunately, the man whose offer I accepted had a wife who was unwilling to become an ex. Unbeknown to me, she too had begun her relationship with this man as his mistress, and she was not prepared to let all her hard work go to waste simply because he had cast his eye on a younger model. She paid me a visit and made it clear that if, as she so nicely put it, I wanted to keep my tits, I had better not only leave her man alone but leave the area completely. A little digging on my part revealed this woman was well-connected and not to be messed with.

So, I gathered together what funds I could and pawned all the jewellery, handbags, etc. that had been gifted to me, and I returned to the good old UK. I'd had enough of the sun by then anyway and Ricky was about to be released from prison.

On my return, I connected with my old forger friend who, as well as providing me with a new ID, also furnished me with a letter purporting to be from a certain police force. It explained that I would be unable to provide references as I was the victim of domestic violence and had been given a new identity to protect me from my abuser and his family. I used this to procure a position with a firm of solicitors in Newhampton, and by the time Ricky was free, I was already working and had rented a flat.

So now we're fast approaching the moment I came into your life, Amy. I'm ashamed to admit it but for the first time, I was outplayed. The firm of solicitors I now worked for was jointly run by a father and son. They were both weak men and I soon had them wrapped around my little finger. They believed the story of my abusive ex-husband and considered me a delicate flower that needed nurturing. It was suffocating but I played along. It wasn't very long before I felt comfortable enough to begin bolstering my income by stealing from clients, just like I had at MRJ. Neither father nor son had the wherewithal to even notice the discrepancies, let alone accuse me of wrongdoing. However, I hadn't taken into consideration the wife and mother.

Although not part of the day-to-day running of the firm, she had access to the accounts and as such she was acutely aware of what I was up to. But she was sneaky. She didn't confront me. I'm not even certain she spoke about it to her husband or her son. No, this woman was much cleverer than the two of them put together and she went straight to the Solicitors Regulation Authority. She provided enough information for them to have 'reason to suspect dishonesty' as they worded it. They took a closer look into my activities, and they discovered I had been transferring clients' money into my own personal accounts. They uncovered the fact that Ricky was staying in the home of a dead man, without the beneficiaries of his will being consulted, and without Ricky paying any rent to the estate. I was also found guilty of not informing certain beneficiaries of their entitlements. The firm was immediately forced to close.

The next few months were horrendous. I had no choice but to declare bankruptcy. I was put into temporary accommodation and the only work I could find was behind a bar. It was so humiliating. There was a tribunal, which I refused to attend, but in mitigation, I told them I had severe mental health issues, as a result of the abuse I had suffered in a previous relationship. I've copied below the conclusion of the tribunal with regard to me:

'Having found that the respondent acted dishonestly the tribunal did not consider that a reprimand, fine or suspension were adequate sanctions. The tribunal determined that the findings against the respondent including dishonesty required that the appropriate sanction was to strike off from the roll.'

Meaning I could no longer work as a solicitor. I was also ordered to pay costs totalling nearly £55,000. A ludicrous sum especially considering I had filed for bankruptcy. The stupid woman who reported me shot herself in the foot too though. Both father and son were fined thousands of pounds for failing to control accounting systems and allowing clients' money to be used inappropriately. As far as I am aware they never re-opened the practice. Who was going to trust them after the results of the tribunal were published? Serves her right for informing on me in the first place. Stupid bitch.

Whilst working for the solicitors I called myself Elizabeth Taylor, but my forged documents were in the name of Elizabeth Tyler, and it was that surname that got printed in the press. I changed to Eliza Taylor, as a way of disassociating myself from the tribunal without having to change my name. That's why you never found me when you went looking, Amy. A small change but enough to keep me out of sight.

I was already seeing your dad when all this came out, and I made up some story of how I had heroically taken the blame in order to try and protect the father from finding out the truth about his son's massive drug problem. I couldn't avoid the issue as my name was all over the local news, but it explained why I changed my name. I have to say your dad was a true gentleman about it all. He offered me his London flat to stay in while he was away filming, and he also negotiated a settlement with the SRA and paid the reduced fine on my behalf. You can understand why I considered him to be wealthy.

Whilst he was in America, Ricky and I made the most of being in the capital and we partied every night, which is how Zac came into existence.

"So, right from the beginning everything we knew about her, everything your father believed about her was a lie," said Marcus.

"Yes, absolutely everything. Nothing she told him was true. Nothing from her past and nothing about what was actually going on when she met him," replied Amy.

"Don't take this the wrong way but I kind of admire her for being able to maintain so many lies," admitted Marcus. "I'd be tripping up all over the place. To have to remember all that detail must have been hard for her."

"But she never gave out that much detail did she," replied Amy. "She kept things simple deliberately and if too many questions were asked, she feigned distress so that the subject was dropped, like with regards to Max. If you started asking too many questions about her past, she closed you down."

I'm not sure how much longer I can go on now, Amy, but I hate to leave you without telling you why I killed your beloved granny, Vi.

By now I'm sure you've worked out how I did it. She went the same way as my mother, only not quite as peacefully. Violet was always too smart for her own good and she had a smart mouth to match. She realised what I was doing but she couldn't stop me. That's when she told me that she was expecting you to call around, and that threw me a bit. I was just starting to go through her paperwork when I heard a car pull up. Luckily for me, it was only one of her 'boyfriends', who I managed to fob off by telling him Vi was out with you and I was just leaving. I wanted to go back inside the house to tidy up after myself, but he wasn't in any hurry to leave, so I drove off. I didn't dare double back in case you had arrived in the interim or we passed each other on the road, so I drove home using a different route enabling me to bypass you.

As to the reason why I killed her. Surely, you've worked that one out too. Money. I could tell that your dad was struggling to find decently paid work and that money was becoming an issue for us. Violet had always appeared wealthy to me, so I thought it was time we received an inheritance from her. I have to admit I was outraged to discover that she wasn't as well off as she made out, but I was incensed when they announced that you, your pathetic brother and your damned kids were all in for a slice. If I'd known that, I might have held off killing her until I could somehow change her will. I could have tried persuading her to cut you off, but I don't think I could have achieved that do you? She was a game old bird was your granny.

"I'm so sorry, Amy," said Kath. "I don't just mean about the fact she murdered Violet but because I didn't believe you when you said something was off about Vi's death."

"It's ok," said Amy. "No one believed me. I'm not even sure I believed it myself. I think I just wanted an excuse to hate her. I wasn't really myself at the time."

"I think, instinctively you knew that your granny hadn't made a mistake. Maybe, if we had taken you more seriously, we could have done something about it."

"Honestly, Kath, think about it. What could we have done? What I was saying didn't make any sense. There was no proof, no evidence. It's not surprising that no one took my suspicions seriously. Why would Edith have harmed Granny? What would she gain? It's only after reading her confession that we understand why she killed her."

"True," said Kath. "But that doesn't stop me feeling guilty about how I treated you at the time. If I remember rightly, I didn't exactly disguise my scepticism. I wish I hadn't been quite so fucking terse with you."

"You're terse with everyone," laughed Amy. "It's one of your many special qualities."

I really was surprised that I got away with passing Zac off as your dad's. *I broke the news of my pregnancy to him when he flew back to London for a few days. Once I learnt about his vasectomy – something he'd failed to mention at any point – I thought our relationship would be over. I was angry with myself for making such a stupid mistake and I turned that anger against him. I accused him of lying. Of using it as an excuse to back out of his responsibilities. Was he calling me a slut? I hadn't slept with anyone else but him, I informed him. I told him to get checked out if he needed proof. I didn't think for one minute he would go ahead. We hardly spoke to each other for the remaining time we spent together.*

After he left for the US, I made myself an appointment with the abortion clinic – it's amazing the hoops you have to jump through – appointments with counsellors and that sort of thing. I also began to case your dad's apartment, sorting out items I could sell because I would need to put a deposit down on somewhere to live and I was skint. It was during this time that a letter arrived and from the postmark, I could tell it was from a private clinic. Steaming it open, I realised your dad had followed my advice and got himself checked. This was indeed proof that the baby I was carrying was not his. And that's when I hatched my brilliant plan.

My forger friend made me a new letter which I scanned and sent off to your father. Oh, Amy, I wish you could have witnessed his reaction, his complete turnaround. He phoned me full of apology for ever doubting me. What a gullible dick. I had too much fun with that letter from the clinic. I was too cocky, wasn't I? You certainly spotted it, but far too late. Not your dad, he fell for it hook, line and sinker. Within the next few days, he sent flowers and a plane ticket for me to fly out and join him and well, you know the rest, we came back married.

Now I feel compelled to correct you regarding your assumption that I concealed Zac's natural hair colour so that your father didn't suspect that he wasn't the Daddy. You are so wrong. Why would I be worried about that? I'd already convinced your father with that counterfeit letter. It wouldn't have mattered one iota to your dad that Zac was ginger. No, you stupid girl, I was hiding the fact from Ricky.

Ricky had never got over losing Max from his life. Of course, he never suspected Max was dead. He'd accepted what I had told him about the kid going to live abroad with Tom. But losing contact with Max had driven him further down the addict path and whereas once I would have trusted him with my life, that was no longer the case. I couldn't risk him knowing that he had fathered another son. It was safer for me if I kept Ricky in the dark. If he was convinced your dad was Zac's dad, he had no leverage over me. I admit it was a pain in the arse having to dye Zac's hair all the time and bribing him to stop him from saying anything, but I still believe it was worth the effort.

I'm not entirely sure why it took me so long to ditch Ricky. Maybe it's because I'd known him most of my life and we'd shared so much. In the end, though he let me down just like everyone else. You were so surprised to discover I'd had sex with Ricky weren't you, Amy? How could she sleep with that scumbag you asked yourself? And it wasn't as if she just did it just once. You're right, I've been shagging Ricky on and off since we were kids. You see I like sex but when it came to my choice of husbands, it turned out they were both vanilla in the bedroom department. Your own father, Amy, was possibly the most boring, unimaginative man I've ever slept with. To stop me from going insane I used Ricky. I trained him early on to satisfy my needs. I never intended for him to get me pregnant though. There's another side to me. One that's rarely seen. One that I usually manage to suppress, but after bouts of severe stress, I lose control. The pressure becomes too much. On occasion, it has turned into anger before I can control it and the red mist descends, as Max and your dad would be able to testify to, had they survived. But most times I can feel the pressure rising and I'm aware of what's happening. Taking copious amounts of drugs and alcohol acts like a release valve that allows me to get rid of all the unwanted tension instead of the anger consuming me. Ricky was always a willing partner on these occasions. We'd go on binges lasting several days, throwing caution to the wind. Birth control was the last thing on my mind.

Murdering my mother was the catalyst that resulted in Max. Zac was conceived during the investigation that led to me being struck off as a solicitor.

"Okay so all of this is horrible," said Amy. "But that bit when she admits to dyeing Zac's hair – I mean what the fuck! She must have started doing that from the moment he was born. It's not just me, is it? That's weird. And a lot of work. How did she get Zac to cooperate for such a long time? I know she says she bribed him but even so, how could she guarantee he would stay quiet? Our two would have raised the roof if I tried to dye their hair every six weeks or whatever. I know out of everything she's done it is an odd thing for me to fixate on, but I can't help it. I've never known anyone who dyed their child's hair. It freaks me out."

"I guess the fact that she started doing it as soon as he was born meant Zac never questioned it," said Marcus. "You know, it was just something that happened – like going to the dentist."

The end is close now, Amy, I can feel it. I've hardly any strength left. Ironic, isn't it? I grew up submerged in religion and I loathed it, turned my back on it as soon as I possibly could, and yet here I am dying immersed in it. Nuns praying every day for my soul – a complete waste of their time don't you think?

I'm sure it's clear that I'm not remorseful for what I've done, but I never set out to kill your father. That was due to the red mist that descended when I discovered what a total imbecile he was. To tell you the truth, had I known the full extent of his debt, I would have done everything in my power to keep him alive – at least until his life insurance policy was reinstated. In fact, I'd have insured him up to the hilt before I even entertained the idea of knocking him off. And it would have been so much tidier to do it that way. His heart condition meant he could have keeled over at any time without arousing suspicion. There would have been no need for the overly elaborate plot I concocted to conceal my involvement in his death. I admit it was a stunningly clever plan, but it left me vulnerable. And if there's one thing I hate, it's feeling vulnerable. I can't tolerate being powerless, not in control. Leaving my fate in the hands of a 9-year-old boy and a drug addict was not ideal, to say the least. When the police took Ricky in for questioning, I knew they were onto me, and it was time to run.

Your father was weak, Amy. Weak and stupid. He left me nothing. He'd pulled 80% of the equity on the house leaving it virtually worthless. He was in arrears with everything including his maxed-out credit cards. Anything of value had already been sold. I had nothing. I was planning to sell my story as the battered wife of a household name to the highest bidder to raise some cash, but now I couldn't risk it. I had to get out fast.

Hiding is expensive. I had to keep running and keep changing my appearance. I felt persecuted. I only dared to risk taking temporary work. I couldn't afford to get too close to anyone. Each time the publicity about me went quiet, something else would trigger it. Ricky's death, finding Max, your stupid book. I didn't notice that I was ill. I put it all down to stress. I blame your father for the mess I was in and you for perpetuating the situation. Why couldn't you just let me be? By the time I sought medical help, the cancer had spread. Treatment seemed pointless. What would I gain by living a few more months? I chose this hospice because it's so remote. I've avoided prison – I've won.

July 2017

"So," said Matt, "what's all this excitement about then?" When he'd returned Amy's call, she had asked him to come to the farmhouse as she had something to show him.

Amy opened her laptop, gesturing for him to take a seat at the kitchen table, she turned the laptop screen to face him and without saying a word, went back to finish making the tea.

Amy sat down opposite him as she let Matt read the pages of Edith's confession that she had photographed before handing the journal over to DI Mason.

"Wow," he exclaimed, having read the first few pages.

"Keep going," she told him. She sat silently sipping from her mug, watching how his face reacted to what he was reading. When she saw a look of pure horror, Amy asked,

"Where have you got up to?"

"Max," was all he answered.

Amy nodded. "So surreal," she said.

"So utterly appalling," answered Matt.

They then once again sat in silence until Matt had finished reading completely. It was an indication of how close they had now become that the silence wasn't at all awkward. Amy got up and made another round of tea.

"How did you say you got this?" Matt asked her.

"Some bloke from the solicitors turned up at the door. They hand-delivered it. I had to sign for it. I should have taken pictures of how it arrived, but I forgot. Don't suppose it matters. The journal is with forensics now, so Mike tells me. They're testing for prints."

"And are you sure she's really dead?" asked Matt.

"As far as Mike can ascertain," answered Amy. "He and Leah are currently on their way to Scotland to visit the retreat where she apparently died. It appears she entered some sort of Catholic hospice/convent. I'm not sure what it is exactly."

"This is incredible, Amy, how are you feeling about it?" Matt looked up at her as she placed more tea in front of him. She could still see the anguish on his face from what he had read.

"I have to admit it was a shock," Amy told him. "It was the last thing I expected to receive. And I had to read her introductory letter a couple of times before I could take it in. Then after I'd finished the whole thing, I went through every emotion possible.

"To start with there was disbelief. Had she really killed so many people? Her grandad/dad, her own child! Her own mother! Then I cried – a lot. I mean, you understand, that was *my* dad, that was *my* grandmother. Those poor people, I was so sad for all of them. I think, stupidly, there was also a kind of sense of relief. To know what really happened to her victims. To finally hear the truth."

"That's not stupid. I feel exactly the same. There's a sense of vindication for writing the book now we know a lot of what we speculated about was actually true," said Matt. "And a whole lot more besides," he added. "I feel there's still so much that we don't know. Was it Ricky who tried to knock Tom off his bike? You know what I'm talking about; it's what made Tom decide to get his name taken off Max's birth certificate. I always considered it too much of a coincidence that the driver had red hair, and like Trevor, I don't believe in coincidences, but Edith doesn't mention it. So, was it really a coincidence or did she just not know about it?"

"I have no idea," Amy told him. "It's not something I've even considered. Right now, at this very moment, all I can think about is how she got away with so much. It just makes me so incredibly angry," Amy admitted. "Having read everything she's confessed to, knowing she's got away with it Scot-free, even if it is because she died, is just so unfair. She should have received some sort of proper punishment."

"I can understand that," said Matt.

"I think she was getting really poorly towards the end and that's why the parts about Dad are quite short. I'll admit I'm grateful for that.

I think she would have preferred to go into far more detail if only to torment me, but I sense she became too ill. I feel like I got spared the worst of it. The hardest part for me to accept is that she's confessed that Dad was never violent, but no one will ever know. The public will never see her confession, will they?"

"Why not?" asked Matt.

"Well, it's with the police now and they won't publish it."

"But you can," Matt told her. "She wrote this for you. She sent it to you. She addressed it to you. It's yours to do what you like with. Publish it, Amy. Let her show the world in her own words just how vile a human being she actually was."

After Keith's Memorial

Flopping down on the sofa, trying to kick off her high heels and unravel her hair from its French plait all at the same time, Amy let out a huge sigh of relief.

"Well, that was quite something wasn't it?" she said to Marcus.

"An amazing turnout. Your Dad would have been bowled over," he replied.

"Yeah, I think he would have been secretly pleased; apart from hating the attention," she answered. "I'm relieved that it's over though. Do you know all the way through I expected Edith to make an appearance."

"What?" said Marcus incredulously. "Even though we know she's dead?"

"Do we though? Know for sure I mean? Look how many times she's reinvented herself over the years and how many people she's fooled. I had this feeling that I might catch a glimpse of someone I didn't know, someone who bore a passing resemblance to her. She would obviously be in disguise, lurking in a dark corner, giving me a knowing nod before disappearing again. And if she didn't turn up in person, I thought she might get to me another way. That she might send a note or get someone to deliver a message."

"I think darling, that is what is generally referred to as paranoia. I personally believe she is as dead as the proverbial Dodo. Now, do you fancy a drink?"

"Can I just have a cup of tea?" asked Amy. "I drank a bit too much wine this afternoon and I've got that fuzzy, headachey feeling."

Marcus came into the room a few moments later with a mug of tea, some aspirin and a glass of water.

"You're a star, thank you," said Amy.

Putting the tea down in front of her and handing her the glass and tablets, he said, "You did good today honey. I'm so proud of you."

Their day had been spent attending a Memorial Service for Keith followed by a form of a Wake at a nearby hotel. Amy had pictured when contemplating holding a service in memory of her father, that it would take place in the local village church. But when it came to actually organising the event, the sheer number of people wishing to attend was far too great for the small church to accommodate. Fortuitously, the local Bishop was a friend of Trevor's, and he gave permission for them to use the Cathedral. Amy smiled as she thought about how proud and pleased her grandmother would have been if she had been alive to witness such an event. Her father, on the other hand, would dismiss it all as overblown nonsense and totally unnecessary.

The guest list had included many well-known figures from television and theatre, a delegation of behind-the-scenes staff, a large contingent from the local police force and representatives of the many charities that Keith had been associated with, as well as friends and family. Rather than following a religious ceremony with bible readings, etc, the service had been far more personal, comprising several people climbing up to the pulpit and talking about Keith. These included a moving tribute to his father by Adam, who had flown in from his home in Australia for the occasion, Lucy Campbell who had played Keith's on-screen wife in Prospect Road, Keith's best friend Terry, who made the congregation laugh with tales of their golfing shenanigans, Trevor Harrison who talked about Keith's charity work and Keith's long term friend and agent Marsha Scott-Williams who gave a précis of his career.

As well as Keith's favourite hymns, some of his favourite music was played too including AC/DC's Highway to Hell, much to the amusement of the congregation. It had been a happy affair full to the brim with good memories. A true celebration of Keith's life. Amy and Kath, when organising the event, had made it abundantly clear that no mention was to be made of Edith, Zac or the manner in which Keith had died and everyone adhered to this directive.

People had been pestering both Amy and Adam to hold some sort of service for their father ever since his death. Having been laid to rest during a shabby funeral organised by Edith, to which hardly anyone had been invited, not only Keith's family members but also his friends and colleagues had requested a chance to say goodbye personally. It wasn't until Amy had received Edith's confession and even then, only after DI Mason had personally certified that Edith was most definitely dead, did she feel comfortable enough to contemplate the idea. For Amy, the Wake at the hotel afterwards had been even more pleasurable than the service. After all the months of deliberately not speaking to anyone outside of her close-knit group about her father for fear of their reaction, she had forgotten just how many people had loved him. It was so gratifying to share treasured memories of her dad with other people and to hear their stories about him. It reminded her just how many of those attending today had played a part in her life and had known her father for who he really was. How many had been supportive of her family, even after the terrible accusations that were circulating about him.

Only a very small number of Keith's actual acquaintances had ever considered the possibility that Edith wasn't lying. These people had only known Keith in passing. They could never be considered as having been close to him, and yet Amy had let these naysayers get to her as much as the trolls who had spread such vicious lies about her dad across all forms of media. There had been people from the village too who had upset Amy. People she had considered friends up until they betrayed her by selling their fabricated stories to the newspapers, in an effort to achieve their 15 minutes of fame. Or the neighbours who had known both her father and her for years yet began to treat her like a pariah, crossing the street to avoid having to speak to her.

On the advice of Matt, Amy had released just a small section of Edith's confession to the press, keeping the rest back for the book she intended to publish in the near future. The excerpt that had been made public had been Edith's testimony to what a decent man Keith had actually been, and her admission that her accusations of violence were a lie. People's attitude changed within days of this assertion being published, and people who had been studiously ignoring her for months now publicly acknowledged Amy in the street. Amy, however, was having none of it and now she was the one to shun these fair-weather friends.

She had also not wanted to invite to the memorial service those few who had known her father and yet still vilified him, but Marcus had vetoed the idea, saying it was better to forgive and forget than bear a grudge. Amy had reluctantly issued invitations and had then gone to great pains to avoid having any contact with these certain individuals. She only got caught out once when she was cornered by an ageing actress, who had only ever appeared in a single play with Keith over twenty years ago. That hadn't stopped her from doing a character assassination on him in a piece for a tabloid newspaper. Now, blissfully unaware of the effect her words were having on Amy, she was trying to convince his daughter that she had never taken Eliza's accusations seriously.

"Well, you seemed to take them seriously enough when you did that hatchet job on Dad for the Sun," Amy told the woman. "You'd better hope you never need me to defend *your* character you backstabbing bitch," she spat, before turning and walking away leaving the woman open-mouthed trying desperately to think of a retort. Her parting shot would have appalled Marcus had he heard it, but Kath would be proud, thought Amy.

Amy had also spent time chatting with the recently promoted DCI Mason. She was pleased that he had attended today along with Danny Hobbs and Leah Cooper. It had given her the opportunity to thank them properly for all their hard work and she asked them to pass her thanks on to the rest of the team, who had worked tirelessly throughout the investigation.

Now that the service and Wake were behind her, Amy was pleased to have gone ahead with it. She finally felt at peace having given her father the send-off he deserved, a proper goodbye.

"I've been thinking," she said.

"Oh, good job you're sitting down," said Marcus.

'*What is it with these men? They think they're hilarious*'

thought Amy ignoring him and carrying on with her theme.

"All the way through her confession, Edith goes on about how clever she was. How she was so smart to outwit everyone and escape punishment."

"And?" asked Marcus, unsure where this was leading.

"Well," said Amy, "that just wasn't true, was it? It wasn't because of her intelligence that she was never caught, it was sheer luck. The majority of the murders she committed were either by accident or, in the case of her mother and Granny, fairly easy crimes to cover up."

Marcus raised his eyebrows.

"What I mean is, imagine if Betty and Granny hadn't had diabetes. What would she have done then? Would she still have killed them? And if so, how? Any other method and it might not have been so easy to get away with it. And what if Tom hadn't moved abroad at that precise time? He would have demanded to know where Max was. He certainly would have notified the police when she disappeared. She was lucky that no one who lived in that house after her ever decided to dig the garden up. She never intended to kill Rachel or Debbie or even, for that matter Sue Ruddick. She certainly never intended to kill either Max or Dad – she 'just lost her temper and the red mist descended' to use her own words. It was just pure luck she was never caught."

"When you put it like that, I see what you mean, a lot of what happened was down to luck. Especially as regards the timings; like when Tom left for that job overseas," agreed Marcus.

"Exactly. Maybe I should call the book "It's All in the Timing - Memoirs of a Second-rate Serial Killer," said Amy.

Marcus laughed. "She did plan her first one though," he said, "the arson attack which killed Ricky's family. And she planned the fire that Ricky started. He was only following her instructions."

"That's true," acknowledged Amy. "Also, horrifying to think she was only 11 when she did it. To me that just shows she had to be born evil. And anyone who beats their own child to death can't exactly be described as sane. She got away with murdering two members of my family but that still doesn't make her a genius."

"So, you've decided to go ahead with the book then?" asked Marcus.

"Yes, I think so," Amy told him. "It's like Matt said. The best way to get justice for her victims is to tell their stories and let her own words show what she really was. Also," Amy wasn't quite finished with the point she had been trying to make before Marcus distracted her, "according to Edith, the point of all this murder and mayhem was to be wealthy. She talks about how clever she was at exploiting both people and situations for money. Well, not every murder was for money but nonetheless, money was all she was interested in. That didn't exactly work out for her, did it? All the grief she caused, and she still died penniless, destitute, surrounded by strangers, unloved and unmourned. Then look at today, all those people who came out to express their love for Dad. All those people whose lives he made a difference to in such a positive way. Who's even going to miss Edith? Certainly, no one we know. I doubt very much if even Zac thinks about her anymore. Perhaps I should subtitle the book "A Rags to Rags Story."

Epilogue

Amy hurried from the car park down the path that ran alongside the church leading towards the cemetery. Aware of how far behind they were running she'd set off leaving Marcus to lock the car knowing he'd soon catch her up. Suddenly, she pulled up short. Spinning round, she almost knocked Marcus over.

"I forgot the-" she never got to finish what she was going to say, as Marcus waved the bouquet of roses under her nose. Smiling gratefully at him as he took her hand, they hurried on to where they could see a little group gathered at the far end of the graveyard, underneath the boughs of an elderly Elm tree.

Even from that distance, Amy was able to make out who was in attendance. There was Peggy, with her daughter-in-law Sharon and a man who could only be Peggy's son, Adrian. Standing next to them was Tom and his wife, Lizzie. Lizzie was holding a bouquet of yellow flowers and Amy could just make out a Buzz Lightyear toy, catching the sunlight as it dangled from Tom's hand. Next to Tom stood Matt and his wife Jasmine, who was holding what looked to Amy like a bunch of lilies in her arms, cradling them as if they were a baby. On the other side of what Amy assumed was the hole that had been dug to receive the ashes, stood Mason, Leah and Danny. Mason too was clutching flowers, the small posy looking a little lost in his massive fist. As if sensing what she was thinking, Mason shoved the posy under Leah's nose so that she took them from him as he knelt to tie his shoelace. He was just standing back up as Amy and Marcus reached the graveside, but he made no effort to retrieve the flowers from Leah. Amy was pleasantly surprised to see that Sylvia had accompanied Trevor, and delighted to spot that the unfailingly elegant lady had her arm entwined with his. Both of them smiled over to her as the Vicar began to speak.

"Right, now that we're all here," he said pointedly, causing Amy to grimace and Matt to shake his head at her in mock disapproval whilst pointing to his watch.

"We have come together today to pay our respects..." continued the Vicar.

"Why are we always late for everything?" Amy whispered to Marcus, who shrugged his shoulders. He had no intention of pointing out that she was the reason why they were always late. Now was not the right time or place. In fact, he knew there would never be a right time or place!

After a poignant speech, a short reading and the saying of prayers, the Vicar asked the small band of mourners to join him in the Lord's prayer. He then brought the proceedings to an end saying,

"Although they never knew each other in life, we can be certain of the love that would have existed between this grandmother and her grandson. Betty would have doted on Max and Max would have adored his granny. May you take comfort in the knowledge that they are now united and will rest together in the most deserved peace for all eternity."

Already feeling emotional, Amy could no longer prevent the tears from falling. Scrabbling to find a tissue in her bag, she heard a sob beside her and turned to see Peggy flinging herself into the arms of her family, her shoulders juddering as she wept. The small wooden boxes containing the ashes were laid into place and Amy heard a moan escape from Lizzie, as Tom placed Buzz on top of the box containing Max's remains. Looking around through a haze of tears Amy saw that both Sylvia and Leah, like herself, had tears streaming down their faces whilst even the burly Mason and the austere Trevor were surreptitiously wiping tears from their eyes.

Acknowledgements

With thanks to Neil, my soulmate and almost better half, who was the first to read the entire book and gave the immortal words of praise, "I kept forgetting it was you who had written it!"

To Joe for his continued belief that I could finish this work.

To Robyn for her encouragement and enthusiasm, and without whom there would be no Trevor.

To Chloe for being so supportive and enthusiastic, for always being willing to listen to and discuss a plot twist, no matter how far-fetched, and for giving up so much of her precious free time to edit the finished work.*

I wouldn't have got this far without you all.

– *Sally Fisher* –

*Any mistakes are my own!

About the Author

Sally Fisher lives on the Dorset coast with her husband of forty years. She has 3 grown-up children and 3 grandchildren.

This is her first novel.

Michael Terence
Publishing
www.mtp.agency

mtp.agency

@mtp_agency

Printed in Dunstable, United Kingdom

75019516R00251